# Death-Watch

## John Dickson Carr Mysteries

# Death-Watch

John Dickson Carr

**PERENNIAL LIBRARY**

Harper & Row, Publishers, New York
Grand Rapids, Philadelphia, St. Louis, San Francisco
London, Singapore, Sydney, Tokyo, Toronto

First PERENNIAL LIBRARY edition published 1990.

ISBN 0-06-081640-8

90  91  92  93  94  WB/OPM  10  9  8  7  6  5  4  3  2  1

# Contents

Spilled across the threshold, a man lay partly on his right side and partly on his back. The yellow light showed him clearly, making a play with shadows on the muscles of the face and hands that still twitched. His eyelids still fluttered and showed the whites underneath. His mouth was open; his back seemed to arch a little as though in pain. . . .

Just above the first vertebra, from which something thin and sharp had evidently taken an oblique downward course through the throat into the chest, projected a hand's breadth of metal. It was not a knife whose like any of them had ever seen before. What they could see of it through the blood had been painted a bright gilt; it was about an inch and a half wide at the head, of thin steel, and the head was perforated in a curious rectangle rather like a car-spanner.

Eleanor Carver screamed.

"Yes," said Dr. Fell. "Somebody got him from behind just before he reached the head of the stairs. And that thing——"

He followed the girl's pointing finger.

"Yes, I shall be very much surprised if it's not the minute hand of a clock. A big, outdoor clock."

—from chapter 2, *Death-Watch*

# Death-Watch

# 1

## An Open Door
## in Lincoln's Inn Fields

"Odd crimes?" said Dr. Fell, while we were discussing that case of the hats and the crossbows, and afterwards the still more curious problem of the inverted room at Waterfall Manor. "Not at all. Those things only seem odd because a fact is stated out of its proper context. For instance," he rumbled, wheezing argumentatively, "consider this. A thief gets into a clockmaker's shop and steals the hands off a clock. Nothing else is taken or even touched; only the hands from a clock of no especial value. . . . Well? What would you make of that if you were the policeman to whom it had been reported? As a matter of fact, what sort of crime would you consider it?"

I thought he was merely indulging in fancies, as is the doctor's habit when the tankards are filled and the chairs comfortable. So I said weakly that I should probably consider it killing time, and waited for the snort. None came. Dr. Fell sighted along his cigar; the beaming expression of his vast red face and many chins became as thoughtful as a chin can conveniently be; and the little eyes narrowed behind their glasses on the broad black ribbon. For a time he wheezed in silence, stroking his bandit's moustache. Then he nodded suddenly.

"You've hit it!" he declared. "Harrumph, yes. You've hit it exactly." He pointed the cigar. "That's what made the murder so horrible when it happened—there was a murder, you know. The idea of Boscombe's intending to pull that trigger merely to kill time! . . ."

"Boscombe? The murderer?"

"Only the man who admitted he intended to commit murder. As for the real murderer— It was rather a nasty case. I'm not much given to nerves," said Dr. Fell, a long sniff rumbling in his nose. "Heh. No. Too much padding—here. But I give you my word the damned case frightened me, and I seem to recollect that it's the only one that ever did. Remind me to tell you about it one day."

I never did hear about it from him, for he and Mrs. Fell and I went to the theatre that night, and I had already arranged to leave London the next day. But it is doubtful whether he would have ever gone fully into the matter of how he saved the face of the C. I. D. in the most curious manner on record. However, anybody who knows Dr. Fell would be alert to discover the facts of a case which could make him uneasy. I finally got the story from Professor Melson, who had followed him through it. It took place during the autumn of the year before Dr. Fell moved to London in his advisory capacity to Scotland Yard (the reasons for which move will be understood at the conclusion of this narrative),

2

and was the last to be officially handled by Chief Inspector David Hadley before his scheduled retirement. He did not retire; he is Superintendent Hadley now, and this also will be understood. Since a certain person prominent in the story died just four months ago, there is now no reason for silence. Here, then, are the facts. When Melson had finished telling his story I understood why Melson, not himself a nervous man, will always have an aversion to skylights and gilt paint; why the motive was so diabolical and the weapon unique; why Hadley says it might be called, "The Case of the Flying Glove"; why, in short, a number of us will always consider the clock-face problem as being Dr. Fell's greatest case.

It was on the night of September 4th, as Melson well remembers, because he was to sail for home exactly a week later for the opening of the autumn term on the 15th. He was tired. It is not a vacation when you attempt that vague extra-faculty necessity known as "publishing something" to uphold your academic standing. *An Abridgement of Bishop Burnet's History of His Own Times, Edited and Annotated by Walter S. Melson, Ph.D.*, had been dragging on for so long, and he disagreed with the old he-gossip so violently on every point, that not even the frequent pleasure of catching him in a lie could stimulate enthusiasm now. But he found himself grinning, nevertheless. There was the presence of his old friend, stumping along beside him in his usual shovel hat, his vast bulk and his billowing black cloak silhouetted against the street lamps; fierily argumentative as usual, his two canes clicking by emphasis on a deserted pavement.

They were walking back along Holborn towards twelve o'clock on a cool and breezy night. Bloomsbury being unexpectedly full, the best lodging Melson had been able to find was an uncomfortable bed-sitting-room up four flights of stairs in Lincoln's Inn Fields. They were late in returning from the theatre; Dr. Fell, a slave to the charms of Miss Miriam Hopkins, had insisted on sitting through the picture twice. But Melson had that afternoon picked up at Foyle's a genuine find, a dictionary of mediaeval Latin script, and the doctor sternly refused to go home without seeing it.

"Besides," he rumbled, "you don't mean to say you actually want to go to bed at this hour? Hey? Man, it's discouraging. If I were as young and spry as you——"

"I'm forty-two," said Melson.

"The man," said Dr. Fell, fiercely, "the man past thirty who mentions his age at all is already beginning to sprout moss. I survey you"—he blinked through his eyeglasses—"and what do you look like? You look like a sort of incurious Sherlock Holmes. Where's your sense of adventure and eager human curiosity?"

"'Great Turnstile,'" said Melson, seeing the familiar sign. "To the right here. I intended," he went on, taking out his pipe and tapping it on his palm, "to ask you about your sense of eager human curiosity.—Any new criminal cases?"

Dr. Fell grunted. "Possibly. I don't know yet. They may make something out of that shopwalker murder, but I doubt it."

"What happened?"

"Well, I had dinner with Hadley last night, but he didn't seem to know the details himself. Said he hadn't read the report; he's got a good man on it. It seems to have started in an epidemic of shoplifting through the big department stores by one woman they can't identify——"

"Shoplifting doesn't appear to be very . . ."

"Yes, I know. But there seems to have been something devilish odd about those robberies. And the sequel is bad. Blast it! Melson, it bothers me!" He wheezed and rumbled for a moment, the eyeglasses coming askew on his nose. "The sequel happened about a week ago at Gamridge's. Don't you ever read the papers? There was a special sale, or something of the sort, in the jewellery department, and the place was crowded. Along came a shopwalker, inoffensive chap with the usual morning coat and plastered hair. Shopwalker suddenly grabs somebody's arm; turmoil, milling about, cries, a tray of paste jewels spilled all over the floor; then, in the middle of the rumpus and before anybody knows what's happened, shopwalker collapses in a heap. Shrieks. Somebody notices blood under him. They turn him over and discover his abdomen's been ripped wide with some sort of knife. He died not long afterwards."

It was uncomfortably cool and damp in the narrow passage called Great Turnstile. Their footfalls echoed on the flagstones, between rows of shuttered shops. Signs creaked uneasily, with a gleam or two where an anaemic gas-lamp caught their gilt lettering. Something in the bald recital, or the night noises stirring under the mutter of London, made Melson look over his shoulder.

"Good Lord!" he said. "You mean to tell me somebody committed murder just to avoid being nabbed for shoplifting?"

"Yes. *And in that manner*, my boy. Humph. I told you it was nasty. No clue, no description, nothing except that it was a woman. Five dozen people must have seen her, and every description was different. She vanished; that's all. There's the worst of it, d'ye see. Nothing to work on."

"Was anything valuable taken?"

"A watch. It was out of a tray of curiosities they were using for display purposes; models used to show the progress of watchmaking from Peter Hele down." A curious note came into Dr. Fell's voice. "I say, Melson, what's the number of that place you're staying at in Lincoln's Inn Fields?"

Without conscious intent Melson had stopped, partly to light his pipe, but also because of some memory that stirred and startled him like a touch on the shoulder. The match rasped across sandpaper on the box. What brought back the memory may have been the expression in Dr. Fell's small bright eyes, turned down on him unwinkingly as the match-flame rose; or it may have been the fact that a muffled clock from the direction of Lincoln's Inn began to strike midnight. To Melson's rather fanciful brain there was something almost goblinlike in the doctor's big figure in its cloak, with the breeze blowing the ribbon on his eyeglasses, peering down at him in the narrow passage. The clock striking—supersition. . . . He shook out the match. Their footsteps went on echoing in the gloom.

"Number fifteen," he said. "Why?"

"Then look here. You must be next door to a man in whom I'm rather interested. Queer old chap, by all accounts; name of Carver. He's a clockmaker, and a very famous one. Harrumph, yes. Do you know anything about clockmaking, by the way? It's a fascinating subject. Carver loaned the department store several of his less valuable pieces—one of his was the stolen watch—and I believe they even coaxed a few out of the Guildhall Museum. I was only wondering . . ."

"You damned charlatan!" said Melson, explosively. Then he grinned, and it was reflected in a broad beam across Dr. Fell's moon face. "I suppose you didn't want to see that dictionary at all? But I—" He hesitated. "As a matter of fact I'd forgotten it, but a queer thing happened there today."

"What sort of queer thing?"

Melson stared ahead between the dark walls, to where street lamps showed the pale green of trees in Lincoln's Inn Fields.

"A joke," he answered, slowly. "A joke of some sort. I didn't follow all of it. It was this morning. I'd come out for the after-breakfast smoke and constitutional; it was not quite nine o'clock, anyway. All those houses have a high stoop, with a cramped little porch under a couple of white pillars, and a bench along each side. There were very few people around, but a policeman was coming along our side of the street. I was sitting there smoking and feeling lazy . . . well, yes, I was looking at the house next door. It interested me because your clockmaker has a plate in his window that reads 'Johannus Carver.' I was curious about anybody who would have the nerve to turn his name into 'Johannus' in this day and age."

"Well?"

"Well—this is where it gets ridiculous," Melson said, uncomfortably. "All of a sudden the door popped open and out came a hard-faced old party (woman), who ducked down the steps and ran for the constable. First I gathered she wanted to report a burglary, and then that she wanted several kids in the neighborhood sent to the reform school; she was in a devil of a stew, and shouting. Then out after her came another woman, youngish, quite a girl; good-looking blonde. . . ."

(Very good-looking, he reflected, with the sun on her hair, and not too thoroughly dressed.)

"Naturally I didn't like to be seen sitting on the porch gaping at 'em; but I pretended not to be listening and just sat there. So far as I could understand it, the hard-faced lady was Johannus Carver's housekeeper. Johannus Carver had spent weeks building a big clock which was to go in the tower of Sir Somebody-or-other's country house; and that wasn't his type of work, and he only did it to obilge Sir Somebody-or-other, who was his personal friend . . . that was how she went on. So the clock was finished only last night, and Johannus painted it and left it in the back room to dry. Then somebody got in, mutilated the clock, and stole the hands off it. — Joke?"

"I don't like it," said Dr. Fell, after a pause. "I don't *like* it." He flourished one cane. "What did the law do?"

"Seemed pretty flustered, and took a lot of notes, but not much happened. The blonde girl was trying to quiet the other woman down. She said it was probably just a prank; pretty mean one, though, because the clock was ruined. They went inside then. I didn't get a glimpse of Johannus."

"Humph. Girl belong to Johannus's family?"

"I should imagine so."

Dr. Fell growled: "Hang it, Melson, I wish I'd questioned Hadley more closely. Does anybody else live in the house, or haven't you been observing?"

"Not closely, but it's a big place and there seem to be several people. I did notice a solicitor's plate on the door as well. Look here. Do you think it has any connection with . . . ?"

They emerged on the northern side of Lincoln's Inn Fields. The square itself seemed more vast than by daylight; housefronts swept and sedate with only a few cracks of light showing behind drawn curtains, and even the trees a sort of orderly forest. There was a watery moon, as pale as the street lamps.

"We turn to the right," said Melson. "That's the

8

Soane Museum there. Two doors farther on...." He ran his hand along the damp iron of the area railings, looking up at flatchested houses. "There's where I live. Next door is Johannus's place. I don't know exactly what good we can do standing and looking at the house...."

"I'm not so sure," said Dr. Fell. "The front door is open."

They both stopped. The words came to Melson with a sort of shock, especially as No. 16 showed no lights. Moon and street lamp showed it mistily, like a blurred drawing—a heavy, tall, narrow house in red brick that looked almost black, its window-frames etched out in white, and a flight of stone steps going up to round stone pillars that supported a porch roof nearly as small as the hood of a clock. The big door was wide open. Melson thought that it creaked.

"What do you suppose—?" he asked, and found his whisper rising.

He stopped, because he noticed a darker shadow under a tree just before the house, where there was somebody watching. But the house was no longer quite silent. A voice there had begun to moan and cry, and there were indistinguishable fragments of words that sounded like accusation. Then the shadow under the tree detached itself. Moving across the pavement, Melson saw with a jerk of relief the silhouette of a policeman's helmet; he heard the steady tread, and saw the beam of a bull's-eye lantern strike up ahead as the policeman mounted the steps to No. 16.

# 2

## Death on the Clock

Dr. Fell was already wheezing as he lumbered across the pavement. He reached up with one cane and touched the policeman's arm. The beam flashed down.

"Is anything wrong?" asked Dr. Fell. "Take that light out of my eyes, can't you?"

"Now, then!" grunted the law, noncommittal and vaguely annoyed. "Now, then, sir—!"

"Keep it in my eyes a second, then. What's the matter, Pierce? Don't you recognize me? I recognize you. They used to have you on station duty. Heh. Hum. You were outside Hadley's office———"

The law erred, and assumed that Dr. Fell's presence here was intentional. He said, "*I* don't know, sir, but come along." Beckoning to a reluctant Melson, Dr. Fell followed Pierce up the steps.

Once you were past the door, it was not altogether dark in the long hallway. At the rear was a flight of stairs, and a glow showed down them from the floor above. The eerie voice had stopped, as though some-body were waiting and listening. From somewhere on his left, behind one of the closed doors, Melson could hear what he at first took for a nervous, insistent whis-pering, before he identified it as the confused ticking of many clocks. At the same time a woman's voice from upstairs cried:

"Who's there?" A stirring and rustling; then the voice cried: "I can't go past him. I can't go past him, I tell you! He's all over blood." And it whimpered.

The words brought a harsh sound from Pierce before he ran forward. His light preceded him to the staircase, his two companions following closely. It was a prim stairway, with heavy banisters, dull-flowered carpet un-derfoot, and brass stair-rods; it was a symbol of solid English homes, where no violence can come, and did not creak as they mounted it. Facing its top, double doors were opened at the back of the upper hall. The dull light came from beyond them—from a room where two people were staring at the threshold, and a third person sat in a chair with his head in his hands.

Spilled across the threshold, a man lay partly on his right side and partly on his back. The yellow light showed him clearly, making a play with shadows on the muscles of the face and hands that still twitched. His eyelids still fluttered, and showed the whites under-neath. His mouth was open; his back seemed to arch a little as though in pain, and Melson could have sworn his nails made a scratching noise on the carpet; but these must have been nerve-reflexes after death, for the blood had already ceased to flow from his mouth. His heels gave a final jerk and rattle on the floor; the eyelids froze open.

Melson felt a little sick. He took a step backwards suddenly, and nearly missed his footing on the stairs.

Added to the sight of the dead man, the trivial slip came close to unnerving him.

One of the people in the doorway was the woman who had cried out. He could see her only as a silhouette, the gleam on her yellow hair. But now she darted round the dead man, losing a slipper, which tumbled out grotesquely across the floor, and seized the constable's arm.

"He's dead," she said. "Look at him." The voice rose hysterically. "Well? Well? Aren't you going to arrest *him*? She pointed to the man standing in the doorway, who was staring down dully. "He shot him. Look at the gun in his hand."

The other roused himself. He became aware that he was holding, by one finger through the trigger-guard, an automatic pistol whose barrel looked long and unwieldy. Nearly letting it fall, he jammed it into one pocket as the constable stepped forward; then he wheeled out, and they saw that his head was trembling with a horrible motion like a paralytic's. Seen sideways in the light, he was a neat, prim, clean-shaven little man, with a pince-nez whose gold chain went to one ear and fluttered to his trembling. He had a pointed jaw, which ordinarily might have been determined like his sharp mouth; dark tufts of eyebrows, a long nose, and indeterminate mouse-coloured hair combed pompadour. But now the face was wrinkled and loose with what might have been terror or cowardice or pure funk. It was made grotesque when he tried to assume an air of dignity—a family solicitor?—when he raised one hand in a deprecating way, and even achieved a parody of a smile.

"My dear Eleanor," he said, with a jerk in his throat. . . .

"Keep him away from me," said the girl. "Aren't you

going to arrest him? He shot that man. Don't you see his *gun*?"

A rumbling, common-sense, almost genial voice struck across the hysteria. Dr. Fell, his shovel-hat in his hand and his big mop of hair straggling across his forehead, towered benevolently over her.

"Harrumph," said Dr. Fell, scratching his nose. "Are you sure of that, now? What about the shot? The three of us were outside the house, you know, and we heard no shot."

"But didn't you see it? There, when he had it in his hand? It's got one of those silencer-things on the end. . . ."

She turned away quickly, because the policeman had been bending over the body. He got up stolidly and went to the fascinated little man in the doorway.

"All right, sir," he said, without emotion. "That gun. Hand it over."

The other let his hands fall to his sides. He spoke rapidly. "You can't do this, officer. You mustn't. So help me God, I had absolutely nothing to do with it." His arms were twitching now.

"Steady, sir. The gun, now. Steady on; you'll catch your hand—just give it to me butt foremost, if you please. Yes. Your name, now?"

"It is r-really an extraordinary mistake. Calvin Boscombe. I—"

"And who is this dead man?"

"I don't know."

"Come now!" said Pierce, giving a snap to his notebook wearily.

"I tell you I don't know." Boscombe had stiffened. He folded his arms and stood back against the side of the door as though in a defensive posture. He was wearing a neat grey wool dressing-gown, its cord carefully knotted into a bow. Pierce turned heavily to the girl.

"Who is it, miss?"

"I—I don't know, either. I never saw him before."

Melson glanced down at her. She was standing now with her face to the light, and he compared the impression he had received that morning, when she ran into the street, with this Eleanor (Carver?) at close range. Age, say twenty-seven or eight. Decidedly pretty in the conventional way which is, *pace* the motion pictures, nevertheless the best way. Of medium height and slender, but with a bloom towards sensuality of figure that was reflected also in eye and nostril and slightly raised upper lip. Something also about her appearance struck Melson as at once so puzzling and so obvious that it was several moments before he realized what it was. Presumably she had been roused out of bed, for her long bobbed hair was tousled, one lost slipper lay within a few feet of the dead man, and she wore red-and-black pyjamas over which was drawn a rather dusty blue leather motoring coat with its collar turned up. But she wore fresh rouge and lipstick, startling against her pallor. The blue eyes grew more frightened as she looked at Pierce. She yanked the coat more closely about her.

"I tell you I never saw him before!" she repeated. "Don't look at me like that!" A quick glance, changing to puzzlement. "He—he looks like a tramp, doesn't he? And I don't know how he got in, unless *he*," nodding at Boscombe, "let him in. The door is locked and chained every night."

Pierce grunted and made a note. "Um. Just so. And your name, miss?"

"It's Eleanor." She hesitated. "That is, Eleanor Carver."

14

"Come, miss please! Surely you're certain about your own name?"

"Oh. Well. Why are you so fussy?" she demanded, pettishly, and then changed her tone. "Awfully sorry, only I'm shaken up. My name's Eleanor Smith, really; only Mr. Carver is my guardian, sort of, and he wants me to use his name . . . ."

"And you say this gentleman shot——?"

"Oh, I don't know what I said!"

"Thank you, Eleanor," Boscombe said, suddenly and rather appealingly. His thin chest heaved. "Will you—all of you—please come into my rooms, and sit down, and—shut the door on that ghastly thing?"

"Can't be done yet, sir. Now, miss," continued the constable, in patient exasperation, "*will* you tell us what happened?"

"But I don't know! . . . I was asleep, that's all. I sleep on the ground floor, at the back. That's where my guardian has his shop. Well, a draught was blowing my door open and shut. I wondered what caused it, and I got up to close the door; then I looked out and saw that the front door in the hall was wide open. That frightened me a little. I went out a little way, and then I saw the light up here and heard voices. I heard *him*," she nodded at Boscombe; there was something of fading terror and shock in the look, more terror than seemed accountable, and also a flash of malice. She breathed hard. "I heard him say, 'My God! he's dead. . . .'"

"If you will allow me to explain—" Boscombe put in, desperately.

Dr. Fell had been blinking at her in a vaguely bothered way, and was about to speak; but she went on:

"I was horribly frightened. I crept upstairs—you can't hear anybody walking on that carpet—and peeped over. I saw *him* standing in the doorway there, bending

15

over *him,* and that other man was standing at the back of the room with his face turned away."

At her nod they became for the first time conscious of the third watcher over the dead. This man had been sitting in Boscombe's room, by a table that held a shaded lamp, one elbow on the table and his fingers plucking at his forehead. As though he had gathered to himself an extreme quietness of manner, he rose stiffly and strolled over with his hands in his pockets. A big man with somewhat projecting ears, whose face was in shadow, he nodded several times to nobody in particular. He did not look at the body.

"And that's absolutely all I know," Eleanor Carver declared. "Except what *he*"—she stared at the dead man—"meant by coming in here and—and frightening . . . I say, he does look like a tramp, doesn't he? Or, come to think of it, if he were washed and had decent clothes on, he might look a bit like—"

Her gaze strayed from the body up to Boscombe. But she checked herself, while they studied the thing on the floor. It could not have been a pleasant object even in life, as Melson could see when individual details obtruded themselves through the one hypnotic picture of murder. Over the man's tattered suit, rubbed to an indeterminate colour and pulled in with safety pins until his arms and legs flopped out of it, there was a greasiness like cold soup. The unknown was a man of about fifty, at once scrawny and bloated. His brass collar-stud bulged on a neck red and wrinkled like a turkey's, and the stumps of teeth gaped wide in a three days' stubble of beard where the blood had not obscured them. Yet (in death, at least) he did not look altogether like a tramp. As he felt this and tried to puzzle out the resemblance, Melson noticed the one incongruous detail—the man was wearing white tennis shoes that were almost new.

16

Suddenly Pierce turned round to Boscombe.

"This deceased, now," he said, "is he a relation of yours by any chance, sir?"

Boscombe was genuinely startled. He was even a little shocked.

"Good Lord, *no*! A relation of mine? What—what on earth ever gave you that idea?" He hesitated, fidgeting, and Melson felt that this idea would upset Mr. Calvin Boscombe nearly as much as a suspicion of murder. "Constable, this business is growing fantastic! I tell you I don't know who he is. Do you want to know what happened? Nothing! That is, to be precise, my friend and I"—he nodded towards the big man, who stood motionless—"my friend and I were sitting in my living-room, talking. We were having a nightcap and he was just getting his hat to go . . ."

"One moment, sir." The notebook came to attention. "Your name?"

"Peter Stanley," replied the big man. He spoke in a heavy, dull voice, as though some curious memory had just stirred in his mind. "Peter E. Stanley." The whites of his eyes flashed up, as though he were repeating a lesson into which had come a tinge of sour amusement. "Of 211 Valley Edge Road, Hampstead. I—er—I don't live here. And I don't know the deceased, either."

"Go on, sir."

Boscombe glanced rather nervously at his companion before he continued: "As I repeat, we were merely sitting like—like two law-abiding citizens." Something in this speech struck even Boscombe as incongruous and absurd; and he achieved a pale smile. "That is, we were sitting here. These double-doors were closed. That pistol of mine you seem to consider suspicious. Not at all. I did not fire it. I was only showing Mr. Stanley what a Grott silencer is like. He had never seen one before. . . ."

Stanley began to laugh.

It was as though he could not help it. He clapped a hand over his chest, for the laughter seemed to strike him like a bullet and hurt him. Bending sideways, one thick-sinewed hand on the doorpost, he peered at them out of a cadaverous face whose heavy fleshiness and putty colour had the effect of a clay mask. It was split with that choking mirth, which screeched with horrible effect as he gulped and winked. And its echo was worse. Eleanor Carver shrank back, crying out.

"Sorry, old man," Stanley shouted, the roar dying into a shudder as he clapped Boscombe on the back. "S-sorry, constable. Everybody. Beg pardon. It's so damned funny, that's all. Ho-ho! But it's quite true. He was showing *me*."

He wiped his eyes, grotesquely. Pierce took a step forward, but Dr. Fell laid a hand on his arm.

"Easy on," said the doctor, very quietly. "Well, Mr. Boscombe?"

"I don't know who you are, sir," Boscombe responded, in the same quiet tone, "or why you are here. But you seem to be that rare phenomenon, a sensible man. I repeat that Mr. Stanley and I were sitting here, examining the pistol, when—without any warning— there was a knocking and scratching at these doors." He laid his hand on one of them, quickly drew it away, and looked down. "That man knocked them open, slipped, and fell down on his back as you see him now. I swear to you that is absolutely *all* I know of it. I do not know what he is doing here or how he got in. We have not touched him."

"No," said Dr. Fell, "but you should have." After a pause he nodded to Pierce and pointed at the body with one cane. "You've looked at that gun, and you've probably seen it hasn't been fired. Now turn him over."

"Can't do it, sir," snapped Pierce. "Got to phone through to the station and get the divisional surgeon here before we can——"

"Roll him over," said Dr. Fell, sharply. "I'll be responsible."

Pierce thrust pistol and notebook into his pocket. Gingerly he bent over and heaved. The dead man's loose left hand flopped over with a knocking of knuckles against the carpet; knees and chin sagged as he came round. Wiping his hands, the constable stood back.

Just above the first vertebrae, from which something thin and sharp had evidently taken an oblique downward course through the throat into the chest, projected a hand's breadth of metal. It was not a knife whose like any of them had ever seen before. What they could see of it through the blood had been painted a bright gilt; it was about an inch and a half wide at the head, of thin steel, and the head was perforated in a curious rectangle rather like a car-spanner.

Eleanor Carver screamed.

"Yes," said Dr. Fell. "Somebody got him from behind just before he reached the head of the stairs. And that thing—"

He followed the girl's pointing finger.

"—yes. I shall be very much surprised if it's not the minute-hand of a clock. A big outdoor clock, a stable clock with an open steel frame, say like the one Carver was building for Sir Somebody-or-other."

# 3

## The Broken Window

"You see," Dr. Fell continued, rather apologetically, "I was afraid it would turn out to be rather more devilish than it seemed. And, much as I detest official moves, I'm afraid that until Hadley gets here I shall have to take charge."

Stanley, who had been brushing one sleeve across his eyes in a sort of wabbling torpor, whirled round. The dull mask was cut with lines round his down-pulled mouth.

"You?" he snarled, and straightened up. "You'll take charge, will you? And what the devil do *you* know about it, my friend?"

"Got it!" muttered Dr. Fell, with an air of inspiration. "Got it at last! It was that particular tone in your voice. I was wondering about you, Mr. Stanley. Humph, yes. By the way, Mr. Boscombe, have you got a telephone here? Good!... Pierce, will you go in and phone straight to Extension 27? I know you've got to send in your divisional station report; but be sure you get the

Yard first. That'll reach Chief Inspector Hadley. I know he's still there, because he's working late tonight. He'll come along with the police surgeon, if only to argue with me. Don't mind if he curses you to blazes. Humph. Stop a bit! Ask Hadley who he's got working on that Gamridge department-store case, and tell whoever it is to come along. I think he'll find something interesting. . . . Miss Carver?"

She had retreated a few steps downstairs, into the shadows, and she was rubbing her face with a handkerchief. When she thrust the handkerchief into her pocket and came up to join them, Melson saw that the fresh make-up was gone. It gave her a more intense pallor, and the blue eyes had turned almost black when she glanced at Boscombe; but she was absolutely composed.

"I haven't deserted you," she observed. "Don't you think I'd better wake up auntie and J.?—my guardian, you know." She held hard to the newel-post and added, "I don't know how you know it, but that *is* the hand off the clock. Can't you throw something over him? That's worse than looking at his face." She shuddered.

Boscombe caught the expression eagerly; he bustled out of the door, and returned with a dusty couch-cover. At a nod from Dr. Fell he settled it over the body. "What," the girl cried, suddenly, "does it *mean*? Do you know? You don't, do you? I suppose the poor man was a burglar?"

"You know he wasn't," said Dr. Fell, gently. He blinked about the hallway, humped over his canes; he looked at the pale face of Boscombe and then at a very subdued Stanley. But he did not prompt them to speak. "I could make a guess as to what he might be doing here. And I only hope I'm wrong."

"Somebody," Stanley muttered, speaking in a gruff

monotone to the corner of the door, "followed him from outside, up the steps, and—"

"Not necessarily from outside. I say, Miss Carver, may we have some lights on here?"

It was Boscombe who moved over and pressed a central switch beside the double doors. A chandelier in the roof illumined the spacious upper hallway, sixty feet long by twenty feet wide, carpeted throughout in the same flowered reddish design. The staircase, some eight feet broad, was along the right-hand wall as you looked towards the front. In the front wall, overlooking the street, were two long windows with patterned brown draperies closely drawn. Along the right-hand wall, between these windows and the staircase, were two doors; another closed door was on the landing side of the stairs, almost against the angle of the rear wall where the double doors led to Boscombe's rooms. Three more doors, all closed, were in the left-hand wall. They were white-painted, like the plain white panelling of the walls, and the ceiling kalsomined a dull brown. The only ornamentation was a wooden long-case clock whose dial bore a single hand (to Melson's eye a dull enough object) between the two windows. Dr. Fell blinked vacantly about the hall, wheezing to himself.

"Heh," he said. "Yes, of course. Big house. Admirable. How many people live here, Miss Carver?"

She went over gingerly and snatched up her lost slipper before Boscombe could retrieve it. "Well . . . J. owns it, of course. There's J. and auntie—Mrs. Steffins; she's not an aunt, really. Then there's Mr. Boscombe, and Mr. Paull, and Mrs. Gorson, who takes care of the place generally. Mr. Paull is away now." Her short upper lip lifted a trifle. "Then, of course, there's our solicitor. . . ."

"Who is he?"

"It's a she," Eleanor replied, and looked downstairs

indifferently. "I don't mean she's ours, you understand, but we take a great deal of pride in her."

"A very brilliant woman," declared Boscombe, with shaky authority.

"Yes. L. M. Handreth. I dare say you saw the shingle downstairs? The L is for Lucia. And I'll tell you a secret." Under the nervousness against which she was speaking rapidly, a flash of devilment showed like a grin in her pale-blue eyes. "The M is for Mitzi. It's amazing how she has slept through all this row. She has one whole side of the ground floor."

"It's amazing how everybody has," agreed Dr. Fell, with easy affability. "I'm afraid we shall have to rouse them out before long, or my friend Hadley will draw sinister inferences from the mere fact that people have healthy consciences. H'm, yes. . . . Now, where do all these people sleep, Miss Carver?"

"I told you Lucia has one side of the ground floor." She waved her hand to the left as she faced the front. "Opposite, the two front rooms are J.'s showrooms— you know he makes clocks? There's a sitting-room behind those, and then auntie's room, and mine at the rear. Mrs. Gorson and the maid are in the basement. Up here—

"That door on the right at the front goes to J.'s bedroom. The one next to it is a sort of clock lumber-room; he works there when it's cold weather, but usually in a shed in the back yard, because sometimes there's noise. Just across the hall are Mr. Paull's rooms; I told you he was away. That's all."

"Yes. Yes, I see. Stop a bit; I nearly forgot," said Dr. Fell, blinking round again. He pointed to the door at the head of the stairs, in the same wall as the stairs, and near the angle of the rear wall. "And that one? Another lumber-room?"

"Oh, that? That only goes to the roof, I mean," she

explained, rapidly, "to a passage, and another door, and a flight of steps with a little box room; then the roof. . . ." Dr. Fell took an absent-minded step forward, and she moved with her back to it, smiling. "It's locked. I mean, we always keep it locked."

"Eh? Oh, I wasn't thinking of that," he said, wheeling round and peering down in his vague way. "It was something else. Would you mind, just as a matter of form, showing me where you were standing on the stairs when you peeped over the top and saw our late visitor lying on the floor? Thank you.—Mind switching out those centre lights again, Mr. Boscombe? Yes. Take your time, Miss Carver. You were down on the sixth— fifth; sure of it?—fifth step from the top, looking over as you are now, eh?"

With only that weird yellow light from Boscombe's living room falling against the dark, Melson felt uneasiness closing in again. He peered down the broad staircase to where the girl's pallid face looked over, her hands closing on one tread. In the darkness of the lower hall below, her head and shoulders were silhouetted against the glow of a street lamp that fell through a narrow window at one side of the front door. The outline trembled for a second while Dr. Fell bent forward.

A voice behind cried out with such abruptness that she stumbled.

"What the hell's the meaning of all this drivel?" demanded Stanley. He strode out into the hall. Dr. Fell turned round to face him, slowly. Melson could not see the doctor's face, but both Stanley and Boscombe stopped.

"Which of you," said Dr. Fell, "moved the right-hand side of those double doors?"

"I—I beg your pardon?" asked Boscombe.

"This one." He lumbered over and touched the leaf

of the door just behind the dead man's head, which was folded back nearly against the wall inside. He moved it out so that a broad bar of shadow ran across the twisted figure under the couch-cover. "It was moved, wasn't it? It was like this when you first found the body?"

"Well, I didn't touch it," Stanley told him. "I wasn't near old—I didn't come near that thing at all. Ask Boscombe if I did."

Boscombe's hand fluttered to his pince-nez and adjusted it.

"I moved it, sir," he answered, with some dignity. "I was, if you will excuse me, not aware that I was doing anything wrong. Naturally, I moved it to get more light from the room."

"Oh, you weren't doing anything wrong," Dr. Fell agreed, amiably. He chuckled a little. "Now, if you don't mind, we'll accept the hospitality of your room, Mr. Boscombe, to ask a few more curious questions. Miss Carver, will you wake up your guardian and your aunt, and tell them to be in readiness?"

When Boscombe fussily ushered them in, apologizing for the disorder of his place as though there had been no dead man across the threshold and as though the place were really disordered, Melson found himself even more puzzled and disturbed. Puzzled, because Boscombe did not look the sort of man who would be interested in pistol-silencers. A shrewd little man, Boscombe; shrewd, probably hard under his surface mildness; bookish—if the walls of the room were any indication—and with a way of talking like a butler in a drawing-room comedy. Many nervous and self-conscious people talked just like that, which was another indication. Very neat, in his black pyjamas and grey wool dressing-gown and thick fleece-lined slippers;

what the devil was the suggestion? Like a cross between Jeeves and Soames Forsyte.

And Melson was disturbed because both these men were lying about what they knew. Melson felt it; he would have sworn to it; it was a palpable atmosphere in the room as well as in the hostility of Mr. Peter Stanley. He grew even more uncomfortable as he looked at Stanley in full light. Stanley was not merely hostile: he was ill, and he had been ill long before this night. A big shell of a man, with nerves jerking like wires at the corners of his eyes, he worked his heavy loose jaw with a loose chewing motion. His baggy clothes were good, but frayed about the sleeves, and his tie was skewered round under the corner of a high old-fashioned collar. He sat down in a Morris chair at one side of the table and took out a cigarette.

"Well?" he said. His bloodshot eyes followed Dr. Fell as the latter peered slowly round the room. "Yes, I suppose the place is comfortable enough—for a murder. Does it tell you anything?"

It told Melson nothing, at the moment. It was a big room with a high ceiling, a ceiling sloping slightly towards the rear, and pierced by a skylight. All but a little of the skylight, where two panes were open for ventilation, was shrouded by a black velvet curtain held against it on sliding wires. Curtained also were two windows at the rear of the room. In the left-hand wall was a door which apparently led to a bedroom. Bookshelves ran around the rest of the wallspace, to the height of a man's shoulder; above them hung irregularly a series of pictures which Melson noted in some astonishment to be Hogarth's "Rake's Progress" in skilful copies. You noticed irregularities in this room's neatness—or certain other things might have gone unobserved. The circular centre table had its student's lamp exactly in the middle; on one side stood an hour-glass and on the other an old brass box into whose filigree design were woven curious greenish crosses. At the left of the table was a great padded chair, a sort of throne with large wings and a high back, across from the chair in which Stanley sat. Although there was a scent of tobacco smoke in the room, Melson noted the curious fact that all the ash-trays were scrubbed clean; and no glasses were set out, despite the array of bottles and glasses on the sideboard. . . .

Damn it, the whole picture was somehow *wrong*; or, reflected Melson, was he merely being a fool with too much subtlety? From the direction of the bedroom he could hear Pierce's voice, presumably on the telephone. As he glanced round, those queer greenish crosses on the discolored brass of the box were reflected again. Up against the wall of the doors by which they had entered, and folded round so as to make nearly a complete enclosure, was a gigantic screen in panels of stamped Spanish leather. The panels, enclosed in a design of brass studding, were alternately black, with gilt figures of flames painted on them, and yellow with red or saffron crosses.

A doubtful memory stirred in Melson's brain: the word *sanbenito*. Now what was a *sanbenito*? For this screen interested Dr. Fell. The seconds ticked; the uncomfortable silence began to grow, while Dr. Fell stared owlishly at the screen. They could hear his asthmatic wheezing, and an inexplicable draught flapping a curtain at the window. He lumbered forward, poked at the screen with his stick, and peered round behind. . . .

"Excuse me, sir," Boscombe said, rather shrilly, and took a step forward as though to ease strain, "but surely you have more important interests than—"

"Than?" prompted Dr. Fell, his forehead wrinkled.

"My culinary arrangements. That is a gas-ring, where I prepare my breakfasts sometimes. An unsightly thing, I fear. . . ."

"H'm, yes. I say, Mr. Boscombe, I'm afraid you're devilish careless. You've spilled a tin of coffee and there's milk all over the floor." He turned round, and waved his hand as Boscombe involuntarily stepped forward in a rush of domestic agitation. "No, no; please don't attend to it now. Look here, do we understand each other if I say this is not a time for crying over spilt milk? Eh?"

"I don't think I understand."

"And there's chalk on the carpet there," rumbled Dr. Fell, pointing suddenly towards the throne chair. "Why should there be chalk-marks on the carpet? Gentlemen, I'm worried; this thing makes *no* sense whatever."

Boscombe, as though he feared Dr. Fell would take his chair, had sat down in it. He folded his thin arms and regarded the doctor sardonically.

He said: "Whoever you may be, sir, and whatever official position you hold, I have been waiting to answer your questions. I confess I anticipated—um—an ordeal. This is pleasantly informal. I fail to see why it makes no sense that I should spill a jug of milk. Or even get into the carpet an odd bit of broken chalk. You see that flat object over behind the couch? It is a folding billiard table. . . . I don't want to hurry you, sir, but will you tell me what you want to *know*?"

"Excuse me, sir," said a voice in the doorway to the bedroom. Pierce, looking stolid but perturbed, saluted Dr. Fell. "I think there's some questions you can ask 'em, if it's not out of place my saying so."

Boscombe straightened up.

"I came in here to telephone," continued Pierce in

a rush, squaring his shoulders as though to go down a football field (at the end of which were sergeant's stripes), "before that gentleman came to get the couch-cover. It was that couch. Sir, there was things on the couch. He shoved 'em down behind. Like this."

As Boscombe got up very quickly, Pierce pushed past him, crossed to the couch, and groped behind it. He produced a battered pair of shoes, their toe-caps gone and worn soles sagging, the laces knotted over a few remaining notches, and plastered with still soft mud. Into one shoe had been thrust a pair of grimy cotton gloves.

"I thought I'd better tell you, sir," he insisted, dangling the shoes. "Those gloves—they're cut round the knuckles, and they've got little pieces of glass sticking in 'em. All right! And then this window"—he strode over to the window where the curtain was swaying in the draught. "I looked at it first because—well, sir, I thought there might be somebody 'iding behind that curtain. There wasn't nobody 'iding. *But* there's bits of glass under it. And I lifted the curtain, like this. . . ."

It was not quite closed. One of the panes, just under the catch that would have locked it, was smashed out. And even at a distance they could see marks on the white sill where mud had been scraped across by a sliding foot.

"Eh, sir?" demanded Pierce. "These are more like the boots that dead man 'u'd be apt to wear. Aren't they, now, instead of the white things he's got on? All right, sir; then you'd better ask these men if he didn't come in by the window, after all . . . Especially as—look there—just outside this window there's a tree that a baby could climb in its sleep. Now!"

After a long pause Melson jerked round.

Stanley was laughing again horribly, and beating his hand against the back of the chair.

# 4

## The Man Across the Threshold

"My friend is ill," Boscombe remarked, very quietly. At the back of his eyes, the eyes that the inscrutability of the sharp dry face could not control, he looked startled out of his five wits; not at the implication of guilt, but at something crashing and unforeseen.

Which, thought Melson, made it worse. The man who overlooks a smashed window and mudstains on the sill is not a criminal who makes a slip; he must be stark insane.

"My friend is ill," repeated Boscombe, clearing his throat. "Allow me to get him some brandy. . . . Brace up, will you?" he snapped.

"By God! are you apologizing for *me*?" the other asked, his mirth choked off. "Ill, am I? And of course I can't take care of myself. Look here, I think I'll blow the gaff." He grinned widely. "Hadley will be here in a minute, and he'll appreciate it. . . . Robert, my lad," he said to the constable, with a kind of bravado that was not supported by his twitching eyelids, "blast you—you and all your kind—the rotten lot and bag of them—the whole filthy—." His voice rose and he gulped. "Do you know who I am? Do you know who you're talking to?"

"I was wondering," said Dr. Fell, "how long it would be before you told us. If I remember rightly, you were once chief inspector of the Criminal Investigation Department."

Stanley looked slowly round. "Retired," he said, "with honour."

"But, sir," protested the constable, "aren't you going to *ask* them?"

Dr. Fell did not appear to be listening.

"Tree!" he roared, suddenly. "Tree! O Lord! O Bacchus! O my ancient hat! Of course. This is terrible. Tell me—" He checked himself, and turned to Pierce. "My boy," he continued, benevolently, "that was fine work. I'll ask them right enough. But now I've got a commission for you." He had taken out notebook and pencil and was scrawling rapidly as he spoke. "By the way, did you get Hadley on the phone?"

"Yes, sir. He's coming over straightaway."

"And the chap on the department-store case?"

"Yes, sir. Inspector Ames, Mr. Hadley said. He said he was bringing him if he could be found."

"Right. Take this," Dr. Fell ripped out the note-sheet, "and don't ask questions. It's a step towards promotion. Hop it, now." He regarded Stanley with a sombre eye while Boscombe brought the latter a tumbler half full of brandy. "Now, gentlemen, I don't want to hurry you, but I can't help feeling my friend the chief inspector is going to cut up rough when he finds those shoes. Don't you think an explanation is in order? And I shouldn't drink that brandy, if I were you."

31

"You go to hell," shouted Stanley, and drained the glass at a a gulp.

". . . Steady," said Dr. Fell. "Better send him into the bathroom. I don't like the imminence of—That's it." He waited while Boscombe urged Stanley, wavering, through the door. Boscombe, rubbing his hands together, returned as unsteadily as his companion. "That man," continued Dr. Fell, "is as close to a nervous breakdown as he's ever likely to be. Suppose you tell me—what happened here tonight?"

"Suppose," returned Boscombe, with a mild flash of ugliness, "you reason it out for yourself." He went softly to the sideboard, his face an unpleasant length; he drew the stopper of a decanter and turned. "I'll give you only one hint. I don't want that lunatic to strangle me when he finds I was trying to play a joke. . . . Admit, if you like, that the fact of the broken window is curious—"

"Somewhat. It could hang you."

Boscombe's hand jerked. "That is nonsense, of course. A perfect stranger, a burglar, climbs in that window. We stab him with the hand of a clock; we take all the trouble to put a pair of new shoes on him and drop him outside the door. Really, that is an extraordinary procedure, isn't it? Why do we do it? One shoots burglars."

"I seem to remember that you did have a gun, at that."

"So far as I am aware," Boscombe said, meditatively, and cocked his head to one side, "there is nothing illegal about smashing one's own windows and owning old shoes. The shoes are mine. I smashed the window. Why I did it is neither here nor there. I smashed the window."

"I know you did," said Dr. Fell, quietly.

32

Melson thought, Is *everybody* insane? He stared first at the doctor, and then at the little man who seemed suddenly more perturbed at these words than at anything that had been said before. Dr. Fell raised his voice.

"I want to know the whys and wherefores of a number of other things, too. I want to know why Stanley was hiding behind that screen there, and you were sitting in the big chair, when Mr. X walked up the stairs tonight. I want to know why you prepared those gloves and shoes; why you so carefully cleaned the ash-trays and washed the glasses. I want to know who it was Eleanor Carver was afraid had got hurt when she saw Mr. X lying over your doorstep. . . . In short," said Dr. Fell, with an offhand wave of his hand and a curiously cross-eyed glance at the Spanish screen, "I want to know the truth. And in this house, where everything is topsy-turvy, it seems an uncommonly tortuous process. Heh. Heh-heh-heh. I shall not be at all surprised to find somebody walking on the ceiling. As a matter of fact, it would seem apparent in literal truth that somebody has—"

"I beg your pardon?"

"That somebody has already walked on the ceiling," said Dr. Fell. "Do I make myself clear? No. I perceive that I do not. Oh, well, dammit," he added, affably, "allow the old man to be a bit of a charlatan! . . . Good evening, sir. You are Mr. Johannus Carver?"

Melson whirled. He had heard nobody approach; the muffling carpet gave to everybody a quality of sudden and disturbing appearance. The man in the doorway did not look like Johannus Carver as Melson had pictured him. He had imagined something small and grandfatherish and dusty. Johannus was on the muscular side, and over six feet, although a stoop took away much of his height. When they first saw him he was staring down at the body under the couch-cover, rubbing one sleeve across his forehead with an expression less of horror than of concern and perplexity; as though he were looking at a child's cut finger. He had a domed skull, with a close stubble of that hair which looks blond even when it is grey; a pair of mild light-blue eyes puckered in wrinkles; a heavy jaw, an indecisive mouth, and a wrinkled neck. He wore striped pyjamas, their trouser-tops tucked into ancient elastic-sided boots.

"This," he said, and seemed to search his memory for an elusive word—"this is . . . Good God! I suppose there's no doubt he's—?"

"Dead enough," said Dr. Fell. "Miss Carver told you how it happened?—So. Will you lift up the edge of that cover and see if you know him?"

Carver replaced the cover hastily. "Yes, yes. Of course. I mean, no; I don't know him. Stop a bit, though." . . . With an effort he lifted the cover again. "Yes, that's the fellow, or I think it is. I'm not very good at faces." He frowned vacantly at the same time that his eyes seemed to wander about the room. His square, spatulate fingers tapped at his cheek. "I don't know his name, but I've seen him. Pubs, of course! He hangs on at the pubs hereabouts. Cadging drinks, you know. I'm very fond of pubs. Er—Mrs. Steffins does not approve." Carver woke up. "But look here! Something's got to be *done*," he announced, with a sort of vague firmness, and again he took a look. "So it is, so it is! Eleanor told me he was stabbed with the hand of Paull's dial. But why? I know he didn't get any of my collection. As soon as Eleanor woke me up I looked at the burglar alarms. All sound and intact. Ha! Yes. Well, then?"

He broke off to cough, and then his eyes widened.

"Wait a bit! Boscombe! That Maurer. You've got it safe?"

Boscombe tapped the brass box on the table. "Quite. Safe and sound in here. Er—have you had the pleasure of meeting our inquisitor, Carver? I confess I should rather like to meet him myself. We have been having a most interesting talk."

Again Carver woke up. "But, man, that's Dr. Fell! Dr. Gideon Fell! How do you do, sir? Eleanor recognized him from a picture in a newspaper. Don't you remember discussing his book on the history of the supernatural in English fiction? You disagreed with some of the points. . . ." Again Carver's ideas wandered, and he had to pull them together with an effort. "Show him the Maurer, Boscombe. He'll be interested."

Boscombe was too reserved to start perceptibly, now that the little grey shell had been drawn over him. But he blinked his eyes.

"This—this is unfortunate," he said, with a jerk in his throat. "I must beg your pardon, sir. I had no idea . . . May I offer you something to drink? A brandy?"

"Heh," said Dr. Fell. "Heh-heh-heh. Let me introduce Professor Melson, who has the thankless task of editing *Gilbert Burnet*. A brandy? Why, I don't mind if I do. Only don't put nux vomica in it, please."

"Nux vomica?"

"Isn't that what it was?" Dr. Fell inquired, affably. "I saw you putting it into Stanley's drink, you know. I rather wondered whether even a depraved taste for cocktails could go quite so far."

"I am afraid you see everything," said Boscombe, coolly. "Yes. I fancied it would be best if Stanley, hum, withdrew for a while.—A brandy, Dr. Melson?"

The other shook his head. What made the whole thing so ugly was the contrast between these two, the mild-mannered clockmaker and the mild-mannered little student, and their attitude towards death.

"Thanks," he said. "Some other time." He tried to force a smile. "I'm afraid my ancestral habits aren't strong enough. I could never get used to drinking at a wake."

"It bothers you, then? And yet why should it?" asked Boscombe, lifting his upper lip slightly. "Consider my own case, for example. Dr. Fell assures me that I am in a very bad position. And yet—"

Carver interrupted, in a heavy voice that was suddenly close to fright: "Do you seriously mean that somebody in this house is under suspicion of killing that—that poor devil?"

"He wasn't a poor devil," said Dr. Fell. "He wasn't a tramp, and he wasn't a burglar. Have you looked at his hands? He came in quietly, and in shoes that would make no noise, but not to steal. He was intended to come in. That's why the front door was unlocked and unchained for him."

"I tell you it's impossible," declared Carver. "The front door? No. I have a distinct recollection of locking and chaining that door myself, before I went to bed. . . ."

Dr. Fell nodded. "Yes. Now let's get down to questioning. Do you usually lock up for the night?"

"No. Mrs. Gorson does. But Thursday is her night off, you see. Usually she locks up at eleven-thirty, but—er—not on Thursdays. Obviously. She goes to visit some friends, I believe in a *suburb*," explained Carver, hesitantly, as though he were describing some remote mysterious haunt. "And when she returns, rather late, she comes in through the area door below. Yes. I locked the door, as I distinctly remember, because Mrs. Steffins said she was tired and wished to turn in early, and would I lock up?"

"And you locked the door . . . when?"

"At ten o'clock. I remember, because I called out, 'Is everybody in?' But I recalled seeing Miss Handreth's light, and Mr. Boscombe coming upstairs earlier; Eleanor I knew was in, and Mr. Paull is away."

Dr. Fell scowled. "But you say the place is usually locked up at eleven-thirty. What if somebody gets home later than that? Aren't there any latch-keys?"

"Latch-keys? No. Mrs. Steffins says they are always getting lost, and dishonest people pick them up. Besides"——he tapped his forehead lightly, and the mild eyes showed a gleam of amusement—"she has the impression that all sorts of vice ensue when people are given a latch-key. 'The devil's tool,' she calls it. This affords Miss Handreth much amusement. Miss Handreth is moving out at the end of the quarter. . . . What was it? Oh yes. If people are late, they press Mrs. Gorson's bell. We have a line of bells beside the door. And Mrs. Gorson gets up and opens the door. It is very simple."

"Very," said Dr. Fell. "You didn't know, then, that Mr. Stanley was in the house tonight when you locked up?"

Carver frowned, and then blinked across at Boscombe.

"Ha! That's queer! I'd forgotten all about poor Stanley. He must have got here late . . . Yes! Don't you remember, Boscombe? I came up and tapped at your door and asked for something to read in bed. You were sitting over there reading and smoking. And there was nobody else here. As a matter of fact, you showed me a sleeping-powder and said you were going to take it and go straight to bed. Ha!" exclaimed Carver, with a noisy breath of relief. He pointed a big finger at Dr. Fell. "There's your explanation, my dear sir. Of course. Stanley got here late, rang Boscombe's bell—why, it's as plain as dammit!—Boscombe went down to let him in; forgot to relock the door; and this burglar sneaked in. . . . Eh? Eh?"

Dr. Fell seemed about to make a comment that would blast the roof; but he controlled his puffing, looked at Boscombe, and said, sourly:

"Well?"

"It is quite true, Doctor," agreed Boscombe, with composure. "I am sorry it slipped my mind, ha-ha." The timid malice flashed a little. "An unpardonable oversight, but true. I was not expecting Stanley. When he arrived, I, unfortunately, left the front door ajar. . . ."

He paused as, clear in the night stillness, the humming of a car in the street roared up and stopped in a squeal of brakes. There were voices, and a trampling of feet up the front stairs. For a brief time—which seemed a very long one in that quiet, chilly room—Dr. Fell blinked at Boscombe and Carver. He said nothing. He only set down on the table a glass of brandy he had not tasted, nodded slowly, and stumped out of the room.

There was a row of sorts going on in the lower hall. Melson, following Dr. Fell downstairs, saw that it was brilliantly lighted. A sombre-clad group stood out against the white panelling; and, amid the photographer's tripods and the green satchels of the fingerprint men, his bowler on the back of his head, trying unsuccessfully to nibble one end of his clipped grey moustache like an annoyed brigadier, was Chief Inspector David Hadley.

Melson had met Hadley, and liked him. Dr. Fell always said that he would rather argue with Hadley than almost anybody else, because each on various points supplied the common sense that the other lacked. They differed violently on everything each of them liked, and agreed only on what they disliked, which is the basis of friendship. Hadley had the manner and bearing of a brigadier, but with quieter (almost repressed) speech. He tried, sometimes painfully, to do his duty, and he was doing it now.

At his elbow was a woman talking vehemently in a low, rapid voice. That morning Melson had not had a good look at the strong-minded Mrs. Steffins, and again his mental pictures had gone awry. She was a contrast: a small woman hard and thick about the body, bulky as though with muscle. Yet (under artificial light, at least) her small face was of a delicate Dresden-china prettiness. The violet eyes and the fine white teeth— she flashed them a good deal—were those of a young girl. It was only in her moments of anger or excitement that you noticed the skin roughening under powder, the faint thin wrinkle wandering down each cheek, the darkened flesh that grew pouched. She had stopped to dress herself completely; and she was, it seemed to Melson, well dressed, as she had not been that morning. Her hair was rather more brown. She could be— he felt—a terror. But she would not resort to terrorism until charm had first failed.

". . . Yes, certainly, madam. Yes, I quite understand," Hadley was saying, making a faint gesture as though he were troubled by a fly. He peered up the stairs rather angrily. "Where's the old blighter got to, anyway? Betts! See if you can find him. . . . Ah!"

Dr. Fell rumbled a greeting from the stairs, saluting with one cane. Mrs. Steffins broke off in the middle of a mechanical smile, the smile with which she was moving her head from side to side and setting off the somewhat loud voice. "And I have something," she insisted, "of the utmost importance—" Hadley raised his hat absently, replaced it on his head, and strode forward. Behind him doddered the glum little figure of Dr. Watson, the police surgeon. Hadley scowled at Dr. Fell.

"Very well, my excellent windbag," he said, with a grim settling of his jaw. "Oh, good evening, Professor! I don't know what he's got you in for, Melson, but I rather fancy *I'm* on a hell of a wild-goose chase. Look here, what makes you think that the knifing of a burglar in Lincoln's Inn Fields is tied up with Jane the Ripper?"

"Jane the Ripper?"

"Newspaper talk," Hadley said, irritably. "Anyway, it's easier than saying the-unknown-woman-who-slit-the-shopwalker's-stomach-at-Gamridge's. Well?"

"Only," answered Dr. Fell, wheezing, "that I'm more worried than I think I ever have been before. And I need a few facts. Did you bring along the man who's on the case—what's his name?—Inspector Ames?"

"No. I couldn't find him. He's out on it somewhere. But I've got his latest report. I haven't read it yet; but it's here in my briefcase. All right! Where's the body?"

Dr. Fell drew a deep breath and led the way up the stairs. He went slowly, one stick knocking against the banisters. At the top Carver and Boscombe were standing in the doorway; but Hadley gave them only a glance. Drawing on a pair of gloves, he propped his briefcase up against the wall and lifted the cover across the body. Something portentous, something fierce and hushed in Dr. Fell's manner, made Melson's flesh crawl uneasily during the instant of silence while Hadley bent over. . . .

Hadley muttered something, sharply, from deep in his throat. He knocked one side of the door open to give him more light.

"Watson!" he said. "Watson!"

When he straightened up again, not a muscle in Hadley's face moved; but it was quiet with rage and hatred.

"No," he said, "I didn't bring Ames." He jabbed a finger stiffly down at the figure under the couch-cover and added, "That's Ames."

# 5

## Two on a Roof

In the past-service files at the C. I. D. there is now a card which reads:

> Ames, George Finley, Detective-Inspector sr. rank. Born Bermondsey E., March 10th, 1879. Constable, K Division, 1900. Promoted Sergeant; K Division, 1906. Transferred D division, plain-clothes, 1914. Promoted, Hope-Hastings case, signal mention by Mr. Justice Gale, Detective-Inspector central bureau at reorganization in 1919. Ht. 5ft. 9in. Wt. 11st. No distinguishing marks or features. L. 'Restvale,' Valley Road, Hampstead. Married. Two children. Abilities: Expert at disguise, trailing, extracting information. Special mention for ability at disguise. Patient, discreet, well-educated by own efforts.

At the bottom of the card is written in red ink, "Killed on duty, September 4th, 1932."

That is the most complete information we are ever likely to have about Detective-Inspector George Finley Ames. In the whole clockhand case, the least conspicuous figure was the victim. His name might have been Smith or Jones or Robinson; he might never have been a human, breathing entity who liked his glass of bitter and was proud of his home; he might or might not have had those who hated him as George Ames; he was killed for another reason.

Although his term of service had been as long as Hadley's, Hadley did not know him well. He said that even after all these years Ames was still hopefully ambitious, and liked to talk of the vacation he would take in Switzerland when he got his next promotion. But he was not of the stuff which gets far ahead; the Yard liked him, Hadley said, but he was not highly intelligent and he was rather too trustful. Put it at a sort of intuitive animal cleverness; he was a bulldog whose tenacity on a tough Limehouse beat had first gained him promotion in the days when Limehouse really was tough—despite his stature being the smallest possible for entrance into the Metropolitan police. But he was trustful, and he died.

All these things, of course, Hadley did not say when he looked down at Ames dead. He did not comment or even curse. He only told Dr. Watson, who was gabbling under his breath, to go on with the silent work that had to be done; he picked up his briefcase, and walked slowly towards the stairs.

"Usual routine," he said to his followers. "You'll probably recognize who it is, but don't gossip. I'll come up there again when you get him out of the way. Meantime—" he beckoned to Dr. Fell and Melson.

In the lower hall Mrs. Steffins was craning her neck from side to side to peer up the stairs. With one outstretched arm she held back Eleanor, who looked sullen; she was smiling mechanically and charmingly over her shoulder at Eleanor, for its effect on the audience. But when she saw Hadley's face, wrinkles struck through the china prettiness. She cried out a foolish, wild remark.

"Is it," she said, "very *bad*?"

"Very bad," he told her, brusquely. His expression said that he did not want to be bothered with fools at that particular time. "I must ask you for some assistance. This may be an all-night job. I intend to take over the room upstairs presently. For the moment I want a room—anywhere—where my friends and I can talk."

"Well, of course!" she agreed in some eagerness. But there was calculation behind her eyes and she seemed to be wondering how to turn this to her advantage. "And we're *so* honoured to have *the* Dr. Fell in our house, although things are so perfectly horrible and—and all. Aren't they? Eleanor my dear, I wonder . . . There's our sitting-room, but then Johannus is so untidy and it's so cluttered up with his wheels and works and things. There'd be Miss Handreth's front room, her office, you know; she's a solicitor and that would suit you, surely, if she didn't mind; which of course she wouldn't . . ."

In the middle of her breathless speech, before they knew what she intended, she had scuttled across and was knocking at the second of the line of doors on the left-hand side.

"Miss Handreth!" she called, ingratiatingly, applying vigorous knuckles and then applying a delicate ear. "Lucia dear!"

The door opened instantly, with such suddenness, in fact, that Mrs. Steffins came close to losing her balance. The room behind was dark. In the doorway stood a woman who could be no older (if anything, rather younger) than Eleanor. Her dark hair was down over her shoulders and she shook it back as she looked at them coolly.

"Er—oh!" said Mrs. Steffins. "Excuse me. I wondered if you were awake, Lucia . . ."

"You knew perfectly well I was," said the other. She spoke in a clear voice, as though everyone were hostile, and as though she were in an uncomfortable position which she defied them to make her feel as uncomfortable. The brown eyes glittered behind long lashes partly lowered. She looked at Hadley, drawing closer her blue dressing-gown. "I presume you will have a doctor here. You had better send him in, please. There's a man here who may be rather badly hurt."

"Lucia!" said Mrs. Steffins in one tone, and then, with an entirely different expression she looked over her shoulder at Eleanor—a kind of beckoning triumph, with one eyebrow raised.

Lucia Handreth also looked at Eleanor. "I'm sorry," she told her quietly. "I'd have concealed it, only he's hurt. And they'd be bound to find out, anyway. It's Donald."

"Oh, dear me!" said Mrs. Steffins. "And are *you* entertaining Donald now, my dear?"

Her triumphant ha-ha's were almost a burlesque, gurgling queerly as she wagged her head and patted her hands together. Eleanor was staring, very pale, and Lucia breathing hard. With an effort she added:

"He seems to have had a bad fall—hurt round the head or something—and I can't quite bring him round. I heard him moaning in the back yard and dragging himself along. I dragged him in. Naturally, I didn't want to arouse . . . Oh, *can't* anybody do anything?"

"This is important, Hadley," Dr. Fell muttered. "Get

Watson. At once. The other can wait. Will you take us in, Miss Handreth?"

He gestured fiercely to Hadley, who nodded and hurried for the stairs. Snapping on the light, Lucia Handreth led them through a little sitting-room to a bedroom behind. The shade had been removed from the bright electric lamp beside the bed, and made a naked glare. Sprawled out on the yellow silk counterpane, a figure lay face downwards, twitching a little. A towel, wet and streaked red, had slipped round the corner of his head and half displaced a brownish bandage fixed with sticking-plaster; there were more towels, a bottle of iodine, and a bowl of water tinged with blood on a chair by the bed.

Eleanor Carver ran to him. He muttered something in a hoarse voice as she tried to lift him up, and suddenly began to fight.

"Steady," said Dr. Fell, putting his hand on her shoulder. "Watson will be here in two ticks. He'll have him round—"

"He kept on bleeding so at the nose," Lucia Handreth appealed to him, in a breathless voice. "I didn't know what to do. I—"

The figure on the bed ceased struggling. Only a faint creaking of springs disturbed the silence in that harsh-lit room; a scratching of clothes, as of someone crawling, against the yellow silk, or they might have thought life had gone. The clothes were grimy and ripped down from one shoulder; and red abrasions showed up bluish points along one wrist. Then even the creaking stopped, so that they could hear a clock tick. Eleanor Carver screamed, and Mrs. Steffins walked over and struck her across the mouth.

Then the man on the bed spoke.

*"It looked round the corner of the chimney,"* he said,

clearly, as though obeying a prompting. The words startled them as though a dead man had spoken. "*It had gilt paint on its hands.*"

There was an intrinsic horror in those unemotional words which seemed to affect even the man on the bed. One of his legs straightened out and struck the chair. The bowl of stained water crashed and broke on the floor like spilled blood.

A sane and very testy voice spoke from the door as Eleanor whirled round on Mrs. Steffins.

"All right, now; all right," squeaked Dr. Watson. "Out of here, now, all of you. None o' my business, but if you will order me about . . . Harrumph. Warm water."

Then Melson found himself standing in the cool of the outer hall. The police surgeon, naturally, did not get rid of the women. Both Eleanor and Mrs. Steffins went hurrying to Lucia Handreth's bathroom for the warm water; in a crazy scramble which looked ludicrously like a fight; and Mrs. Steffins was smiling over her shoulder at an unobserving Dr. Watson. Lucia Handreth began quietly to pick up the fragments of the bowl and mop up the spilled water with a towel. And in the outer hall, with a banged door behind them, Dr. Fell faced an irascible Hadley.

"Now would you mind explaining to me," said the latter, "what all this row is about?"

Dr. Fell took out a violently coloured bandanna and mopped his forehead. "So," he grunted, "you find the atmosphere getting thick, hey? Well, I've had more of it than you. I don't know what 'Donalds' last name is, my boy, but I suspect he's going to be our chief witness. Point number one: Donald is in all probability Eleanor Carver's *caius*—"

"Kindly talk sense," interrupted Hadley, with as-

47

perity. "I don't know why it is, but the very sight of a murder seems to rouse all your worst tendencies towards scholarship. What in hell is a *caius*?"

Dr. Fell wheezed. "I use the word," he said, "in preference to employing the nauseating modern term 'boy friend.' Be quiet, will you? Anyway, I'm jolly certain he's not her fiancé, since she is apparently compelled to meet him on the roof in the middle of the night—"

"Rot," said Hadley. "Nobody meets on roofs. Which is Eleanor, the blonde?"

"Yes. And that's where you underestimate either somebody's romantic spirit or somebody's sense of extreme practicality. I'm not sure yet, but . . . Aha! Well, Pierce?"

The constable, a man of extreme thoroughness, looked guilty and somewhat nervous when he saw Hadley. He saluted. His flush of success with the shoes and broken window had stimulated him; but he was a grimy and somewhat bedraggled object. Hadley's eye raked him.

"Now what the devil," he said, "have *you* been doing? Climbing trees?"

"Yes, sir," replied the constable. "It was Dr. Fell's orders, sir.—There was nobody up there. But there has been, sir, several times. Cigarette ends all over the place, especially in a big flat place in the middle of all the chimneys. There's a trap-door that leads down into the house, not very far away from the skylight in Mr. Boscombe's room."

Hadley looked curiously at Dr. Fell. "Naturally," he remarked, "it never occurred to your subtle mind to send him up through the trap-door to the roof, instead of climbing a tree?"

"Well, it occurred to me that it would have given

whoever might have been on that roof an excellent chance to make a getaway—if he were still on the roof. He must have missed his footing, got his fall, and been dragged into the house some time ago . . . H'm. Besides, Hadley, the door going up to that roof is locked. And I suspect we're going to have a devil of a time finding the key."

"Why?"

A voice struck in: "Excuse me, gentlemen—" and even the stolid Hadley, with Ames's death heavy upon him, was so jumpy that he whirled round with a curse. The big, mild-eyed Mr. Johannus Carver seemed taken aback. He had drawn on a pair of trousers over his pyjamas, and his hands plucked at the braces.

"No, no," he urged. "I wasn't eavesdropping. Not at all. But I overheard you asking Mrs. Steffins for a room. Allow me to place our sitting-room at your disposal. Over this way." He hesitated. The big head and overhanging brows made shadows under his eyes. "I don't know much about such things, but may I ask whether you have made any progress?"

"A good deal," said Dr. Fell. "Mr. Carver, who is 'Donald'?"

"Good God!" said Carver, jumping a little. "Is *he* here again? Tell him to leave, my dear sir! At once! Mrs. Steffins will—"

Hadley sized him up, and did not seem impressed.

"We'll use that room, thanks," he said. "And I shall want to ask everybody in the house some questions presently, if you will round them up . . . As for friend Donald, I don't think he'll be able to leave for some time. The general opinion seems to be that he tumbled out of a tree."

"Then—" said Carver, and caught himself up. He hesitated, with a deprecating eye on them as though he were about to say that boys will be boys and tumble out of trees sometimes; but he only coughed.

"Well?" Hadley asked, sharply. "*Was* he in the habit of spending his evenings on the roof?"

Melson had a sudden feeling that this cryptic old clockmaker was pulling all their legs good and hard. He would have sworn there was a gleam of amusement under those brows. Johannus peered round to make sure they were not overheard.

"To tell you the truth, I think he was," he admitted, doubtfully. "But, so long as they didn't disturb the neighbours and made no noise, they certainly didn't disturb me."

"Hell's *fire*!" said Hadley, under his breath. "Is that all the explanation you have to offer?"

"Mrs. Steffins has her reasons," explained Carver, nodding sagely. "Donald is a very pleasant young man, with an intelligent interest in my profession, but (to be candid) he is stony broke. So Mrs. Steffins says; and he is studying law, so I have no reason to doubt it. However, I make it a rule never to interfere in disputes between women. No matter whose side you take, each is convinced that you must be wrong. Hum. I am for a quiet life . . . However. What has this to do with the— the unfortunate demise?"

"I don't know. And I must be rather flustered," growled Hadley, "when a witness has to correct me. I want *facts*. Come on. Let's get to this room."

Carver led them across the hall, and showed a disposition to linger; but Hadley was curt. It was a spacious room in the same white panelling, with the curvilinear shield-back chairs of Heppelwhite, and a broad fireplace in which embers still smouldered. Above the mantelpiece hung framed a faded print of a man with long hair curling to his broad linen collar, possessing that greyish ethereal look which seventeenth-century artists could give to the fattest men, and inscribed round the margin: *"Wm. Bowyer, Esq., through whose Efforts was Founded ye Royal Company of Clockmakers, Anno Dom. 1631."* In glass cases along the line of windows were curious objects. One was a discoloured metal shell like a bowl, pierced with a hole in the center; another a tall bracket bearing on one arm a floating-wick lamp, just opposite a cylindrical glass upright down whose side ran a board notched in Roman numerals from 3 to 12, from 12 to 8; finally, a heavy open clock behind whose dial and single hand hung a hollow brass cylinder on a chain, the dial inscribed, *"John Banks of ye towne Chester, Anno Dom. 1682."* While Hadley threw his briefcase on the table and sat down, Dr. Fell stumped across to peer at these. Dr. Fell whistled.

"I say, Hadley, he's got some rarities here. It's a wonder the Guildhall hasn't snaffled 'em. These are landmarks in the development of the *clepsydra*, the water-clock. The first pendulum clock, and you know, wasn't built in England until 1640. And, unless I'm much mistaken, this bowl is a Brahmin device somewhat older than Christian civilization. It worked—" He turned round, the black ribbon on his eyeglasses swinging aggressively, and added: "Oh, and don't say I'm merely lecturing, either. I dare say you noticed poor Ames was stabbed with the hand of a clock?—You didn't?"

Hadley, who had been fumbling in his briefcase, threw two long envelopes on the table. He said: "So that's what it was? I couldn't make out—" and sat staring dully at the fireplace. "But the hand of a clock, man!" he snapped, making a wild gesture. "Are you sure of that? It's fantastic! In the name of all unreason,

51

why the hand of a clock? who would ever think of using a thing like that to kill anybody?"

"This murderer would," said Dr. Fell. "That's why it rather scares me. You're quite right. The ordinary person, flying into a rage, seldom thinks of wrenching off the hand of a clock for a weapon, like a little dagger all ready to hand. But somebody in this house looked at the stable clock Carver was making . . ." Rapidly he told Hadley of the theft. "Somebody with a brilliantly devilish imagination saw it as a literal symbol of time moving to the grave. There's something unholy in the very thought that he couldn't even look at an object he must have seen a dozen times every day of his life without looking at it crookedly. He didn't see it as a reminder of dinner or closing-hour or a dentist's appointment; he didn't even see a clock-hand. What he did see was a thin steel shaft, something under ten inches long, barbed with a sharp arrowhead and admirably weighted at the handle for stabbing. And so he used it."

"You're getting into your stride at last," said Hadley. He knocked his knuckles against the table in irritable meditation. "You say 'he.' There are Ames's last reports, and as much information as I could get about the department-store case. I was wondering . . ."

"About women? Certainly. That's our objective. I use 'he' because it's convenient, where I should have said 'it.' As that young chap on the roof did—and I tell you again he'll be our star witness—when he said, 'It had gilt paint on its hands.'"

"But that sounds like a *real* clock," protested Hadley. "I tell you the fellow must have been delirious and got things mixed up. I hope you're not trying to tell me that a clock is human and can get up and walk about on a roof?"

"Now I wonder—" muttered Dr. Fell, as though struck with an idea. "No, don't snort. We're trying to follow the workings of a very lucid crackbrain, and we shall be no forrader until we find out what he meant by using that sort of weapon. There is a significance, blast it! There's got to be . . . Human? Look here, has it ever struck you that in fiction and poetry, even in everyday life, the clock is the only inanimate object that *is* considered human as a matter of course? What fictional clock doesn't have a 'voice,' and even human speech? It speaks nursery rhymes, and clears the way for ghosts, and accuses of murder; it's the basis of all startling stage-effects, and a note of doom and retribution. If there were no clocks, what would happen to the tale of terror?—And I'll prove it to you. There is one particular thing, *vide* the cinema, which is good for a roar of laughter at any time—a cuckoo clock. You have only got to have that little bird popping out to warble, and the audience thinks it's uproariously funny. Why? Because it's a parody of something we do take seriously, a burlesque of the solemnity of time and clocks. If you will imagine of the effect on the reader provided Marley's ghost had said to Scrooge, 'Expect the first of the three spirits when the cuckoo clock chirps one,' you will have some faint notion of my meaning."

"Very interesting," said Hadley, without enthusiasm. "But I can't help wishing you'd tell me what *happened* here tonight, so that I could form my own theories. This metaphysical business may be all very well—"

Dr. Fell took out his battered cigar-case, wheezing.

"You want proof, do you," he said, quietly, "that I'm not talking through my hat? Very well. Why were *both* hands stolen off that clock?"

Hadley's fingers closed over the arms of the chair . . .

"Now, now, steady. I'm not hinting at more stabbings. But let me follow it up with another question. There's probably nothing in your life that you've seen more frequently than clocks, and yet I wonder if you can answer one question with absolute certainty before you look: Which hand is outside and which inside, the long minute-hand or the short hour-hand?"

"Well—" said Hadley. After a pause he growled something and reached after his watch. "H'm. The long one is outside; on this watch, anyhow. Confound it, yes! Bound to be. Common sense would tell you that. It has the bigger arc of the circle to travel—the longer distance, I mean. Well? What about it?"

"Yes. The minute-hand is outside. And," continued Dr. Fell, scowling, "Ames was stabbed with the minute-hand. A further fact: if in your childhood you ever spent joyous carefree hours taking apart your old man's best parlour clock to see if you could make it strike thirteen, you will know that each hand is devilish difficult to take off... Ames's murderer presumably needed only the minute-hand. He could remove it without disturbing the other. Why, then, did he take the time and trouble—and in those steel stable clocks it's no easy job at all—to pinch the *other hand*? I can't believe it was any instinct of tidiness. But why?"

"Another weapon?"

Dr. Fell shook his head. "That's the trouble; it couldn't be, or the whole business would be understandable. By the looks of things, that minute-hand is approximately nine inches long. Therefore, in usual measurements, the short hour-hand couldn't possibly be long enough to serve as a weapon. when any normal fist gripped round it, there would remain at most an inch and a half of steel at the business end. You're not going to do any serious damage with that, especially as the barb hasn't a cutting edge. So *why, why, why* pinch the little one?"

He stuck a cigar in his mouth and passed his case to Hadley and Melson. Then he broke off the heads of several matches trying to strike a light. Hadley, with an irritable gesture, drew some folded sheets of paper out of one envelope on the table.

"And that's not the worst puzzle," said Dr. Fell. "Most of it lies in the behaviour of a certain gentleman named Boscombe and another named Stanley. I intended to ask you about that. I dare say you remember Peter Stan . . . What's the matter?"

Hadley uttered a satisfied snort. "Only a fact, that's all! In the first line of this report. Three words of Ames tell more than six chapters of other people I could mention. Can you understand this?

"'Following up my report dated 1st September, I now believe I can establish conclusively that the woman who murdered Evan Thomas Manders, shopwalker, at Gamridge's Stores August 27th last, lives at Number 16 Lincoln's Inn Fields . . .'"

# 6

## Inspector Ames's Reports

"Go on," said Dr. Fell, as Hadley stopped abruptly. "What else?"

Hadley was running his eye down the short, laboriously written sheet. He threw off his hat and loosened his overcoat as though to assist him. His annoyance grew.

"Damn the secretive little blighter! He says... H'm, 'm. Not a definite word in the whole business, unless there's something in an earlier report. He'd never talk until he was ready to ask for a warrant, ever since Stanley nearly stole his thunder in the Hope-Hastings—" Suddenly Hadley looked up. "Is my hearing getting as muddled as my brain, or did I hear you mention a name like Stanley just a moment ago?"

"You did."

"But it's not—?"

"It's the Peter Stanley who had your position about twelve or thirteen years ago. He's upstairs now. And that's what I wanted to ask you. I remembered in a hazy sort of way that he resigned, or something of the sort, but I couldn't fix the details."

Hadley stared across at the fireplace. "He 'resigned' for shooting dead an unarmed man who was making no resistance at the arrest," Hadley said, grimly. "Furthermore, for precipitating an arrest to get the credit when poor old Ames hadn't worked out all the details. I ought to know. I got my promotion in the shuffle; that was at the reorganization in 1919, when the Big Four were created. It wasn't entirely Stanley's fault. He'd insisted on active service in the war; his nerves were shot to blazes, and he wasn't in shape to be trusted with anything bigger than a cap-pistol. That was why they let him 'resign.' But he put four bullets in the head of old Hope, who was a bank-absconder and timid as a rabbit—" Hadley shifted uncomfortably. "I don't like this, Fell. Not a little bit. Why didn't you tell me he was mixed up in this thing? It—well, it reflects discredit on the Force if some newspaper happens to dig it up. As for Stanley—" His eyes narrowed and he stopped uneasily.

"You've got more pressing worries for the moment, my lad. What does Ames say in the report?"

With an effort Hadley jerked his thoughts back.

"Yes. I suppose so—no, of course it can't be. Curse the luck, this thing would have to happen when I'm within a month of retiring!—Well. Hum. Where was I? There's not much. He says:

"Following up my report dated 1st September, I now believe I can establish conclusively that the woman who murdered Evan Thomas Manders, shopwalker, at Gamridge's Stores August 27th last, lives at Number 16 Lincoln's Inn Fields. Pursuing the anonymous information received, as indicated in report 1st September—'"

"Have you got that?"
"Yes. But wait a bit:

"'—I have taken a room at 21 Portsmouth Street, Lincoln's Inn Fields, adjoining the Duchess of Portsmouth Tavern, in the character of a down-at-heel ex-watchmaker with a weakness for spirits. The private bar of this tavern is visited by all the men and one of the women living at 16 Lincoln's Inn Fields, and the jug-and-bottle by two others—'

"By the way," interpolated Hadley, "how many women are there in the house?"
"Five. Three of 'em you've seen." Dr. Fell sketched out the household. "The other two would seem to be a Mrs. Gorson, a housekeeper of sorts under the direction of La Steffins, and a maid, name unknown. I'll lay you a tanner it's the last two who visit the jug-and-bottle. It will be interesting to discover which of the other three ensconces herself in the private bar. I know the 'Duchess of Portsmouth.' It's a musty enough place, but full of atmosphere and rather swank. . . . Well?"

"'Two days ago (2nd September) my hitherto anonymous informant paid a visit to me at my room, disclosing knowledge of who I was and how I came to be there. (I must ask leave to be excused from supplying further details at this time.) Whatever the motive, informant offered even further assistance. Informant deposed to having seen in

58

possession of certain woman two articles listed as stolen in department-store robberies (see report 28th August for complete list). These articles were (1) Platinum bracelet set with turquoises, value £15; and (2) Early eighteenth-century watch, gold case, inscribed "Thomas Knifton at the X Keys in Lothebury Londini fecit," exhibited in Gamridge advertising-display and loaned by J. Carver. Informant also deposed to having seen, evening of 27th August, same woman burning in a fireplace a pair of brown kid gloves stained with blood—'"

"WOW!" said Dr. Fell.

"Yes. Rather a nasty household altogether. Somebody," grunted Hadley, "is very anxious to get somebody else hanged, and yet makes a dark and secret pact with the police officer. No, not quite. Let me read on:

"'It will be seen that my position up until this morning was as follows. Informant was quite willing to testify in the witness box to the above statements, but refused to make the accusation that would give us a warrant, in case evidence should be destroyed. Information stated that this responsibility must rest with us, so far as making the arrest was concerned—'"

"Clever lady," said Hadley, "or gentleman. I've known a good many of these amateur narks, and they're the meanest devils on two legs. Or was the whole thing a trap? I doubt it. Well . . .

"'I therefore suggested to my informant that we arrange means for getting me (secretly) into the house, where I could examine the possessions

59

of the accused in private and satisfy my superiors
that there was evidence for the issuing of a warrant—'

"Blasted fool! He shouldn't have put that into a report. This thing will have to come out, and every ass
will be braying in the newspapers for the next six
months. Good old plodding, serious-minded Ames!
And the rest is worse:

"'—but my informant, although concurring in
the idea, refused to give active assistance on the
ground that informant might be compromised. I
therefore determined to get into the house on my
own responsibility.

"'This afternoon, just previous to the writing of
this report, stroke of good fortune has rendered
this easy. Another occupant of 16, L. I. F. (not my
previous informant), who had promised to give me
some cast-off clothes, suggested that I call round
for them tonight. I had a good excuse for scraping
his acquaintance at the beginning, as I did with
other occupants of the house; in this case since he
and I were of a similar height, and I said that I
was in need of suitable—'"

"Boscombe, of course," nodded Dr. Fell. He had lit
the cigar and was puffing at it in a sort of puzzled
obstinacy at the report. "Personally, Hadley, I don't
like the sound of the whole thing. It's fishy. It may have
impressed Ames's mind; but then Ames died because
it did. The question is, what damned sort of trick were
Boscombe *and* Stanley going to put up on him? There
was something, I'll swear. And it's a new confusing set
of tracks that runs side by side with Jane the Ripper's

footprints. . . . No, no. Boscombe didn't intend to give a derelict any new clothes. Boscombe, in a pub, would only have cursed such a seedy beggar and had him chucked out. There was a game he and Stanley played, right enough. What else?"

Hadley ran his eye down the reports.

"That's about all. He says that he arranged to call on Mr.—whoever it is, his benefactor—at a late hour. Then he sketches out what he intends doing. He will call on this Boscombe, receive the clothes, pretend to leave the house, hide, and then indulge in a little burglary in the room of the accused woman. He trusts that this slight irregularity will meet with the approval of his superiors—Bah! Why *write* that?—and concludes at 5 p.m., Thursday, the 4th inst., G. F. Ames. . . . Poor devil!"

There was a silence. Hadley threw the report on the table; he discovered that he was rolling to pieces an unlighted cigar, and made an ineffectual attempt to light it.

"You're absolutely right, Fell. It does sound fishy. What I can't do is put my finger on the exact point where its fishiness is most apparent. Maybe that's because I don't know enough facts. So—"

Dr. Fell said, meditatively, "I suppose he really did write that report?"

"Eh? Oh yes. Well, there's no question of that. Even aside from his handwriting, he brought the thing in himself. He wrote it right enough.—Besides, I don't want you to get the impression, from whatever I've said, that Ames was anybody's fool; far from it. He had good reason for writing what he did. He had—"

"Did he have a sense of humour, for instance?" enquired Dr. Fell, with owlish blankness. "Was he above juggling facts a bit and indulging in a little leg-pull, if he thought he did it in a good cause?"

Hadley scratched his chin.

"Suppose he had? Ames would have needed a very remarkable sense of humour to invent a story about a woman burning blood-stained gloves merely to get a hearty laugh out of the C.I.D. Look here," said Hadley, querulously, "you don't doubt that this woman, this Jane the Ripper, is really in the house, do you?"

"I haven't any reason to doubt it. Besides, there's no need to be charitable in our suspicions; there's certainly a murderer here, and as nasty a one as I'd ever thought to meet. . . . Listen, now. I'll tell you exactly what happened, and you can draw your own conclusions."

Dr. Fell spoke briefly and sleepily; but he omitted nothing. Cigar smoke began to thicken in the room, and Melson felt his wits thickening with it. He tried to fasten on the essential points that puzzled him, to ticket them in readiness for Hadley's questions. Long before Dr. Fell had finished, Hadley was pacing the room. As Dr. Fell waved his hand and uttered a long rumbling sniff to indicate that the picture was complete, Hadley stopped by one of the clock-cases.

"Yes," agreed the chief inspector, "it makes some things straight, and a lot more crooked. But it's fairly clear now why you thought there was a man on that roof, and that the blonde was going up to meet him. . . ."

Dr. Fell scowled. "The *first* part of it," he admitted, "is easy. She said her bedroom door was slamming in a draught; that she thought the front door might be slamming, and got out of bed to see about it. But—to do this—she had carefully decked out her face in fresh cosmetics. That seemed unusual, as though a man were to rise from his bed and array himself in evening-clothes to throw a boot at a yowling cat. She didn't turn on any lights whatever, although this would be the natural thing to do; and she hastily rubbed out the make-up when somebody suggested waking up the others in the house. It naturally suggested a clandestine appointment . . . where?

"Now," said Dr. Fell, vigorously, "comes the interesting part. She crept up those stairs, hearing Boscombe say, 'My God, he's dead'; she saw a body lying on the floor and immediately became so hysterical that she kept on wildly accusing Boscombe of murder long after she saw he wasn't guilty. Ça s'explique, Hadley. It wasn't just the shock of seeing a dead burglar."

The chief inspector nodded.

"Yes, that's evident. She expected to find it was somebody else. H'm. But, with that light shining on his face, she would have seen Ames wasn't the man she thought had been hurt or killed—unless one of the doors had been so half-closed that the shadow hid his face. Hence the shock and terror. So you made her reconstruct the scene. . . . Not bad, confound you!" said Hadley, grudgingly, and beat his fist into his palm. "Not at all bad, for a quick guess."

"Guess?" roared Dr. Fell, removing his cigar. "Who said anything about a guess? I applied principles of the soundest lo—"

"All right, all right. Carry on."

"H'mf! Ha! Burr! Very well. Which brings us to the whole crux of the matter. Although she was rather startled to find this man (presumably the one with whom she had the appointment) in the house at all, nevertheless she wasn't surprised to find him *upstairs*. She was going upstairs, to begin with, and the very fact that she did mistake him for the dead man proves it. When I see, not six feet from the dead man, a door leading straight to the roof, and when this girl makes determined efforts to steer me away from it at my first sign of curiosity, then I begin to have a strong suspicion. When I reflect that the girl, although alluringly got up with regard to cosmetics and pyjamas, nevertheless wears a dusty, shabby leather coat with a warm fleece lining . . ."

"I see all that," returned Hadley, with some dignity. "Except that the whole thing's still far from sensible, and only a lunatic would—"

Dr. Fell shook his head benevolently.

"Heh," he said. "Heh-heh-heh. It's our old difficulty again. You don't mean that only a lunatic would spend hours of rapture on a breezy roof. You only mean that *you* wouldn't. I am willing to venture a small wager that, even in your courting days, the present Mrs. Hadley would have been a trifle astonished to see you swinging up to her balcony through the branches of a maple tree. . . ."

"She'd have thought I was balmy," said Hadley.

"Well, so should I, for that matter. Which is the point I am patiently trying to make. But there are young men, aged twenty and twenty-one—I shrewdly suspect Eleanor of being older and wiser, but what of it?—who would. And try to drive it through your head that this crazy comedy is the most desperately serious thing in their lives. Why, man," boomed Dr. Fell, his face fiery with controversy, "the young fellow isn't worth his salt who doesn't want to show off his muscles climbing trees in romantic situations, and half hoping he'll break his damnfool neck, but very much surprised if he does. You've been reading too many modern novels, Hadley. . . . The ironical part is that in the middle of these story-book dreams and rescues from romantic dangers, down dropped a real corpse; and young gallantry did nearly break his neck when he faced reality. But I said Eleanor was older and wiser, and there's the revealing part of the whole thing. . . ."

"How so? If you've not any *facts*—"

"She saw on the floor, dead, somebody she took for this young chap. And over him she saw Boscombe, with a gun in his hand. That was why she went hysterical. She never for a second doubted Boscombe had shot him."

Hadley ran a hand across his dull-coloured hair. "Then Boscombe—"

"He's in love with her, Hadley; I almost said bitterly in love, and I rather think she hates him. That little soft-footed nervous fellow is full of a kind of iron and water, and she may be a bit afraid of him. If she thought he would kill or had killed our friend Donald, there's a curious inference to be drawn with regard to the other—"

Hadley peered at him from under lowered brows.

"There's also the inference," he pointed out, almost idly, "that Ames, in the darkness of that hall, might have been mistaken for Boscombe. . . . We have enough complications already, I admit; but Boscombe interests me."

"The shoes and gloves and the broken window, and Stanley?"

"Oh, I'll get the truth out of them," said Hadley, quietly. There was something in the commonplace words, and in the very faint smile that accompanied them, which made Melson shiver. He had a feeling that something would be smashed, as though the chief inspector were to bring his gloved fist down on one of the glass cases and scatter its brittle contents. Hadley moved over easily and stood with his inscrutable dark eyes in the lamplight. "I have an idea that Boscombe and Stanley were going to put up a bit of a fake 'crime' to pull Ames's leg. You'd thought of that?"

Dr. Fell made an indistinguishable noise.

"And the most significant thing in the whole affair," Hadley went on, "was the testimony as to who did or did not know Ames. And I promise you that I'm going to sweat out every filthy lie that's ever been told in this house, by God! until I find the swine who came up and stabbed a good man in the back!"

His fist crashed down on the table; and, with the eerie effect of an answer, there was a knock at the door. Hadley was his old impassive self when Sergeant Betts appeared, carrying something wrapped in a handkerchief.

"The—the knife, sir," he reported. He looked white. "There was nothing in his pockets, nothing at all, except a pair of gloves. Here they are. Old Busy never . . ." Checking himself abruptly, he gave an unnecessary salute and waited.

"Take it easy, old son," said Hadley, trying not to show that he looked uncomfortable. "We none of us like it. We—Shut that door! Hum. Er—you didn't talk? You didn't let anybody find out who he is? That's important."

"No, sir, although two have been asking a lot of questions—the stoutish lady with the dyed hair and the fussy little bloke in the grey dressing-gown." Betts regarded him with some sharpness under a wooden exterior. "But a queer thing happened only a minute ago. While we were going after fingerprints—there aren't any on that arrow-headed thing, by the way—"

"No," Hadley commented, sourly. "I didn't suppose there would be. I'd like to find somebody in this day and age who did leave finger-prints. Well?"

"—While Benson was doing that, and we were standing in the doorway, out of another doorway comes a

66

big bloke, you see, sir, with a funny shambling walk and a queer look in his eyes. And Benson says, 'Good God,' under his breath, and I said, 'What?' and Benson says (under his breath, you see, sir, because the lady was looking on and saying she wasn't nervous and she was always good in sick-rooms anyway), Benson says, 'Stanley. *He* ought to recognize Old Busy. . . .'"

Hadley remained impassive. "Mr. Stanley," he replied, "was a former police officer. You didn't let him tell the others about Ames?"

"He didn't seem to know Old—the inspector, sir. At least, he wasn't paying any attention. He went over to the sideboard and swilled a lot of brandy out of the decanter, and then turned around without looking at us and went back where he'd come from, with the decanter in his hand. Like a blooming ghost, sir, if you know what I mean."

"Yes. Where is Dr. Watson now?"

"Still with the young chap over in the lady's bedroom," answered Betts, not without a curious glance at the chief inspector. "Doctor says he got a nasty knock, but there's no concussion, and he should be in passable state shortly. The kid—"

"Kid?"

"He's about twenty-one, sir," Sergeant Betts pointed out, from the austerity of a probable twenty-six. "He keeps laughing and saying something about 'hope deferred, hope deferred.' The two other ladies are with him.—What now?"

"Find Mr. Carver," said Hadley, "and send him in here. Stand guard yourself."

When the sergeant had gone Hadley sat down by the table, taking out notebook and pencil. He carefully unwrapped the handkerchief, so that the bright gilt of the clock-hand, which had been cleaned, glittered under the lamp. Along the heavy end the gilt was streaked and blurred with what appeared to be the smudges of gloved hands, and similar streaks brushed faintly down its entire length.

"Stolen off the clock before the paint was dry," observed Hadley. "Or—I wonder if the stuff's thoroughly dried and set even yet? The thing's still damp from washing, but it feels sticky. It should be dry, if the paint was put on last night. May be some sort of waterproof varnish that takes a long time to dry. Note," he wrote down. "The look of these blurs lower down makes me think they might have been caused when it was pulled out of Ames's neck. Therefore may be stains on murderer. . . ."

"And what a cheerful blighter it is," said Dr. Fell, admiringly. He lumbered over to the table and blinked through cigar smoke at the blade. "H'm. Hah. Now, I wonder. It looks as though the thief had *deliberately* messed up the gilt, Hadley. He could have pinched that blade without so much of a mess, d'ye think? Or is it only that the fiend of subtlety is stalking this old brain again? I still wonder."

Hadley paid no attention.

"Length—" he muttered, and measured it on the sole of his shoe. "You were a little out, Fell. This thing is eight and a half inches at the most; nearer eight. . . . Ah! Come in, Mr. Carver."

Hadley sat round in his chair with a sort of dangerous politeness. The wheels were in motion now; the inquisition had begun; and sooner or later, Melson knew, they would interview a murderer. In the room of old clocks. Hadley tapped the gilt minute-hand slowly on the table as Carver closed the door behind him.

# 7

## The Noise of a Chain

Every time they saw Johannus Carver, Melson thought
he had put on one additional article of clothing. Now it
was a frogged smoking-jacket over the pyjamas, in addition to the pepper-and-salt trousers. Melson had a
picture of him frequently wondering what to do when
his house was invaded; and each time putting in the in-
terval by tramping upstairs to struggle into another gar-
ment, if only for an appearance of activity. His first
glance was at the glass cases containing the clocks. Then
he peered sharply at the panels on the right-hand side
of the room—a glance which they did not interpret
then, or understand at all until the case had taken a
more terrible turn. His wrinkled neck looked scrawny
without a collar, his head too big for it. The mild eyes
blinked in the cigar smoke. His smile changed suddenly
when, apparently for the first time, he saw the clock-
hand.

"Yes, Mr. Carver?" prompted Hadley, softly. "You
recognize it?"

Carver stretched out his hand, but withdrew it.

"Yes, certainly. Without a doubt. That is, I think so. It's the minute-hand off the dial I made for Sir Edwin Paull. Where did you find it?"

"In the neck of the dead man, Mr. Carver. He was killed with it. You looked at the body. Didn't you see this?"

"I—Good God, no! I don't look for such things in—well, in burglars' *necks*," returned Carver, a note of protest in his voice. "This is appalling. And ingenious, by George!" He fell to musing, and peered at a shelf of books over a writing desk. "I cannot recall, in the whole history of . . . extraordinary! The more I think of it—"

"We can return to that later. Sit down, Mr. Carver. There are a few questions . . ."

He answered the first of them somewhat absently, sitting with his big body stooped over in a chair and his eyes wandering towards the shelf of books. He had lived in this house for eighteen years. He was a widower, the house having belonged to his wife. (By certain vague digressions Melson gathered that the Carver household had been supported by an annuity which had died with his wife.) Eleanor was the daughter of an old friend of the late Mrs. Carver's—herself an invalid—and had been taken in on the death of Eleanor's parents because there seemed to be no prospect of having children of their own. Mrs. Millicent Steffins was also a heritage, having been a friend who faithfully attended Mrs. Carver through all her illness. You gathered that the late Mrs. Carver had surrounded herself with people as though with trinkets.

"And the lodgers?" pursued Hadley. "What do you know of them?"

"Lodgers?" Carver repeated, as though the word

startled him. He rubbed his forehead. "Ah yes. Mrs. Steffins said it was necessary to rent a part of the house. You want to know something about them, is that it? Hum. Well, Boscombe's intelligent. Got a lot of money, I believe, but, frankly, I certainly would not have sold him that Maurer watch if Millicent—Mrs. Steffins— hadn't insisted." He brooded. "Then there's Mr. Christopher Paull. Quite an amiable young man. He gets drunk and sings in the hall sometimes, but he's very well connected socially and Millicent likes him. Hum."

"And Miss Handreth?"

Again the faint gleam of amusement showed in Carver's eyes.

"Well," he said, deprecatingly, "Miss Handreth and Millicent don't get along, so I hear quite a lot about her. But I don't suppose it would interest you to know that she has no law clients and does not wear undervests in winter and is probably leading an immoral life; hum, especially as most of the statements are matters whose truth or falsity my age prevents me from verifying. . . . Um, she has been here only a short time. Young Hastings brought her here and helped her unpack. They are old friends, so I fear Millicent suspects the worst—"

"Young Hastings?"

"Didn't I tell you? That's the 'Donald' you were asking about, the young man who falls out of trees when he comes to see Eleanor. I must speak to him about it. He might hurt himself. . . . Oh yes, he and Miss Handreth are old friends. That was how he met Eleanor."

Here Carver seemed to stumble over a memory, as though he were trying to recall something; but he blinked, rubbed his cheek, and forgot about it.

"Finally, Mr. Carver," Hadley went on, "you have

an under-housekeeper here—a Mrs. Gorson—and a maid?"

"Yes. Extraordinary woman, Mrs. Gorson. I believe she was once an actress. She speaks in rather a lofty strain, but she has the utmost cheerfulness about doing all work no matter how heavy, and gets along well with Millicent. Kitty Prentice is the maid. . . . Now, sir, that you know the household, will you answer me a question?"

Something in the man's voice arrested Melson. He did not raise his voice, he did not move. But he suddenly took on the cool alertness of a fighter behind a shield.

"You believe, I understand," he said, abruptly, "that one of the people in this house stole the hand off that dial and, for some fantastic reason, killed the man upstairs. Doubtless you have some cause for thinking so, even if it happens to be ludicrous. What I should like to know, sir, is which one of us you suspect?"

This time he glanced at Dr. Fell, who was sighting down the stump of his cigar, piled dangerously into a light chair. The sudden challenge did not startle Hadley.

"Perhaps you can tell me better," he suggested, leaning forward. "A number of people in this house, I understand, are in the habit of frequenting a public house in Portsmouth Street?"

Mildness—but a watchful mildness—had again taken possession of Carver.

"Oh yes. I frequently go with Boscombe myself, and Miss Handreth sometimes goes with Mr. Paull. Now I wonder," he said with a faint frown, "how you knew that? I have been thinking back, and I remember that the man upstairs made frequent and often painful efforts to draw all of us into conversation."

"Yet you had trouble in recognizing him when you saw him dead upstairs?"

"Yes. The light—"

"But you did recognize him? Yes. He was a watchmaker, Mr. Carver, and introduced himself to you as such. But you didn't recognize him upstairs, or said you didn't, even a member of your own profession. Why didn't that occur to you? Why did you say 'the burglar' and not 'the watchmaker'?"

"Because he wasn't a watchmaker, you see," Carver explained, mildly. His brow was ruffled. "Whereas there seemed good evidence of his being a burglar."

Hadley's expression hardly altered; yet Melson knew that he had caught one of the most difficult witnesses of his career, and was just beginning to realize it.

"I know he introduced himself in that capacity," Carver went on, clearing his throat. "But I couldn't help seeing he wasn't, the first words he said. He pointed to the timepiece in the pub and referred to it as a 'clock.' Every watch-and clock-maker says 'dial.' It is the customary word, the only word. Then he asked me for work. I happened to have in my pocket a watch I was repairing for, hum, a client of mine, and I said, 'My friend, you will see that I have got to set a new hair-spring in this. It is a valuable watch,' I said, 'so don't tamper with it; but tell me how you would go about setting a hair-spring.' He mumbled some nonsense about taking out the main-spring."

Carver's deep, chuckling laugh echoed in the smoky room. For the first time he showed some enthusiasm.

"'Well,' I said, 'then tell me how to put in a new cylinder and balance-wheel? Come, that's simple enough,' I said. 'But you don't know it. You don't, in fact, know a blessed thing about watches, do you? Then,' I said, 'pray accept this half-crown and go into the public bar and don't bother me.'"

There was a silence. Hadley swore under his breath. But Carver was not through.

"No," he affirmed, shaking his head, "he wasn't a watchmaker. Um, at the time, sir, I rather suspected he might be a police officer or a private detective."

"I see. You had some reason to think, then," said Hadley, "that a police officer might be interested in your movements?"

"In all our movements. No, no, not at all. Tut, sir! But I noticed that when Boscombe spoke to the landlord about keeping this fellow from dogging us and bothering us (especially as he seldom paid for drinks)—in short, to keep him out altogether—the fellow remained." Carver rubbed his cheek reflectively. "I have observed, um, that only cats and policemen can remain in pubs without paying for drinks."

Muscles tightened along Hadley's jaw, but he still sat quietly.

"Mr. Boscombe," he said, "wanted this man thrown out of the bar, although he later offered to give him a suit of clothes and didn't recognize him when he saw him dead upstairs?"

"Is that so?" enquired the other, with a sort of polite interest. "Well—er—you'll really have to ask Boscombe. I don't know."

"And since you've observed things so closely in pubs, you will have noticed whether any of your party ever had a private conversation with the man?"

Carver meditated, seeming mildly harassed. "I'm fairly certain nobody did. Oh! With the possible exception of Mr. Paull. But then Mr. Paull, as he says, would drink with an archbishop if there were nobody else handy."

"I see. . . . And this terrible persecution you were being subjected to, did anybody comment on it?"

"Feelingly. I—er—I believe Miss Handreth said that he would get himself killed one day. She seemed quite bitter about it."

"He bothered her?"

From under thin wrinkled eyelids Carver threw a curious glance at the chief inspector. "No. I believe he rather avoided her. But then . . . it is scarcely permissible . . ."

"Did either Mrs. Steffins or Miss Carver ever visit the 'Duchess of Portsmouth'?"

"Never."

"We come to tonight. I think you told Dr. Fell that you locked and chained the front door at ten o'clock. Then you went upstairs . . ."

Carver fidgeted. "I know, Inspector—is it Inspector?—I know the police wish people to be painfully exact. I did not go *instantaneously* upstairs; hum, like an explosion, you know. I first went into my showroom," he nodded towards the left, towards the front room giving on the street, "to see that the alarm was set. Then I came in here to be sure the alarm was set on my wall-safe. Lastly, I went to Millicent's room," he nodded towards the right-hand wall, "to wish her good-night. She had been occupied with some chinapainting, and said it had given her a headache and she was going to bed directly; in fact, as I told Dr. Fell, she had asked me to lock up. . . ."

"Go on."

"I went to Boscombe for something to read. We exchange hobbies, and . . . ah! This would interest you, Dr. Fell. I borrowed his *Lettres à un gentilhomme russe sur L'Inquisition espagñole*, Lemaistre's book. I had been plodding through Pelayo's *Historia de los Heterodoxos Españoles*, but my Spanish is poor and I much prefer Lea."

Melson stifled a whistle. He had it now, the elusive

fact which would explain the curious designs painted on Boscombe's leather screen and the brass box on the table. The hobby of this enigmatic Mr. Boscombe was the Spanish Inquisition. Melson glanced at Dr. Fell, who opened his eyes and let out a wheezy sigh as though he were being roused from sleep.

"He got rid of you quickly, didn't he?" enquired Dr. Fell.

"I didn't stay long, no. Then, Inspector, I went to my room at the front, read for about an hour, and went to sleep. That is all I know up until the time Eleanor woke me."

"You are sure of that?" asked Hadley.

"Of course. Why not?"

"When you went to Mr. Boscombe's room, you told Dr. Fell, Mr. Peter Stanley had not yet arrived. . . . We don't question your powers of observation there," said Hadley, never taking his eyes from Carver's face, "but only your statement."

"I—I certainly did not see him."

"No. In fact, you definitely stated that he arrived later. You said he rang the bell, Boscombe's bell, and Boscombe went down to let him in. There's an elaborate lock on that door, and a chain that makes a good deal of noise. This is your explanation of how the door came to be accidentally open so that the 'burglar' could get in afterwards. I suppose you sleep with a window open? Just over that door, didn't you hear somebody being let in?"

Carver stared past him at the glass cases, rubbing his cheek.

"I did," he said, suddenly. "Come to think of it, by Jove! I did! I thought I heard somebody fumbling at that door much later, when I was dozing off. Perhaps about half-past eleven."

He seemed excited, but puzzled. Hadley watched him narrowly.

"Half an hour, then, before the murder was committed? Yes. You heard voices, footsteps, the door open and close?"

"Well . . . no. I was half asleep, you know. All I can swear to is that the door was opened, because the brass slot in which the knob of the chain fits is bent. It gives a kind of screech unless it's handled gently. That's what I remember. I've heard it on certain nights when people have come home late."

"And this didn't surprise you, although you knew that everybody in the house was in when you locked up?"

Melson had a feeling that Carver's nerves were wearing thin, despite his air of muddled ease. Possibly Hadley thought so too.

"Mr. Paull was not in," Carver answered, after a hesitation. "He has been spending some days with his uncle, Sir Edwin, in the country. Sir Edwin ordered the dial that was . . . yes. I thought Christopher might be returning unexpectedly. I wanted to tell him it would take me several more days to replace the hands. Otherwise it was not damaged, except that the pin and washers—holding the hands to the spindle, you see— were also stolen."

Hadley leaned forward.

"We come to that clock, now, and also something else that was stolen from you. You finished and painted the clock yesterday . . ."

"No, no. I finished and tested it two days ago. That is, in the interests of strictest accuracy. It gave some trouble, although it was the ordinary short-pendulum movement; nothing of a job. The day before yesterday I applied the waterproof enamel. . . . No, no," he explained, rather irritably, as Hadley's eyes strayed to the minute-hand, "*not* the gilt. The enamel that will keep an outdoor clock from rusting in all weathers. So that it should dry more quickly, I put it out in the scullery, in the cold air, two nights ago. I hardly thought any thief would carry off a mechanism weighing over eighty pounds. In that exposed place, where anybody could have got at it, *nobody touched it*. . . ."

Melson heard Dr. Fell give a muffled exclamation.

". . . and yesterday evening I applied the gilt. I had it wheeled in here, put in that closet over there, and I covered it with one of the bigger glass cases so that the fresh gilt should not catch up dust. And I always lock the door of this room in addition to the burglar alarm on the safe. On the night, then, when the door was locked and the key upstairs with me, somebody picked the lock of this door and removed the hands. Inspector, it is fantastic! Shall I show you?"

There was a somewhat wild expression on Hadley's face. But he waved his hand as Carver started to get up.

"In a moment. Who knew that the clock was here last night?"

"Everybody."

"Would removing the hands have been a difficult task? For an unskilled person, I mean?"

"Not at all. In this case, extremely simple. I had fitted the pin with a groove so that a heavy screw-driver would remove it. True, it might take some time and man-oeuvring to remove both hands from the spindle, but . . ." Carver lifted his big shoulders and gestured wearily. He looked now only weak and worried.

"There is just one more question, then, that I want to ask you for the moment. But it's important. So very important," insisted Hadley, with a suavity that caught

Carver's wandering attention, "that if you don't answer me frankly it may be damned dangerous for you." He waited. "I'll make it absolutely definite. I want to know where you and all the other members of this household, especially the ladies, were on a certain date at a certain time. Tuesday, the twenty-seventh of August, between five-thirty and six o'clock in the afternoon."

Carver looked genuinely bewildered. After a silence he said:

"I'd like to help you. But I frankly don't know. Tuesday the—I can't keep track of dates. I don't know. How can I tell a particular day; to fix it definitely, I mean?"

"You'll remember this one," said Hadley, stolidly, "if you forget every other day in the calendar. It was the day on which a valuable watch belonging to you was stolen out of a display at Gamridge's in Oxford Street. You haven't forgotten *that*, have you?"

"I don't know. I still don't know," repeated Carver, after a rather terrible silence. "But I understand a little better now. That man was a police officer. You believe that the same person killed him who killed the poor fellow at the department-store." He spoke in a dull, trancelike voice, and his hands closed over the arms of the chair. "And you think it was a woman. You're *mad!*"

Hadley made a significant gesture to Melson; a gesture of one turning the knob of a door and leaving it an inch open, enjoining silence. Standing with his back to the door, Melson felt his heart pound when he softly eased it a little open. He had a feeling that the whole house was waiting and listening.

Then Hadley spoke. His words were clear in the night stillness.

"Somebody in this house," he announced, "accused some one else of murder. Thanks to Inspector Ames's last report, delivered to Scotland Yard this evening, we know the name of the accuser. If the person cares to repeat that charge to us now, very well. *But that's the most I can promise you, Mr. Carver.* Otherwise we must put that accuser under arrest for being accessory after the fact and suppressing vital evidence in a capital charge."

He gestured swiftly to Melson, the door closed, and Hadley resumed his normal tone.

"If you should happen to remember how your household spent that half-hour, Mr. Carver, I will give you tonight to think it over," he said. "That's all, thank you."

Carver rose. His steps were not steady when he went out of the room, and he made several attempts before he snapped shut the latch of the door. Melson was conscious that the house stirred; that the loud words were still ringing, and had brought terror with them. In a quiet thick with suspicion, Dr. Fell tossed the stump of his dead cigar into the fireplace.

"Was that wise, Hadley?"

"I've thrown a bomb. Damn it, I had to!" retorted Hadley. He began to pace the room. "Don't you see it's the only way to use our advantage? It would be all very well if I could conceal the fact of Ames's being a police officer—then it's an ace in the hole. But I can't. It'll have to come out tomorrow. Even if it doesn't come out tomorrow, there's *got* to be a public inquest the day after. They're all going to know why Ames was here. . . . And before they realize we don't know which one of 'em accused a woman here of stabbing the shopwalker, we've got to scare the accuser into talking. Why shouldn't he—or she—talk? He accused somebody of murder to Ames. Why not to *me*?"

"I don't know," admitted Dr. Fell, ruffling his big mop of hair. "It's another of my worries. But somehow I don't think he—or she—will."

"You don't disbelieve the report, do you?"

"Oh no. It's this excessive caution on the accuser's part that bothers me. He might be willing to sneak in and make his accusation confidentially. But now that you've broadcast a public appeal, and everybody knows, you've created an uproar. . . ."

Hadley nodded grimly. "An uproar," he pointed out, "is what we want. If anybody in the house has seen anything suspicious whatever, we shall hear about it. And if what I said doesn't put the fear of God into whoever made that accusation, I'm no judge of human nature. He'll have to have a cast-iron caution to keep silent now. Fell, I'll give you odds that somebody knocks at that door within five minutes with a piece of information for us. . . . Meanwhile, what did you think of what Carver said?"

Dr. Fell poked moodily at the edge of the table with one cane.

"Two things," he growled. "One that I didn't understand and one that I did. *Imprimis*, as Carver said, nobody bothered to steal the hands off that clock when it was in an open place where anyone could have got at it without difficulty. The thief waited until it was locked up, and worst of all, *until it was painted*. If he intended to use it for murder, why run the unnecessary risk of having his gloves and clothes smeared up with a turpentine-thinned oil varnish that you'd need petrol to efface? Unless, that is . . . unless . . ."

He cleared his throat with a rumbling noise. "Harrumph. Suggestive, hey?" he said, and leered round at Hadley. "But this is the point I do understand. At half-past eleven Carver heard the chain drawn on the front door. At first he said he thought it might be this chap Paull returning unexpectedly. Later, when he heard of Stanley's presence in the house, he thought it must

81

have been Boscombe admitting Stanley. Boscombe confirmed this . . ."

"And lied?"

"And lied," Dr. Fell agreed, "if you look at it as I do."

Wheezing, he took out his cigar-case again. Melson looked from one to the other of them.

"But why?" he demanded, finding his voice for the first time.

"Because it's fairly clear that Stanley was already in the house," said the chief inspector. "I'm afraid Fell's right. The suggestion about that leather screen in Boscombe's room has good sound sense to it. What was the state of affairs? There was a gas-ring on a table behind the screen and somebody had newly split a bottle of milk and over-turned a tin of coffee. It wasn't Boscombe. His tidy soul made him want to rush to clean up as soon as Fell spoke about it. Yes, Stanley had been hiding behind that screen. . . . They had been smoking and drinking, but all the ashtrays were emptied and the glasses cleaned, to give the impression that only one person, Boscombe, was in the room."

"Merely to deceive Carver?"

"Not only to deceive Carver," said Dr. Fell. "To deceive—"

There was a knock at the door.

"May I come in?" asked a woman's voice. "*I have something rather important to tell you.*"

# 8

## View Through a Skylight

Lucia Handreth.

Without knowing why, Melson felt a shock at seeing her. Within five minutes, Hadley had predicted, there would be an answer to his bomb-throwing. Standing by the table, a smile tightening under his clipped moustache, Hadley had with apparent casualness taken out his watch and exhibited it to the others. Its hands, Melson noted, pointed to five minutes past two. Then he looked round at the woman who stood with her hand on the knob of the door.

She wore now a grey tailored skirt and jacket, her hands thrust into its pockets. Her heavy black hair was coiled about her head; it had a rich gleam and lustre in the light, and contrasted with the white face. A good face, not altogether beautiful, full of those impulses and sympathies and passions which she seemed trying to repress by thining her broad humorous mouth and making dull the brown eyes that were fixed on Hadley.

"Come in, Miss Handreth," said the chief inspector. "We have been expecting you."

This suave lie seemed to startle her. Her fingers rose and fell on the knob of the door, which was still only half open.

"Expecting me? You're a bit of a mind-reader, then. I—I've been trying to decide whether to come. I know I'm running a risk, but, don't you see, I've *got* to explain something that he'll never tell you, and if you don't hear it you'll never understand. Legally you'd have a right . . . and he insists on seeing you." Her palm beat up and down on the knob. "It's about the death of that man Ames."

Hadley glanced sideways at Dr. Fell.

"You knew, then, that it was Inspector Ames," he stated.

"I've known it," she answered, wearily, "ever since he began to hang about the pub. I was only thirteen when I saw him first, but I wasn't likely to forget. Oh no! He wasn't much different, except that he'd lost some teeth and hadn't shaved." She shivered. "I think he—felt something, too, although, of course, he wouldn't know me. Anyway, he jolly well kept away from *me*."

"And you know who killed him."

"Good Lord, no! That's what I wanted to tell you. . . . I only know who didn't kill him. Although I wish they had killed him, and then we could have disposed of the lot. Still, as Don is my first client"—suddenly a harsh smile flashed across her face—"I may be able to institute proceedings for him. . . ." She stepped inside the door, threw it open, and spoke outside. "Come in, Mr. Boscombe. This will interest you."

"*What the devil*—!" shouted a bewildered Hadley.

"It's funny enough," said the girl, "and low enough,

and mean enough, to be a fit end for Ames. It has a nasty sort of simplicity about it. Mr. Boscombe here, and that man Stanley, intended to kill Ames. At least, Calvin Boscombe was to kill him, with Stanley looking on.—Don Hastings saw the whole thing through the skylight. They intended to be—oh, so cool and detached and scientific, and show up the police for such bunglers when the perfect murder was committed! They had the stage all set. Only somebody beat them to it. And when that happened the two perfect murderers nearly fainted with fright and haven't been able to talk sense yet."

She stood back from the door, and they saw Boscombe.

He was bending forward near the door, restrained by Sergeant Betts's arm, and his face wore a sly and witless look as he tried to peer into the room. It was a queer little tableau: Boscombe with his mouse-coloured hair and his sharp face and his dark-grey dressing-gown against the white panelling, the gold chain of his pince-nez dangling down from one ear as he tried to fight his way into the room past Betts. The sergeant set him back on his heels with a jar. Then, at a sign from Hadley, he shoved him forward; and Boscombe, imperturbable, came softly into the room.

"Am I to understand," he said, jerkily, and shook himself to settle his clothes, "that that man upstairs was a police officer?"

"Didn't you know it?" asked Hadley, with silky quietness. "You offered him a suit of clothes, you know. Yes, he was a police officer."

"Good *God!*" said Boscombe. He turned round and began to swab at the beads of sweat on his upper lip.

"And I'm sure, old boy," said Miss Handreth, studying him with an air of detached interest, "that you and

85

Stanley would have swung for him if the business had gone through as you planned it. The perfect murder. . . ." She turned to Hadley. The flood of words had brought a tinge of colour to her cheeks. "That's what I meant by the funny part of it; that's why the plan ought to have gone through, Don says. Boscombe didn't know Ames was a policeman. And Stanley didn't know who the victim was to be." She began to laugh, her arms folded, and a strange beauty suddenly glowing through her face. "And you preaching on coolness to that nervous wreck upstairs, and him swilling brandy, and your hand shaking so you could hardly hold the gun—!"

Boscombe was a trifle dazed, as though he found himself surrounded and penned in by unexpected enemies. He turned round helplessly.

"I hardly expected," he said, "from *you*, Lucia . . . I—you don't understand! I only meant to give that overgrown braggart a scare, with all his talk of his own nerve. . . ."

"Don't lie. Don," she retorted, "followed every move you made, through that skylight, and a jolly lucky thing he did. He knew about the idea a month ago, when you were first talking to Stanley about 'the psychology of murder,' and 'the reactions of the human brain when its owner is face to face with death,' and all the rest of that poisonous bilge . . . to prove what a superman you were. . . ."

Hadley hammered on the table. Lucia Handreth, who was breathing hard, backed away, and Hadley glared round the circle.

"I *will* have some sense out of this!" said Hadley, with an effort. "Now," he added, after a pause and in a voice of shaky ease, "suppose we make some sort of effort to get this straight. You, Miss Handreth, accuse this man and old Pete Stanley of a conspiracy to murder.

You say this Hastings was not only on the roof and followed it, but knew about it beforehand?"

"Yes. Not who the victim was to be—they didn't know that themselves. But that they would probably have a shot at it."

Hadley sat down again and looked at her curiously.

"This is something new in my experience. By God! I thought I knew all the tricks, too! Hastings was on that roof, saw preparation for a murder, and didn't make the slightest effort to prevent it?"

"He did not," she replied, in a very clear voice. "And he never would have. That's what I wanted to explain to you. You see—"

A voice through the half-open door said:

"Let me explain it myself.

"I've got a statement to make," pursued the voice, "and I want to make it before I go off my onion again. Help me through, me hearties."

He came in unsteadily, watching the progress of his own feet in some surprise. He was a lean young man with a powerful pair of shoulders, large hands and feet, and a good-looking but rather absent-minded sort of face which must ordinarily have worn an expression of deadly seriousness. Now—to counteract the fact that he looked shamefaced—he was trying to grin casually, with a man-of-the-world's air. Eleanor Carver was on one side of him, and Betts on the other.

"But you *shouldn't*!" she was protesting, wildly, even while she helped him. "That doctor said—"

"Now, now," he said, paternally. His eyes, as he peered round the group, were affable but hazy. The abrasions on his face were brown with iodine, and a padding of bandages ran up the back of his head. They got him into a chair, where he slid back with a grunt of relief while his colour took on a less greyish tinge.

"Listen," he said, earnestly. "The fat's in the fire now, and I'm afraid I made a mess of the whole business by falling on my neck; but there's one thing I want understood. I didn't, believe it or not, I didn't fall out of that tree because I'd got the wind up, or anything like it! I could go up or down there with my eyes bandaged and one hand tried. I don't know how it happened. I was rushing to get down and round to the front door; and somehow—*whack . . . !*"

Hadley swung round his chair to study the newcomer.

"If you feel well enough to come in here," he said, "you probably feel well enough to talk. I am Chief Inspector Hadley, in charge here. And you're the young man who sees a murder ready to be committed and says nothing?"

"Yes," Hastings said, calmly, "in this case I am."

But it was a harsh calmness, an abrupt change in the young man's demeanour as though from a kind of monomania, which nearly made the blood gush again. He twitched out a handkerchief, threw back his head, and pressed the handkerchief hard to his upper lip. When it was under control, he said, shakily:

"Near thing, that. Aunt Millie wouldn't have liked it. Sorry.—I'm ready to talk, sir. But I want you to go out, Eleanor; and you too, Lucia. Mr. Boscombe had better stay."

"I won't go!" Eleanor cried, and jumped up from where she had been sitting beside his chair. Her pale-blue eyes were struggling with tears, and the voluptuously pretty face had hardened. She looked from Lucia to Hastings. "You f-fool," she added, as though she could not keep back the words. "I think you might have told me; I think you might have come to me, or done something or said something, and not to *her*!"

"Oh, stop it," Lucia said, sharply. "Go out, do, and don't bring a family quarrel into a murder case."

"While you stay?" enquired Eleanor, and laughed.

Lucia said, "I happen to be his legal adviser—" and stopped short, flushing, as Eleanor laughed again. The words, Melson thought, undoubtedly did sound foolish at that time, however correct they happened to be. He renewed his belief that the only time women lawyers seemed impressive was before they had graduated from law school. Brilliant Lucia Handreth might be, capable she certainly looked; but in this particular rough-and-tumble you thought only of a good-looking brunette stung to anger by a feminine gibe. Hadley took an even shorter view of the matter.

"I don't propose," he said, " to turn this place into a nursery or a playground. You will please go, Miss Carver. If Miss Handreth insists on her legal rights, I suppose she must stay." His voice became harsh as he saw Boscombe move out softly to take Eleanor's arm.

"*You're* not leaving, my friend? Doesn't this interest you at all?"

"No," returned Boscombe, coolly. "I am seeing to Miss Carver's rights. I will escort her out as another member of the nursery should, and return presently. Nor am I interested in the testimony of—of copper's narks who listen at skylights. This way, Eleanor. Now, now! Don't you know who I am? Gently! . . ."

When, after they had gone, quiet was restored amid vast chucklings from Dr. Fell, Hastings settled back in his chair.

"I've often wanted," he said, rather wistfully, "to land that blighter one under the jaw, but it would be too much like infanticide. So he calls me a nark, does he?" demanded Hastings, flaring up again. "I hadn't any particular grudge against *him*, and I was going to let him down easily, but if that poisonous little—"

"What I like about this house," observed Dr. Fell, in sleepy admiration, "is the spirit of love and trust and wholesome jollity which animates everybody. Ah, the solid joys of English home life! Carry on with your story, my boy."

"—and I've got a dashed good idea he's been trying to paw Eleanor . . ." Hastings went on broodingly. He stopped. After a pause he grinned at Dr. Fell, as most people did in the latter's comfortable presence. "Right you are, sir.

"The—the first part of it's the hardest to explain," he went on, uneasily. "You see, I'm reading in chambers with old Fuzzy Parker here at Lincoln's Inn. I'm supposed to be rather good at chin-wagging, and everybody said I should make a first-rate barrister; but it isn't as easy as that. You have to learn a hell of a lot of bilge, it seems. I'm beginning to think I should have gone into the Church, instead. Anyway, I don't seem to be making much progress, you see; and after I've paid the fees, and Fuzzy's hundred guineas on top of it, there isn't much left. I'm telling you this because then was when I met Eleanor, and—you see—well, in short"— his neck squirmed—"sometimes we began seeing each other up on the roof. Of course nobody knew about it . . ."

"Rot!" interposed Lucia, with judicial directness. "Nearly everybody in the house must have known it, except maybe Grandma Steffins. Chris Paull and I both knew about it. We knew you were up there reciting poetry. . . ."

Hastings' iodine-blotched face turned dull pink.

"I was not reciting poetry! You little dev—don't lie about it! O good God! I wish I'd never . . ."

"I was merely trying to be charitable, old boy," she

90

informed him, with a slight sniff. "Very well, if you like. Doing whatever you were doing, then, although I should fancy it was rather an uncomfortable spot." She folded her arms. Despite her pallor and nerves, a faint smile twitched the full lips. "And you needn't be nasty about it. Chris Paull wanted to go up and stick his head through the trap-door, and groan a couple of times, and say, 'This is Your Conscience. Aren't you *ashamed* of yourself?' But I prevented him."

Curiously enough, this did not seem to stir his anger. He stared at her.

"Look here," he said, in a low voice, "do you mean it was Paull who's been up on that roof?"

Hadley, who had been patiently waiting, leaned forward. There had been an indefinable note like horror in Hastings' words. It did not sound like the echo of a joke; it conjured up a vision of dark chimneys above the town, and something moving there with soft, deadly purpose.

"You've had enough latitude," Hadley said, sharply. His words rang in the white room. "Explain what you mean."

"Every once in a while I've thought I heard it walking," said Hastings, "or thought I saw it slip round the corner of a chimney. I supposed it was somebody spying on us, but nothing ever happened, you see; so naturally I thought I must have been mistaken. And I didn't mention it to Eleanor. No good alarming her.

"Our first rule, you see, was that I should take my books up there and Eleanor should help me study. Don't smile!" He glared round the circle. "That's true, and why not? There's a flat space up there, with the chimneys shutting it in all around. Eleanor had some pillows and a lantern that she kept in a chest in that little attic just before you get to the roof; and the chim-

neys kept the light from being seen anywhere about.
. . . Sometimes, when the light was on, I thought I could
hear something scraping and rustling; and once something I thought was a chimney-pot suddenly moved to
one side, so that I could see starlight through a gap in
the houses. Up there at night in the quiet, as though
you were shut off from everything sane in the world,
you get crazy fancies and a feeling of somebody watching you even when there's no one there. So I never
really saw anything—until tonight."

He paused, uncertainly. The handsome face, decked
out in iodine as though for a wild masquerade, looked
dull and weak. He peered over his shoulder; he lifted
a bandaged hand to straighten his necktie in the masquerade wreckage of his clothes, winced as though it
hurt him, and dropped it again.

"Now, then . . . about that skylight. I only noticed it
at all, or thought of fooling about there, because of this:
I was usually to meet Eleanor at a quarter past twelve.
The house was locked up at half-past eleven, and that
gave everybody time to settle down for the night. But
I was always ahead of time. Half an hour ahead of time.
Oh, damn it!" he fidgeted, "you know how it is. So I'd
poke about softly; I always wore tennis shoes. I noticed
that skylight over at one side . . ."

"Just a moment. When was this?" interrupted Hadley, whose pencil had been busy.

"A month and a half ago, at least. During the warm
weather, when a good deal of the skylight was lifted.
You can't hear much from that room unless you have
your ear close to it. And when Boscombe has that curtain clear drawn, there's nothing at all. But on this night
I climbed round the chimney and crawled over, because I could hear something. Whoever else knew I
was on that roof at any time, I'm jolly certain *they* never

did. And when I heard those first words . . ." He swallowed hard. "Boscombe said—and I'll never forget it—he said: 'The question in my mind is only whether you now have even the courage to watch a killing, Stanley. Otherwise the thing is simple. It fascinates you to kill. You love it.' Then he'd laugh. 'That was why you shot that poor devil of a banker, because you thought you could do it safely.'"

There was a long silence. With his undamaged hand Hastings fumbled in one pocket and got out a cigarette-case, as though to keep himself very steady.

"Those," he went on, quietly but more rapidly, "were the first words I heard. I stretched out and looked down through the part of the glass that was uncovered. I could see the back of that big blue chair turned facing the door, where it usually is, and a part of somebody's head over the back of it. Boscombe was walking back and forth in front of the chair, smoking a cigar, with an open book in his hands. The lampshade was tilted and I could see his face distinctly. He kept walking back and forth, back and forth, as he talked, with that little smirk of his, and he never took his eyes off the fellow in the chair. . . .

"It's a queer thing," Hastings said, suddenly. "He was wearing those little glasses, and the light reflected on them so that I couldn't catch his whole look. But when I was a kid I had an aunt who was an anti-vivisectionist, and she used to have a lot of posters to stick in odd places. One of the posters showed a doctor— Anyhow, that's what the expression on Boscombe's face reminded me of, and he was smiling.

"I listened to all the smooth poison he was talking. He was going to kill somebody, not for any good reason, not because he hated anybody, but to 'observe the reactions' of the victim when he got him in a corner, and played on his nerves, and told him to get ready for death. Or some such horrible rot. . . . He wanted Stanley to join him. Didn't Stanley like the idea? Yes, of course he did. And didn't Stanley want to do the poor stupid police in the eye for chucking him out, by committing a perfect murder or just assisting at one? *He* would plan the details, Boscombe said. He was only interested in Stanley's reactions when confronted again with the bogey that had wrecked his career in the first place.

"I could see one side of that chair, and a part of the fellow's face turned away. But most of all I could see his hand on the arm of the chair. When Boscombe began talking about doing the police in the eye, the hand began opening and shutting. Then it bunched into a fist and got a queer bluish colour and began to un- clench again. And Boscombe kept on walking back and forth, in that long robe of his, past a funny-looking black-and-yellow screen that had flames and imps painted on it; and he was showing his teeth."

Melson felt again the dull, creepy sensation that came to him whenever he thought of the screen that was painted in the design of the *sanbenito*, the robe worn by the sufferers of the *auto-da-fé* on their way to the place of burning. Figures were vivid in the white room; not a person moved; and Lucia Handreth said in a low voice.

"Dear Mr. Boscombe's hobby, I think, is the Spanish Inquisition."

"Yes," said Dr. Fell, "but I was wondering. If you people still hold to the popular notion that the Spanish Inquisition was a mere piece of senseless brutality, you know as little of it as Boscombe. Never mind that now. Go on, young man."

Hastings got a cigarette shakily into his mouth, and Lucia struck him a match.

"Well, I crawled back to the other place. I was nervous; I admit it. The whole business made me half afraid of the roof and whoever might be walking on the roof. Of course I didn't think they really meant it. When Eleanor came up I didn't tell her, but she noticed I was edgy and I asked her who Stanley was . . . . One thing I remembered was that Boscombe had said, 'It will have to be a Thursday night.'

"That stuck with me; it kept me thinking and puzzling—yes, and half *hoping*; I admit it . . . ."

"Hoping?" interposed Dr. Fell.

"Wait, sir," Hastings said, curtly; "wait a bit. My work went to the devil; on other evenings I'd go over to the skylight, but never a word about it even on a couple of the evenings when Stanley was there. I won't say I forgot it; but the hard thoughts stopped tormenting me and that 'It will have to be a Thursday' stopped ding-donging through my head.

"Until tonight. The most persistent thought, the thing that kept after me like a little blue devil, was: '*How are they going to get away with it? How are they going to commit this perfect murder and keep from being hanged?*' But even that had faded out until tonight.

"I climbed up the maple tree at just a quarter to twelve. I remember that because the bell at the Hall was striking the quarter-hour. And I didn't have any books; all I had, queerly enough as you'll see, was a newspaper stuck in my pocket. That tree—did you notice it?—runs up past one of Boscombe's windows. That never gave me any difficulty, because the windows were always closed and covered with thick black curtains. But tonight I noticed a queer thing. There was a moon out, shining on the windows, and I saw that the window by the tree had one of its panes smashed and wasn't quite closed.

"Funny how the mind works. I didn't any more than notice that pane, except to think I'd have to be quiet in case Boscombe heard a noise. But when I swung off to the gutter of the roof it put it in my mind to have a look down Boscombe's skylight.

"I waited till I'd got my breath again, and crawled over. I had to keep low in the exposed places, because there was bright moonlight and I didn't want to be seen from another house. Then I heard something, very low and whisperish, from the room. It suddenly turned me cold and half sick in the stomach, and my arms shook so that I nearly fell forward on the sharp edge of the pane. Boscombe said: 'We'll do the business in just fifteen minutes, or never. It's too late to back out now.'

"I was shaking so much that I had to lie down at full length on the upward slope of the roof. My coat got caught up under my arms, you see, and twisted round so that the damned newspaper was twisting out of my pocket. When I put my head round I could see it as—as close as somebody who's going to shoot you. The moon was on it, and I read across the top, 'Thursday, September 4th.' . . ."

He drew a deep breath. The fire had eaten crookedly down one side of the cigarette. In absolute stillness he continued:

"Then Boscombe spoke again, and I learned how he was going to do it. . . ."

96

# 9

## The Imperfect Crime

This Hastings, Melson reflected, might never become an outstanding barrister. But as a story-teller he unquestionably had his points. He seemed to realize that he had snared his audience, so that no creak came from a chair and even Hadley's pencil was motionless. And Hastings' face wore a crooked smile that made him look older than his years. They heard his breath whistling thinly.

"When I looked down there again," he went on, "I hadn't any consciousness of time or place, or anything except the rectangle of light that wasn't covered by the curtain. I could see the right-hand side of the chair-back as it faced the door, just as before, and the double-doors themselves, and a part of the screen to the right of them.

"Stanley was standing with his hand on the screen; his face was a greenish colour, and he was shaking as much as I was. Boscombe stood over by the lamp, putting bullets in the clip of an automatic. He seemed a bit queasy, but he was smiling and his hand was as absolutely steady as that table. He reached over and picked up the gun itself off the table—it seemed to have rather a long barrel, but I understood that a minute later—and shoved in the clip: *click*. Then Stanley said, 'O Christ! I can't watch it! I'll dream about it if I do!' All Boscombe did was patiently go over the whole plan again, to make sure everything was set, and then I understood.

"He had gone on the principle he'd laid down a month before—that nobody was to be selected for the 'experiment' who was likely to be 'a loss to the enlightenment of the human race.' Which," said Hastings, turning and throwing his cigarette into the fireplace, "was uncommonly decent of him. Secondly, the victim had to be a seedy down-and-outer, well known in the neighbourhood who might be thought likely to commit a burglary.—So he'd selected the likeliest man, a hanger-on at a pub near by, whom he'd been considering for a week. He had been careful to present this man with a grudge against him, in public, by ostentatiously asking the landlord to keep the man out of the private bar."

Somebody in the group uttered a stifled exclamation, but Hastings did not notice it.

"He'd already dropped hints in the bar about the amount of cash and valuables he kept lying about loose. . . . Come to think of it, from what Eleanor told me," Hastings reflected, dully, "he *had* bought a valuable watch from the old man; he didn't use any burglar-alarm devices like the old man; he kept it lying loose in a brass box. Eleanor said she liked it better than anything in the old man's collection.

"Anyway, he was ready. This evening he trailed the

down-and-outer, was sure nobody saw them, pretended to relent, and offered him a suit of clothes if he'd come to the house that night for it. Then he was just about prepared for the fake 'burglary,' because . . ."

Dr. Fell opened his eyes and interposed, sharply:

"Steady on, son. Wasn't this ingenious gentleman afraid that the tramp—always supposing the tramp was what he seemed—would tell somebody Boscombe had invited him to the house for a suit of clothes?"

Lucia Handreth stared. "But, Don," she cried, "don't you *know*? Were you too groggy to hear what I told you in the other room? That tramp was—"

"I repeat my question," snapped Dr. Fell. "Steady, Miss Handreth. This is no effort at concealment. It's simply that we don't want any digressions now."

Hastings had been moodily considering the previous question.

"Oh, Boscombe had thought of that, too. He said he didn't mind if the fellow told anybody; in fact, he rather hoped he would. Then, after the whole business was over, it would be taken as an extra lie on the man's part—told to excuse his presence in case he should be seen hanging about the house, and clearly a lie because Boscombe had disliked him.

"One funny thing, though. I remember Boscombe said to Stanley about that: 'This is what I don't understand, but I'll let *you* worry about it. When I was spinning an excuse to have him come here late at night after the clothes, *he* suggested it himself.' Boscombe said he supposed this man really did intend to pinch something, if he could find an easy crib.

"He told the fellow to come round exactly at twelve; not before or after. He was to ring Boscombe's bell. The house would be dark, but he wasn't to mind that. If Boscombe didn't come downstairs to answer the bell himself, that would mean Boscombe was engaged in an intensive piece of work upstairs, and would have left the door unlocked. So, if the man got no response from the bell, he was to come in quietly; not wake up the house by striking matches or going after lights, but walk straight back to the staircase he would see at the rear, and go upstairs. . . .

"Boscombe, naturally, never had any intention of venturing out of his room to meet the tramp. *His* trick was to make everybody else in the house believe he had gone to bed at half-past ten. And now," said Hastings, beating one hand softly on the table, "now comes the devilish ingenuity.

"Earlier, about half-past eleven, Boscombe had already sneaked downstairs in the dark, to unlock and unchain the front door. Asking this fellow to ring the bell at midnight, of course, was merely to warn him when the man was coming upstairs. . . . Eh? Pardon?"

He looked round blankly as Hadley uttered an exclamation. Hadley turned back a page of his notebook as he looked across at Dr. Fell.

"That," he said, "was what Carver heard at half-past eleven. You notice he didn't hear voices, or footsteps on the pavement, which is what you do hear if somebody is being let in; he only heard the chain rattle. But that's not the important thing. Do you see what the important thing is?"

"*I* see it," said Lucia Handreth, unexpectedly. Hadley started round, his eyes narrowing, and she faced him with defiant composure. "It means that if Inspector Busy Ames found that open door—and he was the sort of person who *does* find open doors—he had some little time to prowl about this house before he rang Boscombe's bell at twelve o'clock."

"Quite," agreed Dr. Fell, blandly. "He was curious about somebody's room. And that was why he was murdered."

Hadley struck the table. "By God! you've got it!... The question is, Miss Handreth, how *you* know not only who he was, but even his nickname. Have you anything to say about that?"

"One thing at a time. Don is talking.... Now, now, Don, don't be so stupid and look so wild! I told you a while ago, even if it didn't register. That tramp was *Inspector* Ames, and in case the name means nothing to you...."

Hastings stared. Then he put his head in his hands, his elbows on the table, and kept on laughing in a way that sounded horribly like sobbing. "Quit ragging!" he choked out, and then peered at her half-fearfully. "You don't really mean—mean that one cop was waiting for another, and neither of 'em knew...! My head— easy—where's that handkerchief?

"Listen," he went on, presently, with a thin edge of amusement in his voice, "whatever this means, it's sauce for the rest of the joke. It repays me. I'm happy. I'm happy for ever now, in spite of the scare I got.

"I told you about Boscombe unlocking the door. Well, when I saw Boscombe through the skylight, he was setting out the rest of his properties. An old pair of dilapidated shoes, stolen; a pair of cotton gloves and two pistols. One pistol was a Browning revolver, bought at a pawnshop, its numbers effaced, and fully loaded. The other was his own thirty-eight calibre automatic, with a German silencer on the barrel, loaded with several real cartridges and one blank.

"In his bedroom he had a couple of potted plants. After he'd unlocked the front door, he took some earth out of one pot, made a paste of mud with water in the washbowl of the bathroom, and spread it on the soles of the shoes. He then walked into the study, opened the window nearest the tree, sat on the window-sill, and put the shoes on his own feet. With the gloves on, he leaned out backwards like a window-washer, smashed one pane, lifted his feet and made marks on the sill of one climbing in. There was very little mud— just enough to make those marks and leave a very faint trail to the table where the brass box was. He'd done this with the lights out, of course; and the crazy thing was, I gathered from what he and Stanley were saying, it must have been only ten minutes or so before I climbed up.

"They'd had the lights out all the time after Boscombe was supposed to have gone to bed at ten-thirty, so that *nobody* could later have said a light was seen; and they only flashed 'em on briefly to make sure everything was ready. Boscombe had the gloves and shoes, upside down, laid out on a couch. He had his own gun in his bare hand; and the other, which he hadn't touched except with a handkerchief, in the pocket of his dressing-gown.

"When they heard the bell ring at midnight, they'd arranged that Stanley was to get behind the screen again with his eyes to a crack, so that he could see. So that there'd be no chance of anybody seeing a light, or catching this tr—this *copper*. . . ."

At the word, which startled him anew, Hastings began to show those inexplicable signs he had demonstrated before.

"Go on!" Hadley snapped.

". . . Sorry. Or of catching this copper coming upstairs, Boscombe had told him that he'd be working in another room; the outer room would be dark, but not to mind that. Boscombe said for him just to open the door, walk in, and call out quietly. . . . Then, by God! the fun was to begin; the screaming mirth and the beautiful experiment on a man about to die." Hastings' voice rose. "As soon as he came inside, Stanley was to pop out from behind the screen, switch on the lights beside the door, and turn the key in the lock.

"They'd catch the rabbit before it squealed, you see. The victim would see Boscombe sitting in the big chair, with a gun in his hand, grinning at him; and Stanley, six feet three and also grinning, just behind him. Boscombe had even rehearsed what was going to be said. The victim would say something like, 'What's all this?' or 'What do you mean?' And Boscombe would say, 'We are going to kill you.'"

Hastings pressed the back of one hand across his eyes.

"Blast it! even to hear Boscombe talking down there—and hopping back and forth and making oozy gestures while he rehearsed it—was . . . well, it was like one of those ghastly nightmares in which people don't strike you as human beings at all, but as implacable robots you can't reason with. You only see them coming closer and closer, and know that they're going to kill you as a matter of course.

"Boscombe explained how they were going to lead him gently over to the other chair, and make him sit down, *and put on the old shoes he was to be found dead in.* Then Boscombe would say, 'You see that pretty box on the table? Open it. There's money in there, and a fine watch. Put it all in your pocket. You won't keep it long.' He would explain exactly what they intended to do, after they'd squeezed all the blood out of their victim's nerves, and got all his 'reactions,' and seen him crawl and pray. They would debate *where* they would shoot him, and after that game had been enjoyed in tortuous ways, then Boscombe would stand back and drill him through the eye with a silenced gun.

"'I don't wish him to suffer any pain'—so help me, I heard Boscombe say that! He said, 'It's not in the nature of my object.'"

Lucia Handreth, who was standing by the mantelpiece, turned away suddenly and thrust her hands over her eyes. She cried:

"He *couldn't* have . . . not even Calvin Bos—You see . . . well, it's too horrible! It must have been a joke, as he said, on that man Stanley's nerves. . . ."

During the heavy, sickly silence Hadley said:

"I don't see that there's much difference, if that's the fellow's idea of a joke on a neurotic cripple." He cleared his throat and finally added: "Well, Mr. Hastings? What were they to do then?"

"Oh, the fun was over then, with just a little more work to be done. They would spread him out on the floor, wearing the shoes and gloves, beside the rifled box. They would put in his hand the Browning revolver, unfired. Stanley would shake hands with Boscombe, thank him for a pleasant evening, and slip away while Boscombe relocked the front door. Boscombe would then go and rumple up his bed. Leaving the exploded cartridge-case on the floor, he would go back to the room, hide the silencer and the man's shoes, and fire a blank cartridge at nothing. . . . When the crash of the shot awoke the household, Boscombe (the blank cartridge-case slipped out and its place filled) would explain that he had been aroused by a noise, and . . .

"Oh, you see it. He would not only have been instantly exonerated; he would even be praised. 'Courageous Householder Shoots Armed Burglar in Self-defense. *Picture inset*, Mr. Calvin Boscombe, who was a fraction of a second quicker on the draw than the desperate criminal who threatened his life.'" Hastings choked off his gurgling laughter and leaned forward.

"That was what was supposed to happen. Now I'll tell you what did happen."

The door to the room softly opened and Boscombe came in. Nobody moved or spoke. Each person glanced at him, briefly, without seeing him at all, and then looked back to Hastings; but Melson could feel in the air a sort of rustling, a repulsion as though each person had moved a little back from him. The atmosphere was thick with it, the more so as Boscombe's face wore a sickly smile and he was rubbing his hands together. He glanced at each one, but nobody would look back. Dr. Fell alone studied him, a puzzled blankness in his eye. Boscombe's lip twitched, and he folded his arms.

"One thing I noticed," Hastings went on, although his stamina was ebbing and he looked even paler than when he had come in—"one thing I noticed," he said, heavily, "was that as the zero hour came closer Stanley began to shake less and grow a little more human—or inhuman. He'd lost some of his flabby jaw-twitching. And the minutes kept on ticking, until all of a sudden the big bell over at the Hall began to strike midnight. My God! it sounded loud!—like thunder and dooms-day. I thought I couldn't move at all, but I nearly jumped out of my skin at that. Directly on top of it Stanley said, in a voice that sounded as loud as the bell: 'You're going through with this? You do mean it?' And Boscombe said, 'Yes.' He said, 'Get behind that screen, and don't bungle your part when you come out. You'll be able to see the light-switch, because there's a bright moon and I've left the—'

"There was where he looked up."

"He saw you?" demanded Hadley, and jerked forward as though Boscombe were not there at all.

105

"No. The light was in his eyes, and he was thinking about other things, anyway. His face looked like a blind man's behind the glasses. What distracted him just then, and put the wind up me, was that on the same second his doorbell buzzed.

"That buzzer must be up near the ceiling somewhere, because the blasted thing seemed to go off like a rattlesnake sounding directly under my hands. I jumped and nearly rolled. Boscombe said: 'Behind the screen. I give him five minutes before he's here,' and switched off the lamp on the table.

"The moonlight came into the room with a pale bluish colour. I couldn't see Stanley, who was bumping about behind the screen, but I could see Boscombe distinctly—and ahead of him the moonlight on the double-doors, with the shadow of the big chair strong and black. Boscombe stood in that weird light, moving his shoulders up and down, and I heard the safety catch click on the pistol when he released it. The doorbell started in again, horribly, and buzzed out a couple of bursts—the victim clamouring to come into the trap. When the buzzing stopped—and it seemed incredibly loud and nervous—Boscombe backed into the big chair and sat down. I could see him leaning forward, his hand getting nervous on the pistol, and the moonlight trembling a little on the long blue barrel. . . .

"He'd said he would give the victim five minutes. It seemed like three times as long as that, although it couldn't have been, because I'll swear I held my breath the whole time. It was the dead silence of the place—everywhere. Not even a motor horn outside, or a creaky fire grate inside. I thought, now he'll be opening the door downstairs, looking inside. Now he'll be coming across the hall. . . .

"Minutes, hours. . . .

"The strain was growing too much. I could hear Boscombe rustle in the chair, I could even hear his breathing; but he still had a pretty steady grip on the gun. Once Stanley rattled a tin or something behind the screen. It was as though you could hear a watch ticking the minutes in your own head. I felt that I couldn't stand it much longer, when Boscombe spoke. It wasn't much more than a whisper, but the man was losing his nerve and the gun had begun to wabble. He said:

"*'What the hell's delaying him?'*

"And there was a kind of agony in it, the voice gone to a crazy key and shooting out that whisper. It seemed to propel him out of the chair. He got up and took a couple of steps, stiffly, towards the double-doors. The bluish light was clear on the doors and I suddenly thought I saw one of the knobs starting to turn. But I know I heard a noise. . . .

"It was a *scratching* noise on the outside of the doors, like a dog trying to get in. It wavered and fumbled for about ten seconds. Then with a crash the left-hand door was knocked open. Something or somebody pitched through, went forward on his hands as though he were salaaming, kicked himself round and lay writhing half inside the room. It was a man with something shiny sticking out of the back of his neck, and trying to talk as though he had his mouth full of water. . . .

"Boscombe ripped out a curse and jumped back. There'd been a kind of sodden *flap* as that man hit the floor, and Stanley cried out something behind the screen. For a second nobody moved except that man twisting on the floor and rattling his heels. Boscombe stumbled around before he got back to the table and switched the lamp on.

"The shiny stuff was gilt. I looked once. Then I put my face down against the roof, and I was so weak that

I couldn't move. I think my own shoes rattled. . . . "

Hastings stopped, twisted in the chair, and got his breath. He went on, more quietly:

"What made me look up I don't know. It may have been a sound on the roof, but I don't think I was in much condition to pay attention to sounds then. But I did look—towards a chimney on my right, and I saw it.

"It was standing by the chimney, staring at me. I don't know whether it was a man or a woman; the only impression I got was of a white face, and (I don't know if I can make this clear) of a malignancy so powerful that its very wave may have roused me like a noise. And I did see one hand along the side of the chimney. As I moved my body to one side, a little of the glow from the skylight fell on this hand just as the person slid back out of sight. On the hand there was a smear of gilt."

His eyes moved over to the shining clock-hand on the table, and then he closed them. He was silent for so long that Hadley prompted:

"Well? What then?"

Hastings made a gesture. "You know the rest of it. . . . The first coherent thought I had was that Eleanor mustn't come upstairs, past Boscombe's door, and see what was there if I could prevent it. I could have gone down through the trap-door in the roof—but I didn't see any reason for betraying where I was to Grandma Steffins. I thought if I got down, ran to the front door, and . . . I don't know; I'm not sure what I did have in mind, except that it was to rush blindly somewhere and get that sight out of my mind. I'd got into the tree safely. I remember swinging over to it. That's all I do remember except hearing leaves ripping and suddenly seeing the tree upside down, until I woke up. Some

108

old chap with a grey chin whisker was bending over me in Lucia's room, and the next minute he seemed to be pounding iron spikes in my head while I was talking. I think I was telling all this to Lucia . . ."

Hadley glanced over at her with sharp enquiry. She made a half-cynical gesture and anticipated his question.

"Yes, of course, Inspector," she said. "You'll wish to know about *me*. I don't know how long it was after he fell that I picked him up; I didn't hear him fall. . . . I'd been reading in my bedroom, and I must have fallen into a doze. . . ."

"You heard nothing of what went on in the house, either?"

"No. I told you I must have been dozing in the chair." She hesitated, and shivered a little. "Something woke me; I don't know what it was, but I know it startled me. I looked at the clock and saw it was well past midnight. I felt chilly and—well, dispirited, and I didn't want to bother making a fire. So I went out to my kitchen to heat some water for a toddy before I turned in. The kitchen window was open, and I heard somebody groaning in the yard. I went out . . ."

"You showed great coolness of mind, Miss Handreth," Hadley told her, evenly. "And then?"

"I didn't show great coolness of mind, and I don't think you need to be sarcastic. I got him in. He was bleeding horribly. I thought I might wake up Chris Paull or Ca—" She looked towards Boscombe, checked herself, and a glitter showed under the drooping eyelids, although her face remained palely set—"get Chris to help without waking the others up. I opened my sitting-room door to the hall, but there was a light shining down the stairs and I heard voices. I also saw Mrs. Steffins. She was standing in the light, looking upstairs and listening. I noticed she was fully dressed. She saw me, and I closed the door and went back to Don. That was a few minutes before *you* arrived. When the doctor came to see Don, Mr. Carver came with him and told me what had happened. When Don came to himself he insisted on speaking, too."

She spoke the words with the meaningless sing-song inflection of a policeman giving evidence before a magistrate. Then the voice came alive.

"Of course he only fell thirty feet, and of course the branches *did* rather break the fall," she added, hotly. "And of course he must give the evidence. But will you let him go now?"

"There's nothing wrong with me," Hastings snapped. His voice grew querulously high. "For God's sake, Luce, will you stop treating me like a kid?" He was in such a weakened state that small things assumed a monstrous hue, and strained almost to the point of a grotesque blubbering. "You've done it ever since the old days, and I'm getting sick of it. I've got one purpose in telling this, whatever they think of it. I've nothing in particular against Boscombe. I don't like him"—his eyes flashed round briefly., "but I've got nothing against him. It's that swine *Stanley*. Whoever killed the fellow, I know damned well they didn't; but they meant to, and I want to see that everybody knows what kind of swine Stanley is. I want 'em to know that he encouraged a murder; that he stood by and watched while—"

"Yes," said Hadley. "But so did you."

Hastings grew very quiet, and for the first time very sure of himself. A quiet, rather terrible smile grew on his face.

"Oh no," he said. "That's different. Didn't I make it clear?" The smile grew crooked. "That's what conked my nerves, you see—the joyous anticipation. I had it all planned out. I had plenty of time. When they'd talked their fill to the victim, and prepared to fire that bullet, I was going to drop through the skylight. I hoped the victim could deal with Boscombe; if he couldn't, old Bossie looked as though he couldn't add much punch to the two of 'em. Maybe I ought to explain that I skippered the boxing-team at my college. First I was going to beat Stanley; beat him to such a squashed jelly that—" he stopped, drew a deep breath, and the smile grew to a murderous ecstasy. "Well, never mind. Then I was going to give 'em both in charge, with the testimony of the victim *and all the supporting evidence they couldn't destroy*—for attempted murder. They wouldn't hang. But I'm willing to bet you that even yet they'll burn in effigy on the highest bonfire that's built for Guy Fawkes' Day."

"But *why*? Steady, Mr. Hastings! What have you got against—?"

"You'd better tell them, Don," Lucia suggested, quietly. "Things are so mucked up that it will come out, anyway. And if you don't, I will."

"Oh, I'll tell them. I'm not ashamed of it . . .

"My full name," he said, harshly, "is Donald Hope-Hastings. And that swine shot my father."

He jerked himself up out of the chair and made for the door. When it had closed behind him, they heard a startled exclamation from Sergeant Betts, and the thud of knees collapsing on the floor.

# 10

## Gilt Paint

"Attend to him," Hadley said, curtly, to Lucia Handreth, "and come back here. I want all the ladies in the house to come here immediately." He stared at the door as it closed after her, and listened to the commotion in the hallway. Then he growled to Dr. Fell: "It's becoming more of a nightmare, complicated by the fact that that young fellow loves melodrama. I suppose he *is* telling the truth? H'm. I seem to remember that old Hope—that's the fellow I was telling you about, who looted his own bank for something like a quarter of a million—did have a child about seven or eight years old then. If this youngster didn't love melodramatics so much . . ."

But Hadley did not feel easy. He mopped his forehead with a handkerchief, and stared at his notebook as though it contained only useless information.

"That's where you're wrong, Hadley," Dr. Fell contradicted in a heavy voice. "He doesn't love melodrama;

he only lives it. That's because he's one of the real, breathing, erratic human race, and not a character study. Emotion scares you, my boy, so much so that you've driven into saying it doesn't exist unless somebody talks about it in terms of the weather. All you can understand are the chaste feelings of the burglar who wants somebody else's property. When somebody really does have a large human chunk of hatred or grief in his shaky soul, he doesn't treat it as an interesting metaphysical problem like a character in Ibsen. That's why all Ibsen's houses are dolls' houses. On the contrary, he goes off his onion and talks stark raving melodrama. The same as—" He rumbled to himself, smoothing his moustache, and seemed more puzzled than ever.

"I believe I know what you are thinking about now," said Boscombe, softly.

Dr. Fell started a little. "Hey? Oh! Oh, you're still here, are you?" he enquired, blankly, and wheezed as his little eyes flickered over the other. "To be candid, I was hoping you had gone."

"So I am under a cloud?" asked Boscombe, rather shrilly. His self-consciousness was showing again, although he tried to assume an air of cynical pleasantry. "You regard me as a monster?"

"No. But I think you'd like to believe you were one," said Dr. Fell. "That's your trouble and your amiable phobia. You're stuffed full of unpleasant nonsense, but I believe you're a fraud. Your brains aren't one-two-three with the *real* devil who's behind this, and of course you never really intended to kill Ames. . . ."

"Which I told you," Boscombe pointed out. "I told you it was a joke on that overstuffed braggart upstairs, and that I was a bit tired of hearing him gabble about his iron personality in the old days."

"Uh! Yes. That was when you thought you might be had up for murder. But now that we've learned what really did happen, and you're in no danger, you may be apt to get some pleasure out of making a howling bogey of yourself. You may maintain you really did mean murder, and go and gibber on the stairs to celebrate yourself. Somehow you annoy me, my friend."

Boscombe laughed, and Hadley swung round.

"You think you are in no danger, eh?" he snapped. "Don't count on it. I think I shall just give myself the pleasure of taking you up on an attempted-murder charge."

"You can't," Dr. Fell said, dully. "I know it'll be bad for his reputation as a bogey, but I looked at that gun when Pierce had it. . . . The silencer is a dummy."

"What?"

"It's not a silencer at all; it's a tin cylinder painted black, with a nozzle at the front to give the design beauty. Blast it, Hadley, don't you see it's only another bit of fiction-fed imagination? You ought to know there are only half a dozen real silencers in England; they're too hard to get; but every good bogus murder-plot entails the use of one. *Bah!* Your whole case against Boscombe and Stanley would have to depend on Ames's being shot with a silencer, and they could give you the merry ha-ha the moment you produced Exhibit A. It's a good thing, Boscombe, you didn't give Stanley a close look at it. He may strangle you yet for your little joke."

Hadley got to his feet and looked at Boscombe.

"Get out," he said, heavily.

"I should like to suggest—" Boscombe began.

"Get out of here," said Hadley, taking a step forward, "or in just one minute more . . ."

"Before the end of this case," Boscombe told him, his nostrils pinched as he backed away, "you will come to me for advice. I can tell you something, with which I don't feel inclined to assist you now. Enjoy yourself until I do."

The door closed. Hadley muttered something, rubbed his hands together, and turned back to his notebook. "What bothers me most," he exploded, "is the mess this whole thing's got into by such an unholy series of coincidences piled one on top of the other. Look at them! Somebody in this house—anonymous—tells Ames that the woman who stabbed the shopwalker lives here, hiding damning evidence somewhere, but refuses to help Ames get in. Subsequently somebody else invites Ames in—so that he may walk into a casual murder-trap arranged for amusement by Boscombe *and* a former police officer who was once closely associated with Ames. While walking into this trap, Ames is stabbed by still another person—presumably the woman who killed the shopwalker to begin with. Watching the whole infernal business through the skylight is a young man whose father was shot by Stanley fourteen years ago, *and* whose father had also been tracked down and proved guilty by Ames!—Fell, if coincidence can go any farther, I never want to hear of it. If the thing were fiction and not fact, I would flatly refuse to believe it."

"You think they're all coincidences?" enquired Dr. Fell, musingly. "Because I don't."

"How do you mean?"

"And I don't believe them, either," the doctor affirmed with a sort of obstinacy. "Miracles may happen. But they don't come in batches like a conjuring performance. Similarly, most real criminal cases (I regret to say) are solved by a coincidence or two—the fact that somebody looks out of a window unexpectedly, or hasn't enough money for his cab fare, or any of the other points that hang the shrewdest murderer. But mere chance couldn't produce such a string of whoppers as we've got here."

"You mean—?"

"I mean it was *arranged*, Hadley. There's one poor little bedraggled coincidence that is real, and the rest was contrived by the imagination of somebody beside whom Boscombe's shabby little murder-joke is tame. That person is the real devil. Somebody knew the histories and background of everybody connected with this house. Somebody shifted these people about like a chess-gambit, and produced this twisted state of affairs as a background for the final blow with the clock-hand. I say, Hadley, I think I'm going to be half afraid of everybody I meet until . . ."

"Excuse me, sir," interposed Sergeant Betts, putting his head into the room. "Will you come here a moment? There's something . . ." He woodenly checked his expression of excitement as Lucia Handreth came in. "Benson and Hamper and the doctor have got through now, and they'll report to you before they go."

Hadley nodded and closed the door when he hurried out. Lucia eyed him speculatively. She was smoking a cigarette in short jerky puffs, and dislodged a bit of paper from her lower lip with the nail of her little finger. It showed white sharp teeth when the lips were drawn apart. The long, luminous brown eyes passed over Melson and fixed on Dr. Fell.

"I'm quite ready for the women's third-degree," she announced. "Eleanor and Steffins will be here in a moment. They're still fighting, you see. Don is—as well as can be expected."

"Sit down, ma'am," urged Dr. Fell, in that beaming and benevolent fashion which radiated from him on all good-looking females. "Heh-heh-heh. I'm glad to hear it. I dare say you've known him a long time and that

116

was how you came to spot the late Inspector Ames."

She smiled. "Quite a lot of cats have been let out of the bag tonight. So I don't mind admitting that I'm his first cousin. At least it'll do *some* good if it persuades our little Nell that she's no longer any grounds for jealousy." A swift contempt showed in her eyes; she concealed it, and examined her cigarette. "My mother was the sister of Carlton Hope, or Hope-Hastings, the man they landed—"

"Landed?"

She jerked her cigarette away from her lips. Melson saw the sharp teeth again. "He was no more guilty of embezzling that money than you were. Less so, if you belong to the police. Do you?" She inspected him, and a smile began to grow. "I'll pay you the compliment of saying you don't look it. They couldn't find a victim, and so they framed him. Then they knew they could never convict him in open court, so . . ." She flung the cigarette into the fireplace. Then she began to walk up and down, quickly, with her arms folded about her as though she were cold.

"Don," she added, "was only eight then, and I was thirteen, so I know rather more about it. The funny thing is that Don really believes his father was guilty—that's because his mother brought him up to think so; and he's morbid about it, so morbid that he keeps the whole relationship dark, and when I came here, and he fell for Eleanor, he wouldn't even let it be known we were related for fear Steffins should somehow find out. Yet he hated the police violently. Whereas I know perfectly well Uncle Carlton was innocent, and I . . ." She stopped and shrugged wearily. "No good going on, is there? Some are crooked and I dare say some are honest; but in any case there really isn't much I can do about it. I'm a bit of a fatalist, I fancy."

Dr. Fell blew the ribbon of his eyeglasses off his nose, and grunted amiably.

"You may be, of course," he admitted, "although you may not be certain of what the term means. When a person says he's a fatalist, he very often means merely that he's too lazy to try changing the course of events; whereas I rather suspect you're a fighter, Miss Handreth." Upheavals animated his several chins, and his little eye twinkled. "Now tell me, when you saw Inspector Ames nosing about the pub over there, what did you really think?"

She hesitated, seeming to change her mind, and made a gesture of acknowledgment. She confessed:

"Frankly, I got the wind up. I knew I hadn't done anything, but—! It was his presence there, that's all." She looked at him sharply. "Why *was* he there, as a matter of fact?"

She broke off as Hadley, with suppressed excitement tightening round the muscles of his jaw, ushered in Mrs. Steffins and Eleanor. Both were flushed. Mrs. Steffins, wagging her head and not looking at Eleanor, but staring straight ahead as though she were imparting a rapid confidence to one of the glass cases, was continuing a soliloquy through lips that scarcely opened.

"—not enough," she pursued, in this ventriloquist fashion, while her colour mounted, "to conduct a common seduction on the very roof of this house, where anyone might be looking on; to break your poor guardian's heart while he works his fingers to the bone for you, and keep all, every penny, of the money you make while never contributing one halfpenny towards the support of this house where I work my fingers to the bone"—short drawing of breath—"up over the roof on our very heads in front of the neighbours, a thing I warn you I shall never live down until I come to my deathbed"—here tears shone in her eyes—"and you might think a little of us sometimes, but do you? No, and not only that," said Mrs. Steffins, suddenly coming to the full attack and whirling round, "You ask that your paramour be kept all night in this house, after you deliberately, on that roof—"

"Rot. Those buildings," said Eleanor, with curt practicality, "are mostly offices, and who is there to see? I found that out."

Mrs. Steffins became coldly grim.

"Very well, my young lady. All I can say is that he will not stop *here*. Of course you would be the one to discuss all this before strangers," she pointed out, raising her voice unconsciously in the apparent hope of getting support from somebody there, "but, since you do, I can assure you that he will not stop here. Where should we put him? Not with Miss Handreth, I assure you. Haa-aaa no!" exclaimed Mrs. Steffins, shaking her head and smiling a grim tight smile, as though she saw the cunning and sinister design but was shrewd enough to frustrate it. "Haa, no; not with Miss Handreth, I assure you."

"Put him in Chris Paull's room, of course! Chris wouldn't mind."

"We will do nothing of the kind.—Besides," she hesitated, "the room is occupied, so you see . . ."

"Occupied?" demanded Eleanor.

Mrs. Steffins shut her lips firmly. Hadley, who had been letting them talk for a quiet reason of his own, interposed.

"*I'm* interested in that, Mrs. Steffins." He grew sharp. "There seems to have been a misunderstanding somewhere. We were told that this Mr. Paull was away, and certainly not of anybody occupying his room. If anybody is still there, he must be deaf or dead. Who is it?"

The change was as remarkable as it was swift. One

moment she had stood with her chin drawn in, simmering; in the next, a wholly new assortment of wrinkles had shaped themselves across the once-pretty face, like an effect by one of those lightning-artists making a charcoal sketch on the stage. Out of the pouches and hollows of her faintly darkened face gleamed perfect teeth. A wide smile, a dental smile; a deprecating expression of the violet eyes; a different, insinuating carriage of the thick shoulders to indicate charm. Even her voice acquired a different timbre. And, in her effort to shovel out charm, for the first time she looked rather sinister.

"But of course it must have slipped my mind," she said in a voice of eager cultural overtones that sounded like somebody burlesquing the B.B.C. "Why, my dear Mr.—my dear Inspector—who would be in dear Mr. Paull's room but dear Mr. Paull himself?"

Eleanor regarded her suspiciously. "Oh? *I* didn't know he was here. And he's a light sleeper. He certainly would have . . ."

"Of course, my dear. You know about all of them, don't you?" enquired Mrs. Steffins, twitching her head round briefly to look. "But I really don't think it will be necessary to wake him. I didn't think it was at all necessary to tell Johannus or Eleanor or even his friend Miss Handreth. And I do think it is so awf'ly nice for a young man to belong to nice clubs, don't you? for then they're with really nice people, you see, and don't go to those filthy, nasty pubs or to the other kinds of clubs where they say those abandoned women dance most immorally"—a quick breath—"though of course if they are in clubs and talking to members of the nobility—perhaps you know Sir Edwin's place, Roxmoor, in Devon; three hours and fifteen minutes, by a good train—then perhaps they *will* stay a wee bit long over the refreshments and I know perfectly well . . ."

Dr. Fell struck his forehead. "Got it!" he boomed, with a sudden air of inspiration. "I begin to see this at last! You mean that he's paralyzed drunk!"

Mrs. Steffins said this was vulgar, and disclaimed it. Under pressure she acknowledged that Christopher Paull, with a remarkable cargo aboard, had arrived about seven-thirty that evening, that for some mysterious reason he had come in by the back door, and that she had found him sitting on the stairs in a disconsolate mood. She had assisted him up, nobody else being aware of his presence, and so far as she knew he was still in his room. She snapped at Eleanor for making her tell this now, after which she sulked. Hadley went to the door and gave instructions to Sergeant Betts. When he returned something about the expression of his face subdued even Mrs. Steffins' charm. Her volubility trickled off, and she seemed to be girding herself for a refuge in hysteria if matters took an uncomfortable turn.

"I have several important questions to ask each of you," said Hadley, looking at the three women in turn. Lucia was casual, Eleanor defiant, and Mrs. Steffins snuffling a little. "Sit down, please." He waited until Melson had pushed out chairs; then he sat down himself and folded his hands. "It's late and I shall not detain you too long tonight, but I should like all of you to be absolutely sure of what you say. Miss Carver."

There was a rustling pause while he looked at his notes. Eleanor straightened up.

"Miss Carver, about that door leading up to the roof. It was locked tonight, and you say that it is usually locked. Now we have reason to believe that the murderer himself was on that roof tonight a few minutes or immediately after the stabbing.—Who has the key to that door?"

Somebody in the group gasped, but their backs were

towards Melson and he could not tell which it was. He moved unobtrusively round so that he could see them.

"I *did* have it," Eleanor replied. "Now that you know the whole affair, I don't mind telling you. Somebody stole it from me."

"It will be padlocked tomorrow. Padlocked and nailed—" Mrs. Steffins broke out wildly, but Hadley's look silenced her.

"When was it stolen, Miss Carver?"

"I—don't know. You see, I usually keep it in the pocket of this coat." She touched the leather motoring-coat. "I thought I had it tonight. I—when I put on the coat tonight I didn't even bother to make sure it was there. I suppose I must have put my hand into the pocket as I went out; you know, automatically; but I had a handkerchief and a pair of gloves and some coins and things in the pocket, so when I didn't feel it I simply supposed it was among them somewhere. I didn't discover it was gone until I went upstairs . . . went upstairs the first time." She was having difficulty, between anger and fear.

"The first time?"

"Yes. When those two," she nodded towards Dr. Fell and Melson, "came in and saw me, that was the second time. I admit I'd gone upstairs for the first time about fifteen minutes before—I remember, because the clock was striking a quarter to twelve. I was early, because the house had been locked up early and naturally I was sure everybody was in bed . . . Oh, stop looking at me like that!" she broke off to glare at Mrs. Steffins. Then her heavy eyelids fluttered, and she resumed with quiet defiance as she faced Hadley. "So I went up in the dark, and then I discovered I didn't have the key. I thought I'd mislaid it. So I came down and searched my room, and the more I searched the more I was *sure*

I'd put it in that pocket, so I thought—"

"Well, Miss Carver?"

"That somebody was playing a filthy joke on me," she replied, fiercely. She looked straight ahead, her hands opening and closing. "I was jolly *certain*, because I remembered putting it in one finger of a glove the last time—in case somebody should come snooping, as they do—and, anyway, that's a habit I have with keys. So I didn't know what to do. I went out in the hall again, and by that time I saw the light upstairs and heard . . . you know."

"Yes. We'll come to that in a moment. When was the last time you saw the key?"

"Last Sunday night."

"And your room is not locked?"

"Oh no. Locks on the doors," she said, and laughed sharply, "aren't permitted to anybody except J."

"I see no reason," interposed Mrs. Steffins, lifting her shoulders and bridling in a sort of hollow astonishment—"I see no reason, really, why a woman of thirty, with her own salary—and more salary, I'm sure, than I ever dreamed of asking when *I* was companion and *confidante* to a splendid refined woman like dear dead Agnes Carver, although doubtless you have different ideas with an employer in the theatrical profession— why a woman of thirty should remain here at all, if she doesn't like it after all the gratitude she ought to have."

Eleanor turned. The soft face had grown more flushed.

"You know why it is," she said, bitterly. "You creeping about with all your talk and tears; and how could I be so ungrateful to a guardian who had saved me from the parish when I hadn't any parents and how poor we were—you liar—and you needed the money and . . . Oh, I know what you are, and I'm sick of it! I've learned

123

a lot tonight, and I've been a wishy-washy sentimental ass, but from now on . . . !"

Hadley had let her go on because Hadley knew that these things beget an admirable frankness in witnesses. He interposed now:

"We'll go back to that second visit upstairs, Miss Carver. When you heard Boscombe say, 'My God, he's dead,' and saw somebody lying on the floor in the shadow of the door"—he looked at her quickly—"you thought it was somebody you knew, didn't you?"

"Yes." A hesitation. "I don't know how you guessed that, but I did. Donald."

"And you also thought Boscombe had killed him?"

"I—yes, I fancy I did. I—It was horrible, and that was the first thing I thought of . . ."

"*Why?*"

"He hates Donald. He's been sidling about me, which is awfully funny because it took him so long to say what he meant; he was nervous or something, and finally he came up to me determined to be, oh, so devilish; and he put his hand on my knee and said how would I like a nice two-seater and a flat of my own—"

Mrs. Steffins was simmering, so taken aback that she could not speak; and Eleanor looked at her while she talked at Hadley, impishly. "—and I said, jolly nice, provided the right person offered them to me." She laughed. "Then he made the jump and said, 'I'd even marry you'; but that was so funny that I couldn't control myself."

Hadley studied her.

"But, even so," he cut in, as she was about to go on, "what made you think that Hastings might be *in* the house? He didn't usually come in, did he? And how did you think he could get in, if the door was locked?"

"Oh, well . . . that! It's a spring lock, you see. You can open it from the other side just by turning the catch. And, you see, Don's so—so foolish about some things he might even have been mad enough to come in."

Hadley glanced over at Dr. Fell, who had muttered something in an absent fashion, and turned back.

"You mean to say, Miss Carver, the lock is so arranged that anybody—a burglar, for instance—could walk in from the roof? What about the trap-door to the roof itself?"

She frowned. "Well, come to think of it, there was a bolt on that once, a rusty one; and one night it stuck while I was trying to get up, so Don yanked the whole thing out. . . ."

"He did indeed," said Mrs. Steffins, in such a tone of cool fury that she seemed to be confirming a statement. "He did indeed? Then I think *I* shall have something to say to the police about this clever young man wantonly—"

Hadley turned on her. "It's your evidence, Mrs. Steffins," he interrupted, curtly, "that I do happen to want now. I want an explanation. You know"—he reached under the papers on the table, and suddenly held out the glittering clock-hand—"that a man was killed with this tonight?"

"I don't want to see it, whatever it is!"

"And you see that traces of this paint would probably have remained on the murderer's hands or clothes?"

"Would they? I refuse to be looked at like that. I refuse to have you address me in any such fashion, and I will not have you trap me into admitting that *I* said anything at all."

Hadley tossed the clock-hand on the table and bent forward.

"You'll be required to answer," he said, "about traces remaining in an emptied washbowl which Sergeant Betts found in your bedroom. There are traces of soap, and also traces of gilt paint. *Well?*"

# 11

## The Impostor

Melson, comfortably married for nine years, had never yet witnessed a complete attack of feminine hysterics. The mere shrillness of it made him uncomfortable; but that was not the important thing. What Millicent Steffins said in the course of the next ten minutes he always tried to remember, as an example of the devious progression of thought in a neurotic, possibly dangerous woman, absolutely without a sense of humour and in the dangerous early fifties.

It never occurred to her (he was willing to swear) that she might ever for a moment seriously be suspected of a crime. Her imagination, so far as considering things of which she might seriously be accused, did not go beyond a suggestion of selfishness or petty lies. If she were to be found with a bottle of poison in a house where half a dozen people had died of that poison, it would simply strike her as an unfortunate circumstance. Since unfortunate circumstances were always being

caused by other people, and she was always being lured
into them by either the malice or the thoughtlessness
of these other people, then she must explain this one,
too, by denouncing the person responsible.

Her first coherent words to this effect were to rage
against Hadley and against Johannus Carver. The first
since he obviously believed she was an inefficient, slov-
enly housekeeper who did not keep washbowls clean,
and sent his officers snooping into rooms. The second
because Carver was at the root of all the trouble—her
china and pottery painting.

She painted pottery, she said, and it had always been
affirmed that she did beautiful work (quoting authorities) until this fact had been used as a serpent to sting
her. But she would paint no more. This evening she
had been engaged on a vase, festooned with gilt hy-
drangeas, and had acquired a severe headache from the
eyestrain of her selfless devotion. Carver knew that.
Carver had encouraged her at the work, since he had
first suggested, years ago, that she take it up. Tonight
when he callously went up to bed he had seen her at
work, using an oil paint which cost one and threepence
the tube and was thinned with turpentine in a dish.
She bought it out of her own pocket money. But since
Carver not only did not appreciate her domestic econ-
omy while he treacherously urged her to paint, but
even conspired with the police to accuse her of the
murder of a filthy tramp, then . . .

It was an uncomfortable business, whose unpleas-
antness obscured the ludicrous side. It was intensely
real (or it seemed so) to her. And it did not have the
effect this time which Melson supposed it customarily
had in that house. Events had grown so big that more
than hysterics would be required now to subdue those
about her. While she was wiping her eyes furtively after

128

the storm, and peering about through the dark-pouched lids, Eleanor remained stolid and Lucia Handreth looked wearily contemptuous through the smoke of a fresh cigarette. But, obscurely, Melson felt that there was a deeper cause behind the whole tempest. . . .

"I'm sorry if it distresses you, Mrs. Steffins," said Hadley, stiffly. "If the paint came from that, it can easily be proved. But in the meantime I must insist on your answering some further questions. Suppose you tell me everything you did tonight, from the time Mr. Craver locked up, spoke to you while you were at your painting, and went upstairs."

She was listless, with the air of a martyr who minds nothing now, and her smeary eyes showed over a handkerchief.

"I—I worked until about half-past ten," she replied, the tears coming into her eyes as she thought of it. She dabbed at them. "I was too tired even to put away my work, which I always do otherwise. I"—something occurred to her, and she shut her eyes before she went on jerkily—"I do think you might let me alone. I know nothing about your beastly old murder. I went to bed after that, and naturally I washed my hands after I got a little of that paint on them. I don't know anything more until I heard a commotion outside, people going up the stairs and talking. So I put my head out of the door, and from what I heard—upstairs, it was, and Eleanor was there talking to that stout gentleman . . ."

Dr. Fell beamed and inclined his head, this being the most modest description he had probably heard in some time; but she eagerly took it as the gesture of an ally.

". . . yes, you'll agree with me, I know. Well, I gathered that a burglar had been hurt or killed, or something trying to get into the house, and it was horrible, especially as Eleanor was there before all those men with almost nothing on; but I didn't know *what* had happened, so I was going to call out to her, but I didn't, and I got dressed."

She came to such an abrupt halt, sniffling, that Hadley waited for her to go on. But it appeared to be the end.

"You took the trouble to get fully dressed," prompted Hadley, "before you came out to discover what was wrong?"

She nodded absently; then stiffened as the question seemed to occur to her, and compressed her lips. "I most assuredly did."

"And now one very important question, Mrs. Steffins." Hadley raised his eyes slowly. "Do you by any chance remember Tuesday a week ago—Tuesday the twenty-seventh of August?"

Mrs. Steffins, evidently thoroughly startled, stopped dabbing at her eyes. Then her face twisted up in new wrinkles of pain; she swallowed, and cried: "Do you pick out everything just for the sheer pleasure of torturing me? *However* did you know—that Horace—that was the day of his funeral. He died on the twenty-fourth; the twenty-fourth of August, nineteen-twelve, the—the year the *Titanic* went down, and the funeral was on the twenty-seventh at Stoke-Bradley in Bucks. I'll never forget that day. The whole v-village—"

"Then," said Hadley, grimly, "if that was the day your husband died, you will surely remember—"

"My late husband," interrupted Mrs. Steffins, her mouth growing grim despite the tears that had begun to well again, "was a c-cad and a rotter, although I will never speak ill of the dead and gone. He took to drink and was killed in the war. I did not mean Mr. Steffins.

I meant his poor brother Horace, who was just like a husband to me. . . . So many people I have known have died. It makes me sad to think of it, even. On the anniversaries I like to have my dear ones about me, to comfort. Of course I remember Tuesday a week ago. Johannus and I had tea in this very room. I wanted all the family; but, of course, on an occasion like that, Eleanor *would* be late."

Lucia Handreth remarked softly:

"I begin to understand this now. Tuesday was the day . . . that poor devil—and the watch. Well, well."

Hadley ignored this and kept his gaze fixed on Mrs. Steffins while he went on quickly: "You and Mr. Carver had tea here. At what time?"

"Why, it was rather late. About half-past four; and it was really hours later when we left the table, as you know it always is when you begin to talk of old friends. Yes, I remember because it was half-past six when I rang for Kitty to clear away the things and Eleanor hadn't come in yet."

"Kitty is the maid? Exactly. . . . Miss Handreth, do you mind telling us where you were on that afternoon; say, between five-thirty and six o'clock?"

She seemed to be trying to make up her mind about the exact attitude she should take. But when she replied her voice was colourless, with just the proper note of polite attention, and she did not look up at him until she had finished.

"Tuesday the twenty-seventh. Did it rain that day, or didn't it? I rather think it was the day I went to a cocktail party in Chelsea."

"The name of the people who gave the party?"

"Steady on, Inspector. You needn't write that down. It's rather difficult to say offhand, isn't it?" She frowned, and hunched her shoulders as though she were cradling

131

the cigarette. "I'll have a look at my diary and let you know for certain." She looked up. "One thing I'm sure of, though. I wasn't anywhere in the neighborhood of Gamridge's."

"Well, *I* was," said Eleanor, unexpectedly and with such complete casualness that Melson jumped. "What about Gamridge's, anyway? You mean the day when somebody killed that poor fellow and pinched all the things off the jewellery display? I must have been in the place when it happened, although I didn't know about it and didn't hear anything of it until I saw it in the paper next day." She seemed to take some alarm from the expression of the faces round her, and stopped nervously. "What of it? What's it got to do with *us*?"

Hadley was stumped. He looked from one of them to the other with a somewhat wild expression on his face, and then over at Dr. Fell, who himself did not appear comfortable. Somebody, Melson thought, was a magnificent liar. A liar of such dexterity that—Hadley barked an answer in reply to a knock, and Sergeant Betts hesitated when he saw the room full of people.

"Well?" demanded the exasperated chief inspector. "Speak up. What is it?"

"About that drunk fellow . . ." Betts commenced, dubiously.

"Yes?"

"He's in there right enough, sir. I can hear him snoring through the keyhole. But I don't get any result with knocking, and he's bolted the door. Shall I make a row or force the door open or something?"

"No. Let him alone for the present. Yes, what else?"

"There's an old party just come in through the area door downstairs, and a good-looking little girl with her. Old party says she's the housekeeper. She's had her drop of stout and she's amiable. Do you want to see her?"

"Yes, I do. We'll have the lot of them in here," said Hadley, grimly, "and those two are the last. This thing is going to be thrashed out now. Send 'em up, Betts. Don't mention what's happened—just say a burglary."

He motioned the others to silence while they waited. Melson found himself looking forward in some tenseness to the arrival of Mrs. Gorson and Kitty Prentice, as a sort of final ghoulish hope, but their appearance was an anti-climax. It presented to his mind little hope in the way of suspects. They both entered in something of a flutter, Mrs. Gorson with eager dramatic haste. She was a solid-built woman who might once have been a genuine beauty, but only amiability now remained. She wore a plumed hat running into many curves like a roller-coaster; she had intense, rather protruding brown eyes like those of a spiritual cow; and missing front teeth made more conspicuous by one or two upper ones which still remained. Her most outstanding trick of speech was to throw back her head and slowly bring it forward with her eyes fixed on the listener, while her voice rose to hollow dramatic quality like somebody imitating the rising of the wind. Gestures were appropriate.

"I see you have the police in, ma'am," she said to Mrs. Steffins, agreeably, as though she were referring to a social gathering; and then resumed her dramatic manner. "It is terrible, although I am informed that nothing was stolen. I must tender our apologies at being so disconcertingly late. The fact is that our omnibus collided with a lorry in the Fulham Road, at which the pilot and conductor of the omnibus had words with the lorry-driver, and dreadful words they was, too."

"Ooo!" agreed Kitty, nodding vigorously. Her face was flushed and her hat on one side.

"I won't detain either of you long," Hadley said,

casually. "I am in charge here, and I must ask you one or two questions as a matter of form. Your name?"

"And we were compelled to walk home. Henrietta Gorson. Two 't's," she added, amiably, as she saw Hadley write it down.

"How long have you been in this house?"

"Eleven years." The wind began to rise as she put back her head. "I was not always as you see me now," she said, shaking her head with wistful nostalgia. "I have Trod the Boards."

"Yes, yes. Now, Mrs. Gorson, I should like to hear a full account of both your movements this evening."

"Is that what the police like to know? Is it, now?" said Mrs. Gorson, admiringly. "We had a lovely evening, I assure you. We met Kitty's faithful knight, Mr. Albert Simmons, at Lyons'. Then we betook our way to the Marble Arch Pavilion to see a musical film of light romantic comedy, 'The Princess of Utopia.' The onsombil was lovely. I will not say," observed Mrs. Gorson, folding her hands judicially, "that the unfolding of the plot emphasized the three dramatic principles of Unity, Coherence, and Emphasis, but the onsombil was lovely."

"Ooo!" agreed Kitty, nodding vigorously.

"You were together all evening?"

"Yes, indeed. Afterwards we then betook our way to the home of Albert's parents in Fulham, and reely it is remarkable how we took no track of the flight of time until close on midnight, when . . ."

"Thanks," grunted Hadley, and looked more worried. "One last question. Do you recall Tuesday before last, the twenty-sev—"

"The day, Henrietta," Mrs. Steffins broke in, eagerly, forgetting her past tears, "the day I told you of, you remember, that dear Horace—"

134

"Day of the 'orrible murder," said Kitty, with relish. "Oo-er!"

A harassed chief inspector finally extracted the information. On that day, between five and half-past, both Kitty and Mrs. Gorson had taken tea downstairs with a Miss Barber, who worked next door. Kitty had taken up tea to Mrs. Steffins and Carver at half-past four, had gone up again at a little past five with more hot water; and had removed the cloth at half-past six. Hadley made a last note.

"There's somebody you may have seen at the 'Duchess of Portsmouth'; you may even have talked to him. This man is here tonight. . . . Betts!" called Hadley, who evidently did not intend to face more hysterics. "Take them to see Ames, and then get anything they may like to say. That's all—thank you."

When they had gone, Hadley glared round again.

"You all understand it now. Somebody in this house accused one of five women of being the thief who killed that shopwalker in Gamridge's. One of you has been accused of murder; can you get that clear? Well? I'll give the accuser a last chance to speak up now. Who was it?"

Silence.

"Who saw a woman burning a pair of bloodstained gloves? Who saw a turquoise bracelet and a stolen watch in the possession of one of you?"

He struck his knuckles sharply on the table, and it roused them.

"I don't know what you're talking about," Eleanor cried. "This is the first *I've* heard of it. And I certainly didn't kill anybody at that store. If I had, do you think I'd have been fool enough to admit I'd been there?"

After her first apparent fright, Mrs. Steffins had been considering.

"Isn't it fortunate," she murmured, with cold sweetness, "that you know where I was all afternoon on the anniversary of Horace's funeral? This is really outrageous!"

"And I also plead not guilty," Lucia put in, with a mocking grin. "Don't worry; I'll produce that alibi . . . All that bothers me is the liar who made a remark like that, if somebody did accuse one of us and you're not pulling our legs."

Hadley said, gently: "You'll give us permission, then, to make a thorough search of your rooms? Now?"

"With pleasure," replied Lucia.

"I'm sure I don't mind," said Eleanor, sniffing a little. "Search as much as you like, but mind you put everything back where it was."

Mrs. Steffins sat up. "I'll allow nothing of the kind!" she cried, and her eyes grew smeary again. "You'll search over my dead body. I'll scream. I'll yell for the p—I'll carry it to the Home Office, I'll see that every one of you gets the sack, if you dare have the insufferable—oh, my nerves! Oh, can't you let a poor . . . Besides, aah! You know I didn't do it. You know where I was. So what reason can you have for wishing to search my room?"

Wearily Hadley got to his feet.

"That's all for the moment," he said, and waved his hand. "We shall have to leave it there for tonight. The body is being removed now, and you may go to bed if you like."

But the damage was done in that last suggestion of suspicion; the air, already poisoned in this household, had grown so tense that they seemed reluctant to go. Mrs. Steffins waited for Eleanor, and Eleanor waited for Mrs. Steffins, until Hadley said, "Yes, what else?" and they both hurried out. Lucia Handreth alone preserved a callous cheerfulness. At the door she looked back over her shoulder.

"Well, good luck, Mr. Hadley," she nodded. "If you're going to search my digs I hope you'll be quick about it. I want to turn in. Good night."

The latch clicked. It was for a time the end of the strain. Melson sat down drowsily, and the room felt cold.

"Fell," said Hadley, "I must be losing my grip. I have a suspicion that so far I've bungled this thing badly. The murderer's here; the murderer's under this roof, and within reach of me at this minute. They're all here. *Which one of them is it?*"

Dr. Fell did not speak. He had propped an elbow on the crook of his cane, and his chin in his big hand. The ribbon on his eyeglasses fluttered in a draught that blew through the white room, but it was the only sign of motion. Faintly, with the curtness of finality, the bell at Lincoln's Inn tolled half-past three.

# 12

## The Five Riddles

Friday, September 5th, was cool and autumnal. The landlady tapped on Melson's door at the usual hour of eight o'clock, and brought in his breakfast without more than the usual comment on the weather. Although she must have been aware of last night's disturbance, she did not connect her lodger with the events next door. On his own part, being secretly inclined to worry about his health, his surprise that he felt bright and refreshed after only four hours' sleep induced in him a rather swashbuckling mood.

He was forty-two; in the history department of his college he was second only to the internationally famous scholar who was at the head of it; he had a good home, he worked with intelligent people, and nothing roused his wrath except the expounders of the "Theory of Teaching." Well, then? Smoking his first after-breakfast pipe by the open window, he found himself smiling in that obscure fashion which, he suspected, merely

138

meant to his students in History 3a ("The Monarchical Prerogative and Its Opponents in English Constitutional History from the Civil Wars to the Accession of William III") that old Melson was going to crack one of his mystifying jokes, and to get ready for it.

He frowned, glancing across at his image in the mirror of the wardrobe. "A sort of incurious Sherlock Holmes," Fell had said. Well—he had himself to blame for that slight standoffishness, although he wasn't standoffish at all. In his earlier days he had thought it was necessary. If you got too much of a reputation as a *raconteur* and good fellow, you might be popular, but the authorities were not inclined to take you seriously. This stiffness was now so established a part of his reputation that he never dared use, in his lectures, the fireworks or unconventionalities of more spectacular faculty-members. Secretly he would like to have done it. But he had only cut loose once. It was a lecture on Cromwell, and he had flayed that old villain all over the classroom with a sudden richness of oratory and drama whose reception disconcerted him. The class had taken it first in dazed silence, and then with discreet mirth. Subsequent rumours about it made him uncomfortable for the rest of the semester. His dry cough returned to him; he never tried it again.

Gideon Fell, now—that was different. To Fell this sort of thing was as frankincense and gunpowder. Melson remembered the two semesters in which Dr. Fell had been guest-lecturer from England, and the most uproariously popular figure who ever disrupted the campus. He remembered Fell's roaring chuckle, the massive gesture with which he singled out a student to argue, his trick of hurling his notes about when excited; he remembered Fell's famous five lectures on "The

Effect of Kings' Mistresses on Constitutional Government," or that equally famous one in the Queen Anne series, which began abruptly and thunderously: *"Flew now the eagles of bloody Churchill, black in honour and war, on to an ever-glorious damnation!"*—and lifted the class straight from their seats at the end of the battle of Oudenarde.

Now he was again in a criminal case. As many years as he had known Fell, Melson had never seen him at work on any of these puzzles. One of Melson's honour students, to whom he had introduced the doctor, had told Melson of the Chatterham Prison case[1] and only a month ago the newspapers had been full of the Depping murder near Bristol. This time Melson had stumbled into it. Chief Inspector Hadley had intimated that he would not object to Melson's presence, and, if he could pacify his own conscience about neglecting Bishop Burnet's History, he meant to follow it up.

Damn Burnet, who was always dashing off to Scotland when you wanted him to stay in England. Melson looked over at the littered writing-table: he felt a sense of freedom in damning Burnet. It suddenly seemed to him that he might be making too much of Burnet after all. Fell had invited him round to the rooms the doctor usually rented in Great Russell Street during his fits of work at the British Museum on materials for his great work, *The Drinking Customs of England from the Earliest Days*. He had said to come for breakfast, if Melson could manage it, or any time that was convenient. Well, then—

Melson picked up his hat and hurried downstairs.

He glanced at No. 16 as he passed, quickly and with a sense of guilt. Its white pillars and red-brick sedate-

[1] See *Hag's Nook*.

ness looked different in the morning light, so remote from terrible events that he half expected to see Kitty sweeping the steps with the utmost composure. But the blinds were drawn and nothing stirred there. Refusing to put his mind to the puzzle, Melson turned off into the rattling traffic of Holborn, and ten minutes later he was ascending in the creaky lift of the Dickens Hotel nearly opposite the British Museum. From behind Dr. Fell's door came the sounds of violent argument, so he knew Hadley was already there.

Swathed in a bathrobe of lurid colors, Dr. Fell sat placidly disposing of one of the largest breakfasts Melson had ever seen, in a room littered with books. Hadley, jingling keys in his pockets, stared moodily out of the window at the crowd of idlers already accumulating at the gates of the Museum.

"For a man who lives at Croydon," Melson said, "you're on the job remarkably early."

Hadley was bitter. "What was left of the night after half-past five," he said, "I spent at the Yard. That obese blighter you see shovelling down the bacon and eggs ran away and left me to do all the dirty work. If that's coffee you're pouring out for me, make it good and strong."

"I wanted to think," replied Dr. Fell, placidly. "If the process is unknown to you, you might at least tell me what you did. I'm like you last night: I want the facts and not grousing. What happened?"

Hadley passed a cup of coffee to Melson and took one himself.

"Well, we searched the rooms of every woman in that house, for one thing. We found nothing. But neither Hamper nor myself is much of an expert at that, so it doesn't mean much. However, I've a chap at the Yard who's first rate at the business; and I'm going to

141

rush him round there this morning. Those ladies are watching one another so closely that, if one of them *has* got something concealed, she won't have a chance to get rid of it without being seen. All the same—"

"You searched Madame Steffins' room as well?"

"Yes, finally. The others cut up such an unholy row that I think it scared her. She exploded into tears, said to go ahead, and finally asked me why I didn't cut her throat. I have since been wondering why. . . . And d'you know the reason for the row? She had a couple of pornographic books stuck away in the bottom of the bureau drawer. I pretended not to notice 'em and everything went more smoothly afterwards."

"Any trouble from Mrs. Gorson and the maid?"

Hadley grunted. "Not so far as searching their stuff was concerned. The girl was rather a problem after she discovered murder had been committed, but Mrs. Gorson calmed her down. I like that woman, Fell; she's all right . . . except that she kept on going in that ghost-story way of hers, with a lot of philosophical remarks about life and death. If anything, she gave me too much coöperation in the search. She dug up all her old theatrical photographs, and showed me at least a trunkful of poetry she'd written, with side remarks on the iniquity of publishers. It seems she wrote a three-volume novel and sent it to the biggest firm in London; and after rejecting it they basely pinched the plot and wrote it up themselves, which was proved because the heroine's name was the same as in hers, and it sold a million copies. . . . I tell you, I felt my brain giving way."

He drew a deep breath, jingled the keys moodily, and added:

"By the way, there was just one queer thing about Mrs. Steffins' belongings that I forgot to tell you. I don't suppose it means anything, but after all that commotion about the gilt paint—"

142

"Hey?" said Dr. Fell, looking at him curiously.

"I looked at the paint-tubes she's been working with. The gilt one was squashed nearly flat on the end towards the mouth, as though she or somebody else had accidentally leaned one hand on it. You know, the way you do sometimes with a tube of toothpaste, and it spurts out? She denied having done it, and said the tube was intact when she last used it. . . ." At this point in the recital Dr. Fell stopped with a loaded fork halfway to his mouth, and his eyes narrowed. Hadley went on:

"Anyway, it makes no difference. The paint we found traces of in the washbowl, and the paint on the hand of the clock, are altogether different. Sergeant Hamper—he started life as a house-painter, and claims to be an authority—swore to it last night. And I've had confirmation this morning; one's an oil, and one's an enamel. So that's washed out. But Steffins carried on about it for the rest of the night. Deliver me," said Hadley, violently, "from any more cases where there are too many women concerned!—To conclude the night pleasantly, I had trouble with Stanley; but at least it was somebody I knew how to deal with."

Dr. Fell laid down his knife and fork.

"What about Stanley?"

"Watson said he was laid out with nervous shock and wasn't responsible. So I was the goat. I took him home to Hampstead in a cab. After all, damn it," Hadley protested, uncomfortably, "he was once a member of the Force, and it was war service that did for him. Besides, I had to question him, whether I liked it or not. But did he appreciate it? Not half!—if you call it appreciation. He turned nasty, refused to answer questions, began raving against the Force. Finally he tried to fight, and I had to land him one on the jaw and put him to sleep until I could get him home to his sister." Hadley made a gesture of distaste, drained his coffee-cup, and sat down. "It was broad daylight by the time I got back to the Yard, and I hope somebody appreciates it."

"Yes, you had rather a night," admitted Dr. Fell, with absent-minded encouragement. He leaned back from the table with an expiring sigh of satisfaction, fished up his old black pipe from a pocket of the lurid dressing-gown, and beamed on the chief inspector. "I imagine it would be an insult to ask you whether you've learned anything more since then?"

Hadley reached for his briefcase. "I've been collecting all the evidence Ames left us about the murder of the shop-walker . . ."

"Aha!"

"And also the notes of Sergeant Preston, who worked with Ames at collecting the facts before Ames went off on his own. And still what puzzles me most is which of those five women in that house—! They all told such infernally straight stories, Fell! or at least natural stories. It beats me to the extent that I've been getting all sorts of fantastic ideas. For instance, I thought, suppose the murderer at Gamridge's had been a man disguised as a woman?"

Dr. Fell looked at him.

"Don't gibber, Hadley," he said, austerely. "I detest gibbering. The men at number sixteen Lincoln's Inn Fields may have their faults, God knows; but at least none of 'em would be apt to run about dressed up as a woman. Besides—"

"I know, I know. That was knocked on the head straightaway. It seems that when the killer was making a getaway"—he fumbled among his papers and found a typewritten *précis*—"a Miss Helen Gray (address given) made a grab to stop her. The woman was wearing some sort of blouse or jumper arrangement under her

144

coat, and the whole thing was ripped down from the neck when she tore away from Gray. Both Miss Gray and two men near by testify that there's no question about its being a woman. The men seem enthusiastically positive on this point. Their testimony is—"

"Tut, tut, Hadley," said Dr. Fell, reprovingly. "Sometimes there is a limit even to the thoroughness of Scotland Yard. What I don't understand is this. Do you mean to say that—in spite of all this—nobody, those people or anyone else, could give you a passable description of her?"

Hadley made a noncommittal noise.

"Did you ever have any experience with a mob of excited people all trying to testify to the same incident—when there's a motor-smash, for instance? The more people there are, the more confusing the story is. In this case it's worse. In the confusion and milling about, each person was describing somebody else and swearing it was the right person. I've got a dozen descriptions, and only a few of 'em remotely tally."

"But what about Miss Gray and the two cavaliers? Are they reliable?"

"Yes. They're the only real witnesses we have, because they actually saw the murder done." Hadley glanced down the sheet. "They saw the woman standing near the counter; they were to the right and behind, but they had a good view. They saw the shopwalker come past them, walk up and take this woman's arm, saying something to her. She instantly whirled with her other hand towards the counter next to the jewellery display, which unfortunately happened to be silverware. There were a number of table sets in boxes lying exposed on the counter—among them sets of carving-fork, whetstone, and carving-knife. They saw her snatch a knife from one; all are positive she had gloves on. Then it happened. They saw some of the blood go out against the glass front of the showcase, which had lights inside it; and saw her drop the knife. She ran, ducking her head, and Gray made a wild grab at her when the shopwalker collapsed. This is our only clear evidence. . . . Just then the screaming and rushing began."

Melson, putting down his cold coffee, felt an ugly shiver. That detail about the blood splashing the lighted showcase. . . . Dr. Fell said:

"Harrumph, yes. It's nasty. What about their descriptions, aside from the details of physiology?"

"She had her head down, as I told you. Gray says she was a blonde, rather young. Of the two men, one says she was a blonde and the other a brunette; you see, she had a close-fitting hat on. Gray says the hat was dark blue, the two men say black. Further descriptions—" Hadley's frown deepened as he turned the page. "Gray says she wore a blue-serge tailored-suit business, with a white blouse, and no coat. Of the two men, one thinks she had on a blue or brown coat, rather long; the other isn't sure which it was. But all agree absolutely on the white blouse that was torn."

Hadley flung the papers on the table, and Dr. Fell carefully removed the marmalade from their neighbourhood.

"Which," declared the chief inspector, "is the devil of the whole thing. Almost any woman you could find would be bound to have any or all of those things in her wardrobe. The torn shirt thing might be a lead— could she pin it together in the washroom, or something like that? I suppose so. Also, if she did wear a long coat she could have concealed it easily. I didn't have these details last night, or it might have helped me a good deal. . . . Well? What is it?"

146

"I say, Hadley," the doctor rumbled with an air of suppressed excitement, "were these details in the newspapers?"

"Probably. At least, they're marked, 'Bulletin to Press Association may contain, etc.' Speak up, will you? What the hell's that got to do with it?"

Dr. Fell was beginning to recover his good-humour. He lit his pipe, and his vast red face was beaming and shining as the breakfast settled. But he closed one eye meditatively as he looked down the pipe.

"The design is forming, my boy. But you've already realized since last night, of course, that—if you accept the alibis of Mrs. Steffins and Mrs. Gorson and Kitty Prentice—you have only two remaining suspects?"

"Lucia Handreth and Eleanor Carver. Naturally. I've also realized," Hadley pointed out, with some bitterness, "how neatly this new evidence is divided between them. . . . Last night we saw the Handreth woman wearing a tailored suit. It was grey instead of blue, but suppose business-like young professional ladies have a habit of wearing them? And one of the reliable witnesses says the killer was a brunette. On the other hand, two of the witnesses—one of them Helen Gray, whom I suspect of being the most reliable of the three so far as observing a woman is concerned—say the killer was a blonde like Eleanor Carver, and last night Eleanor was wearing a blue coat. Right. Fine. Pay your money and take your choice."

"Steady, my lad," Dr. Fell suggested, benevolently. "You're willing, then, to accept the alibis and exclude the other three women?"

"I'm not quite so gullible as all that. No, no! It's unbeatable in a court of law; but, so far as common sense is concerned, an alibi is the most untrustworthy defense of all—because it only takes two liars to make

147

it. I'll try to break them, of course. But if I can't . . . well, I can't."

Dr. Fell pushed the tobacco-jar towards him. He continued to smoke meditatively.

"We'll let it go at that for the moment, then. The next thing I want to ask you, Hadley, is so simple that we're apt to lose sight of it. Are you absolutely positive that the same person who stabbed the shopwalker also stabbed the police inspector last night?"

Hadley shifted. "I'm not positive of anything. . . . But certainly some sort of crazy thread joins them! What else have we got to go on?"

"As a matter of fact, that was my next question; question three," said Dr. Fell, nodding owlishly. "What have we got to go on? Well, chiefly we have Ames's report, which concerns a nameless accuser. Hadley, it's remarkable just how nameless that person has been from start to finish. Ames is put on the scent from some anonymous source, so that he first takes up quarters in Portsmouth Street to watch the Carver household. For an anonymous suggestion, it must have been very convincing to make Ames go to all that trouble. The same X next visits Ames, and—I don't have to outline to you the course of the whole ghostlike, intangible affair from there on. And yet now, with another murder committed and the killer still undetected under that one roof, still the accuser hadn't spoken up! . . . Have you spent sufficient reflection on the monstrous implications of that?"

"We argued all that last night," returned Hadley, with something like a groan. "Hang it! you can't think that somebody was merely pulling Ames's leg? That would be too fantastic even for this business. And, on the other hand, you certainly can't imagine that Ames was merely pulling ours!—"You don't, do you?"

"No. There may be still a third, and a simple, explanation. I'm trying to suggest it to you by linking up a series of facts by means of questions. I may be wrong," muttered Dr. Fell, setting his eyeglasses more firmly on his nose, "and, if I am, there'll be a roar of laughter at my expense that will cave in the walls of Scotland Yard." He growled to himself for a moment. "But let me indulge the vagary. I have two more questions—numbers four and five. Number four—"

Hadley shrugged. Melson, with his methodical habits, had taken out an envelope and was jotting down the "series of facts."

"By the way," Melson said, "talking of things so obvious that nobody has mentioned them: I don't know anything whatever about the art of detection, but it strikes me that the simplest reason why the accuser hasn't spoken up may be . . ."

"Eh?" said Dr. Fell, rather eagerly. "What?"

"That he (or she) is afraid. The woman who stabbed that shopwalker is about as playful as a cobra. She struck so fast once that almost nobody saw her. The accuser might think twice about beginning to intimate in public, 'I saw So-and-so with a stolen bracelet, or burning a pair of gloves.' That may be the reason for not being willing to testify until the murderess was in the hands of the police."

Hadley sat up. "That's a possibility," he acknowledged. "If—"

"It's a possibility of rubbish, I'm afraid," said Dr. Fell, shaking his head. "Grant everything you've said. If fear is behind it all, it works in rather a curious sort of way. If X, the accuser, were originally afraid of the murderess when X saw her burning blood-stained gloves, I should think X would get the wind-up at the possibility of being caught eavesdropping on several occasions, and wouldn't feel safe until everybody at Scotland Yard *had* been told. But granted X does act in this fashion, and quietly tells Ames. What happens? Ames, the *second-hand recipient of the secret*, is instantly knifed. By this time I fancy X's case of the wind-up must be blowing a howling hurricane. Still, X doesn't speak, but goes on peacefully living and sleeping under the same roof with this pet cobra. If that's the state of affairs I shouldn't call it fear; at the most modest estimate, I should call it fat-headed recklessness."

There was a silence. Hadley nodded grudgingly.

"Something in that," he conceded. "All right; let's hear the last two points or questions or whatever they are. Then we'll try to make a sense of the whole."

"H'mf. Ha. Where was I? AH! Well, I've already mentioned my fourth point, but I stress it again so that it can come in the group where it belongs. That's the little matter of the stolen clock-hands: why this apparently lunatic thief should pinch both hands, and wait until the completed clock was safely locked up instead of getting at it when it was freely exposed. Eh?"

"And the last?"

Dr. Fell chuckled wryly. "The last is in a sense a corollary of the fourth, but it seems even more insane unless properly interpreted by the others. To emphasize it, let me first ask you what articles—all of them— were stolen from Gamridge's on the day of the murder."

"I've got all that," said Hadley, looking at him dubiously and then down at the typewritten sheets. "Let's see. 'Bulletin to Press—Gamridge Official List—' Here we are. Pair of pearl pendant earrings, value ten pounds. Opal ring, set with small diamonds, value twenty pounds. And Carver's watch. That's the lot."

"Was Carver's watch ticketed as such in the display?"

"You mean with his name? Oh yes. There was a little

card on each curiosity, with the name of the owner and a brief history . . ." Hadley's hand fell with a flat smack on the table, and he sat up. "Good God! of course! I told you I was losing my grip. I see what you mean. Your last point, then, is, 'Why should a member of Carver's household who wanted that watch run the insane risk of shoplifting it in a crowded department store when it would have been much easier to steal it at home?'"

"Exactly. And the more so as Carver's burglar-alarms weren't meant for his own household. I suspect he's glad enough to exhibit his collection to anybody who'll listen—We'll test that out, by the way. So what do you make of it?"

After a pause Hadley said: "I don't know what to make of it." He shook his head and stared blankly out of the window. "The whole business has now reached the last point of insanity. If you can find a simple little clue that will connect it all up, you're a better man than I think. These questions of yours. . . . Read out what you've got," he added, abruptly, turning to Melson. "Let's have the lot. Now I've forgotten how they run."

Melson ran his pencil doubtfully down the list.

"If I haven't misunderstood, it goes something like this:

"*Points to be considered in Department-Store Murder, as Linked up with Murder of Inspector George Ames.*
1. That, since the alibis of all others are at present to be accepted, the suspects narrow down to Lucia Handreth and Eleanor Carver as the department-store murderer.
2. That there is no concrete evidence definitely

151

to show that the murderer of Evan Manders, shopwalker, is also the murderer of Inspector Ames."

"Bravo!" said Hadley, gloomily. "That's a fine way to begin working up a case against anybody, isn't it? You first announced that according to the evidence either the Handreth or the Carver woman must have killed the shopwalker. Then you throw cold water on the whole thing by saying that the murderer of Ames might be somebody else. . . . Look here, Fell, don't ask me to believe that there are *two* murderers in that house, each addicted to walking about and stabbing people; because I won't believe it. It's too much. It's an *embarrass de richesse*. No, no. If I can prove that one of those two women definitely is the department-store killer, I'm not going to have much doubt that she also killed Ames."

Dr. Fell thundered for a moment, and then toned himself down to mere fiery controversy.

"I was afraid you'd say that," he declared, flourishing his pipe. "What I want to get through your head is that I'm not trying to make out a case against anybody. Keep repeating to yourself those words, 'According to the evidence, according to the evidence.' This is what the evidence tells us, and I'm setting it out because I want you to interpret it and see what the whole devilish business means. . . . Carry on, Melson."

"We go on, then, to the next point.

"3. That the whole accusation and case against one of the women for murdering Evan Manders comes from an unidentified person, who now under circumstances of the strongest pressure refuses to communicate with us.

4. That, in procuring a weapon, the murderer of

152

Inspector Ames (a) stole both hands off a clock when only one could have been used for that purpose; and (b) did not perform this theft when it was easy, but waited until the clock was locked up in Carver's room.

5. That the department-store murderer did not steal a watch belonging to Carver when the theft must have been easier at home, but took the dangerous risk of stealing it out of a display in a crowded department store."

"Heh," said Dr. Fell. "Heh-heh-heh. There's a donnish flavor about that document, Melson, which makes me want to preserve it. H'mf, yes. But it's a fair statement with which to explain the glimmer of reason I have. I'll let you consider it while I dress. Then we'll go to the Carvers'."

# 13

## The Skull-Watch

It was half-past ten when they drove up in Hadley's car
to the clock-maker's house. A crowd had assembled
outside the door: a tractable crowd which was shoved
aside by a policeman, moved back respectfully, closed
in again, and kept repeating this process as the policeman paced back and forth with the silent regularity of
one of Carver's pendulums. A group of newspaper men
argued with Sergeant Betts, and cameras flashed into
view as the car stopped. From this group a burst of
approval went up at the sight of Dr. Fell, and the press
charged in. With some difficulty Hadley hustled away
Dr. Fell, who showed a tendency to stand up in the
front seat of the car and hold forth affably on any subject
about which he was asked questions. Hadley said,
curtly, "A statement will be issued," as Betts cleared
a lane for them. Impelled forward, his figure mountainous in the black cloak, his shovel-hat lifted above
his head in salute, Dr. Fell beamed over his shoulder

amid a clicking of cameras and a chorus of invitations to the nearest pub. Kitty—looking nervous—opened the front door, and closed it behind them against the roar of noise.

It was cool and quiet in the dimness of the hallway. Hadley turned to a sharp-faced, swarthy young man who had followed Betts in.

"You're Preston? Yes. You know the instruction; a thorough search of these women's rooms, with every trick and device you know."

"Yes, sir," said the swarthy young man, nodding in pleased anticipation.

Hadley turned to the girl. "Where is everybody, Kitty? All up and about, I hope?"

"Not all," Kitty said. "Mr. Carver and Mrs. Steffins were up. Mr. 'Astings, who had spent the night on the couch in Mr. Paull's sitting-room and was feeling much better"—here Kitty gave a nervous giggle—"had gone out for a breath of fresh air with Miss Eleanor. That was all."

"I'll see Mrs. Steffins," Hadley decided, not without reluctance. "In the dining-room, you said; back of the house? Right." He hesitated. "Do you want to watch us dig in, Fell?"

"I do not," the doctor returned, firmly. "H'mf, no. A little *causerie* with Carver is indicated. Also I want to see the convivial Christopher Paull and get our list of people straightened out, if he isn't needing the hair of the dog too badly. Come along, Melson. I think this will interest you."

He knocked at the door of the sitting-room where the conference had been held last night, and Carver's placid voice answered. Against a dull and chilly morning there was a bright fire burning in the white room. Carver, a cup of tea beside him and a half-eaten piece

155

of toast balanced on the saucer, had moved the centre table nearer the windows. With a jeweller's lens in his eye he was bending over an object on the table. He rose uncertainly and with some annoyance, which changed as his pale eyes recognized Dr. Fell. Big and stoop-shouldered against the discoloured hues of the old timepieces under their glass cases along the windows, in his smoking-jacket and slippers, he showed some pleasure at seeing them.

"Ah!" he said. "Dr. Fell and Dr.—Melson, is it? Good! good! I was afraid it might be ... Sit down, gentlemen. I have been trying to distract my mind, as you see. This little example," he touched with the lens a curious flattish clock whose bronze hood was ornamented with the small figure of a negro in turban and once-bright Oriental costume, a dog standing beside him, "is, as you can see, a dial of French manufacture. The English craftsmen have mostly neglected such things as being mere toys. I do not agree with Hazlitt's plaint about the French 'crochets and caprices with their clocks and watches, which seem made for anything but to tell the hour,' or call it quackery and impertinence. I like the little figures which move with the striking of the quarters, and I have seen some remarkable examples, from the humorous to the ghastly.

"For example,"—enthusiasm crept into his look, and one big finger drew a design in the air—"there is the common device on the hood of the figure of Father Time seated in a boat rowed by Eros, with the motto, '*L'amour fait passer le temps*'; which, as has been remarked, was turned into, '*Le temps fait passer l'amour.*' On the other hand, I have seen in Paris a not-too-pleasant device by Grenelle, with a striking-mechanism whose figures represented the flagellation of Our Saviour with the hours struck to the fall of the whips."

156

He hunched his shoulders. "Er—I don't wish to bore you, gentlemen?"

"Not at all," said Dr. Fell, amiably, and produced his cigar-case. "I have only a smattering of knowledge on the subject, but it has always interested me. Smoke? Good! I'm glad you mentioned the matter of mottoes. It reminds me of something I had intended to ask you. I don't suppose by any chance you inscribed a motto on that clock you built for Sir Edwin Paull?"

The interest faded out of Carver's expression and was replaced by a dogged patience.

"I had forgotten for a moment, sir," he replied, "that you were affiliated with the police. We always come back to it, don't we?—Yes, there is a motto. It's not customary, you see, on dials of that sort; but I could not resist a little conceit. See it for yourself."

He shambled over to the door of the closet in the wall by the fire-place, opened it, and nodded inside. Melson and Dr. Fell, standing to one side so that the dull light should fall within, peered at the yellow glimmer of the squat, heavy, handless mechanism on the floor. There was a look of ugly mutilation about it, almost as though the thing had been alive, which brought back again the terrors of last night. Then with something of a shock Melson read the Gothic lettering that curved round the top of the dial.

"*I shall see justice done.*"

"A conceit of my own," repeated Carver, clearing his throat slightly when the other two stood silent. "Do you like it? A little banal, perhaps; but it seemed to me that only clocks, as a symbol of eternity, can establish the just order of the future. Er—" he went on, as there was still silence, "the whole force of the motto, as you see, is the use of the word 'shall.' The 'will' of determination, as of fate or an avenger, has no place

157

in it. It is the impassive, patient, vast 'shall' of mere futurity. I am interested in subtleties, like my friend Boscombe; in the devious . . ."

Dr. Fell looked over his shoulder. Slowly he closed the closet door.

"You are interested in subtleties," he said, flatly. "Is that all this inscription means to you?"

"I am not a policeman," he answered, in such a quiet voice that Melson nearly missed the flicker of intelligence in his look. "You may make of it what you like, my dear Doctor. But now that we are on the subject (briefly, I hope) I might ask you . . ."

"Yes?"

"Whether you made any headway with that rather infamous suggestion Mr. Hadley was hinting at last night. I don't listen at doors, but I gathered that there was some difficulty about where all the ladies were—in that Gamridge business—the twenty-seventh of August. If you understand me?"

"I understand you. And I mean to return question for question. When Hadley asked you about that afternoon, and the whereabouts of everybody, you said you couldn't remember it. Just between ourselves, Mr. Carver," said Dr. Fell, blinking at him, "that wasn't strictly true, was it? Mrs. Steffins' panegyrics on her dead Horace would hardly have allowed you to forget the date. Eh?"

Carver hesitated. He opened and shut his hands, examining them. They were big hands, with knotted spatulate fingers which nevertheless conveyed a look of delicacy, and well-trimmed nails. He still held unlighted the cigar Dr. Fell had given him.

"Just between ourselves, it was not."

"And why did you forget it?"

"Because I knew that Eleanor was not here." The hint of formal statement went out of his voice. "I am

158

very fond of Eleanor. She has been with us a long time. I am nearly thirty years older, of course, but at one time I had hoped—I am very fond of her."

"Yes. But why should the mere fact that she was late coming home to tea make you forget the whole afternoon?"

"I knew that she would probably be late. As a matter of fact, I knew that at one time or another she would be at Gamridge's. You see, she-ah—is employed as private secretary to a Mr. Nevers, a theatrical impresario, in Shaftesbury Avenue. She had told me that morning"—he opened and shut his hands again, staring at them—"that she would try to get off early, for some shopping, and to 'smooth down' Millicent in case she were late getting home. . . . I remembered particularly because I paid a brief visit to Gamridge's myself in the middle of the afternoon, along with Boscombe and Paull and Mr. Peter Stanley, to inspect the collection of watches they had just put on display; and I wondered whether I should see her. But, of course . . ."

"If you are fond of her," said Dr. Fell, with sudden sharpness, "explain what you're hinting at."

"We had some difficulty with her as a child—" Carver checked himself. The film disappeared from his eyes. The hard practicality which sometimes flashed out of him overcame his worried look, and he spoke crisply. "It worries me to lie or distort the truth. Not because I object to a lie; but simply because it disturbs my peace of mind afterwards. Shall we call it selfishness?" He smiled grimly. "I lied last night, but I have told the truth this morning and I have told all I know. I do not intend to say any more, nor do I think any artifices can drag out of me what I do not wish to say. If you really have any interest in my collection, I shall be happy to show it to you. Otherwise . . ."

Dr. Fell studied him. Dr. Fell was looking partly

over his shoulder, a heavy wrinkle in his forehead; otherwise his face was impassive and almost dull. His dark cloak vast in the white room, he stood with a clipped cigar in one hand and an unlighted match poised in the other. For the space of perhaps twenty seconds he stood thus, while Melson had a feeling of deadly things brewing and of some terrifying import in the little eyes blinking behind the eyeglasses. Then—with a suddenness that made Melson jump—there was a crack and the rasping flare of a match-flame as Dr. Fell kindled it with a jerk of his thumb nail across its head.

"Can I give you a light?" he boomed, jocularly. "Yes, I'm much interested in the collection. Those water-clocks, now . . ."

"Ah, the *clepsydrae!*" Carver was trying to mend that silence. He drew about him again his own vague dignity and enthusiasm, and indicated the glass cases. "If you are interested in the early means of marking time, the whole history of it begins here. And to understand them you must keep in mind the divisions of time used by the ancients. For example, the Persians divided the day into twenty-four hours, starting from sunrise; the Athenians had the same method, but starting from sunset. The Egyptian day was twelve hours. The Brahmin time-schedule was more complicated. This"—he touched the case containing the big metal bowl with the hole in its centre—"this, if it is genuine, must be one of the oldest timepieces now existing in the world. The Brahmins divided the day into sixty hours of twenty-four minutes each, and this was their Big Ben. It was placed in a vat of water in some public spot, and beside it was hung a great gong. In exactly twenty-four minutes the bowl sank, and the gong was struck to tell the passing of an hour.

"That is the most primitive principle. All of them,

160

before the invention of the pendulum, consisted in a regulated flow of water, whether only to sink past a series of notches numbered with the hours—"

He indicated the device Melson had noticed last night, the upright glass tube with the Roman numerals carved on a board, and the tallow-lamp on one bracket.

"—like that, which is a night-clock with the lamp always kept burning. It purports to be early seventeenth century, the work of Jehan Shermite, and is probably the same design as the one Pepys describes as being in Queen Catherine's room in 1664."

Melson's dry, curious brain was again at work. He saw that for some obscure reason Dr. Fell was encouraging Carver in his hobby; and he took advantage of it.

"Water-clocks," he enquired, "were in use as late as that? I always associated them chiefly with the Romans. There's an account somewhere of how, in lawsuits or senatorial debates where the orators were allowed only a specified time, the water-clocks would be tampered with so that the orator had a greater or less time to speak."

Carver was caught fully by enthusiasm now. He rubbed his hands.

"Quite right, sir. Quite right. It was done with wax. . . . But the *clepsydrae* were certainly known up to the 1700's. I should explain that, although a primitive form of our modern dial-mechanism was known in the fourteenth century, there was an enormous revival of interest in the *clepsydrae* towards the middle of the seventeenth—if only as ingenious toys. They were alive, those people! They were as clever as brilliant children at mechanics and chemistry. The Royal Society did its first vague groping towards a steam-engine then; we got the tinder-box, the burglar alarm, mezzotint

161

engraving, Prince Rupert's drops. . . .

"This water-clock, for example." He indicated the frame-work with dial and one hand, from the back of which a brass cylinder hung on a chain. "*This* I know to be authentic. As the flow of water from this cylinder decreased, the decreasing weight of the cylinder moved the hand at exactly the specified speed. Its date is 1682, but it is commonplace if you are looking merely for ingenious mechanisms. Consider, for instance, the clock run by steam, which you may now see at Guildhall—"

"Just a moment, please," interposed Dr. Fell. "Humph, ha. You seem to doubt the genuineness of most of these things. But let's consider some of the authentic pieces in your collection. Watches, for example."

Carver was now at the requisite pitch of enthusiasm.

"Watches!" he said. "Ah, *now* I have something for you, gentlemen! Let me see. I don't usually do this, at least for strangers; but if you like I'll open my safe and show you some real treasures." His eyes moved over to the wall on the right as you entered the room—the same glance, Melson remembered, that he had instinctively given when he entered the room last night. His face clouded a little. "Of course you must remember that the gem of my collection is gone, although it remains under the same roof—"

"The watch you sold to Boscombe?"

"The Maurer skull-watch, yes. I have another of the same design and equally perfect as a piece of craftsmanship, but not one-tenth so valuable because of the inscription and the associations of the first. You must see it, Doctor. Boscombe will readily show it to you."

Dr. Fell scowled. "That's what I was coming to. I'm exceedingly curious about that watch, because it seems to me that there's been a devil of a lot of fuss concerning it," he growled. "For a watch, even an antique watch, it has upset others besides yourself. Is it valuable? Very valuable, I mean?"

Carver's eyelids flickered. He smiled faintly.

"Its value, Doctor, is far greater than its price. But I can tell you what Boscombe gave for it. It was the same price I paid when I bought it some years ago—three thousand pounds."

"Three thousand pounds!" said Dr. Fell, violently, and let out a great gust of smoke as he twitched the cigar from his mouth. He coughed, his face grew more red, and presently the upheavals gave way to a chuckle. "Three thousand quid, hey?" he added, more mildly, and his eye twinkled. "O my sacred hat, wait till Hadley hears about this! Heh. Heh-heh-heh."

"You—er—you see now why Mrs. Steffins sometimes thinks we are in need of money. But surely you know what the watch is?" demanded Carver. "You shall judge for yourself, then."

He shambled over to one of the long panels in the middle of the right-hand wall. Although Melson could not follow the movement of his hand, he must have touched a spring, for a gap appeared along the edge and he pushed the panel back. Inside was a high gloomy aperture like an alcove, fronted by a door parallel with the wall. On the right-hand side of the alcove they saw the outline of a wall-safe, and on the left-hand side another door.

"One moment while I disconnect the alarm," Carver was continuing. "As you may know, the skull-watch was an early and curious development in the sixteenth century. Don't think of watches as we know them now. The skull-watch could never be carried, at least with any convenience: it weighed three-quarters of a pound.

There are specimens now in the British Museum. This one is a good deal smaller—"

He twirled the combination knob with his left hand, unostentatiously shading it with his right. After opening an inner door, he drew out a small tray lined with black velvet and carried it to the centre table.

The watch was shaped like a flattish skull with an underhung jaw, so that in its very length there was something sinister. Outside, the daylight had become more murky; bright yellow firelight made a changing play on the skull-face, and its dull silver-gilt hue shone against the black velvet. In its own way it was beautiful, but Melson did not like it. What lent it a touch of the *macabre*, and even of the terrible, was the maker's inscription engraved in curling script across the forehead and round the eye-sockets—a man writing his name on a death's head.

"You like it?" asked Carver, eagerly. "Yes, you may handle it. You see: the jaw opens. Open the jaw—reverse it—so. There is the dial. The works are in the brain, as they should be." He chuckled. "It is quite small and fairly light, as you see. Isaac Penard made it, nearly a century after Boscombe's, of course, but the two are similar. Except—"

"Except?" prompted Dr. Fell, who was weighing the watch in his hand.

"Except its history. Yes. Except," said Carver, his faded eyes shining, "what is written across the forehead in its own symbolic way. Have you a pencil? Thank you. I have an envelope here. I will write it for you. Ha! You gentlemen should have no difficulty in . . ."

The pencil wrote jerkily, and Carver drew a deep breath. He glanced up under the shadow of his big forehead, bending forward to smile harshly in the firelight as he pushed the envelope across the table. The fire crackled and fell a trifle. Melson stared as he deciphered what was written. "Ex dono Frs. R. Fr. ad Mariam Scotorum et Fr. Regina, 1559."

There was a pause.

"'The gift,'" read Dr. Fell, suddenly putting up a hand to his eyeglasses, "'the gift of Francis, King of France, to Mary, Queen of France and Scotland, 1559.' Then—"

"Yes," said Carver, nodding. "The gift of Francis II, on ascending the throne, to his bride—Mary Queen of Scots."

# 14

## The Last Alibi

"That," continued Carver, pointing to the watch in Dr. Fell's hand, "is a good specimen. But it has—if I may use the word—no personality, no suggestion with those who have used it. It is dead metal. But the one upstairs is not. And there is nothing which keeps touches of past people like a watch. It is personal as a mirror. Think of it," he continued, quietly, and stared at the fire. "In 1559 Mary was seventeen, queen of the earth, and Elizabeth only a raw red-haired vixen just mounting a shaky throne. There was no shadow of scheming, and butchered lovers, and her hair showing white when the wig fell off with her head under the ax. And yet, gentlemen, you can look at that watch upstairs and imagine it all reflected in the face."

Melson, professor of Constitutional History, did not like this sort of thing. Automatically he uttered his dry cough, as though he were about to deal with it. At any

166

other time it might have roused him to battle. But he was silent. Something in the muffled terror of the house made him unable to take his eyes off the watch gleaming in Dr. Fell's hand. Besides, there was a curious expression on the doctor's face. He put down the skull-watch on its velvet tray.

"I presume," he remarked, "that everybody in the house has seen it—the other one? Eh?"

"Oh yes."

"Did they all like it?"

Suddenly the shell of reserve was back on Carver. He picked up the tray.

"Very much. . . . But let us go on. You will wish to see some others." A small crash. "Damn it, I'm a clumsy beggar! Will you pick up that teacup, Doctor, or what's left of it? I'm always knocking china off tables. Um, yes. Yes. Thank you. My enthusiasm has carried me away, I fear." Again he was talking against a silence, ducking his big head, wrinkling up his face, and nearly blundering into the door-post. He went on rapidly: "I suppose you think me unduly cautious for having all these alarms on my collection. It's true that the safe is a good one, and that any burglar who stole something of mine would have difficulty in disposing of it. But—it makes me feel safer. Especially, you see, as this door," he nodded towards the one on the left of the alcove, "leads to a staircase going up to the roof; and, although it is strongly bolted . . ."

*"To the roof?"* said Dr. Fell.

His words were still echoing when the door to the hall was thrown open and Hadley strode in. He looked perturbed, and he was trying to conceal in the palm of his hand something that looked like a handkerchief. He had begun, "Look here, Fell—" when he caught the expression on the doctor's face and stopped.

"Don't tell me," he rasped, after a pause, "that something else has happened. For God's sake don't tell me that!"

"Harrumph. Well, I don't know whether you'd call it happening. But there appears to be another way up to the roof."

"What's that?"

Carver was again hard and quiet. "I did not know, Inspector," he said, "that you were interested. At least, you did not take the trouble to tell me so." He put away the tray in the safe, closed the door with a decisive clang, and twirled the knob. "This door opens on a staircase. The staircase goes up between the walls past two rooms, now lumber-rooms, on the floor above, and then on to the roof. I believe it was used in the early nineteenth century, when this room was a dining-room, as a private stairway for carrying the master of the house up to bed when he had finished his port-drinking. . . . I repeat, what of it! You see, there are double-bolts on this side, and bolts on the inside of the trap-door. No outsider could get in."

"No," said Hadley, "but an insider could get out. To the roof, eh?" He pointed to the door behind Carver, the door in the far side of the alcove parallel to the wall of this room. "And that—yes, I was in there just a moment ago. That's Mrs. Steffins's room, isn't it, on the other side of the door?"

"It is."

"What about these lumber-rooms on the floor above? Do they open on the staircase, too?"

"They do," Carver told him, without curiosity.

"I say, Hadley," interposed Dr. Fell, "exactly what is on your mind?"

"Any member of this household, with access to this stairway either down here or from the rooms above,

168

could get up to the roof. Once on the roof, he could go down again through the *other* trap-door—you remember the girl said it once had a bolt on the inside, but the bolt was broken—then on again to the door at the head of the main staircase, open that door by the spring lock from the inside, and . . ." Hadley made the gesture of one stabbing. "That had occurred to you, hadn't it? You seem to have become unusually dense all of a sudden."

"Perhaps I have," grunted Dr. Fell, pulling at his moustache. "But why all the elaborate hocus-pocus? If you were going to kill jolly old Ames, wouldn't it have been much simpler to walk up the stairs behind him, do the business, and then go comfortably off to your room?"

Hadley regarded him in some curiosity, as though he sensed a trick or a hidden purpose. But he discarded the idea.

"You know damned well it wouldn't. First you've got the possibility of a fight or an alarm that would rouse the whole house. Second and most important, after the work was done, you could go straight back to your room by the same way without a chance of being seen."

"Well, now—!" urged Dr. Fell, deprecatingly. "Don't say that. It would strike me that with Miss Carver and Hastings up there taking the air and the moonlight, you would run much more chance of being seen than in a a nice dark comfortable hall. Hey?"

Hadley looked at him in some suspicion. "Look here," he said, "is this your idea of a subtle leg-pull? You're using to back up your theory the evidence that proves mine. Namely, that somebody *was* seen on the roof, and that somebody the probable murderer. Eleanor Carver and Hastings didn't meet regularly on that roof; the murderer likely didn't know they met there at all. Come along. We're going to explore that roof now."

Dr. Fell had opened his mouth to reply, when Carver, who had been regarding them in ironical amusement, made a great show of drawing the bolts to the staircase door.

"By all means," he suggested, gesturing, "you must—hum—explore. Yes, yes. I should hate to damp your ardor, Mr. Inspector. All I know is that your theory is wrong."

"Wrong? Why?"

"Millicent was much exercised last night, you remember? Particularly about Eleanor's saying that young Hastings could not, um, control his temper, and had broken the bolt on the trap-door. She told me about it. To be frank," the corners of his mouth were drawing down, "I did not like it myself. It was unnecessary. And dangerous, after all my precautions. So naturally I went up and had a look at it—"

"At the trap-door on the other side of the roof? This is interesting," said Hadley. "Last night the door at the head of the stairs, leading up to it, was locked. And your ward said that the key had been stolen from her. . . . Did you find the key? Or how did you get through?"

Carver drew a bunch of keys out of his pocket and inspected them.

"I have duplicates," he replied, "to every door in the house. You did not ask me, or I should have told you. Do you want that one? With pleasure. Here you are."

Detaching one key, he suddenly tossed it. It glittered in the air, as though with a flick of contempt, and Hadley caught it. Carver went on:

"I inspected the trap-door. And Eleanor has somehow made a mistake. The bolt was not smashed. It was in perfect order, and the trap was firmly bolted with

170

three inches of steel.—Nobody on the roof could possibly have entered the house through that trap. Consequently, your whole picture of the murderer coming up through one trap and going down through another like a character in a pantomime happens to be rubbish. Hum. Yes. If you doubt me . . ." He gestured towards the key.

There was a silence, broken by Dr. Fell's wheezy sigh.

"It's no good talking about deep waters, Hadley," he volunteered. "This whole affair is gradually swamping the boat. So—people on the roof are eliminated, eh? Apparently, apparently." He reflected. "Yes, we shall have to go up and explore the roof, Hadley. But not at this precise moment. . . . I have a fancy to see a watch."

"Watch?"

"Boscombe's. I don't want to examine it," the doctor insisted, with rather unnecessary emphasis. "I just want to see it and make sure it's there. It's like this. . . . H'mf? Ah! Good morning, Miss Handreth."

He broke off at the knock, and remained beamingly dull as she entered. Lucia Handreth looked alert and even cheerful. Dressed for going out, in a tight fur-collared coat and grey hat, she was briskly pulling on a pair of black gloves and had a briefcase tucked under one arm. No shadow remained of last night's defiant uncertainty. Her eyes had the strained appearance of one just risen from brief sleep, but she brought health and vigour into the room along with a scent of wood-violets which somehow seemed as brisk and business-like as the briefcase.

"I'm going out on business, surprisingly enough," she said, smiling at Hadley. "But I thought I could catch you here before I went. D'you mind coming to the telephone?"

"Right. Tell them to—"

"Oh, it's not your office. It's about that alibi of mine," she explained, composedly. "You know, for the afternoon of Tuesday a week ago. I told you I would look it up in my diary, and I was right. It *was* the day of the cocktail party. So this morning I rang up the man and his wife who gave the party; I remember now that I got there about half-past four and stayed until seven. Ken is on the wire now, and both he and his wife are willing to give me corroboration. He's an artist, but he does magazine covers and should be respectable enough for you. There are others, of course. . . . I know you'll have to check up all this in person, but I wish you'd speak to him now and let me get it off my mind. It's been worrying me, rather."

Hadley nodded, with a significant glance at Dr. Fell, and Hadley seemed pleased as he followed her out. Dr. Fell did not look pleased. He lumbered out after them, but he went no farther than the hallway. When Melson closed the door behind him, after a word of thanks to Carver, he found the doctor standing broad-legged in the gloom, his shovel-hat stuck on the back of his head, pounding one cane slowly on the carpet with a sort of repressed fury. Melson had never seen him like this. Melson felt again the sense of unknown terrors gathering and darkening. Dr. Fell started when he spoke to him, and peered round.

"Eh? Oh! I can't stop it," he said, with a baffled stamp of the cane. "I see it coming. I've seen it gradually drawing near every hour we've been in this damned place, and I'm as helpless as a man in a nightmare. The devil never is in a hurry. And how can I stop it? What tangible evidence have I got to lay before twelve good men and true, and say—"

"Look here, what ails you?" demanded Melson, who

was beginning now to feel jumpy at each footfall or opened door. "You seem upset because this Handreth girl has proved her innocence with regard to the department-store murder."

"I am," nodded Dr. Fell. "But then I am always rather upset when I see an innocent person in danger of being hanged."

Melson stared at him. "You mean that the Handreth girl really—"

"Steady!" said Dr. Fell, sharply.

Hadley, his jaw muscles tight with satisfaction, bowed Lucia Handreth ahead of him out of the room opposite. She settled her gloves between the finger-joints, gave her hat a final pat, and said:

"You feel better now, Mr. Hadley?"

"I shall have to check up, of course, but—"

She nodded quietly. "Yes. Still, I think it will do. I may go now? Good. You may still search my rooms, if you like. Good morning."

The pointed teeth showed in a broad smile, and her brown eyes gleamed. Then the hollow slam of the front door, the rattle of its chain, went up in echoes that were caught by the heightened murmur of the crowd still milling outside. Through the narrow side-windows on either side of the door fell faint light. Melson could see the area rails, and eager faces, open-mouthed, swaying back and forth over them like heads on spikes. A camera was raised high, and a flash-bulb glared against the autumnal sky. Then Melson became aware that Hadley, behind him, was humming some fragment under his breath as though he was pleased. Melson was not well acquainted with popular songs, but he could not help knowing that one. Words stood out:

"—*din' for the last round up* . . ." Then Hadley spoke incisively. "That woman's out of it, Fell. Aside from

173

that artist fellow, there seemed to be a whole crowd there having rather a noisy breakfast. They all tried to talk, and they all said the same thing. So——"

"Come upstairs," said Dr. Fell. "Don't argue; come upstairs. There's one last thing, and we must find it out."

He stumped ahead, making little noise on the muffling carpet, and they followed him. Hadley, seeming to remember the handkerchief he had been holding in his hand for some time, began to speak; but Dr. Fell silenced him with a fierce gesture. The double doors of Boscombe's room were slightly open. After a perfunctory knock he opened them. The remnants of a breakfast were on the table, and the curtains drawn wide. Boscombe, fastidiously dressed, looking sallow and withered against the daylight, was pouring himself a whisky and soda at the sideboard. He swung round, his hand on the syphon.

"Good morning," said Dr. Fell. "We've been talking to Carver—an exceedingly interesting conversation. He's been telling us all about watches, and we're rather interested in that skull-watch you bought. Would you mind letting us see it?"

Boscombe's eyes darted to the brass box. He hesitated, and suddenly looked even more sallow and withered, as though he could not get his breath, and nevertheless fought for something.

"Yes," he said, "I would mind. Get out."

"Why?"

"Because I don't choose to show it to you," the man returned with an effort. His voice rose harshly. "It happens to belong to me, and nobody is going to see it unless I say so. If you imagine that merely because you have police powers you can do as you bloody well like, then you'll find you're mistaken."

Dr. Fell took a tentative step forward. Boscombe yanked open the drawer of the sideboard and slid his hand inside. He braced himself backwards.

"I warn you what you're doing is robbery. If you so much as touch that box, I'll—"

"Shoot?"

"Yes, damn you!"

Something in his voice cried out in a sheer pale fury of humiliation that his bluff had been called once, but he did not mean to have it called again. Hadley muttered an oath and jumped forward. And then Melson realized that Dr. Fell was chuckling.

"Boscombe," said the doctor, quietly, "if anybody had told me last night that at some future time I should rather like you, I'd have called him a liar.... I am changing my mind a little. At least you have guts enough and affection enough in that little soul of yours to protect *somebody*, even if you happen to be wrong about who—"

"Look here, what the devil is all this about?" demanded Hadley.

"The Maurer skull-watch has been stolen," said Dr. Fell. "But not, I suspect, by the person Boscombe is afraid stole it. You'll be interested, Hadley. That watch happens to be worth three thousand pounds. And it's gone."

"That's a lie."

"Don't be a fool, man," said Dr. Fell, sharply. "You'll be questioned about it at the inquest, and if you can't produce it . . ."

Boscombe turned back to the sideboard and reached for the soda-syphon again. "I shall be under no necessity to produce it. If I happened to have loaned it to a friend of mine before this affair occurred, that is my own concern and nobody else's." The hiss of the soda-syphon rose loudly. He turned to face them.

"In fact," observed Dr. Fell, blankly, "it shakes you up when somebody stalks boldly into your room and accuses you of a decent act. It must upset your pride in yourself. Come out of it, man! The world isn't such a miserably rotten place that you've always got to keep kicking it because you're afraid it may kick you. As for—"

A voice in the doorway behind said in a quick, shaky, confidential tone,

"I say, old boy . . ."

Then it gulped. They looked round, to see a stoutish young man peering forward into the room. With one hand he clutched round his throat the collar of a rumpled silk dressing-gown and held hard to the door-post with the other. His thin blond hair was ruffled; his face, which must ordinarily have been fresh-coloured, was pale and hazy, with gummy eyes which held a rather horrorstruck look. Although he was not wavering, his expression conveyed that if he let go the door-post he would rise and hover in the air. His voice was quick, slurred, and jerky, even now when it had taken on a hoarsely confidential air.

"I say, old boy," he repeated, clearing his throat, "could you give me a spot, by any chance? Rotten luck. I—I seem to have smashed the last bottle or lost it or something. Appreciate it frightfully. . . ."

He appeared chilled. Boscombe looked at him, then took up the bottle, spilled more whisky into the drink he was carrying, and held it out. The newcomer, who Melson supposed could be nobody else than Mr. Christopher Paull, let go the door-post and his dressing-gown, and hurried forward with that same vaguely horrified look, as though he could not believe in the existence of any state of nerves so hideous as the one he felt. Mr. Paull was barefoot and his pyjama parts did not match. Mr. Paull seemed full of jangled piano-wires. After accepting the glass from Boscombe, he held it blankly for several seconds; then said, "Well, cheerio," faintly, and drank, and shivered.

"Hhhh-ooo!" said Mr. Paull. His smile was spectral. "I say, old boy. Guests. Most frightfully sorry you have guests. Er—" He wiped his toothbrush moustache with the back of his hand nervously. "You know how it is. Regimental dinner or something. 'Boys of the bulldog breed,' and all that. Or was it? Can't imagine how it happened, or getting home. 'Boys of the bulldog breed, Hooray'—somebody sang that, I know. I say, old boy; frightfully sorry, you know." He drank again. The voice of eager contrition was immersed in gurgles. "Haaa. That's better."

"Then you don't know," Boscombe said, sharply, "what happened last night?"

"Good God! what did I do?" said Paull, and suddenly took the glass from his mouth.

"You didn't," interposed Hadley, "you didn't by any chance commit murder, did you?"

Paull backed away. The glass wabbled in his hand and he had to put it down on the sideboard. For a moment he stared incredulously; then fear came into his sticky eyes. His voice grew querulously uncertain.

"I say. I say, this is no time to pull a fellow's leg." He looked at Boscombe. "I say, old boy, who are these fellers? Tick' em off. Tick 'em off good and proper. Dammit, putting the wind up a man feels like I do; damned bad form, if you ask me. Who are these fellers? Commit murder? My God! What rot!"

He reached for his glass again, and his hand nearly missed it.

"I happen to be from the C.I.D.—from Scotland

Yard," said Hadley, raising his voice as though he were speaking to a deaf person. "And I suppose you are Mr. Christopher Paull. A police officer was murdered here last night while he was coming up those stairs. At the head of the stairs, as a matter of fact . . ."

"Rot! You're pulling—"

"I am not. He was stabbed to death not very far from your own door. We have evidence to the fact that you arrived here last night at about seven-thirty, and must have been in your room at the time. I want to know whether you know anything about it."

Paull looked at Boscombe, who nodded. He became very quiet, whether from sheer shock and fright Melson could not tell; but for a time he could not speak. Several repetitions of the statement were necessary. He went over to a chair and sat down, putting his glass on the table beside him.

"Well, Mr. Paull?"

"I don't know! My God! You don't think *I* did it, do you?"

"No. We only want to know whether you heard or saw anything, or whether you were in a condition to hear or see anything."

Paull seemed a little reassured, and his breathing grew more quiet. Pressing his hands over his eyes, he rocked back and forth.

"Can't *think*, confound it! Can't get a blasted thing straight in my head. Everything in such a muddle; damned bad form spring a thing like this on me. . . . Police officer gettin' killed, what rot. . . . Stop a bit!"

He looked up blearily.

"There was something . . . can't quite get it straight. Some time. When? Let me see. No, I dreamed it. Often think you get up in the dark and you don't. What rot. I thought—"

As though to drive away a phantom of recollection, his hand stole to the pocket of the dressing-gown and fumbled there. It found something, for his expression changed. Out of his pocket, dazedly, he drew a woman's black kid glove, turned partly inside out. As he turned it over a small key fell from one of the glove-fingers and gleamed on the floor; and the palm of the glove was dully streaked with gilt paint.

# 15

## The Flying Glove

Momentarily Hadley stood frozen. Then he bent over and took the glove out of Christopher Paull's limp hand. Carrying it to one window, he examined the palm against dull grey light. Beyond him the branches of the great maple, as yet scarcely tinged with yellow, almost touched the window, and a draught blew through the broken pane. Hadley touched the gilt stains; then he ran his finger along other stains, evidently not yet quite dry.

"Blood," he said.

The quiet word echoed. It seemed all the more ugly uttered in this big room with its sombre books and the leering Hogarth prints on the walls. Returning without hurry, quietly inexorable, Hadley picked up the little key. When he backed away to get the light, this time it was he who stood up against the tall leather screen painted with flames and saffron crosses. Hadley's face looked grey, his eyes hard black, his jaw pleased. From his pocket he took the key Carver had given him downstairs, the key to the door on the landing. He fitted it against the other, holding them both up against the light. They were exactly the same. Then he put the keys into different pockets.

"Now, Mr. Paull," he said, "you will tell us how you happen to have this glove."

"I don't know, I tell you!" cried the other, with a kind of groan. "Can't you give a chap a chance to think? Maybe if I have a chance to think I can get the beastly thing straight. Got an idea—can't think—picked it up somewhere? Did I? Got an idea—talking to some woman. On the stairs. No, that was Aunt Steffins. She put my necktie in my pocket. There were lights on then. Don't know why I remember that."

"Do you know who owns this glove?"

"Good God, its not mine! Take it away, can't you? How should I know?" He regarded it doubtfully, as a man might get closer to a snake he is assured is harmless. "Woman's glove. Might be anybody's. . . . I say, old boy, let me have another, will you? I'm quite sober. I feel like hell, but I'm quite sober. Buck me up if I do."

"You, Mr. Boscombe?"

Boscombe's nostrils twitched; but he remained motionless, his arms folded, against the sideboard. Again he was fighting for something. He barely glanced at the glove.

"I never saw it before."

"You are sure of that?"

"Quite sure. I am also sure that you are on the verge of one of the biggest mistakes of your life. Excuse me." He adjusted the thin pince-nez on his nose and went over softly to take Paull's glass.

"You said last night," Hadley went on, "that before the end of this case we should come to you for advice. You said you had something to tell us. Have you anything to say now?"

"I have question for question." He took Paull's glass, but did not turn round. "What do you make of that glove?"

"I don't need to exercise my imagination very far," the chief inspector returned, "when I find the letters 'E. C.' stencilled inside."

Boscombe turned in dry fury. "It would be precisely like your shallow intelligence to think that. Now I will tell you something. Eleanor's name is not Carver. It happens to be Smith. On things belonging to her—"

"Got it!" said Paull, suddenly. "Eleanor! Of course!"

He had sat up straight, trying to pull at his little moustache. The blotchy colours of his face had begun to sink; he looked stout and ineffectual, but for the first time more sure of himself. "Eleanor! In the hallway—"

"You saw her in the hallway?"

"Now, now! Don't joggle me," Paull urged, with querulous entreaty, as though his memory might be spilled like a pail of water if he moved his head. "Wasn't it? It's beginning to come back a bit. Nothing to do with your blasted old police officer, of course. Eleanor. Ho-ho! But since you're so keen to know . . . I say, what did happen really? Maybe if you told me that—"

Hadley curbed his impatience with an effort.

"Remember what you can remember without any help. We don't want the evidence distorted to fit what you think might have happened. Well?"

"Got it, then. Part of it. What mixes me up is your saying I got back here," Paull muttered with an air of stubbornness, "so early. Hang it all, there was a dinner

182

. . . or was there? Dunno. Anyhow, I woke up—"

"Where?"

"In my room. It was dark, you see, and I didn't know where I was or how I'd got there, and my head was so muzzy I thought I must still be dreaming. I was sitting in a chair and I was cold, so I felt my shoulder and found I was half undressed, with my shoes off, too. Then I stretched out my hand and hit a lamp. I pulled the chain and found I was in my room right enough, but the light looked funny.

"Yes, by God! I've got it now. . . . Remembered there was something at the back of my mind worrying me. All of a sudden I remembered. I thought: 'Dash it all, what time is it? I've got to get to that dinner.' But I couldn't move straight, and the room looked all queer, and I couldn't find the clock, so I thought: 'Kit, you're still drunk as an owl, old boy. Got to get to that dinner.' Then I wandered round and round the room until I heard a clock striking somewhere. I counted it. . . ."

He shivered suddenly. Hadley, who had taken out his notebook, prompted, "You remember the time?"

"Absolutely positive of it, old chap. Midnight. I counted. Remember that, because I got my dressing-gown because it was cold, and sat down on the bed and thought it over. I thought I could still get to that dinner if I had another spot to keep me going. Then—no, there's another blank. Don't remember getting up from that bed. Next thing I knew, you see, I was standing over in the closet among my suits and things, and couldn't keep upright, but I had a flask in my hand. There was a little in it and I drank some, but I thought, 'Look here, old boy, *that's* not enough to keep you going.' Always feel most comfortable with a full bottle.

"Then, somehow, I was out in the hall in the dark . . ."

"How did that happen?"

"I can't—yesbgad! I can!" He was more excited, as slowly the struggling image seemed to come out of a haze. He gestured fiercely to Boscombe, who brought him a very weak drink; but he did not taste it yet. "It was you. Got it. Of course. I thought: 'Old Boscombe. Always keeps a bottle of the best on his sideboard.' Then I thought he might be very shirty if I went in and woke him up to ask for a spot. Some fellers are. But he don't keep his door locked, I thought. Sneak in ever so softly, don't make any noise—like this and pinch a bottle."

"Go on."

"So I did. Quiet. Tiptoe. Turned out my light. But that last drink—bad. Everything was all blurry, even in the dark. Head went round, couldn't find the door. Frightful." He shuddered again. "Then I opened the door, very quiet, you see, and started out in the dark. I had the flask in my hand; remember that . . ."

"And what did you see?" demanded Hadley. His voice was rather hoarse.

"I don't know. Something—somebody moving. Thought I heard something, but I'm not absolutely positive. . . . Eleanor, yes."

"You'll swear to that?"

"I know what it was!" Paull muttered, with an air of inspiration. "It came to me then: Eleanor goin' to meet that chap on the roof. She does, you know. Wanted to play a joke on 'em, time and again. It made me want to laugh. I thought, I say, wouldn't she get a turn if I came up behind and said, 'Boo!' Then I felt bad about thinkin' that. I thought, 'Poor little devil, what fun does *she* get?'—she don't, you know—and I said to myself, 'You're a cad, that's what you are, you cad, to think of interruptin' her. . . .'"

In his overwrought nerves and chivalry, even now

his eyes were moist. His hand trembled when he drank the rest of the whisky and soda.

"Look here, Mr. Paull," said Hadley, with a sort of wild patience, "nobody cares what you thought. Nobody wants to know what you were thinking about. The whole thing is, what did you see? When you have to testify at the inquest—"

"Inquest?" babbled Paull, jerking up his head. "What rot! What do you mean? I tried to do a good turn—"

"What you saw, or thought you saw in the dark, was a man being stabbed to death. Can you understand that? A man being stabbed through the throat—like this—who stumbled up those stairs and died between these two doors." Hadley strode over and flung them open. "You can still see the blood on the floor. Now speak up! Tell us what you heard, how you came by that glove, and how it is that nobody saw you when the doors were opened a few minutes afterwards, or it's just possible that a coroner's jury will bring in a verdict of wilful murder against *you*."

"You mean," said the other, stricken alert and seizing the arms of the chair, "that was what I heard—"

"Heard?"

"It was a funny sort of noise, like somebody choking, and then stumbling a bit. I thought it was because she'd heard me and was frightened. So I ducked down, rather . . ."

"How far were you from the stairs, then?"

"I don't know. It's all a fog. Stop a bit, though. I must have been a goodish distance away, because I hadn't got much outside my door. Or was I? Don't remember. . . . But when I bent down, I touched or kicked something; don't remember which; and it was that glove."

"You are trying to tell us that you found that glove

185

on the floor some distance from the stairs? Come now!"

"I tell you it's true! Damned bad form doubting. Look here, I don't know where it was, but it was on the floor, because I nearly dropped my flask when I picked it up, and it was draughty. I thought I'd duck back to my room and wait till she'd gone. So I did. Softly, you know. On tiptoe. Then I don't know what happened. I don't even remember getting to my room. The next thing I knew it was daylight and I was lying on my bed still half-dressed, and feeling like hell."

"Why did you pick up the glove?"

"I—I was trying to do a good turn, dash it!" protested the other, with weak querulousness. The dull gaze was returning to his eyes. "At least, I think so. Yes, of course. I thought, 'Little lady's lost her glove, poor old girl. Aunt Steffins finds it there, going to be trouble. Poor old girl. Give it to her tomorrow and say, 'Tut, tut, I know where *you* were last night.' Ha-ha! . . . I say, old chap, I don't feel well. Maybe if I have time I can remember some more. I seem to remember——" He ruffled up his hair, and then shook his head blankly. "No. It's gone. But now that I keep on thinking, I seem to remember . . ."

Dr. Fell, who throughout all this recital had kept silent, lumbered forward. Between his teeth he still gripped the stump of a long-dead cigar, but he took it out and put it quietly in an ash-tray before he looked down at Paull.

"Be quiet a minute, Hadley," he rumbled. "Somebody's life depends on this. . . . Let me see if I can assist your memory, young man. Think back. You're in the hall now, in the dark. You say it was draughty. Now think of the door at the head of the stairs, the one on the way up to the roof where you thought Eleanor was going. You'd have noticed that if—Was it draughty because that door was open?"

"Yes, by Gad! it was!" muttered Paull, sitting up. "Absolutely. I know now. That's what I was trying to think of, because . . ."

"Don't lead him, Fell!" snapped Hadley. "He'll remember anything if you suggest it to him."

"I'm suggesting nothing now. It's coming back to you now, young fella, isn't it?" He pointed with his cane. "Why are you sure it was open?"

"Because the trap-door to the roof was open, too," said Paull.

There was a silence. Topsyturvydom had returned again. Melson looked past Dr. Fell's big cape, at the dull gleam on the ferrule of the cane as he held it out, and beyond it Paull's fat pale face against the big blue chair. In the young man's eyes there was a growing light of revelation and more—of certainty. You could not help believing him.

"This is sheer fooling," Hadley said, heavily. "Stand back, Fell. I'm not going to have this sort of thing forced on witnesses . . . It happens, Mr. Paull, that a reliable person—one who happened to be sober at the time—has told us that trap-door was solidly bolted when he looked at it a little while afterwards. In the meantime, the door leading to it was locked and the key missing."

Paull sat back. Into his expression had slowly come a look that was not weak or querulous.

"I say, old chap," he said, quietly, "I'm getting a bit tired of having people call me a liar. If you think I've enjoyed telling how I made a ruddy ass of myself, think again. I'm doing the best I can; I know what the truth is, and I'll face you with it in every coroner's court from here to Melbourne . . . The door was open. So was the trap. I know that because I saw the moonlight."

"Moonlight?"

"Rather. When you open that door there's a straight passage, without windows, that runs back to a sort of

187

staircase-ladder at the end. Above that there's a little box-room, not big enough to stand up in, and the trap-door is just above. I know that. We'd thought of putting a roof-garden to sit in on the flat part of the roof once. We couldn't; too much smoke from the chimneys all about . . . But I know it.

"I know what I saw. It was a sort of line of moonlight on the floor of the passage. If I could see the passage, the door was open; and if I could see the moonlight, the trap was open. That's flat. The trap was open, right enough. Dammit all, now I know what put it in my mind about Eleanor! That was it."

"But did you see anybody to identify?" asked Dr. Fell.

"No. Just—something moving. Or things."

Hadley walked slowly about the table, knocking his knuckles against it, his head down. But he became aware of the glove in his hand, and his indecision did not last.

"I don't imagine it much matters," he said. "Since I found in the finger of this glove—the glove used by the murderess—the key that opens that door. My advice to you, Mr. Paull, is to go to your room, slosh yourself with water, and get some breakfast. If you have any more inspirations, come and tell me." He looked significantly at Dr. Fell and Melson. "I think, gentlemen, that a glance at the trap-door . . ."

"Delighted," said Paull. "Thanks for the drinks, old lad. I'm a new man."

He closed the door so quietly that Melson suspected he had thought of slamming it. Hadley followed a moment afterwards, glancing left towards the door of Paull's own room as it also closed. In the direction of the chief inspector's measuring eye, Melson saw that the staircase was some little distance away from Paull's room—from the trail of the blood-marks, say about fifteen feet. The curtains were drawn back on the big windows at the front of the hall, and harsh light illumined it clearly. Some effort had been made to scrub out the stains, but the wet discoloured rubbing of the nap on the red-flowered carpet showed the trail more clearly than the blood itself.

It would be impossible, Melson thought, to determine on which step of the stairs Ames had stood when the clock-hand pierced his neck. The first stains began on the second tread from the top, but, since he had presumably remained on his feet until he stumbled across the threshold upstairs, then the blow might have been struck lower down. First the trail turned towards the right (coming upstairs), as though the dying man had tried to hold to the banisters for a moment or two; then it zigzagged to the left, passed the top tread, zigzagged right again and grew more plain, as though Ames had gone down on one knee briefly, and at last on to the double doors.

Hadley looked at Dr. Fell, and Dr. Fell at the chief inspector. Both had their minds set on something; battle was coming, but neither would open the subject. Hadley examined the newel-post, peered down the narrow stairwell to the floor below, and glanced back at Paull's door.

"I wonder," he remarked, abruptly, "how long it took him to—make that progress?"

"Two or three minutes, probably." The doctor spoke with gruff abstraction. "It was slow going, or the track wouldn't be so easy to follow."

"But he didn't cry out."

"No. The murderer struck for a spot that made sure he wouldn't."

"And from behind . . ." Hadley peered round. "Any

189

idea where the murderess might have stood? If she came up on him, followed him up—"

"In all probability, the person who killed Ames stood flattened against the wall opposite the banisters, about three treads down. As Ames passed, the killer struck. It's likely Ames was walking up with his hand on the banister-rail: most of us do when we go up a strange stairway in the dark. The blow brought Ames nearly to his knees—that would be where the track turns right, where he grabbed with both hands for the banister-rail. Then he lost his grip, turned left, and kept on as you see."

"Ames walked past, but didn't see the killer?"

"That," said Dr. Fell, a long sniff rumbling in his nose, "is the point in the reconstruction I wanted you to see. It's a question of light. Now this hall, as I think we've heard several times, was pitch dark. Question: how the devil could the murderer see to strike? Well, there's only one way it could have been managed, and I tested it last night . . . Look downstairs; you'll have to go down a little way. So. You see those narrow windows at either side of the front door? One of 'em is directly on a line with the banisters, and there's a street lamp outside. A person coming up in the dark has his head and shoulders faintly but clearly silhouetted, whereas the murderer would be in shadow. As I say, I tested it last night. I asked Eleanor Carver to show me where she was standing when she first saw the body from the stairs, and it worked out."

Hadley straightened up. "So you asked Eleanor Carver," he repeated in a curious voice. "I want to talk to you about that . . . Let's go and see that bolt on the trap-door; to the roof, maybe. Where we can have some private conversation."

There was strain here, the strain between old friends.

Hadley took one of the keys out of his pocket and unlocked the door at the head of the stairs. It opened inwards, and he groped on the left-hand wall inside for a light-switch. A dull electric bulb hanging without shade from the ceiling revealed a narrow passage, dark-panelled and stuffy, with a strip of ragged carpet on the floor and at the other end a steep flight of stairs like a stepladder. The ceiling was low, accounting for the box-room overhead in a sort of loft, and Melson found himself coughing in the dust that trembled round the light. Hadley let the lock click shut. Then he dropped his defences.

"Fell," he said, abruptly, "what's the matter with you?"

Dr. Fell peered at the stepladder, hesitated and then he chuckled. That chuckle, booming out in the musty confines of the passage, eased and then destroyed the strain; a deep and Gargantuan mirth that kept back the terrors of the case. Drawing out his gaudy bandanna, he mopped his forehead, and the twinkle returned to his eye.

"Nerves," he admitted. " Didn't know I could have 'em. It's the result of going until noon without the strengthening influence of beer. And also because I've been through one of the worst interludes I ever hope to put in. Heh. And also—"

"You don't believe that girl is guilty."

"Eleanor Carver? I do not," said the doctor, with a tremendous honking battle-cry as he blew his nose. "Haa, hum. No. But first suppose you look at that trap-door and see what there is to be said for young Paull's evidence."

Hadley climbed the ladder until only the lower part of his legs showed. They heard his hands bumping, the sound of a match struck, and then an exclamation of satisfaction. Dusting off his hands, he descended and stuck his head under the loft.

"That settles it. That most definitely settles it. The murderer didn't come down through here; and, what's more, the murderer didn't slip back up through that trap leaving it bolted on the inside behind him. It *is* bolted, my boy. Hard and fast, and it takes a good wrench to move it."

Dr. Fell twirled the bandanna.

"And so," he observed, musingly, "your star witness was drunk and seeing things?"

"Exactly. This proves that only El . . . Hold on! What the devil do you mean, my star witness?"

"Isn't he? Didn't he prove to you that Eleanor committed the murder? Now I am aware," said the other, with relish, "of your concurrence with Emerson when he says that a foolish consistency is the hobgoblin of small minds. But in this matter I am going to shout for a little consistency. You damned well can't have it both ways. When Paull produced a blood-stained glove which he says he picked up in a pitch-dark hall, you applaud his shrewd presence of mind. When he says he sees a comparatively harmless patch of moonlight—which in the dark is usually more noticeable than a black glove, anyway—then you go off the deep end and accuse him of delirium tremens. Tut, tut. You may believe or disbelieve his story; I don't mind. But you can't accept the part you like and yell scorn on the part that doesn't happen to suit your theory. To my simple mind, there ought to be an equal falsehood or an equal truth."

"I can," returned Hadley, "if the facts happen to support me. The trap is bolted: he was mistaken about that. But on the other hand, here *is* the glove. I've got it in my pocket. You don't doubt the glove, do you?"

"I only doubt its importance . . . See here, now. Do you honestly think the murderer used that glove? Can you picture Eleanor Carver, after stabbing poor old Ames, plucking off the glove and hurling it into the air in pure joyous abandon—for the police to find with her initials inside? It must have sailed some distance, by the way, if it travelled from the head of the stairs to Paull's door. 'The Mystery of the Flying Glove,' a Scotland Yard Thriller, by David F. Hadley . . . Eyewash, my fathead. First-class, guaranteed-British eyewash. Put Paull into the box to tell that story, and a good counsel would laugh you out of court. But what do you do? You swallow that piece of evidence intact, and sternly deny the business of the trap-door! Hasn't it occurred to you that the trap-door may have been open then, and bolted now, for the astounding reason that somebody later bolted it?"

Hadley studied him. His face wore a grim smile. He patted the pocket where he had put the glove.

"You're good enough at ridicule. I've always admitted that . . ."

"But don't you see any reason in it?"

The other hesitated. "Your own type of firework reasoning, maybe. But I don't want any advocacy, and it strikes me you're doing what's known as whistling in a graveyard. You've made up your mind this girl isn't guilty . . ."

"I know she isn't. Look here, what do you mean to do?"

"Face her with the glove. If it really does belong to her . . . Now take it easy and look at the facts of the case. The evidence fits down to the smallest joint, even to her admitting herself that she had a habit of carrying a key in the finger of a glove—where we found the key in this one!

193

"We had decided that suspects in the department-store business narrowed down to Handreth and Carver. Handreth proved an alibi. The witnesses at Gamridge's didn't get a look at the girl's face—but in everything else the description exactly fits Eleanor. She even admitted she was at the store at the time of the murder. . . ."

"Now," interrupted Dr. Fell, bitterly, "I will proceed to give you a piece of evidence which fits into your case and will please you no end. I had a talk with Carver—Johannus. *He* thinks she's guilty, and apparently jumped to the conclusion after the Gamridge robbery and murder, to such an extent that he lied to us last night about remembering the reason, he said, 'We had some difficulty with her as a child—'changed his mind, and shut up. Kleptomania, my lad. Kleptomania, for a fiver."

"Are you joking?"

"Nooo-o!" rumbled Dr. Fell. "Seize the bright objects; that's it. Probably everybody knows about it. The only reason why La Steffins didn't mention it last night was probably because her narrow imagination couldn't connect anybody in her own house with murder. Seize the bright objects: bracelets, rings, watches. . . . If the bright objects happen to belong to your guardian, the inhibitions strongly rooted from the past prevent you from pinching 'em except when they're out of his care—in another person's charge—or *sold to somebody else*. These inhibitions! The clock was sold to Sir Edwin Paull; one watch was sold to Boscombe, and Gamridge's were financially responsible for good care of the other. Seize the bright objects; watches, rings—carving knives."

Hadley was struggling with his notebook.

"Have you gone stark insane?" demanded the chief

inspector. "You're making out an unanswerable case against your own client! I've got—"

Dr. Fell drew a deep breath and quieted down.

"I'm telling you this," he replied, "first', so that you can't say that the defense hasn't been fair; second, to make you see what I've been seeing looming up in one deadly mass on that girl from the first—and third, because I don't believe one single damned word of it. Like some of your other fortuitous circumstances, Hadley, it's much too good to be true . . . Shall I go on and pile up your case for you? There's a good deal more of it."

"What *is* the defence?"

Dr. Fell stumped up and down the passage, which seemed to stifle him.

"I don't know," he answered, dully. "I can't make it—yet. Look here, shall we get out of this place? I'd much rather be overheard than suffocated . . . But if I tell you your case, and drive in all the good stout coffin nails, will you grant me a grace of time to pull 'em out again?"

Hadley walked ahead of him to the door. "You think you know who did commit the murder?"

"Yes. And, as usual, its the last person you might have suspected—No, I'm not going to tell you. Is it a go?"

Hadley fiddled with the spring-latch, clicking it back and forth.

"The Carver girl is guilty. I'm almost sure of that. But I'm willing to admit your confounded positiveness has got me uneasy . . . Well, look here! In default of more evidence, I can hold my hand until I make certain of the glove and test all other possibilities; in the meantime, we'll let her alo—"

With a decisive gesture he was opening the door,

and stopped. He came face to face at the head of the stairs with Sergeant Preston, the swarthy-faced master of search.

"Ah, sir!" said Preston, with a grin. "I've been looking all over the house for you. I wanted to tell you that its all up. Ho-ho!"

"All up?"

"Yes, sir. We've found the stuff—hidden very neatly in her room, but we found it."

Melson felt a constriction in his throat, and he heard Dr. Fell mutter something as Hadley asked the obvious question . . .

"Why, the young lady's room, sir," said Preston. "Miss Eleanor Carver's. Will you come downstairs and see?"

# 16

## Proof Behind the Panel

Hadley did not look at Dr. Fell while they tramped downstairs. Possibly the sergeant also sensed the tension; for, after a curious glance at the chief inspector, he was silent. Melson found himself thinking with something of a shock that the thing had become definite: no mere accusation, but as real as death and thin rope. Before him floated Eleanor Carver's face—the long bobbed hair, the heavy-lidded blue eyes, the eager, voluptuous mouth moving in silent speech . . . She was out walking with Hastings; or had she returned? They gave them short shrift in England. Three clear Sundays after sentence, and then the walk at dawn. In the lower hall Hadley turned to Preston.

"Sewn up in a mattress, I suppose?" he asked, sharply, "or hidden behind loose bricks? We only made a cursory search last night."

"Small wonder you didn't find the stuff, sir. No. It's

cleverer than that. I should have found it eventually, of course—I was just getting round there. But an accident helped. See for yourself."

Eleanor's room was at the rear of the house. And before the door, which was closed, Mrs. Steffins stood back in the shadow of the staircase. She had an air of shaken anticipation, as though a rumour without voice had gone through the house. They saw the whites of her eyes in the gloom.

"Something's going on in there," she said, shrilly. "I heard them talking. They've been too long in that room, and they won't let me in. I have a *right* to go in there . . . this is my house. . . . *Johannus*!"

Hadley's frayed temper broke.

"Get out of the way," he snapped. "Get out of the way and keep quiet, or it will be the worse for all of you. Betts!" The door to Eleanor's room opened a little, and Sergeant Betts glanced out. "Come out here and stand guard. If this woman won't keep quiet, lock her in her room. Now, Preston. . . ."

They went inside, and shut away the noise of shrill cryings. It was a small but high room, evidently once part of a larger one partitioned off. Two high small-paned windows looked out on the desolation of a brick-paved back yard, but the projection of the wooden scullery cut off even that view. The walls were of the same fine white panelling as most of the other rooms; aside from that, the whole room looked pinched and meagre. There was a white marble mantelpiece, its top ornamented with a Krazy Kat doll and two or three photographs of motion-picture stars in flimsy imitation-silver frames. Somehow that expressed everything else. For the rest: a wooden bedstead, wash-handstand, wardrobe—open, to show disarranged dresses on hangers—a dressing-table with a large mirror and a china

198

lamp shaped like an eighteenth-century marquise, and on the floor a small woven rug. Over against the mantelpiece stood Mrs. Gorson, a startled expression in her protruding brown eyes, and the handle of a carpet-sweeper loose in her fingers. They heard her breathing. . . .

"Well?" demanded Hadley, peering round. "I still don't see anything. What did you find, and where is it?"

"Ah! That's the cleverness of it, sir," nodded Preston. "I thought I'd let you see." He crossed to the wall between the two windows. Between them hung a bad picture in blurry colors of a knight in armour straining to his shoulder-plates a scantily clad girl with long yellow hair. Preston's footfalls creaked on the boards. He pulled the picture to one side.

"I was just beginning on this wall, sir, and Betts with me. *That* lady," he nodded towards Mrs. Gorson, "insisted she had to do some cleaning, and we let her go ahead. She was using a mop, and when she turned round the handle of the mop struck against this panel. . . . Well, it was all up then. It took me longer to find the spring. But watch."

He ran his finger along the top. Exactly as had happened in Carver's room, a vertical line appeared at the side of the panel, this one, however, being only about two feet long. Preston hooked his fingers inside and pushed the slide into the wall.

"Like the old man's" Hadley muttered, and smote his hands together. "The architect of this house seems to have . . ." He hurried forward, and they followed him.

"Looks like she'll hang; eh, sir?" enquired Preston, complacently. "I remember when we dug up the cache of that fellow Brixley, the Cromwell Road murderer;

you remember, sir; him that had his wife's arm wrapped up in a bit of—"

"Be quiet!" roared Dr. Fell. "Now, steady, Hadley. . . ."

All the suggestion of the girl's presence gathered in this room to form her image. Inside the opening, which was hollowed out of the bricks about a foot deep, were some objects wrapped up in an old torn jumper and thrust behind a shoe-box as though for more jealous concealment. The shoe-box contained a gilded steel clock-hand about five inches long, and, also smeared with gilt, a left-hand black kid glove which nobody doubted was the mate to the glove in Hadley's pocket. Hadley, with an eagerness that made his hands shake, carried the wrapped-up jumper to the bed before he unfolded it. . . .

A platinum bracelet set with turquoises. A pair of pearl pendant earrings. A flattish skull-faced object, somewhat smaller than a man's fist. They rolled out on the white counterpane as Hadley pulled the jumper from under them, and the light made an ugly glitter on the silver-gilt surface of the skull as it tumbled grotesquely over like a severed head. "*Seize the bright objects . . .*"

"No!" said a husky voice. They heard the rattle of a wooden handle on the mantelpiece, and windy breathing. Mrs. Gorson came forward at a heavy waddle, one hand against her ample bosom, her eyes protruding. "That's not right," she said, with fierce intentness, and pointed to the bed. "I am telling you, God being my judge at this minute, that it's not right. I am telling you they 'ate her."

Hadley straightened up.

"That will be all, Mrs. Gorson," he said, crisply. "Thank you very much."

"But I ask you, sir; I ask you, now"—her breath still whistled, and she reached after his lapel—"now come and tell me if anybody should know better than *I* should? Eh?" It was though she were trying to hypnotize him with cow-like eyes and wagging head. "E-e-eh? When I've lived here eleven years, ever since the old Mrs. Carver died, and I know Millicent Steffins, who does not fool me, wants *him*, and he won't see her. . . . Listen, now! Only a bit, sir, and I could tell you—"

"All right, Preston. Take her out."

"And I'm the one that's done it," said Mrs. Gorson, suddenly. Her eyes brimmed over. She did not resist when Preston impelled her out like a laundry-bag; but Melson steadied his nerves because he thought she was going to scream. She did scream, but not until she was in the hallway.

"Betts!" called Hadley. "Where the devil are you?—Ah! You've seen what's in here? Good. Then hop down after the warrant. We'd better be prepared in advance. If there's any trouble about it, have them phone me here for confirmation. . . . Has she come in yet?"

"No, sir."

"Then tell Preston to keep close to the door and bring her to me as soon as she comes in. But get after that Gorson woman—hurry!—and don't let her say a word about what's happened, not yet."

"Wait a second, Betts," said Dr. Fell. His roaring uncertainty had gone; he looked very quiet, leaning on one cane and waving a vague finger at the sergeant while he stared at Hadley. "You're sure you want to do this, now? Why not simply detain her, and wait until the inquest . . . ?"

"I don't care to risk my pension by passing the buck in the case of an obviously guilty woman."

201

"But you do know you'll ruin yourself if you make a mistake? You know you haven't even given the woman a chance to explain this? You know you're doing exactly what the real murderer wants you to do?"

Hadley lifted his shoulders. Then he took out his watch. "If it satisfies your conscience, I'll do you the favour for all past help. It's now twenty minutes past twelve. She should come in any minute . . ." He hesitated, staring. "Unless—Good God! do you suppose she's bolted? She didn't go to work today; she went out with Hastings—"

He slapped his fist into his palm and turned round uncertainly. "If that's it—"

"Well, if that's it," argued Dr. Fell, "nothing will be simpler than to find her. And then I shall withdraw my objection and you can execute your warrant on a guilty woman. But she'll be here. What was the concession you were going to make?"

"Wait in the hall for a few minutes, Betts. . . . I'll talk to her, yes. You act as though I expected to get a great deal of pleasure out of arresting this girl. I don't, let me tell you. I'm entirely willing to look at your side of the case—in spite of evidence that would hang a saint in the calendar—provided you give me a case to look at. But you haven't done that. All you've done is ridicule the evidence that exists, and complain about my fatheadedness. Yet you can't be working merely on a hunch. I've never known you to use as an excuse any worn-out rubbish like 'intuition'; so, if you have any real grounds for believing she's not guilty, let me hear 'em and I'll try to take my mind off this evidence. . . ."

"Oh, that?" said Dr. Fell, without interest. He glanced at the articles on the bed, and then over at the shoe-box in the aperture. "I knew we should find most of those things, even when I wasn't sure in which room:

so they didn't impress me. On the contrary, they gave me my theory. I knew we should find the clock-hand and somebody's glove, and probably the bracelet and watch. The only thing I was absolutely positive we should *not* find . . ."

"Well?"

"Was the watch taken from Gamridge's display. Here's my position. I have a theory I think is right. There were two overwhelming obstacles to it—not to the theory itself, I should say, but to making you or anybody else believe it. I've found a way over one of those obstacles. But the other is so big that I frankly admit it will take something like a miracle to remove it. . . . On the other hand, there's one very weak place in your theory—"

"It's not theory; there are the facts, the literal hard facts, on the bed and in that box. You've admitted that even lacking them we could convict Eleanor Carver of the department-store murder . . ."

"And Ames' murder, too, don't forget," said Dr. Fell, pointing at him. "It's only Ames' murder that clinches it and proves the whole."

"Well, if a jury believes she stabbed the shopwalker, they're not going to be very reluctant to think she also killed the police inspector. Even suppose they're dubious. If we hang her by the neck for the murder of Evan Manders, it's not going to be much consolation to her to say that the jury, after all, weren't really sure she killed George Ames. . . . And my case against her for the murder of Ames is just as strong."

"I know. But I don't want to hear the evidence. Just to make sure, before I start, tell me exactly what you think *happened* here last night."

Hadley sat down on the edge of the bed and leisurely began to fill his pipe.

"As I reconstruct it—I don't say this is exactly the outline; we can fill it in later with full corrections—Eleanor knew that a police officer was watching this house and trying to scrape acquaintance with its members in that pub . . ."

"A pub, incidentally, which Eleanor has never been known to visit; still less to know of a disguised police officer there."

Hadley regarded him almost genially. "Going to fight every step of the march, are you? I don't mind. Neither of those objections matters a tinker's curse. . . . Carver suspected the man was a police officer (he told us so himself), and Lucia Handreth *knew* he was (also by her own testimony). Now is it likely that either one of those would keep the news locked up secretly, and never comment on it to anybody else? It is not!—it would come out, if only in casual talk. And if Carver had any reason to fear that his beloved ward had been mixed up in the Gamridge affair (as you say he told you), he'd have let slip a hint. In short, there are a dozen ways in any one of which she must have learned. . . . More especially as," said Hadley, struggling to light his pipe, "she was probably aware of somebody spying on her in the house, knowing her secret, preparing to inform the police it might be. . . ."

"*Ah!*" grunted Dr. Fell. "We come back to that mysterious accuser, do we? And who was the accuser?"

"Mrs. Millicent Steffins," replied the chief inspector, placidly. "And I'll tell you several damned good reasons. I'll not insist on the obvious facts that (1) she is the sort of person who writies anonymous letters, spies on those in her household, and goes to the police in secret; that (2) she would know about that secret panel in the wall, which a guest here would not; and (3) she would take good care Carver didn't see she was the first to accuse his ward and put the police on her track. . . . There," said Hadley, with his slow grin, "is *my* explanation for the accuser's silence, without any cloudy nonsense. I'll not say, then—"

"All right, all right," interrupted Dr. Fell, testily. "You may omit all the things you won't say. Wash out and expunge from your mind all the things you wouldn't think of mentioning. What *do* you say about Steffins?"

Hadley tapped his pipe-stem against his teeth.

"I ask you to remember her conversation about Eleanor."

"What about it?"

"You'll admit, won't you, that she's about as talkative a parcel as you've ever met?"

"Yes."

"And that she shouted to the world about Eleanor's love affair on the roof; about Eleanor's ingratitude, Eleanor's selfishness, Eleanor's greed; in fact, everything about Eleanor *except*—"

"Yes, well?"

"Except," repeated Hadley, leaning forward after a pause, "the only things about Eleanor that were at all relevant to this investigation, and which she couldn't help knowing were relevant. She must have known about the kleptomania—which would have been a much better weapon for a sly nasty remark than most of the ones she used—yet she never even hinted at it even before we brought up the subject of the Gamridge robbery. She was very silent on that score. She was *too* silent. Then, when we did bring up the Gamridge question and flatly accused one of those women to their faces, still she didn't utter a word about Eleanor—even though she must have known perfectly well Eleanor had been at Gamridge's; she would certainly have enquired why Eleanor had been late for her tea-party.

All she said was, 'Eleanor was late.' Again she was too silent. And it couldn't have been, as once you tried to hint, that she 'didn't connect one of the household with murder'; as I say, we flatly announced that one of them had stabbed the shopwalker. No, Fell. She went too far, too unbelievably far in the other direction in case she should be suspected of being the one who denounced Carver's beloved Eleanor. She was as silent as the accuser because she *was* the accuser."

After this burst of eloquence Hadley leaned against the footboard of the bed and puffed vigorously at his dying pipe. There was a gleam of amusement in his sombre eyes.

"So we've got the old bear growling, have we?" he asked, examining Dr. Fell's choleric expression. "I'll tell you what. I've got nothing to do until my victim returns, and I feel so strongly on the matter that I don't mind going on to outline my case for the Crown. When I finish, you may rise for the defence if you like. Dr. Melson shall be the jury. Eh?"

Dr. Fell pointed his cane at him malevolently.

"Now I'm mad," he said. "Now I'm good and mad. I didn't suspect you were sneaking about fitting bits of evidence together behind my back, as well as calmly appropriating all the points I gave you. All right; presently I'll tell you a few things even if the time's not quite ripe for 'em. Yes, I'll speak for the defence. I'll tear your flimsy case to blue tatters, that's what I'll do. I'll blow up your house of logic and dance on the ruins. Goo-roo! I'll—!"

"Don't excite yourself," Hadley urged, mildly. He blew a film of ash off his pipe. "Something's just occurred to me. . . . Betts!"

"Sir?" responded the sergeant, poking his head inside. He seemed astonished to observe Dr. Fell violently flourishing his cane.

"Betts, find Mr. Carver—"

"Stop a bit," interposed the doctor. "There are to be no reporters in this courtroom. Slightly to change the metaphor, if you insist on baiting the old bear, it's got to be done in private."

"If you like, then. I can always verify certain things later. Anyhow, Betts, ask Mr. Carver about that clock he built for Sir Edwin Paull. Ask him whether the transaction has been concluded, and whether he received payment. Is Preston still watching out for Miss Carver?"

"Yes, sir."

Hadley waved him away; he settled back, his elbow on the footboard, and stared at the Krazy Kat doll sprawling on the mantelpiece.

"We've established, then, that Eleanor is afraid she is being watched by a police officer . . ."

"And takes steps to murder him?" interrupted Dr. Fell, sharply.

"No, I don't think so. I think she was only at the stage of being afraid, and that the murder occurred in a manner of speaking by accident. Like this—"

"This is the last time I'll interrupt you, Hadley," said Dr. Fell with great earnestness; "and I don't do it now to confute you, but to get something understood. I want to know how you stand on the theft of the clock-hands. That's your thundering difficulty; and, curiously enough, it's also mine on the opposite side. If you can produce even a remotely plausible explanation of why Eleanor should have pinched those clock-hands, I admit the defence will be pushed nearly to the edge. Now, now! Don't say you have one of them found in her possession, so that proves she did steal it and therefore why argue? No! It's the visual evidence I'm attacking.

"Now she stole those clock-hands either (a) out of pure kleptomania, or (b) to execute a deep-laid murder

207

plot—and you must see that either explanation is howling nonsense. Granted that she had a spur-of-the-moment passion for pinching watches and bracelets. But it's a very rummy sort of kleptomaniac who creeps out in the middle of the night, picks the lock of a door in her own house, painstakingly removes two large steel objects which have no value only as scrap-iron, and triumphantly carries them back to secrete with her hidden hoard. Whatever else you may call Eleanor Carver, I presume you don't call her stark crazy. Otherwise you may have difficulty in getting her hanged.

"On the other hand, this deep-laid murder plot—applied to her—becomes nonsense by the every evidence with which you prove her guilty of the Gamridge stabbing. Suppose she is that cobra, after trumpery rings and bracelets, who, when her arm is touched, loses her head, and snatches up the first convenient weapon, and slits a man's stomach, and dashes off blindly like a street-urchin, and only escapes capture by a wild piece of incalculable luck. Very well. If she is that woman," said Dr. Fell, tapping a finger into his palm, "then I'll tell you what she *didn't* do.

"She didn't concoct the devilishly imaginative scheme of using a clock-hand as a weapon. She didn't see its possibilities as a knife, and creep in there, and patiently wait on the off-chance that a prying policeman would pay her a visit in the middle of the night. It's that clock-hand, Hadley, that you can't associate with Eleanor or anything you know of Eleanor—either as a kleptomaniac or a murderess."

Hadley was unimpressed.

"The defence is out of order," he said. "If you'll listen to my explanation . . . What the devil!"

He sat up straight and peered round. From the hallway outside there was a sound of commotion; trampling footfalls, the clash of voices, a sharp sound like a slap, and a thud against the door. Kicking it open, a flustered Sergeant Preston had in his grip a woman who wrenched loose and glared at them. . . . Then Lucia Handreth stopped and stared at the articles on the bed.

# 17

---

## The Case for the Prosecution

It was too late to conceal them, although Hadley made a quick effort to do so without disturbing any finger-prints that might be there. The skull-watch and the bracelet were in plain sight. Lucia Handreth's eyes moved swiftly to the open panel in the wall; then they became veiled.

"I brought her here right enough, sir," Preston announced, in some satisfaction. The red marks of fingers showed across a cheek dull-pale with anger, and he straightened his tie. "She tried to give me something about her name not being Carver, but you told me to bring her in here——"

"You bloody *fool!*" roared Hadley, jarred out of his legal calm. He stumbled up from the bed. " Didn't you know——?"

"Not by sight, sir," Preston interposed during his retreat. "Betts told me a good-looking girl about her height. I wasn't here last night, and——"

"Where was Betts? He should have been out there to see..." Then Hadley seemed to remember he had sent Betts to look for Carver. "All right," he added, gruffly. "Say it wasn't your fault. Get out now. You'd better stay, Miss Handreth."

Melson had been studying her. Her colour had been high when she entered; she breathed heavily, and the fur collar of her coat was disarranged. Now she smoothed herself, with only a small gleam of anger making yellowish the clear brown eyes. And she did not attempt to pass over the objects she had seen on the bed. After adjusting her hat she looked at him levelly.

"So it was our Nell, after all," she said, in a contemptuous voice.

"It was. Why do you say, 'after all'?"

"Oh—well. Reasons. I suppose it's no good keeping quiet now, although I didn't think you sleuths would have much difficulty getting the truth out of poor old Chris Paull. Did you find the other clock-hand, or what made you so sure?"

There was material in this remark which made Melson jump. "The truth out of poor old Chris Paull?" He hoped his face had not betrayed him, for Hadley remained impassive and Dr. Fell poked absently at the floor with his cane. Lucia seemed to find the business mildly distasteful, and to speak without much curiosity. Her eyes wandered over the ornaments of the meagre room; her nostrils twitched, and she gave a faint shudder as at an unpleasant memory. When Hadley indicated a chair she appeared to hesitate about taking it. Then she shrugged, and sat down wearily.

"Poor old Don—" she burst out, the corners of her mouth drawing down. "And it won't be pleasant, and it hasn't been pleasant, for most of us. I'm glad you've

211

been so quick about it. I shouldn't have wanted to spend another night under the same roof with that . . . that mad wild-cat. Oh, it's mucky. But I didn't want to tell you, you see, because it would have looked like spite or something, and I knew Chris would—under pressure. And then again I didn't really *know* . . . What did Chris say?"

They saw that the pose of indifference was trembling over a powerful releasing of nervous tension, as she slowly realized the import of things. She had exaggerated her contempt on that, "I knew Chris would"; and a nerve jerked spasmodically in her arm.

"What did he say, Miss Handreth?" repeated Hadley, and reflectively examined his pipe. "About what particular thing do you mean? He told us a good deal, and he had rather a thick head this morning."

"About getting Eleanor to stop that clock from . . ." She was a shrewd woman. Even as she spoke she caught the echo of a wrong inflection in Hadley's remark, as at the ring of a false coin. "Let's understand each other," she added, sharply. "Do you know what I'm talking about?"

Before Hadley could reply Dr. Fell interrupted.

"We're at a time for pretty plain speaking, Miss Handreth. So there's no point in trying to be cute about extracting information from you. No, we don't know what you're talking about—but you've gone so far now that you've got to speak out. It will be none too good for your future legal career if you are accused of suppressing information. We talked to Paull, yes. If he knows anything about those clock-hands, he didn't tell us, because we didn't ask him. Come to think of it, we never even mentioned the fact that the murder was committed with a clock-hand. . . . It was difficult enough to make him understand the rest of it without introducing that."

"Then you mean," she cried, "that you didn't really find—"

"Oh, we found the short hand, the missing hand, right enough," confirmed Dr. Fell. "It's in that shoe-box over there. Show it to her, Hadley. You needn't worry about the strength of the evidence. Now, then, Miss Handreth?"

She was silent for a time.

"To think," she said, with a kind of savagery, "that after all the resolutions I made I did let the fool police make a fool of me, after all! Well, you had luck, that's all. You . . ." She stared at the cat-doll on the mantelpiece, and suddenly she began to laugh. "But the whole thing's so *silly*! That is, if it hadn't turned out horrible. It was a joke. Anybody but Eleanor would have seen that!" (Mirth, or tears, or terror, or all three? She dabbed at her eyes with a handkerchief.) "Oh, Chris will tell you all about it. He told me the story before I overheard him telling her. I dare say he only told her because I wouldn't sympathize with him, and said it was exactly like a difficulty in a Wodehouse story, and—Oh, well, I know I shouldn't have laughed, but . . .

"Look here. Do you know why Chris went down to see old Sir Edwin? He thought he was in a horrible mess, and I gather that the old man is rather a terror. Well, it was *Chris*, to keep on the good side of a wealthy relative, who insisted on the old man ordering that clock from the finest craftsman in town when any hack would have done as well; Chris said he himself would present Sir Edwin with the clock. Everything would have been quite all right if it had been merely the question of paying for the clock as a business proposition. But the old man said no. He knows Carver, he's tremendously keen on clocks and watches, so what they should do if Chris insisted on making him this gift, he said, was

213

'return a favor from a master' in proper form.

"Well. It seems that somebody in the Company of Clockmakers has for sale an old piece of junk, or what-not, that Sir Edwin knew Carver admired. A watch of some sort. So let Chris buy it. Then, when Carver's clock was finished—it was to be ready by today—in should come Sir Edwin, the old stuffed shirt, present Carver with the watch, receive the clock into his car, and take Carver down to Roxmoor to install it. Chris told me about this part openly, but the rest was in deepest confidence. . . ."

"When was this?" demanded Hadley, making rapid notes.

She was laughing again; and dangerously on the edge of hysteria.

"There—no, four days ago; on the Monday . . . Oh, don't you see how ridiculous it is? Chris has a good monthly income. But then last Sunday night the poor idiot got into a poker game at some club when he wasn't in shape to tell a full house from two pair, and got rid of everything with an overdraft at the bank to boot. He had a whacking big sum coming to him on Saturday of this week—tomorrow. But in the meantime he couldn't afford fifty shillings for the watch, much less fifty pounds or whatever it was. When he was in such a stew I said, 'My dear fathead, why not do the obvious thing? Get this watch, explain your difficulties, and give the chap who owns it a post-dated cheque for Saturday. He knows Sir Edwin and he'll understand.' Of course Chris wouldn't hear of it. He said the owner of the watch was a crony of old Edwin's; and if the old man ever heard he was stony, and learned why, then there'd be bad trouble, and it was trouble he was trying to smooth over by buying the clock. And so on. You know . . .

"I tell you it was so absurd! I said, 'Well, the clock'll

be finished by Thursday or Friday.' I said, 'Your only hope is for a burglar to come in and pinch it, but he'll need a crane and a lorry to go off with it.' Then he got his back up. . . . Then it was Wednesday morning, the morning of the day he went away, that I heard him telling Eleanor, also in strictest confidence . . ."

Hadley, like one who sees an answer to a hitherto impossible question, tried to suppress his excitement when he demanded:

"It was Wednesday night the hands were stolen? Yes! And she didn't hear of Paull's difficulty until Wednesday; in other words, until *after* the clock had been moved from its exposed position into Carver's room?"

"Yes."

"Go on. Exactly what was said about it?"

"I didn't hear all of it. Chris pinched my own words, without telling her where he heard them, about his being done for and that all he could hope for was a burglar with a crane and a lorry. I wouldn't have paid any attention—except it struck me all of a sudden that that little devil was actually taking it seriously! I could tell it by her voice. That's Eleanor. That's Eleanor's sense of humour," Lucia cried, rather wildly. "She said, 'Oh, it needn't be as bad as all that.' Then Chris mumbled something in his self-pitying way, and said, without much meaning, 'Well, all I can say is that I'd *give* fifty pounds to the burglar who'd do something about that clock.' And instantly Eleanor said, 'Do you mean that?'—It was all I heard."

"It was enough," said Hadley.

Something like a groan came from Dr. Fell. The doctor put his big head in his hands and ruffled the hair at his temples. Hadley, regarding him as though in an absent-minded fashion, drove in his words like nails.

"'Can you reconcile the theft of those clock-hands

with anything we know of Eleanor?'" he repeated. "'Why were both hands of the clock stolen? Why were they stolen on Wednesday night when it was locked up, rather than Tuesday night when it was exposed?' You said the answer would be simple, and it is. Fell, the whole case is complete and as blazing clear as daylight. The defence hasn't a leg to stand on."

"Humph, yes. Thanks very much, Miss Handreth. That," said Dr. Fell, dully, "has unquestionably torn it. Thanks very much. It may interest you to know that for the first time in your legal career you will have succeeded in sending somebody to the gallows."

Her eyes widened, and over them spread a glaze of fear. She had difficulty with her words when she said:

"Do you mean you have been tricking me *all* along? O my God! I wouldn't have told you if I hadn't been sure you . . . you said . . . If what I told you has made you alter your opinion . . ."

"You haven't altered my opinion in the least. You've only confirmed the opinion of the only person who matters."

"You—you don't think," she said, breathlessly, "I'd lie about—"

"No."

"Please understand my position," she urged, and began to beat her fist on the arm of the chair. "Could you expect me to keep silent, could you expect me to do anything else with a woman like that at my elbow and thinking about God knows what; with Don, who's wrapped up in her and has had enough horrible trouble already with his father's . . . ! What could I do?"

"You have done exactly right, Miss Handreth," said Hadley, with some curtness, "except that if you had told us this last night you would have saved a great deal of trouble. . . ."

"In front of Don? Not likely! Besides, I wasn't sure. I wasn't sure of anything until you began talking about Gamridge's and the robbery and murder there. Then I thought I saw the whole thing." She shivered. " May I go now? Living—living is a little more complicated than fancied."

She rose, wearily, and Hadley rose with her.

"There are just two more questions I wish to ask you," said Hadley, consulting his notebook. "First, did you know that Eleanor Carver ever had any tendencies towards kleptomania?"

A hesitation. "I've been waiting for that. Yes. I wondered why nobody mentioned it last night, especially Mrs. Steffins. I heard it from her. The old witch hates me, of course, but every time she had a row with Eleanor she had to talk to somebody about it.—Well."

Hadley glanced over at Dr. Fell. "Finally," he went on, "do you have any positive information as to whether Eleanor knew there was a police officer interested in somebody in this house?"

"Yes. I mentioned it myself. One day last week, I've forgotten which, Eleanor and I were walking through the Fields, and I saw Mr. Busy sitting on a bench, reading a newspaper. I was in a foul temper about something then; and, though I'd resolved not to say anything about Ames, it rather burst out. I said something like: 'Watch your step. There's the Great Detective himself in one of his famous disguises.'"

"What did she say?"

"Nothing much. She looked round at him, and wanted to know how I knew. But I caught myself up then, and just said I thought I remembered seeing him in court somewhere. Then I laughed and said it was a joke."

217

Hadley shut his notebook. "Thank you. That will be all, I think. I must caution you, remember, to say nothing to anybody yet. It will be only a matter of an hour or two, but—"

When she had gone, dispiritedly, Hadley did not speak during a time while he ran through his notes. Then he glanced up.

"Yes," he said, "forgive me a little personal vindictiveness in this business. I admit that; it's a clan affair. A member of the Force, in case you've forgotten it, was murdered; a man who carried no weapon was stabbed in the back. I shall take pleasure in hanging the killer.

"Now let me tell you what happened last night. That girl had the clock-hands in her possession; inside the secret panel, which she thought was safe. She wasn't looking for trouble. She had an appointment with Hastings on the roof—and she went up to keep that appointment, according to her own testimony, at a quarter to twelve.

"Now remember what we decided last night. We decided that Ames was watching, and that he got into the house long before he rang the bell at exactly midnight. You recall that? To ring the bell, to have some excuse for coming to this house, was necessary in case he should be caught; he would have to go through with it, even if to keep from arousing suspicion. He was watching Eleanor—probably through these windows, which are on the ground floor. When he sees her leave at a quarter to twelve, in a heavy coat which indicates she will be absent for a while, he gets in, either through the open front door or by a simple matter of burgling one of these windows. We are not certain whether or not the accuser, Mrs. Steffins, told him of the secret panel; in any case, he would make a rapid search of the whole room to make sure of all his evidence.

"But," said Hadley, with a soft, triumphant emphasis, "look at what happens even by Eleanor's own testimony to us. In the ordinary course of things she would have gone up to Hastings on the roof and Ames would have got his evidence. But she reached the door upstairs—and discovered she didn't have the key, which she had mislaid downstairs..."

"Blast your evidence!" growled Dr. Fell. "I'm afraid you're right about her coming downstairs, as she said. But..."

"Ames unexpectedly hears her coming; you'll notice," put in Hadley, setting his foot on the creaky floor, "how they don't have the thick carpet here at the back of the house, or in the hall here. He turns out the light and ducks for cover; under the bed, behind the door—you'll have noticed they all open inwards—anywhere. She comes in to look for her mislaid key, finds it, and suddenly realizes that somebody's been ransacking the room. The most skilful searcher can't do it without leaving a trace, you know. Well, naturally, what does she do? Remembering that police officer, she goes instantly to her secret panel, and opens it to see...

"While her back is turned, Ames, quiet in his tennis shoes but not at all noiseless, gets out of the room. Not quickly enough. She's not going to set up an alarm; she knows quite well it's no burglar and that she's utterly lost if an alarm is given. But this cobra of ours, who snatched the first convenient weapon when she was in danger at Gamridge's, does now exactly what she did then! Right in front of her is the heavy, sharp clockhand of the pair she stole for Christopher Paull, and the gloves she used to avoid getting wet paint on her fingers. And she snatches them.

"But what about Ames? That's what I'm coming to.

219

Have you realized his difficulty? He would probably have had time to duck out the front door and run for it. He wasn't afraid of her. But the danger was—from his viewpoint, since he didn't think anybody knew him for a detective—that she might believe he was a real burglar and set up an alarm. In case of capture, he could exonerate himself; but he would give the Force a nasty black eye for illegal methods, possibly get himself sacked, and certainly let his quarry know she was his quarry prematurely! He couldn't afford capture. And, alarm or no alarm, the surest way to capture lay straight out that front door. He knew that just at that time, just at midnight, there would be a policeman making his round smack outside that door. And any copper who sees a seedy vagrant, in the full light of a street lamp, slipping out of a dark house at midnight . . .

"On the other hand, she might not have seen him at all. She might not even be positive of a burglar, since nothing was taken and (he hoped) nothing disturbed. In either event, to run was foolishness. His best course, and in fact his only course, was—well, gentlemen of the jury?" Hadley suggested.

Melson blinked.

"Eh? Yes, certainly," he admitted. "His best course was to stand out on the doorstep boldly punching Boscombe's bell."

There was a pause. This time it was Hadley who chuckled.

"Exactly. If the copper came along, there he was honestly ringing the bell for an appointment he could prove. If a wide-eyed woman rushed out: 'Burglar, madam? Do you think if I had burgled your room I should be here ringing the bell? I saw somebody come out of here, I saw the door wide open, and I've been trying to rouse you.' So there he stood, with the door

220

wide open, waiting to see if she would come out. If she didn't, it meant he hadn't been seen. Then he could go straight in again, up to his appointment, and later have a shot at the interrupted search."

Dr. Fell hitched his cloak round his shoulders.

"H'mf. Has the learned gentleman," he said, "got any corroborative evidence for his Arsène Lupin episode?"

"The learned gentleman has. Don't you remember for what a *long time* he kept punching that bell (as Hastings told us), even though he'd been told to come up straightaway? He was seeing if the coast was clear. Do you remember that you yourself found the front door *wide open* when you went up with the constable who spotted it? He'd have closed it, naturally, unless he wanted to make sure nobody charged down on him in the dark.

"Now let's go back to our pet cobra. She's come out into that dark hall with the knife and the gloves. And there the enemy is, silhouetted on the street lamp, ringing the doorbell and summoning aid. It must have been the most horrible moment she ever had. If she doesn't act she's caught. If she does act, she's apt to be seen in the act of murder with a stolen clock-hand. She could risk killing him—stabbing him as a burglar who got in—if only he actually would get into the house. Or does she even dare risk that? She's got to do something before there's an answer to that bell. Now he's coming in. Now he's walking across the hall, while she's back under the staircase. Now he starts upstairs—

"And she's got him."

Hadley ended with a sort of pounce and jerk in his words, clenching one fist. He looked at Melson as though every sentence were a blow to avenge the Force.

"Lastly," he said, "and in case you accuse an old salt

like myself of romancing, I'll offer you the final, the absolute, the sealing proof. I'll do that by explaining what you, Fell, tried to ridicule as 'The Mystery of the Flying Glove.' It only occurred to me when I examined that staircase a little while ago, and remembered something I was too blind to see before. But I can explain to you the flying glove and why it flew. Look at it."

He took from his pocket the glove which Christopher Paull had said was lying in the upper hallway, and smoothed it out on his knee.

"Now imagine that you are in Eleanor Carver's place, creeping up those stairs behind Ames. Instinctively she has taken both gloves, but she wears only one. In one hand she has glove and clock-hand; in the other the second glove, into the finger of which, with a gesture to get rid of it, she has dropped the key she has automatically kept from the first. On her left is the wall, on her right the banister rail. Got it?

"Right! At the second tread from the top—where the stains begin—she bears forward with her weight on Ames's back and strikes. The weight carries him nearly to his knees. He instinctively throws up both hands; she throws up her free hand to keep her balance, automatically loosening her grip on the free glove. There is blood. His arm, jerked up, sends the loose glove spinning over the top handrail into the hall . . ."

Melson leaned forward.

"But, my God, man!" he cried, and the academic calm cracked to bits, "in that case her free hand must have been on the right-hand side!"

"And this," said Hadley, "is the right-hand glove. Exactly. This is not the hand that gripped that knife. On this glove the only blood-stain is directly down the palm: a place it could never have been if the hand had been closed tightly round that steel shaft. Therefore—"

He brought his fist slowly down on the footboard of the bed.

"—therefore you see why the angle of the blow carried Ames so much to the right. You understand the statement of the witnesses who saw the shopwalker murdered at Gamridge's: 'We were standing to the *right* of her at one side, when the shopwalker came past us and touched her arm. She reached over with her *other hand* and seized the carving knife.' . . . It means, gentlemen, that the Gamridge murderess was left-handed. And, by the incontrovertible evidence before you, Eleanor Carver is left-handed too."

He rose, went to the fireplace, and knocked out his pipe on the marble edge. Hadley took pride in himself as a relentless logician who was not above a crackle of drama. Smiling grimly, he leaned his elbow on the mantelpiece and looked at them.

"Any questions, gentlemen?" he enquired.

Dr. Fell started to say something, changed his mind, and said:

"Not bad, Hadley. 'What men and what horses against you shall bide, when the stars in their courses do fight on your side?' Humph. Bucephalus has become Pegasus all of a sudden. Man, you talk fine! And yet somehow I'm always suspicious—highly suspicious—of those cases which depend on somebody's being left-handed. It's a little too easy. . . . Just one question. If all this is true, then what becomes of the mysterious figure on the roof that Hastings saw: the figure with gilt paint on its hands? Do you think Hastings was lying?"

Hadley put down his pipe with the air of one who remembers something.

"The handkerchief!" he muttered. "By Jove! I've been carrying it about all morning, ever since I found you looking at watches with Carver."

223

"What handkerchief?"

"Mrs. Steffins's. I didn't tell you, did I?" He took out of a separate envelope a crumpled cambric handkerchief thick with that substance which was cloying Melson's very thoughts by this time. "No, don't stare. This is only the gold oilpaint she used for her china and pottery painting. It has nothing to do with the other stuff. Preston found it shoved far down in the bottom of a laundry-bag in her room. But the stuff's fresh; as fresh as last night.

"Our good friend Steffins was undoubtedly the watcher on the roof. She went up from her own room, which opens on that hidden staircase in Carver's alcove, up the other staircase to investigate this romance on the roof which everybody else seems to have known about.

"Remember that she was fully dressed. Remember also that tube of paint I told you about?—the one squashed *at the top* , as though somebody had put a hand down on it. That's exactly what happened, because it was dark. She went out of her room in the dark, and leaned on that tube of paint while she was blundering about. She wiped her hand on a handkerchief, not realizing how much she'd accumulated in the darkness, and tumbled up hastily to see the evil things on the roof. There she accidentally walked into Hastings at the height of the terror downstairs. The paint on her hand put the wind up him—he ran for the tree, with what results we know. She saw him fall and saw Lucia find him, over the edge of the roof; else how did she know he was in her room? (You remember she called our attention to it the instant I arrived.) Then she blundered downstairs, saw in the light how much paint she'd put on her hand, and had a wash. She shoved the handkerchief into the laundry-bag and prepared to have hysterics before all the high gods if anybody gave her a sinister look . . . Does that strike you as reasonable?"

Dr. Fell uttered a mysterious noise which might be interpreted as either agreement or dissent.

"But that," the chief inspector went on, "is not my chief consideration now. I have stated the case of Rex *v.* Eleanor Carver. This morning you outlined a list of five points or questions in connection with the evidence, and I have answered every one of them. I have done this in spite of your sneering at all the visual evidence: the stolen articles in her possession, the hour-hand of the clock, the blood-stained gloves. I have provided not only concrete evidence, but motive, opportunity, and temperament of the accused; and I have provided the only explanation which satisfactorily fits *all* these conflicting facts. I therefore claim that the evidence leaves no reasonable doubt as to the guilt of Eleanor Carver. You have said you'll tear my evidence to blue tatters, but you haven't a fact to call your own. That, me lord and gentlemen," said Hadley, with a broad smile, "is the case for the Crown. Now break it if you can."

He mockingly sat down. And Dr. Fell, hitching his cloak about his shoulders, rose for the defense.

# 18

## The Case for the Defence

"Me lord," said Dr. Fell, inclining his head absently towards the Krazy Kat on the mantlepiece, "and gentlemen of the jury."

He cleared his throat with a rumbling noise like a battle cry. He hitched his cloak across his shoulders and took up a position facing the bed. With this cloak, and his heavy grey-streaked mop of hair disarranged, he looked rather like an over-fat barrister squaring himself for battle.

"Me lord and gentlemen," he continued, settling his eyeglasses more firmly and looking over the tops of them. "To an unprejudiced listener, it might well seem that on every hand chance and coincidence have conspired to deliver over to my learned friend every corroborative fact and detail necessary for his case; whilst to me, on the other hand, they would appear to have delivered only what might be described in vulgar circles as a kick in the pants. His success in this respect is almost uncanny. He has only to seek for one clue, and he finds six. He has only to open his mouth to hazard a theory, and instantly somebody walks in that door and confirms it. I do not like this. I do not believe that even a really guilty person could leave *so much* damning evidence behind her if she strewed the pavement with clues from here to the Elephant and Castle. I persist in regarding this affair as a murder case and not a paper-chase. And it is on a deduction drawn from this belief that I base my case."

"Hear, hear!" said Hadley, encouragingly.

"And," pursued Dr. Fell, imperturbably, "if my learned friend will consent to stow it and shut his fat head for a brief time, this defence I shall proceed to elaborate. To begin with. Gentlemen, it is a well-known rule in poultry-farming—"

"Now look here," expostulated Hadley, getting up. "You can have all the latitude you like. But I object to your making a farce of this thing. In the first place, I haven't time for jokes, and, even if I had, it seems to me pretty bad taste when a man has really been murdered and somebody's life is concerned. If you have anything to say, say it; but at least have the decency to be serious."

Dr. Fell removed his eyeglasses. Then he dropped his judicial manner and spoke very quietly.

"You don't see it, do you? You won't believe me if I tell you I was never more desperately serious in my life? I am trying to keep that girl from being arrested, if nothing worse—and, incidentally, save your own official head—in the only way you'll understand it—by showing you what you're up against. I'm no authority on law. But I do know a good deal about lawyers and their methods. And I'll show you what a man like Gordon-Bates or Sir George Carnahan, if they brief him,

227

would do to your poor old case when you presented it. I may be wrong. But God knows I was never more practical."

"Very well. Carry on, then," muttered Hadley. He seemed uneasy.

"It is a well-known rule in poultry-farming," resumed Dr. Fell, his voice trumpeting out again as he squared himself, "to avoid two errors which have since become axiomatic, thus: (a) Do not put all your eggs in one basket, and (b) Do not count your chickens before they are hatched. The prosecution has done both, which is a fatal bloomer. The prosecution has made its two charges interchangeable. If this woman killed Evan Manders, she also killed George Ames. If this woman killed George Ames, she also killed Evan Manders. Each charge is built on the other and is a part of it. We have only to throw a reasonable doubt on one of them, and we therefore discredit both.

"For example, we have this glove, the right-hand glove. The prosecution states that this glove could not have been worn on the hand that stabbed Ames. From the wound, as we saw, there was an effusion of blood which would have saturated it; whereas on this glove there is not only a very small blood-stain, but a stain placed in such a position that my learned friend flatly states it could not have been there had this hand held the weapon. Good! My learned friend produces evidence definitely to show that the Gamridge murderess was left-handed. Since Eleanor Carver in killing Ames must have struck with the left-hand glove, then the two killers are one and the same.

"That," said Dr. Fell expansively, and nodded his big head, "is what I call putting all the eggs into one basket. Whereas this"—he lumbered over to the panel in the wall, opened the shoe-box, took out the left-hand glove, and, whirling round, flung it on the bed. "This is what I call counting chickens before they are hatched. There is the glove which the prosecution alleges must have been used in the murder. But examine it, gentlemen, and you will find not one single spot or speck of blood upon it. My learned friend states that the blow could not possibly have been struck without a quantity of blood. Therefore—by the prosecution's own reasoning—we prove (1) that Eleanor Carver is not left-handed like the Gamridge murderess, and (2) *that in the murder of Inspector Ames neither of these gloves could have been used at all.*"

Hadley rose from his seat as though in a process of astral levitation. He seized the glove from the bed and stared at Dr. Fell. . . .

"We wish all this to be understood," the doctor thundered, "because this time the prosecution is jolly well not going to have it both ways. At this late date my learned friend is not going to say that he meant something else, and that the right-hand glove was really used, after all. He himself proved that it wasn't. And I have proved the impossibility of left-handedness. If the free right-hand glove got a splash of blood when it was several feet away from the wound, then—to put it mildly—we must demand that the prosecution show us at least some microscopic trace on the hand that made the wound. There is none. Therefore Eleanor Carver didn't kill Ames. Therefore she wasn't the left-handed woman who stabbed Evan Manders. And those gloves, the only real *personal* evidence against her, must be disregarded when the prosecution's whole case crashes down under the weight of its own logic."

To show he was far from finished, Dr. Fell added, "Ahem!" as he took out the red bandanna to mop his forehead. Then he beamed.

"Stop a bit," said Hadley, with dogged quietness.

"Perhaps I've betrayed myself—a bit. Maybe in the excitement of building up a case (which was only a skeleton outline, as I told you) I may have gone a little too far. But these other pieces of real evidence . . ."

"Me lord and gentlemen," pursued Dr. Fell, thrusting the bandanna back into his pocket. "So instantly is the prosecution adopting the attitude I prophesied it would, that I need not point out how damaged its case has become. But let me proceed. The other side itself has proved she did not use the gloves. But one was found near the body, and another behind that panel. If she did not put them there, it follows that somebody else did—with the sole purpose of getting her hanged—and this I shall attempt to prove.

"In considering these other 'pieces of real evidence' against her, I shall first deal with the Gamridge murder. As somebody has mentioned, I have outlined five points to be considered in connection with these two crimes. . . . Harrumph. Gimme that envelope, Melson. So. . . . And, when I come to discuss them, I shall ask leave to take them backwards."

He looked about suspiciously over his glasses, but there was no hint of a jeer. Hadley sat with the glove in his hand, chewing at the stem of a dead pipe.

"Since we have disproved the charge of left-handedness, the only definite one, what remains to connect Eleanor Carver with the Gamridge murderess? That she was probably a blonde (one says a brunette, but let that pass), that she was young, and that she wore clothes common to most women. This rouses my amazement, not to say my mirth. In other words, it is the very *indefiniteness* of the description which you use to prove it was Eleanor Carver. You say that the murderess must have been a certain women solely on the grounds that there are so many other women in London who look

230

like her. It is as though you said John Doe was infallibly guilty of the Leeds scarf-murder because the man seen sneaking away from the scene of the crime might just as well have been somebody else. Second, you have Eleanor's own admission that she was at Gamridge's that afternoon; which does not sound like the admission either of a murderess or of Eleanor Carver as you have painted her character as a murderess. But I will tell you what it does sound like. It sounds like the effort of somebody who knew she was there that afternoon; who noted the superficial resemblance to her in the newspaper accounts and knew there could be no positive identification; who read a description of the stolen articles and saw that, with one exception, they could not positively be identified, either—to saddle her with the crime."

"Hold on!" interposed Hadley. "This is getting fantastic. Granting that the witnesses couldn't positively identify her, we *have* the stolen articles. There they are in front of you."

"You think they're unique?"

"Unique?"

"You have a bracelet and a pair of ear-rings. Do you think that you couldn't walk into Gamridge's at this moment and buy twenty exact duplicates of those two articles? They're not unique; they're turned out in lots of which no individual bracelet or ring could be absolutely identified as the one stolen on the twenty-seventh of August. You wouldn't think of arresting every woman you saw wearing one of them. No, my boy. There is only one of the stolen articles that could be identified beyond doubt—namely, the seventeenth-century watch of Carver's in the Gamridge display. That is unique. That, and that alone, would infallibly point to Eleanor Carver. And it is very significant," said Dr.

Fell, "that it is the only one of the stolen articles you have not got."

Hadley put his hands to his forehead.

"Do you expect me to believe," he demanded, "that two exact duplicates of the stolen articles happened to be hidden behind that panel by accident?"

"Not by accident. By deliberate design. I am gradually trying to show my learned friend," snapped Dr. Fell, bringing his fist down on the mantel-shelf, "that all the coincidences which trip and befog us have not been coincidences at all. Everything led to it. Eleanor's kleptomaniac tendencies were well known; that was what gave the murderer the idea. He (or she) saw a chance all planned in the Gamridge crime. The loose description of the killer fitted Eleanor; Eleanor was at the store; Eleanor could prove no alibi. But it required a lot of evidence. That was why the person behind this whole damnable design tried to add to it by pinching the Maurer skull-watch out of Boscombe's box. Boscombe was intended to believe she had stolen it—because this devil knew Boscombe would cover her up. You were intended to believe she had stolen it—because you would not believe any story Boscombe told to account for its disappearance. And both of you tumbled straight into the trap. Now, let's go on with these 'real pieces of evidence' you have against her. I've pointed out that the only real piece of evidence, the unique watch that really could damn Eleanor, is missing. Why is it missing? Surely if somebody wanted to put the blame on Eleanor that watch would be the one thing he (or she) would be absolutely certain to 'plant' behind the panel. But it isn't there. And the only tenable hypothesis to account for its absence—whether you still think Eleanor guilty, or whether you believe in my own theory—is that nobody put it there *because nobody had it to put there.*

"I asked you in my fifth point," thundered Dr. Fell, looking at the envelope in his hand, "about that. Melson's note reads: 'The department-store murderer did not steal a watch belonging to Carver when the theft must have been easier at home, but took the dangerous risk of stealing it out of a display in a crowded department store.' Well, why?—Surely it's obvious. The mad impulse did not come over a woman in this house to steal a watch they all must have seen dozens of times before. The mad impulse came to somebody else. The mad impulse came, in fact, to some woman who does not live in this house; some woman of whom we have probably never heard; some woman we may probably never hear of in her hidden namelessness among eight million people! That is the department-store killer. The devil in this house merely used her crime; used it as a lead to spin up the insufficient evidence against Eleanor to bring the police on Eleanor's track, and then murdered the police officer who had been summoned amid faked evidence that should send Eleanor to the scaffold for both crimes!"

Hadley was so excited that he hurled his briefcase on the floor and faced Dr. Fell wildly.

"I don't believe it!" he shouted. "This is some of your damned rhetoric. It's sheer theory, and rotten theory at that. You can't prove it! You can't accuse somebody you can't even prove exists! You—"

"Have I got you on the run?" asked Dr. Fell, grimly. "At least I think you're worried. Why don't you look at that bracelet and that skull-watch and see if there's a single fingerprint on the whole polished surface of either? You say Eleanor thought that panel was safe: then there'll be dozens of her prints on both, if that's true. But it's not. There won't be any at all—that was one thing the evidence-faker couldn't manage. Man, do you understand now why you had only to seek for one clue to find six? Do you understand why you had only to open your mouth to hazard a theory, and somebody walked in that door and confirmed it? Then you know why this case frightened me and why I can believe in evil spirits. There's a real evil spirit here, who hates that girl with a patient, deadly, brilliant guile, hates her as a galley-slave hated the whipmaster and failure hates success. The whole design was to weave a rope for her neck and crack that neck, as somebody would like to do between two hands. . . . Now shall I go on, or are you afraid to hear my case?"

"You still can't prove—" began Hadley, but not loudly. He picked up his briefcase and his voice was growing thoughtful.

"Go on," said Melson, whose dogged hand kept on making notes.

Dr. Fell, wheezing heavily, stood looking from one to the other of them, his face more red and his thumb hooked in the armhole of his vast waistcoat. Beyond him the grey light through the windows showed the dreariness of sky and back yard. He went on more quietly:

"So, in taking those five points backwards, I come to the fourth. That is the recurring, vexing question of why both clock-hands were stolen and why they were not stolen when the clock was exposed. I will tell you why it was done. It was done because all evidence had to point to Eleanor as the murderer of Ames. Merely to steal one clock-hand did not point to anybody. But the hour-hand, the superfluous hand which could not be used as a weapon and whose removal was a pure waste of time—it had to be found in Eleanor's possession, as clear evidence of the thief. This also, but to a greater extent, was the reason for waiting until Wednesday night to steal the hands. It seems to have occurred to nobody here that the thief waited until Wednesday night because not until then had the clock been *painted with gilt*.

"Hasn't my learned friend realized the utter simplicity of that? The whole case is a track of gilt paint! It was meant to be. Where would have been your evidence against Eleanor as Ames's murderer if it had not been for those gold smears ostentatiously plastered over a pair of her gloves, one of them hidden behind the panel, and the other thrown down not too ostentatiously close to the dead man? And, if you care for further confirmation, consider that matter of the key. The real murderer had to steal that key from her. That little key, gentlemen, was the most important thing in the whole plan, because the plan would have been impossible without it. Eleanor was required to turn in early, and would have no alibi for any night you might choose—*unless* she went up to see her lover on the roof. That must be made impossible. She must be trapped without being able to get through that door. And, when the murderer had no further use for the key, it was returned to the finger of the glove to score another crushing point against her."

Hadley interposed with some haste:

"Admitting all this for a second . . . which I don't, mind; but admitting it as a hypothesis . . . then what about the gloves? Hang it! The more I think of it the more I realize how much depends on those gloves! You seem to have proved that neither one of 'em was used—"

"H'mf, yes. That bothers you, don't it, hey?" The doctor chuckled, and then became very grave. "But the fact is I'm not telling you what did happen. I'm only telling you what didn't. No, no. It's not yet time for me to indicate to you who the real murderer is."

Hadley's jaw came out. "You think not, eh? And yet

you're trying to convince me? By God! this isn't the time for your own brand of parlor mystification! I still think I'm right—"

"No, not altogether. At least I don't think so," replied Dr. Fell, studying him with sombre attention. "I've shaken you, but you're in just that uncertain state when I don't dare set out my whole case." He saw the chief inspector opening and shutting nervous hands, and a real ring and thunder of earnestness came into his voice. "Man, this isn't parlor mystification! I give you my word I'm much too worried for my usual observe-gentlemen-there's-nothing-up-my-sleeve tactics. I don't *dare* tell you, or I would. You're in such a state that you'd rush out and try to verify it. We're facing the wiliest devil under an inoffensive mask that I ever hope to be pitted against. One word dropped—then the slippery enemy speaks in return, and in your present state you'll sweep away everything I've worked to build up, and go roaring after Eleanor again.

"Listen, Hadley." He swabbed fiercely at his forehead. "To follow it up, to drive the battering-ram into that brave skull of yours, continue on with my point number three, which reads:

"'The whole accusation and case against one of these women for murdering Evan Manders comes from an unidentified person, who now under circumstances of the strongest pressure refuses to communicate with us.'

"Precisely. That's the core and secret of the whole scheme. Ponder those words deeply while I analyse 'em. What explanation can anybody give of this? The prosecution says, 'Because that accuser was Mrs. Steffins. While hating Eleanor and wishing to reveal her as a murderess, she nevertheless refused to testify openly because she feared old Carver's wrath at an accusation of old Carver's favourite.' I submit that no-

236

body in his five wits could believe this for a moment—
even those who still believed Eleanor guilty. What does
Ames's own report say? It says, ' Informant was quite
willing to testify in the witness-box to the above statements.'

"In the witness-box, you perceive. It's like saying
that you have a secret which you are afraid to whisper
in your own home, but on the other hand you have no
objection to hearing it broadcast over the wireless. If
there were things of which she feared the effect on
Carver when uttered in private, they would scarcely
be rendered more soothing when she spoke them in
open court.

"Hadley, I said there were several things that
sounded very fishy about Ames's report. That's one of
them. Say, if you like, that Mrs. Steffins was the accuser—but in that case you must say she was also the
murderer. Whoever told Ames that whole tissue of lies
did it for only one purpose—to lure Ames to his death
in that house. That person, as Ames says, testified to
having seen in the accused's possession . . . Eleanor
Carver's possession, if Ames hadn't been so secretive,
and it would have built another plank in the girl's scaffold . . . to having seen 'the watch in Gamridge's display
loaned by J. Carver.' Nothing else would have interested Ames. Well, where is that watch? It's not here,
along with the rest of the carefully prepared evidence.
It never was here. It was bait for Ames, intended as a
literal death-watch for him as the Maurer skull was to
be a death-watch for Eleanor. What else did the accuser
see? Eleanor burning a pair of blood-stained kid gloves
on the evening of the Gamridge murder. Hadley, did
you ever try burning kid gloves? The next time you
make a bonfire in your back garden, have a shot at it;
but it would be an extraordinary woman who carried

237

those damning trophies all the way back from Oxford Street and spent the next twelve hours over a roaring blaze patiently reducing tanned leather to ashes. . . . Read Ames's report again. Study the inconsistencies, the too-canny behaviour of the accuser, the insistence on secrecy, the contradiction in the accuser's being willing to tell all this but jibbing at the small point (apparently) of openly introducing Ames into the house. And you will see that there can be only one explanation.

"So we come at as last to the beginning. My second point indicates that the murderer of Ames was not the same as the Gamridge killer, for the reasons I have given. My first point indicates the crux of the case and the whole conclusion to which we were intended to be led: that, if we accepted all other alibis, the weight of suspicion must rest on either Lucia Handreth or Eleanor Carver. Even this could be reduced, and was almost instantly reduced, to a certainty when the Handreth woman produced an alibi too strong to be even attacked. Then I was sure. Eleanor and Eleanor alone was to be the victim of one of the most ingenious and devilish murder-plots within my memory.

"Me lord and gentlemen!" He straightened up, and brought his hand down flatly on the mantel-shelf. "In conclusion, there are several things which the defence cheerfully acknowledges. Nobody has been kind enough to fake evidence for us as has been done for my learned friend. Therefore we are to rely only on truth, and, having neither magical properties nor the cooperation of the police, we cannot produce the real Gamridge killer. We can set forth no 'hard facts' which turn to thistledown under scrutiny. We can tell no rambling tale of police officers who ring bells on their way *out* of a house, and, within two minutes of being caught rifling somebody's room, blithely walk in again for the convenience of a killer waiting in the dark. We do not picture a killer so sartorially fastidious as to carry about two gloves when she needs only one, and then inexplicably fails to use either. It is even difficult for us to imagine a police officer, on the alert for danger, walking up twenty-three steps without ever a suspicion of somebody treading on his heels. But let that pass. What we *have* wished to do is to throw a reasonable doubt on the prosecution's case, the one little grain of uncertainty which must force you to bring in a verdict of 'not guilty'; and I submit, gentlemen, that we have done so."

Both Hadley and Melson were so much on edge that they jumped and whirled round when the door banged open without a knock. Sergeant Preston said sharply: "I don't want to make a mistake this time, sir. But I think she's coming up the front steps now. She's trying to keep off the reporters, and there's a young fellow with her who's got his head bandaged. Shall I—?"

Swift dull-coloured clouds made more shadowy the grey room, and wind had begun to mutter in the chimney. Hadley stood facing Dr. Fell. Both were erect, and looked each other in the eye while Melson heard his watch ticking loudly. Every nerve-force in the room was locked and fighting between them.

"Well?" said Dr. Fell. He moved his elbow backwards on the mantel, and one of the framed photos toppled over with a tinny crash.

Hadley moved forward swiftly. He rolled up the articles on the bed in the old jumper, thrust it all into the opening, and shut the panel.

"All right," he said, in a heavy voice. "All right. No good alarming her if she didn't do it. . . ."

Then his voice rose. "Where the hell is Betts? Don't let her talk to the press! Why isn't Betts out there taking care of—?"

239

Through an almost sickening sense of relief Melson heard the sergeant say: "He's been on the telephone for ten minutes, sir. I don't know what it is. . . . Ah!"

There was a tramp of hurried footsteps. Betts, still stolid, but with his hands shaking a little, pushed Preston to one side and closed the door.

"Sir—" he began, rather huskily.

"What is it? Speak out, can't you?"

"Call from the Yard, sir. It's rather important. The Assistant Commissioner. . . . I don't think we can get that warrant even if we want it. They've found the woman who did the Gamridge job."

Hadley did not speak, but his fingers tightened on his briefcase.

"Yes, sir. It's—it's somebody we know. She tried a raid on Harris' Stores this morning, and they nabbed her. Marble Arch Division says there's no doubt about it. When they took her home, they found about half the jewellery and the rest of the stuff stolen in all the raids for some time. When they found that watch—the one Mr. Carver owns—she broke down and tried to throw herself out of the window. The finger-print comparison showed who she was. They nabbed one of her accomplices, too, but the other . . ."

"*Who is it?*"

"Well, sir, nowadays she goes under the name of Helen Gray. It's a systematic business; she works the big stores and gets rid of the stuff through a fence. She always has two men accomplices to cover her—"

He stopped, probably at the curious expressions on the faces before him. Again it was very quiet. There was a scrape and creak of boards as Hadley stepped back. Breathing heavily, he looked round at Dr. Fell. And across Dr. Fell's face spread a Jovian serenity which slowly broadened into a vast sleepy smile. He hitched his cloak across his shoulders. Clearing his throat, he lumbered out from the fireplace, turned, and swept the Krazy Kat a great bow.

"Me lord," said Dr. Fell in a ringing voice, "the defence rests."

# 19

## Sequel in a Tavern

In the bar of the "Duchess of Portsmouth" tavern, which is in the curve of the little backwater called Portsmouth Street, there is still talk of a lunch given in the smoky, low-raftered back dining-room one afternoon early in September. The lunch was given by a certain enormously fat gentleman to four guests. It lasted from half-past one until a quarter-past four. It was noted not merely for its size—although the stout gentleman himself consumed a steak and kidney pie nearly as big as a washbowl . . . but also for its hilarious noise. The stout gentleman stuck his head into the bar, removed a shovel-hat, and announced that all the drinks for the *habitués* there assembled were on him. He made a speech to the company, which contained incomprehensible references to having his enemy by the hip, or some such nonsense; but it was roundly applauded until a companion of his, tall chap with a military cut, came hurrying in and hauled him away, amid protests from the company.

That lunch was always a pleasant memory to Melson. But what he best remembered was a little scene that preceded it, while Eleanor and Donald Hastings were studying the menu in the dining-room, and the other three had adjourned to the private bar to moisten their sandy throats with a quick one before the beer-drinking. Dr. Fell looked at Hadley, and Hadley looked at Dr. Fell. But neither spoke until the doctor had emitted an expiring and satisfied "Haaa!" as he put down his glass.

"And the beauty of the circumstance," said he, bringing down his first on the bar in admiration, "is the way both of us used the testimony of Gray and her two accomplices—false testimony, to divert suspicion from Gray's own crime. You used lies to condemn Eleanor, and I used the same lies to defend her. Of course we believed Gray. Why not? There were three apparently unrelated people, disinterested onlookers, who all told the same tale. Gray didn't run. She simply dropped the knife, cried out, pointed to a phantom, told an expert lie . . . and was backed up. Why she should have lost her head and stabbed Manders—"

Hadley stared at his glass and swirled round its contents. "Well, it meant certain prison if they took her up on suspicion and compared finger-prints with the files. All the same, it was a fool trick. She'll hang, for a certainty, and maybe the others with her." He scowled. "What interests me is that it's a new trick in super-shoplifting. If anybody grew suspicious, up stepped a fashionably dressed young man. 'You thought you saw this lady—? Nonsense! I was watching her myself, and—' Snuffy-looking respectable man on the other side also shakes his head and timidly agrees. Gray thanks them and departs in a huff before authority can be summoned. Not bad! Costume jewellery at twenty quid a time . . . they must have cleaned up a couple of

243

thousand in a fortnight. The shopwalker'd probably spotted her before, and wasn't going to have any nonsense. If she hadn't lost her head . . ." He set down the glass with a thump. "Oh, yes. We believed her. But now that I come to think of it . . ."

"*Arrière pensée*," agreed Dr. Fell, nodding guiltily. "Yes, I'd thought of that, too."

"Thought of what?"

"That statement which seemed to prove the killer was left-handed. Gray never meant to say that, in all probability. It was a slip in her dramatic recital. 'The shopwalker came up, she reached across with her *other* hand,' and the rest of it. That's the sort of slip that would occur in a hastily constructed lie. She didn't *say* the woman was left-handed. Nobody thought of it or even interpreted it until—hem!"

"All right, all right! Rub it in."

"It was also an excellent touch about the blouse," Dr. Fell pursued, affably. "I'm not rubbing it in. If it's any satisfaction to you, it deceived the old man completely; although I did think it was a bit odd that, although Gray was close enough to tear the blouse, she never saw the girl's face. Humph. She stuffed her gloves in her pocket and waited as coolly as you please. That testimony of hers about the killer wearing gloves—also in the papers—was another hint to our Lincoln's Inn Fields murderer. . . . No, Hadley, the only 'I-told-you-so' that the old man can rake up out of the whole mess is my warning to beware of cases that rest on somebody's being left-handed. They're all fishy. Walk the path of the prudent, and have no traffic with the left-handed blow, the discarded cigarette-end, and the dictaphone behind the door."

"Eleanor's not left-handed, by the way," Hadley observed, musingly. "I asked her to write down her employer's address." His exasperation and bewilderment grew. "The whole thing is, what the devil are we going to do *now*?"

He got no satisfaction, Dr. Fell merely saying that there would be copious talk in good time. Since the corroboration of his defence he had been unusually silent. Before they left the house he borrowed from Hadley one of the keys to the landing-door; nobody went up with him, but he said he wanted a look at the bolt on the trap-door and seemed in unusually good spirits when he returned. He made, however, one good suggestion. When the harassed chief inspector wondered how they should approach Eleanor in the present situation, he outlined a plan which met with Hadley's entire approval.

"Why, we'll take her to lunch, of course; and young Hastings with her," he said. "I have a little experiment in mind."

"Experiment?"

"Like this. Everybody in the house probably knows by this time that you meant to arrest Eleanor. Even if the Handreth woman keeps quiet, there's Mrs. Gorson. The odds are Steffins got it out of her, and what Steffins knows everybody else knows. Good! So much the better! Let 'em go on thinking that. We'll go out and, in a loud voice, invite Eleanor to lunch; she's been out, knows nothing, and won't suspect any sinister sound we put into it. The others will: they'll have only one interpretation. We then go to lunch, where we can explain things to her and see what she has to say about it herself. Afterwards we return—without Eleanor. We interview each member of the household, telling them first that she has been taken into custody, and then flatly announcing that she has been released because the case against her has been broken down beyond any doubt. Hey? Man, I shall be very much interested in watching somebody's face when we spring that latter announcement. It's going to give somebody a horrible jolt, and from then on will be the crucial time of the whole affair."

"Good!" said Hadley. "Damned good! But suppose somebody cuts up a row or interferes when we leave the house with her?"

"We simply insist that we're going to lunch. It's the only way to make 'em believe we're not."

Nobody did interfere, which surprised Melson. He had expected to find Mrs. Steffins flying out from a dark corner like a jack-in-the-box, and flinging the straight question. But nobody was even in sight. It gave Melson a curiously ghost-like feeling in the quiet house; nobody stirred, but he felt that several people were standing motionless against their closed doors, listening. You could hear the crackle of coal fires, but no footsteps . . .

The lunch, at which nobody mentioned the business in hand for at least the first two hours, was a great success. Dr. Fell, as indicated, was in a hilarious mood; even Hadley unbent, although he treated Eleanor with a fumbling and exaggerated politeness and could not seem to keep his eyes off her. For the first time Melson heard Hadley laugh. He even told a mild anecdote from the many current concerning a certain celebrated film-actress whose broad charms were attracting attention, and showed all his teeth with unexpected mirth. Both Eleanor and Hastings were exuberant. They had, she told Dr. Fell, reached a decision.

"I'm leaving that place," she said, "as soon as I can manage it. I told you I'd been a sentimental fool long enough, and I meant it. And then everything will be wonderful, unless the police make a row about my leaving? They won't will they?"

"Haah!" said Dr. Fell, his glowing face dawning from behind a large pewter tankard. "Make a row? No, I shouldn't think so. Haah! Have you made any plans?"

The long, low room, with its bright fire and blue-painted Dutch tiles round the fireplace, had windows with crooked panes looking out on the trees of a garden. *Rus in urbe*, where no sound of traffic came to disturb their own noise. The room had that half-pleasant dampness which brings out the smell of old wood, and beer, and three centuries of steaming roast beef. Melson was content. Like a sensible person, he preferred well-cooked roast beef and full-bodied bitter ale to any other delicacies by the gods conceived; he felt a deep pleasure in the raftered ceiling, the sawdust on the wrinkled board floor, the tall-backed oak benches. The wood of the benches was also wrinkled, and against it Eleanor Carver's prettiness—not beauty, but lusty prettiness—stood out vividly. Her manner was not subdued, but she had not the hysteria of last night. About her was the deep pleasure of a decision reached and ceasing to weigh on the thoughts. Melson studied the pale-blue eyes, their lids slightly lifted at the outer corners, and set rather wide apart; the full earnest lips which could suddenly twitch with laughter; the long bobbed hair that was duskily gold. Beside her sat Hastings, whose clothes were no longer a wreck and whose good-looking if somewhat immature face was more human in the absence of iodine. Both were having the devil of a good time. They looked frequently at each other, and laughed, and both, at Dr. Fell's roaring insistence, were absorbing a good deal of the strong ale.

"Plans?" she repeated, wrinkling up her forehead. "Only that we're going to get married, which is absolutely mad, but Don says—"

"Who gives a damn?" enquired Hastings, affably, and

thereby summed up his whole philosophy. He set down his tankard with a thump. "We can manage somehow. Besides, we should still be starving during the first six years even after I passed my examinations. The law! The law be blowed! I've got an idea that what I ought to go in for is insurance. Look here, sir. Don't you agree with me that insurance is the coming thing; the only thing for a man who——"

"You will *not*," announced Eleanor, setting her lips.

"Ho-ho-ho," said the other. He became confidential. "The whole thing is this . . ." Then he broke off, looking curiously at Dr. Fell, who was shedding the effulgence of his being radiantly over them like the Ghost of the Christmas Present. "I say, sir, it's funny. To be absolutely frank, I've always hated coppers like poison. But you don't seem like—like—you know. Neither do you," he added, turning to Hadley graciously, but in some doubt. "You see, it's no joke when your old man . . . when he gets into trouble, and you've got a name that can be used for a lot of puns, and even the newspaper people do it and make their damned jokes. 'Hope deferred something or other,' and all that. What I mean is . . ."

Hadley drained his own tankard and set it down. Melson had a feeling that the jokes were over and that Scotland Yard was moving slowly towards business.

"Both of you, young man," remarked Hadley, studying them with a sort of tentative beginning, "have good reason to be grateful to the police. Or, if not to the police, at least to Dr. Fell."

"Nonsense!" roared the doctor, highly delighted, nevertheless. "Heh. Heh-heh-heh. Have another drink, you two! Heh-heh-heh."

"How so?"

"Well, there was a good deal of a row this morning..." Hadley played with a fork and looked up as though with an air of sudden recollection. "By the way, Miss Carver. In that room of yours; you remember, you gave us permission to search it—?" As she nodded, her eyes still clear, he frowned at the recollection. "Is there by any chance a secret panel or something of the sort there?"

"There certainly is. I say, how did you know that? Did you find it? It's between the windows, behind that picture. You press a spring—"

"You don't keep anything there, I suppose?" Hadley tried light jocoseness. "Your love-letters, for instance?"

She returned the smile. She seemed absolutely untroubled.

"Rather not! I haven't opened it for years. If you're interested in secret panels, there are several of them there. J. can tell you all about it. It seems that some man who owned the place in seventeen hundred—or eighteen hundred, maybe it was—was an old rip or something like that..."

Hastings was intrigued and enthusiastic. "Hullo!" he exclaimed, and stared round at her. "I say, why didn't you tell me about that? By the Lord," he said, fervently, "if there's anything I've ever wanted, wanted more than anything else, it's a house with a secret passage! Wow! Think of the fun you could have with people when they—"

"There's no secret passage, silly. Just those places. I haven't used mine..."—she looked blankly at the chief inspector, and into her eyes crept hardness—"well, since I was a kid. No, thank you. Not now."

Hadley saw the lip curl. "Why not? Excuse my curiosity, but I should think—"

"What would it be? Oh, I used to use it. When I was a kid and had a bag of sweets I wanted to hide; and

249

when I was fifteen there was a boy, an errand-boy from a shop in Holborn—it's still there," she smiled—"who used to write me letters. . . . Well, and there were other times—" She drove away quickly whatever thought came into her mind, and flushed. "Mrs. Steffins knew it. She knew where I'd hide them. She thrashed me once, horribly, about one of those letters. I've never been such a fool again as to hide anything there I wanted to keep a secret."

"Does anyone else know about it?"

"Not so far as I know, unless some one told them. Maybe J. has." She looked at him sharply. "Why? Nothing's wrong, is it?"

Hadley smiled, with a note of past grimness. "Not so far as you're concerned, certainly," he reassured her. "But if possible I want you to be sure on the matter. It may be important."

"Well . . . I still can't think—Stop a bit. Maybe Lucia Handreth does." She tried to keep the antagonism out of her voice. "Don told me today about their being cousins, which I think he might have told me before, and trusted me . . ."

"Now, now!" interposed Hastings, hurriedly. "What you need is another—"

"Do you think I cared," she asked, with some tensity, "whether your father robbed fifty banks, and shot all the managers, or poisoned people—or did anything! And, after all, you're only a cousin of that woman's, you know. Not really related." She stopped, rather confused, and tried to brush away the subject as she would have brushed crumbs off the table: by missing many. "What was I saying about panels? Oh yes. She may know, because I think there's some sort of apparatus in her room—I've forgotten what—but I think she asked me, and I'm not sure whether I told her. Miss

Lucia Mitzi Handreth wants poisoning."

"Now, now!" said Hastings, hurriedly reaching for his tankard.

"To go on, Miss Carver. Is there anyone in that house who hates you?"

There was a startled silence.

"Hates me? Oh, you mean Mrs. . . . I say, what do you mean? What are you thinking about? Hates me? No. They like me." She added, rather fearfully: "Don't they? Sometimes I've thought that even somebody I like—likes me too much." She hesitated, looking inwards. "What *do* you mean? I can see it in your face; it's something horrible. . . ."

"Steady, now. First I want you to think about all of them. Think of each one in turn before I tell you something you must know."

He let that sink in. Melson himself required time to understand and explore each corner of the theory Dr. Fell had outlined—its possibilities as well as its monstrous significance. 'The wiliest devil under an inoffensive mask—' Every commonplace floated past in his mind, seeming all the more terrible for being commonplace.

The fire crackled, and he shivered as Hadley began to speak.

Long afterwards, the chief inspector maintained that, if he had not stressed one particular part of the recital which in the nature of the evidence he could not help stressing, they might have had a flash of the truth then. But it is a question. In stating the case Hadley was tactful, making it clear at each step that he had no doubt of Eleanor's innocence. But long before he had finished, Hastings got up with a curse and went over to pound insanely on the mantelpiece; and Eleanor sat very quietly, pale and shaking.

She could not speak for a long time, but belief was growing in her eyes. When Hastings came back and sat down at the table with his head in his hands, she looked at him stonily. She said, through stiff lips:

"Well, what do you think of her *now*?"

A pause. Hastings peered up.

"Think? Think of whom?"

"Don't pretend," said the lifeless voice. Then it flared up to fury. "You know as well as I do. So do *you*—so does everybody here. I said Miss Lucia Mitzi Handreth wanted poisoning. I was wrong. She wants hanging. I knew she disliked me, but I didn't realize it was quite as bad as that."

"All I know," Hastings answered, in a quiet shaky voice, "is that my debt to the police is paid. If it hadn't been for you, sir . . ." He looked at Dr. Fell. "God! its hard to understand; don't let's go wrong again, old girl. It can't have been Lucia. There must be some mistake. You don't know her—"

"All right. Defend her!" cried Eleanor. She was stiff and trembling, and suddenly the tears brimmed over in her eyes. "That's what she said, was it, the filthy little sneak? I'll not be like her. I'll not stand about as cool as you please, and make nice, cool, nasty remarks, and turn up my nose. I'll go over and scratch the little sneak's eyes out, and beat her face in!" She was shaking so much that a bewildered and clumsy Hastings put one arm round her, but she shook it off and turned away before she swung back to Hadley with quiet savagery. "You understand it, don't you? Who led you on and told you all those things? She did. Even to that business about the clock-hands. She is after Don, that's all. She *would*" —the real point of wretchedness about the whole thing struck through it with a ring—"she would tell about—what I did—when they beat me

252

for—taking things. Yes I admit it. I don't suppose you want me now, Don, do you?" she demanded. "But I don't care. You can go to the devil, for all I care." She struck the table and turned away.

Dr. Fell did the only possible thing to keep her quiet. He rang the bell for the waiter and ordered brandy against closing-time. They waited for the storm to settle, until Hastings could get near her without her giving a twitch of repulsion. Then Hadley cut in again:

"You really think Miss Handreth is guilty, then?"

She laughed harshly.

"Then you want to help us, don't you? You want to see the real criminal caught?" As she nodded with a flash of eagerness, Hadley pressed his point. "Then pull yourself together and think. That business about the clock-hands, for instance. You did talk to Mr. Paull about it?"

"Yes. Oh, it's *true*! But I never thought twice about it. That is—I might have thought about it, but J.'s door was locked and however could I?"

"Therefore somebody must have overheard you talk."

"Naturally. She did."

Hadley became deprecating. "Of course, of course. Only to make sure of our case, you see, we must make certain nobody else could have overheard. Where did you have the talk with him?"

After reflection Eleanor said, grimly: "And nobody else did or could have . . . except Mrs. Gorson, maybe, and she doesn't count. I'll tell you just when it was. It was at eight o'clock on Wednesday morning, and not a soul was up or anywhere near us. I was leaving for work, you see, and Chris came downstairs with a suitcase to catch the eight twenty-five from Paddington. We went out to the front door, and Chris hailed a boy in the street and got him to run and fetch a cab. While we were waiting on the step Chris told me his difficulty. He was sober. I remember now that that bi—that woman's front windows were open; I remember the curtains blowing. We weren't talking loudly, and there wasn't anybody anywhere near us at any time, except that I think Mrs. Gorson came up once in the areaway to shake out a mop or something. I told him—what *she* overheard. Then the cab came along and I rode with Chris; he dropped me off at the Oxford Street end of Shaftesbury Avenue."

Hadley drummed on the table. He glanced at Dr. Fell, but did not speak until the waiter had cleared away the meal and brought their coffee and brandy.

"There's one thing I'm not quite clear on," he resumed. "Did you say in so many words how the clock could be defaced?"

"She told you that?" demanded Eleanor, with a sort of pounce. "I say, then we have got her!"

"No, she didn't say that. She only intimated—"

"Because I remember now," Eleanor cut in, with brilliant eagerness, "I didn't even mention that at all until we were in the cab where nobody could have heard. Chris had been quiet for a long time, fidgeting. You know how he does. He said, 'Look here, how could you put the thing wonky, anyhow? I mean, you couldn't just go in and dot it one with a sledge-hammer. I mean, I don't want the confounded thing wrecked.' I said, 'No, but you could take a screw-driver and remove one of the hands . . .'"

"Only one of the hands?"

"Yes. But he got gloomier and gloomier. He said he wanted to hurry on to some club or other and write a note in a last attempt to borrow money. So if dear little Miss Handreth told you she heard that—"

"One other thing." Hadley took out of his briefcase

the left-hand glove; he did not make the mistake of showing the one with the blood-stain. His tone became lightly humorous. "Here's part of the evidence prepared against you. Does it belong to you?"

"No. I never buy black." After a momentary repulsion she examined it. "Good gloves, too. Jolly little girl! Eight and six-pence to get herself hanged. A bit too large for me, though."

"Skoal," wheezed Dr. Fell absently. He pushed his glass away. "By the way, while the questions are flapping back and forth, d'ye mind if I ask one?—Good! I don't want to pry into secrets that don't concern the murder, but just how often did you two young ones meet on that roof at night? Did you have regular nights, or what?"

She smiled. She was calmer now.

"I know perfectly well it seems silly," she announced. "And neither of us cares. Yes, we had our nights, Saturdays and Sundays, as a rule."

"But never during the week?"

"Almost never—on the roof, that is. Sometimes we met downtown on Wednesday afternoon; we met this last Wednesday, the day I was telling you about. Don has been trying to persuade me to do what I'm doing now. I was so fed up that we agreed to meet on Thursday night. That was how it happened . . . Dear Lucia knew all about those meetings, too; don't think she didn't! I could see it right enough. She told Chris . . ."

"Hullo!" called a voice from one of the dusky rooms, and a start went through the group. The door closed. Up to them in nervous but amiable mood, a glass in his hand, came Christopher Paull.

"Hullo!" he repeated, gesturing with the glass. "Thought I heard my name mentioned, or did I? I'm not interruptin' anything, am I?"

# 20

# A Letter Under the Floor

The chief inspector, hurriedly stuffing the glove back
into the briefcase, swore under his breath. He had not
forgotten that the "Duchess of Portsmouth" was a ren-
dezvous for the members of the household, as he had
told Dr. Fell; but it was convenient as being close
to Ames's late lodgings, which had not yet been investigated, and he offered odds that none of the
Carver crowd ever bothered to wander back into the
dining-room. Very well, he was wrong. Melson
heard him whisper, fiercely, "Agree-with-anything-I-
say." Then he turned to the newcomer almost with affability.

Mr. Paull was not drunk. He looked as though he
had it in his mind to be off somewhere, for one hand
determinedly grasped hat and rolled umbrella while
the other held the glass. But he was in that dividing
state when, if a boon companion suggests having just
one more quick one before leaving, the balance trem-

bles, the scale-pan dips, and mortal man remains to get drunk. He was freshly shaven to pinkness, his toothbrush moustache was clipped and his thin blond hair brushed straight. He wore blue serge of a dexterous tailoring that made him look less stout, and tie with colours for something-or-other. But his eyes were still bloodshot; he seemed friendly but nervous.

"We should be very glad," Hadley went on, "if you would join us for a few minutes. There are some questions. . . . We were discussing the murder last night—" He glanced at him and left the matter vague.

"Rotten business," said Paull, with some violence. "*Rotten* business. Ain't it? My God!"

He sipped his whisky and soda hastily and drew out a chair. He shot an apprehensive glance towards Eleanor, but did not continue.

"Have you learned exactly what happened?"

"Yes! I can't for the life of me see what it means, dammit!" Again the apprehensive glance. "But I was wondering . . ."

"Wondering what?"

"Well, dash it all! whether you might want to ask me any more questions." Paull returned, in a somewhat aggrieved tone which trailed off. He fidgeted. "Look here. Tell me. I was still pretty well screwed when I talked to you this morning, wasn't I?"

Hadley's tone became sharp. "You're not going to tell us, are you, that you don't remember what you said?"

"No, no. I remember that well enough. All I can say is"—he drew a deep breath—"do you think it was very sporting not to tell me the fellow'd been done in with—what he was? Now I ask you!"

"Why should it interest you?"

"You know. You're makin' it devilish hard, old boy."

He gulped at the drink. "Fact is, I've been talking with Lucia Handreth, and—"

"Have you, indeed," said Eleanor, with that breathlessness which precedes an outburst. Her eyes had a curiously unreal blaze. Then something jarred her body like a shudder, and Melson suspected that some one had administered an ungallant kick under the table. Paull appealed to her for the first time.

"Old girl, on my solemn oath, swear it on a stack of Bibles, I never really said I saw you in that hall! It was what I thought . . ."

"What did you think," Hadley cut in, "when you learned a police officer had been stabbed with the hand of a clock?"

"Not what you think I thought. Word of honour!"

"Especially with the hand of a clock you had asked Miss Carver to steal for you?"

Again Eleanor seemed about to interpose, but Hastings had her by the arm. Hastings' imaginative, intelligent eyes moved between Paull and the chief inspector, and understood. He was leaning forward, one elbow on the table; Melson felt that he was ready to lend a convincing theatrical display to the situation if it were needed.

"But I didn't, old boy," Paull protested, taken aback. He peered over his shoulder. "I say, don't talk so loud. I didn't at all. Besides, I didn't need it. I borrowed the money, you know. Didn't like to face the chap—borrowed money before—went to the club and wrote a note explainin'. Thought I'd better get an appointment with him, you see, so I thought, 'Dammit! the train's gone, but if I get an appointment I can't take the train anyway, can I?"

"Steady. You mean you didn't go down to Devon, after all?"

"Oh yes. But not till Wednesday night. I'd promised the old man, you see, so I had to go. But I had the money, and there was no reason for pacifyin' the old boy about anything, so I simply turned round and came back up to town again. What? Of course I ran into some fellers yesterday afternoon, and when I woke up this morning, dashed if I wasn't stony again, but my money'll be in tomorrow, so everything's quite all right. Absolutely. What?"

Hadley cut short this desperate talking against time. "Let's go back to the subject, Mr. Paull.—Would it surprise you to hear that a warrant has been issued for Miss Carver's arrest?"

Paull had taken out his handkerchief, and it shook in his hands.

"You can't *do* it," he insisted, rather wildly. "Speak up, Eleanor. Say something. What I say is this. Some fellers are murderers, and some fellers ain't. Same thing with women. Dammit! it's too hard to believe—"

"But Miss Handreth believes it?"

"Well, Lucia's different. She don't like Eleanor. But I do."

"Yet you still agree with Miss Handreth, don't you?"

"I—no, I—I don't kn—. Oh, well, dammit!"

Hadley's eyelids flickered. His elbow came forward on the table, and he watched Paull steadily as he said:

"Then you'll be glad to hear that the effort to throw suspicion on Miss Carver has been absolutely discredited and she is the one person we are certain did not commit the murder."

"Eh?" said Paull, after a long pause. The fire fell with a collapsing rattle, splintering weird light about the room, so that the pewter plates in their racks seemed to shift duskily. There were ghostly creaks from old woodwork. Paull sat with his handkerchief halfway to

259

his forehead, as though suspecting a joke. "Eh?" he said, and asked Hadley to repeat. The chief inspector did so. When Paull spoke again, there was a rustle of expelled breath from all around the circle; Melson had a feeling of a shadow come and gone.

"Well, what do you want to pull a feller's leg for, then?" he asked, in a sort of querulous weakness. "Havin' me in here and lookin' at me like a poacher, dash it! But I'm glad you can see sense. Hear that, old girl?"

"I hear it," replied Eleanor, very quietly. She sat with her fingers locked, rigid. Then she shook back her hair, moving her head and throat with unconscious grace, but the eyes never left him. "Thanks for the help, Chris."

"Oh, that's all right," he disclaimed, in vague haste. Some inflection in her tone caught him momentarily, but he disclaimed whatever suggestion of an ulterior meaning it might have had. About him was an atmosphere of amiability and failure. "Do you—do you want me any longer? If not, I'll be pushing off. It's a rotten business, but so long as I haven't got anybody into trouble—"

"I'm afraid you are in need of some recreation. As a matter of fact," said Hadley, in his suavest tones, "you have an invitation. Very shortly my two young friends are going to—to the cinema, and they insist that you go along with them. They feel that the atmosphere at home is a little strained and that your conversation might make it more so. You do insist on his going along, don't you?"

He looked at Hastings, who nodded instantly. Hastings' lean face was expressionless, but his dark eyes moved towards the chief inspector.

"We insist on it," he assented, feeling surreptitiously

in his pocket. "Ha. Ho-ho! Yes, we insist," he went on in a fuller tone. "Nothing like celebrating, is there? It should be a three-hour program. I was only wondering—for instance, whether we ought to start now?"

"Stop a bit," said Dr. Fell, sleepily. "I was wondering . . . Tell me, Mr. Paull. Has anything else emerged out of the mists of last night?"

The other, who was trying to puzzle out the last situation, wrenched his wits back.

"You mean, remember anything? No. Sorry, old—er—sorry. Not a blasted thing. Sorry. I've been trying all day."

"Not even when Miss Handreth told you what had happened?"

"'Fraid not."

"Heh." A small twinkling eye opened in his red and shining face. "But perhaps you've an idea . . . a theory . . . about what might have happened? After, hem, our first theory blew up, we've been rather looking for leads."

Paull grew more confidential, even a trifle flattered. From his inside pocket he took a flat silver flask, made a pretence of offering it about, and took a deep pull. The scale-pan trembled and tipped with that decisive ounce of whisky. His voice grew more hoarsely confidential.

"Not in my line, exactly, is it? No. What I always say is this. There are fellers who think and fellers who do. If I did anything I should be one of the fellers who do, but I don't. Follow me? Well. I don't claim much, but there's one thing I'll tell you." He tapped the table with his forefingers. "I don't like that chap Stanley."

Hadley sat up.

"You mean," he said, in the hush, "you suspect—"

"Now, now! I said I didn't like him," Paull insisted,

261

doggedly, "and I don't. And he knows it, so it's no secret. But when Lucia told me, I thought, 'Hullo!' Nothing in it, maybe. The whisky talking and thinkin'. But why do they put two barrels on a gun? Because there's always more than one bird, or what would the shoot be like? Well. Here's a police officer killed, and rotten business. And in the same house there's another police officer. And the two fellers knew each other and worked together, Lucia says. Ain't they goin' to ask any questions about *that?*"

An eager gleam had come into Hastings' eyes. It faded; he clenched his hands and sat back.

"Lord! how I wish I could believe you!" he said. "But it's no good—you don't know the whole story . . . of what happened. . . . And even aside from that, I—I, of all people!—can give the swine a clean bill of health. He was in the room the whole time. I saw him."

"Did you?" asked Dr. Fell.

He did not raise his voice. But something in his tone arrested them all and made silence a hollow in which a spoon clinked sharply.

"Did you see him in the room the whole time?" Dr. Fell went on, and this time he did raise his voice. "You saw *Boscombe,* yes. But did you see Stanley? Did you notice Stanley? If I remember correctly, he was behind the screen."

Hastings released his breath. He was staring at the memory, and he could find nothing he liked. "Sorry. How much I wish I could support it you'll never know. I mightn't have seen Stanley. But I did see the door— in full moonlight. And nothing, nobody, went in or out."

Dr. Fell lost interest. "Why do you dislike Stanley?" he asked Paull.

"Well, dash it! he hangs about so, if you know what

262

I mean. Always in your way. Sits in Bossie's room drinkin' Bossie's brandy, and not speakin' for half an hour at a time; and when he does speak it's something dashed unpleasant. He's the one, by the way, who's always goin' on about the Spanish Inquisition."

Dr. Fell cocked a sleepily mocking eye at a corner of the ceiling.

"H'm, yes. The poor old Spanish Inquisition again. Gentlemen, how the fiction-writers have flattered it and everybody else has misunderstood it! Remember Voltaire's horror—*'Ce sanglant tribunal, ce monument de pouvoir monacal, qui l'Espagne a reçu, mais elle-même abhorré*—written at a time when in enlightened France people could be checked into the Bastille without trial and kept there till they rotted? Of course, the Inquisition had become doddering by that time and didn't tear out a man's tongue or cut off his hand for a political offence as in France; but never mind. I had a young friend once, a writer, who intended to write the historical novel of his life about the picturesque horrors of the Inquisition. He was enthusiastic. He was going to picture the foul Inquisitors smacking their gums over the ingenuity of newly devised tortures, and the young Scotch hero-mariner struggling in their grasp; as I remember it, the whole thing was to wind up in a swordfight with Torquemada across the roofs of Toledo. . . . Then, unfortunately, he began to read the evidence. He stopped reading fiction and began reading facts. And the more he read the more disgusted he grew and the more his shining illusions fell away. Gentlemen, it genuinely pains me to have to dispel any good blood-thirsty illusion, but I have to report that he gave up in despair and is now an embittered man."

Even Hadley was roused by this.

"I don't want you flying off into a lecture again," he

snapped. "But you don't defend the thing, do you? You don't deny that your Scotch hero would have been in danger of torture and burning?"

"Not at all. At least, not much more danger than he would have run in Scotland. In his home town, the boot and thumbscrew were a legal part of any man's trial for anything. Spain would have burned him as quickly as England would have burned him if he denied the existence of a future life, by the Puritan ordinance of 1648; as Scotland burned two thousand alleged witches and good old Calvin burned Servetus. That is—Spain would have burned him unless he recanted, which at home he wouldn't have the option of doing. Not one person went to the fire who was willing to recant before the reading of the final sentence, I regret to say. . . . No, I don't defend it," said Dr. Fell, rapping on the table with his stick. "I only say nobody attacks it for the real harm it did—the ruin of a nation, the eternal stain on the *mala sangre* family, the secret witnesses at trial (also a cheerful feature of English law), and the certainty of conviction for some offence, however light, on anybody brought to trial. Regard it as a wrong. But don't regard it as a nightmare. Say that the Inquisitors tortured and burned people, as civil authority did in England. But they were men who believed, however wrongly, in the soul of man, and not a group of half-witted schoolboys maliciously torturing a cat."

Hastings lit a cigarette. The match-flame flared in the darkening room, and for the first time he looked older than Eleanor.

"You've got a purpose in telling all this, sir," he stated, rather than asked. "What is it?"

"Because Mr. Paull's attitude towards Stanley interests me, for one thing, and for another—"

"Yes?"

Dr. Fell roused himself from thought and sat up briskly. They had an impression of cobwebs broken and terrors for the moment pushed away.

"That's all," he declared. "H'mf. That is, it's all for the moment. Go along to that show, now, the three of you. I have some last instructions for you. You'll see that they're followed, young fella?—Right." He looked at his watch. "You're all to come back to the house at exactly nine o'clock tonight, and not before then. You're not to say a word when you get there—about anything. Got it? Cheer-ho, then."

They rose hesitantly, and Paull in some haste.

"I don't know what's in your mind," Eleanor said, her hands clenched, "or why you've done all this for me. All I can say is, thanks."

She could not go on. She gripped her coat round her, shut her eyes once, and then hurried away, with Hastings after her. The footfalls faded and died. Three men sat round a table in the sinking firelight, and for a long time nobody spoke.

"We shall have to go and look at Ames's room," Hadley remarked at last, in a dull voice. He opened and shut his hands. "We're wasting time. But I don't know what to do. Somehow everything has been upset. In the last hour or so a dozen new possibilities have been floating about in my mind. They're all possible, they're all even probable—and I can't nail down any one of them! Then what that young fool Paull said . . . that started me thinking too. . . ."

"Yes," assented the other. "I rather thought it would."

"For instance. I keep coming back to one of the points you mentioned this morning, and one of the big difficulties. Ames was brought to this quarter, to interest himself in that household, by an anonymous letter.

265

Could it have been anonymous? That's what I can't swallow. In my own day at that sort of job, I know I shouldn't have paid much attention to an unsigned letter telling me to put on a fool disguise and plant myself somewhere in the hope of hearing something interesting. Lord, no!—not with the flood of crank letters that pour into the Yard about much less important cases than the Gamridge murder. Ames was thorough, yes. But was he as insanely thorough as all that? . . . On the other hand, if the letter came from a source he knew and thought authentic . . . Blast it! nothing works!" He banged the table. "I see a dozen objections, and yet—"

"Hadley," said Dr. Fell, abruptly, "do you want to see justice done?"

"Do I! With what's happened? My God! if we could get some evidence to lay this killer by the heels, then—!"

"I didn't ask you that. I asked you if you wanted to see justice done."

Hadley stared at him, a stare that grew to suspicion.

"We can't have any tampering with the law," he snapped. "You did it once, in the Mad Hatter case, to shield somebody; and you did it with my permission, I admit. But this time . . . what's in your mind?"

The other's forehead had grown sombre.

"I don't know whether I dare do it!" rumbled Dr. Fell. "Even whether it would work. And if it did work, whether it mightn't go too far. Oh, it would be justice! Make no mistake of that! But I juggled with dynamite once, in that Depping business, and—it rather haunts me sometimes." He struck his forehead. "I swore never to do it again, and yet I see no other way out . . . unless . . ."

"Just what are you talking about?"

266

"I'll give my final hope a chance before I try it. Don't worry! It'll be nothing to hurt your conscience. Now, then, I'll go with you to see Ames's lodgings. Afterwards I want about four clear hours to myself—"

"Alone?"

"Without you two, anyhow. Will you follow my instructions?"

"Right," said Hadley, after they had looked at each other briefly. "Well?"

"I want a car and driver put at my disposal, but with nothing to mark it as a police car. Let me have two of your men for special work; they don't have to be intelligent—in fact, I should prefer that they weren't—but they must be discreet. Finally, you're to see that all members of our Carver household are at home by nine o'clock tonight. You are to be there, with two of your men. . . ."

Hadley looked up from snapping shut the catch of his briefcase.

"Armed?" he asked.

"Yes. But they're to keep out of sight, and under no circumstances are they to draw a weapon unless I give the word. They are to be the biggest and nerviest fellows you have, because there's certain to be a roughhouse and there may be slashing. Now let's get started."

Melson, not a man of action, felt an unpleasantly clammy sensation in the pit of his stomach when he followed the others out. But he refused to admit it. He was going to get one glimpse of that killer before he bolted . . . if he did bolt. How did you know what you would do under any such circumstances? After all, it was only a man—or a woman. What the devil! And still he felt ineffectual. . . .

Under swollen grey clouds the little street looked unreal. It had that powdery grey color which comes to the London sky towards twilight or storm; and a high wind was rising across the trees of Lincoln's Inn Fields. Down the curve of Portsmouth Street a few furtive gaslamps were flickering in a nimbus. Here were low brick houses with bulging fronts and windows; and, curiously enough, the spurious Old Curiosity Shop at the corner gave the whole street the look of a Cruikshank print. Consulting his notebook, Hadley led them into a muddy alley between brick walls—one of those unexpected nests of houses within houses, with toppling chimney-pots and withered geraniums in boxes on the windowsills. When he pulled the bell wire of one numbered 16, there was first a stubborn silence; then the noise of a slow clanking approach, like a ghost, from down in the bowels of the house. Then a small fat woman, with a face rather like a greasy cooking-pan, pushed her cap up from her eyes, breathed hard, and regarded them suspiciously. Her keys clanked again.

"Yeza, whattayou want?" she said, without inflection. "You wanna room, eh?—No? You wanna see who? Meesterames? Meesterames heesa not at home," she announced, and instantly tried to shut the door.

Hadley got his foot wedged inside, and then difficulty began. When he had at last made matters clear, there were only two things the woman knew and insisted on—that she and her husband were good people, and that they knew absolutely nothing about anything. She was not in the least frightened. She only remained stolidly without information.

"I ask you, did he ever have any visitors?"

"Maybe. I dunno. Whateesvistors?"

"Did anybody ever come to see him?"

"Maybe," A mountainous shrug. "Maybe not. I dunno. My Carlo, heesagood man; we area bote good, you ask polissman. We don't know not'ing."

268

"But if somebody came to see him, you would have to open the door, eh?"

It did not catch her. "Whatafor? Meesterames hesa no cripple, what you call, eh? Maybe he coulda walk down. I dunno."

"Did you ever see anybody with him?"

"No."

This sort of attack, with variations and repetitions, went on until Hadley fumed. Dr. Fell tried Italian, but his accent was strong and it produced only volubility about nothing. Hadley was beaten before he started, and knew it. The witness who has once lived in terror of the Mafia keeps a close mouth even when the Mafia exists no longer; threats from the mere law are nothing. At last, in accordance with his order, she waddled ahead up a dark flight of stairs and opened the door to a room.

Hadley struck a match and lit an open gas-jet. Out of the corner of his eye he kept watching the woman, who had planted herself composedly in the room, but he did not appear to notice her. It was a small, bare room looking out on a tangle of chimney-pots. It contained an iron bed, a dresser with pitcher and wash-bowl, cracked mirror, table, and straight chair. The place was surprisingly clean; but it contained nothing more except a battered portmanteau and some clothes hung up in the closet, with a pair of ancient shoes in one corner.

As the chief inspector moved about the creaky carpetless floor, Melson found himself watching the woman's impassive mouth, as Hadley was doing. Her eyes were straying somewhere. . . . Hadley went through the clothes in the closet, found nothing; the mouth remained impassive. He examined the dresser; still impassive. He lifted and sounded the mattress; impassive to the point of scorn. The duel went on. There was no

269

sound but the creak of boards and the singing of the yellow-blue gas. When he bent towards one part of the floor, the mouth changed a little. As he approached the baseboard of the wall near the window, it changed still more. . . .

Suddenly Hadley bent down and pretended to find something.

"So, Mrs. Caracci," he announced, grimly, "you've lied to me, haven't you?"

"No. I don' know not'ing, what I tellayou!"

"You lied to me, didn't you? Yes, you did. Mr. Ames had a woman in his room, didn't he? You know what that means. You'll lose your licence to keep a rooming-house, and they'll deport you; maybe send you to a gaol."

"No!"

"Be careful, Mrs. Caracci. I'm going to put you in court, up before the big judge, you know; and he'll know. It was a woman, wasn't it?"

"No. No woman sheesa been in theesehouse! Man, maybe; no woman!"

She struck her breast passionately, and her breathing had become gusty.

"That's allaIknow! I'm poor woman. I don' know not'-ing—"

"Get out," said Hadley. He cut short a storm of lamentations by shoving her through the door, and a full soprano voice rose and fell above beatings on the door as he bolted it. He took out a pocket-knife and clicked open the big blade.

"Over under the window," he explained. "Loose board. There may be something hidden. But I suspect it's only his money. She may have got it."

As Melson and the doctor leaned over him, he pried up the board. From the hollow of the rafters beneath

270

he took out several objects. A pigskin notecase, stamped G.F.A., containing police credentials but no money. A bunch of keys, a silk tobacco pouch and a meerschaum pipe, a penny packet of envelopes, a writing-block, a good fountain-pen, and a paper-bound book with the title, *The Art of Watchmaking*.

"No notes," said Hadley, getting up with a grunt. "I was afraid there wouldn't be." He ruffled the pages of the book. "Studying his last rôle, poor devil. And he never even got away with it. Carver saw—Good *God!*"

Hadley jumped back as a folded sheet of notepaper slid from between the pages and fluttered to the floor: a letter, with its signature uppermost. Hadley muttered something as he fumbled to pick it up, and his shaking fingers could not at first snare it. . . .

"Dear George [said the typewritten note]: I know you will be surprised to hear from me after all these years, and I know you think I tried to do you in the eye over the Hope-Hastings case. I won't say I'm trying to make amends, but I will say that I want to see if I can't do something that will get me back into favour with the Powers, even if it's a uniform job. I have a line on that Gamridge murder case you're handling, and it's HOT. Keep this strictly to yourself and don't try to see me until I write you again. I'll communicate with you. This is BIG."

It was dated, "Hampstead, 29th August," and signed "*Peter E. Stanley*." They looked at each other. The gas sang thinly.

271

# 21

## The Impossible Moonlight

At half-past eight that night, after some hectic business at Scotland Yard, Hadley and Melson shot out on the Embankment in the former's car, and Hadley was raving. He had to tone down his voice, because in the rear seat were Sergeant Betts and a six-foot-six-inch plain-clothes constable answering to the name of Sparkle. But he raved, nevertheless, and his driving style was savage.

"An interview with the Assistant Commissioner," he said, "and nothing to tell him but that Fell was up to some hocus-pocus, and I didn't even know where he was. Desk full of business—some big pot's country house has been robbed, and the Commissioner himself's been phoning in. A mess. You ought to be glad you cooled your heels in the lost-and-found department."

"What about Stanley's letter?"

"Fell took it. *I—I*, mind you—was instructed to say nothing yet. I didn't mind that. My God! do you—does

Fell—realize what this means if Stanley's guilty? One police officer, even an ex-, accused of murdering another? There'll be a scandal that'll blow the lid off the C. I. D. and maybe the government. The Roger Casement case'll be nothing to it! You notice I kept Stanley clear out of today's papers; not a word, not a line about his connection with it? . . . Then all the worse if he's guilty. I'm only praying he isn't. I sounded out Bellchester, that's the Assistant Commissioner, and he went off the deep end. We're paying Stanley a pension. It seems the man's crazy—"

"Literally?"

"Quite literally insane, and several times within an ace of being certified. Ought to be, as a matter of fact. But his sister got around somebody higher up. . . . I don't know the straight of it. Of course he'll never hang if he is guilty; he'll go to Broadmoor, where he belongs. But do you see the leader in the morning *Trumpeter*, for instance? 'Let our readers consider the strange case of the mad policeman who has for some years been supported and coddled by the present authorities, instead of being placed in a position where he can do no further harm. Is it at all strange that the authorities endeavoured to hush the matter up when this man ran amok and killed a senior detective-inspector of whom he had long been jealous, just as he killed, some years ago, a banker against whom nothing has yet been proved,' etc. I tell you—"

The big car swerved to avoid a barrow, and roared on through the light mist and rain that blurred the Embankment lights. Melson felt his heart rise as they skidded; but the whole mad business was lightness and exhilaration, as though the car itself were rushing to a conclusion of the case. His fingers tightened on the door.

"But what," he demanded, "does Fell think?"

"All I can tell Fell," the chief inspector returned, "is that he's got to swallow his own medicine. *He* can't have it both ways, either. If his reconstruction of the whole business is right—I mean about Eleanor—then Stanley can't be guilty! It would be raving nonsense; it would make nonsense of everything else. Don't you see that? If I could only prove that that letter we found is a forgery! But it's not! I showed it to our handwriting man, with a blotter over the letter itself, and he swears it's absolutely genuine. That tears it. It puts Stanley in a corner . . . while all I can do now is follow Fell's instructions, return to the house, and tell the Carver crowd that we've decided to release Eleanor. Seems rather an anticlimax now, doesn't it? Anyhow, there you are. If that young fool Paull hadn't . . ."

He checked himself, and spoke no more until the car drew up in the drizzle outside No. 16. Kitty Prentice, whose swollen reddish eyes attested to recent weeping, opened the door. She jumped back with a queer squeak like a toy, peered over Hadley's shoulder, saw nothing, and seized his arm.

"Sir! Oh, sir, you've gotter tell. 'Ave they arrested Miss Eleanor? *'Ave* they, sir? Oh, it's awful! You *gotter* tell! Mr. Carver's frantic, and 'e's been a-telephoning to Scotland Yard, and couldn't find you, and they wouldn't tell 'im anything, and—"

Hadley evidently feared that premature joy would have the wrong effect in a too-quick revelation for the rest of them. His eye silenced her, even though his expression approved this witness.

"I can't tell you anything. Where are they?"

She was stricken silent, and pointed to the sitting-room. In a moment her face would slowly begin wrinkling up with tears. Hadley crossed over swiftly to the sitting-room door. Into the house had come palpably

274

now a new atmosphere: at once of hurry and tense waiting, of hands that were clenched and faces waiting to wrinkle like Kitty's. In the stillness Melson could hear the rustling noise of clocks ticking in the front workroom, as he had heard them last night; but this time they had a quicker beat. From the sitting-room he heard Lucia Handreth's muffled voice raised:

"—I repeat I've told you all I can. If you keep on I shall go mad. I promised not to tell, but I can warn you you'd better be prepared for—"

Hadley knocked.

The white door, with its porcelain knob and big key, opened like a theatre curtain on sudden silence. Carver, big and dishevelled, still in smoking-jacket and slippers, stopped pacing before the fireplace. His grip on a short pipestem made the jaw muscles stand out, and Melson could see the gleam of his teeth as one corner of his lip lifted. Mrs. Steffins, a handkerchief below her smeary eyes and her face now clearly furrowed, rolled up her head from where she sat lolling by the table; she gave a hiccoughing sob just before she was transfixed by the sight of Hadley. Lucia Handreth stood bolt upright by the mantelpiece, her arms folded, her colour high.

For a second the tableau held, emotion arrested at its climax and in the weird facial distortions of its climax; while the currents of it, hatred or tears or anger or jubilation, flowed out palpably at the watchers. They felt these emotions like the heat of a fire. Then Lucia Handreth released her breath. Carver took a step forward, and Mrs. Steffins's knuckles made a rattling noise as her arm fell on the table.

"I knew it!" Mrs. Steffins cried, suddenly, as at a confirmation. Her face grew to hideous ugliness with tears. "I knew it, remember! I warned you! I told you it would come to this house. . . ."

Carver took another step forward, slowly, his big shoulders against the light of the lamp. The pale-blue eyes were unreadable.

"You have kept us waiting a long time," he said. "Well?"

"What," said Hadley, bluntly, "do you wish to know?"

"I wish to know what you have done. Have you arrested Eleanor?"

"Miss Handreth," the chief inspector replied, without conscious irony, "has undoubtedly given you some idea of what we talked over in Miss Carver's room this afternoon. . . ."

The pale-blue eyes bored in. Carver made a slight gesture. He seemed to grow larger and nearer, although he did not move.

"That is not the point, Mr. Inspector. Not the point at all. The only thing we are interested in is—is it true?"

"It's the *shame* of it!" cried Mrs. Steffins, and began to beat her hands on the table wildly. "It's the awful *shame* of it. Arrested for murder. In this house. Living in this house, and her name in the papers as arrested for murder. I could have stood anything *else*. . . ."

Hadley's impassive look roved round the group.

"Yes, I have something to tell you, if you will be quiet. Where is Mr. Boscombe?"

"He's done no talking. But he's just as much of a fool," said Lucia, and kicked at the edge of the mantelpiece. "He's gone to find his solicitor for her. He says you haven't any case, didn't have a case, and never will have a case. . . ."

"He is quite right, Miss Handreth," said Hadley, very quietly.

Again they were stricken motionless in a hush, in that queer illusion wherein their faces seemed to have been caught as though by a camera. Melson felt a roaring in his ears. In the quiet Hadley's voice sounded loudly.

"The evidence against her," he continued, "is wiped out. We do not have a case, did not have a case, and never will have one. We knew it this afternoon, in time to prepare for—something else." A faintly sinister ring here. "She has been enjoying herself at the theatre, with the young man she intends shortly to marry, and should be here presently."

Melson was watching Lucia and Mrs. Steffins. On the latter's face was only a stupid expression, like a drunken person fumbling with keys. Then realization came and she sagged. Her head went over against the back of the chair in an unconsciously theatrical gesture, and her shaky lips framed words which Melson could have sworn were, "Thank God."

"Are you mad?" said Lucia Handreth.

It was not a question, but a quick, sharp, incredulous statement. She took a step forward. Her breast rose and fell.

"Doesn't it please you, Miss Handreth?"

"Kindly don't try to be suave. I—I am neither pleased nor displeased. I simply don't believe it. Is this a joke? You told me this morning—"

"Yes. But since then we have heard other things. I'm afraid all of your evidence wasn't . . . altogether corroborated, if you understand me? I think you do."

"Yet with all that evidence—?" Her voice began to rise. "What did she say? What did she tell you? You mean Don is really going to m—What *do* you mean?"

Then Carver moved across Melson's line of vision. He put the dead pipe back in his mouth and drew at it noisily. He looked as though a great weight had been taken from him; not angry with the trick, or even curious, but with the energy drawn from his brittle bones now that there was no longer occasion for it.

"Thank you for your good sense," he remarked, rather shakily. "You've given us the worst scare we ever had. At least we seem well out of it now. What—what do you wish us to do?"

They heard the faint slam of the front door, footsteps, and somewhere a telephone insistently ringing. Clearly not knowing what to do, Hadley lifted his hand and waited. There were mumbling voices, and the whisper of the rain grew louder. Then Kitty appeared.

"Dr. Fell's 'ere, sir," she said to the chief inspector. "And they want you on the telephone. . . ."

Through the open doorway Melson had a glimpse of the doctor's rain-spattered cloak as he stood with his back to them muttering hurriedly to Sergeant Betts and Constable Sparkle. They slid back out of sight in a moment. Dr. Fell, his shovel-hat in his hand, lumbered into the room as Hadley went out. They did not speak; the doctor's face was heavy with weariness.

"Ah—good evening," he greeted them, wheezing a little. "I'm just on time, I fancy. It seems we're always setting this house by the ears, but I'm glad to say that tonight will probably be the last time."

"The last time?" repeated Carver.

"I hope so. I hope to make the acquaintance of the real murderer," said Dr. Fell, "tonight. Under these circumstances you must allow me to send you all out of this room, until I summon you here presently. Go anywhere you like, but none of you must leave the house. . . . No hysterics, ma'am!" he added, swinging towards Mrs. Steffins. He seemed to tower. "I think I see it in your eye that you are about to accuse Miss Handreth of being the cause of all your trouble and worry. Perhaps she is; but this is not the time to discuss it. . . . Mr. Carver, will you please take charge of these ladies? All of you are to be within call."

He stood back. Muffled by the falling rain, the voice of Lincoln's Inn bell began to toll nine. In the midst of the strokes, as though at an agreed signal, the house bell began buzzing in bursts under somebody's finger, and the big doorknocker banged out under a vigorous hand. Kitty flew to answer it. The voices of the newcomers were stilled as Eleanor, shaking rain from her coat, moved into the hall so that those in the sitting-room could see her. Behind her loomed Hastings, sullenly jubilant; Boscombe, dryly pleased; and Paull—slightly drunk and very wet, standing puzzled with his rolled umbrella gripped under his arm.

Eleanor faced them.

"Here I am," she said. Her voice could not find the right level, and echoed thinly. But she stood very straight. "Not in gaol. Free—for the first time." She looked at Lucia. "Aren't you sorry?"

"Don, you fool!" screamed Lucia. She dashed her hand across her eyes; hesitated, and then flung out of the room as though she were running for the group. But she passed them, while Eleanor was palely smiling, darted into her own room, and slammed the door. Mrs. Steffins's wail took up the echo of the noise; but Carver paid no attention. He walked out slowly and said something to Eleanor.

"Thanks, J.," she replied. "Come upstairs with us, won't you?"

As in a dream Melson heard Dr. Fell giving instructions; the group fell silent, but terror was here as well as tensity when the doctor returned with Hadley and the hall was cleared. The chief inspector, his back to the door, stood and stared at Dr. Fell.

279

"Well?" the latter barked. "What is it? Anything wrong?"

"Everything—now. Everything. Somebody's blown the gaff."

"What gaff?"

"Call from the office," Hadley replied, heavily. "It's in all the late editions of the evening papers. Somebody at the Yard talked; my instructions weren't understood. Hayes got into a mix-up with the Press Bulletin, but they won't hold that as his fault. It may be my job in my last couple of weeks, and the pension with it. . . . They know Stanley was here last night, mixed up in funny business, and the Assistant Commissioner told me what would happen if it leaked out. I shall be the scapegoat for all of 'em. Even if we do catch the real murderer now—"

"Do you think I didn't foresee all that?" asked Dr. Fell, quietly.

"Foresee?"

"Steady, son. You've been thirty-five years in the Force without losing your nerve, and don't lose it now. Yes, I saw the trouble; and there's only one way to meet it, if we can meet it. . . ."

"Yes, thirty-five years," nodded Hadley. He stared at the floor. "You've got something arranged?"

"Yes."

"You realise what will happen if you bungle it, don't you? Not merely to me, but to—"

He stopped. Kitty was there again, looking more frightened, as though she had darted away from the front door.

"Sir," she said, "*Mr. Peter Stanley is here*. . . ."

For a second the chief inspector stood stonily; then, as he started to move, Dr. Fell gripped his arm. Hadley said:

"That's done it. That's done it now. Somebody'll see

him, and we're ruined. He was to be kept in the background. Now—"

"Be quiet, you fool," said Dr. Fell, very softly. "Sit down there, and whatever happens don't move or speak. I sent a message for him to come. Send Mr. Stanley in here, Kitty."

Hadley backed away and sat down by the table. So did Dr. Fell. Standing in the background by the glass cases, Melson gripped the edge of one to steady himself. . . .

"Come in, Mr. Stanley," continued Dr. Fell, almost drowsily. "Don't trouble to close that door. Take a chair, please."

He entered with a curiously soft step for such a big man. Melson had never yet seen him in full light, and all past feelings and insinuations about him returned now with a sort of shock. He seemed to jerk back from the full glow of the lamp, as an animal might. Wearing a sodden ulster, he was hatless; and when the rain dripped down his face he would twitch his head. His eyes were set and sunken, and the broad face with the projecting ears, which last night had been of a leaden colour, was now of a blotchy pallor—and he was smiling.

"You sent for me," he said, heavily, and opened his eyes wide.

"That's right. Sit down. Mr. Stanley, this afternoon certain accusations—suggestions—were made about you. . . ."

He sat down, his big fingers outspread on his knees. Nor was he really smiling, Melson saw; it was a twitching of the lips he could not control. He sat there as motionless as wax, power and danger poised and growing tense in the white lamplight. Suddenly he leaned forward.

"What do you mean, accusations?"

"Did you know the late Inspector George Ames?"

"I did—once."

"But you didn't recognize him when you saw him dead last night?"

"I didn't recognize him," said Stanley, leaning forward still further. "The way he looked *then*. Pretty, wasn't it? Yes."

He started to laugh.

"But I suppose," said Dr. Fell, "you do know your own handwriting when you see it?"

It was as though he had cracked a whip before the other's face, and Stanley jerked back. Then Melson knew. He knew what Stanley had reminded him of ever since the man came in. The soft movements despite his heaviness, the snarl in the voice, the witless, incalculable stare of the eyes that looked back, the quick jerks. They were in a cage, with something between them and the door.

"Know my own handwriting?" he snapped. "What the hell do you mean? Of course I know my own handwriting. Do you take me for a lunatic?"

"Then," said Dr. Fell, "you wrote this."

He reached in his pocket, took out the folded letter, and flung it across. It landed on Stanley's knees, but he did not touch it.

"Read it!"

Again the whip-crack. Stanley touched the letter, then slowly unfolded it.

"You wrote that."

"I did not."

"It's your signature."

"I'm telling you that I didn't write it and never saw it before. You call me a liar, do you?"

"Wait until you hear what they say, Stanley. I'm your friend, you know, or I wouldn't be telling you this. Wait until you hear what they say."

"Say?" He moved back a little. "What do they say?"

"That you're mad, my friend. Mad. That there's a little maggot up in your head that's eaten away the brain. . . ."

He was leaning forward as Dr. Fell spoke, to throw the letter on the table. From him came a strong odor of wet clothes and brandy. As his hairy hand came forward, his ulster and coat fell a little open, and Melson saw something in the pocket. . . .

Stanley was carrying a gun.

"Mad," said Dr. Fell. "And that was why you killed George Ames."

For a second Melson thought the damned thing was going to turn on them. It switched in the chair, and seemed to grow larger.

"But to show you what *I* think of your brain," Dr. Fell went on, looking straight into the round yellowish eyes that seemed to contract and expand, "I'm going to tell you what the evidence against you is. This is what somebody thinks about you, as somebody said. . . .

"Last night, while Ames was walking up those stairs, you couldn't have gone out through the double doors to the hall. We all know that, and admit it.

"But there was a very odd bit of testimony in the evidence, the oddest bit we have. A man standing out in the dark hall saw a little line of moonlight. The door to the passage, the passage that runs up to the roof, was open—you understand that?—and in that passage he saw moonlight. He said that it came from the trap-door to the roof. But that must have been impossible, because the trap was heavily bolted and nobody could have got at it. Remember that he said 'a line'; not a patch or a square such as an opened trap could make, but a little line . . . like the opening, say, of one of these secret wall panels of which we know there are half a dozen in this house.

283

"Remember the position of the rooms—that your host's bedroom is at the left, and that *its wall is the wall of that passage*. Remember that you could have slipped from behind the screen, also at the left, in your dark-grey suit—slipped unseen into the bedroom—and opened the wall panel to get out. Remember that the back windows face the moon. That moonlight fell into the bedroom, and shone out through the partly open panel as you slipped out, opened the spring lock of the door from the inside, and struck down Ames on the landing!—That's what your enemy says you did, unless you can make him tell different, and his name is—"

"LOOK OUT!" yelled Hadley.

They heard the rest of it as Stanley's big hand smashed forward and swept the lamp off the table. Firelight rose up through the momentary blindness in their eyes; they saw Stanley's eyes, the gleam of metal in his hand, and heard a sob of breath.

"Stand back," said Stanley. "I'll get him."

A big shape blocked the light from the hall as he turned and ran; the light disappeared in the crash of the door-slamming, and the key was twisted in the lock even as Hadley plunged for the knob.

"He's locked us—" Hadley's fists beat the panels. "Betts! You! All of you—get him—open this! Fell, in the name of God, you've turned a maniac loose.— BETTS! Can't you stop—"

"Do—Fell—he said *not* to stop him!" yelled a voice from outside. "You said—He's taken the key!"

"You bloody idiot, stop him! Do some . . . Sparkle! Smash this door!"

A weight crashed against it from the outside, a grunt, and another crash. From upstairs came a scream, and then a pistol-shot.

They heard the second shot just before the lock ripped out in a tearing screech, and a big figure stumbled through on its knees. Hadley knocked the door aside, writhed out, and was off towards the stairs, with Melson after him. A voice was speaking clearly through the house. It was loud, but very cool and level, and it seemed pleased.

"You see, they think I'm mad, so I can kill you slowly without any danger whatever. I may kill you whether you tell the truth or not; that I haven't decided. But one bullet for the leg—one for the belly—one for the neck—the whole thing is, it must go on slowly until you open your lying mouth. You see, don't you, that nobody's interfering with me? There's a police officer at the door, and he does nothing to help you, although he has a gun himself. I saw the bulge of it in his hip pocket, but you observe he does nothing even though my back is to him. Now I'm coming in for another shot. . . ."

A scream, more like a rabbit in a snare than anything human, made Melson's knees turn to water as he staggered on the stairs behind Hadley. The scream was repeated.

"No," said the voice, pleasantly, "you can't run away, you see. A room has only four walls and you're a good deal in a corner. You know, I was a fool when I once shot that banker with four bullets in the head. But then I had nothing against him."

The painful breath gasping in his nostrils, Hadley plunged up the last step. Cordite fumes blurred pale faces there; faces that did not move, that watched, twisted and stricken. Through open double doors Melson saw Stanley's back. Beyond him he saw a face that was not human at all. It was a writhing figure, flapping away, hurling out his arms, trying to bore himself into a tall painted screen as Stanley moved towards him.

"This one," said Stanley, "is for your belly," and raised his arm to fire.

The other man stopped screaming.

"Take him off," a queer voice muttered, not loudly. "It's all right. I killed Ames. I killed Ames, damn you all! I killed Ames, and admit it. Only for the love of God take him off."

The voice rose despairingly. The grey face lifted and strained back against painted flames. Then Calvin Boscombe, his mouth slobbering, tumbled down against the screen in a dead faint.

For a moment Stanley stood motionless; at length he drew a shuddering breath and put the pistol in his pocket. He turned a dull face towards Dr. Fell, who lumbered slowly across the room and stared at the open-mouthed caricature on the floor.

"Well?" asked Stanley, heavily. "Was it all right? He cracked."

"It was a damned good show," said Dr. Fell, gripping his shoulder, "and we couldn't have planned a better one. . . . Only, for Lord's sake don't fire off any more of those blanks or you'll rouse the whole neighbourhood."

He turned to Hadley.

"Boscombe's not hurt," he added. "He'll live to hang. *I wonder what he thinks of the 'reactions of a man about to die' now?*"

# 22

## The Truth

The *Daily Sphere*: "Brilliant Strategy By Retired Police Officer Avenges Murder of Old Comrade!" The *Daily Banner*: "Scotland Yard Again Triumphs by Faith in Disgraced Chief Inspector!" The *Daily Trumpeter*: "Pictures: Left, Chief Inspector David Hadley, who unerringly spotted the solution within twenty-four hours, receiving handshake from Assistant Commissioner the Hon. George Bellchester; and Right, Mr. Peter E. Stanley, the hero of the hour, who, unfortunately, could not be interviewed, as he had started on a long sea voyage for the benefit of his health."

The *Daily Trumpeter's* leader said: "Again has been signally demonstrated the efficiency of the law's guardians, even those who have no longer a connection with the institution they reverence even in retirement. Only in Britain, we may proudly boast, could such a thing—"

Dr. Fell said: "Well, dammit! It was the only possible way to save all their faces. Have another glass of beer."

But, since this is a story not so much of saved faces as of a murder committed by a man who thought himself too shrewd, we must refer for enlightenment to a conversation which occurred in the early hours of that same morning at Dr. Fell's hotel in Great Russell Street. Hadley had to brush up in secret on the facts of his triumph, and only he and Melson were there when the doctor talked.

It was past twelve o'clock when he began, for much had to be done and Boscombe's signature, with witnesses, had to go on a statement before he gathered back enough of his nerve to attempt a denial. But the work was over; a bright fire was kindled, padded chairs were set out, and ready to hand stood a case of beer, two bottles of whisky, and a box of cigars. Dr. Fell beamed on his domain and prepared for the recital.

"I'm not joking," he said, "When I tell you I was honestly sorry to have to deceive you all the way through. I not only had to drop hints to you of my belief in Boscombe's innocence, but even to Boscombe himself. You remember I told you, just after we went to his room this morning and found missing the watch he had stolen from himself, that I had just been through one of the worst interludes of my life. When I even had to stand there and pay compliments to that fish-blooded devil, they choked me like castor oil. But it was necessary. If he is the meanest murderer in my experience, he is also one of the cleverest; he left *no* tangible clue to work on. My only chance to trap him was the chance I took. You were in such a state this morning that, if I had let you know what I thought, you would have tried to verify it and let him know he was under suspicion. Then he would have begun to slip and twist away from us again, and he would certainly have been suspicious of the trap I planned to lay with Stanley. Boscombe didn't fear the law: it was Stanley he feared, Stanley's poor goblin-ridden brain turning with claws to tear him. And I saw it was *all* he feared."

"But the alibi—!" protested Melson. "Hastings saw—and why did he—?"

"Stop a bit," interposed Hadley, his notebook on his knee. "Let's get this in order. When did you first become suspicious of him?"

"Last night. I wasn't morally certain until this morning, when the skull-watch disappeared, and I wasn't absolutely certain until I went upstairs just before lunch (you were carefully kept from coming along) and discovered that sliding panel in the passage wall which was also the wall of his bedroom. There *had* to be a panel there, or there could have been no sense to Paull's story of moonlight in the passage at all.

"But we'll take it in order. I first believed in Boscombe's guilt because of one of those *coincidences* which have been bothering us so much. There were some of them, and especially one of them, which I *could not* believe to be accidents. The minor ones were easy to credit, since they were not really coincidences at all, but logical outcomes from the habits and characters of the various people concerned. For example:

"I could believe that by accident, on that fatal Thursday night, Eleanor and Hastings had agreed to meet on the roof even though they were not accustomed to do so in the middle of the week. There had been turmoil in the house over the clock, Eleanor was at the end of her emotional tether, Hastings was depressed: a meeting sooner or later was inevitable. It was a possibility which Boscombe foresaw and anticipated by stealing

289

the key, even though he did not really believe they would choose the middle of the week. This, then, was not a startling coincidence.

"I could believe, further, that Mrs. Steffins had been on that roof investigating the two lovers (we shall return to this presently), because—as you pointed out in your reconstruction which was the only true part of your case against Eleanor as murderess—that was exactly like Mrs. Steffins. Thursday night was the logical night for her to choose; Mrs. Gorson was out, and Steffins could lock up the house early and go a-sleuthing without danger of being sought out over some belated household point.

"*But*," said Dr. Fell, stopping to tap the arm of the chair, "there was one thing too monstrous for anybody to swallow.

"I could not believe that *Boscombe, putting on a fake 'murder-plot' as a harmless bit of amusement, as the victim of this plot accidentally chose a disguised detective who was out to prove a murder on somebody else in that same house*! That, Hadley, is the coincidence which makes the mind reel and the stars turn upside down. If chance can play tricks like that, then chance is not only frightful, but frightening. It savours not only of something supernatural, but something supernatural managed by the powers of darkness. That is, if it were accident.

"But I looked again, and saw it backed up and apparently supported by another coincidence just as astounding as the first. Boscombe has not done merely this. As the sole (intended) witness for his bogus murder, *he has accidentally chosen a former police-officer who was once a close associate of the disguised detective he doesn't know is a detective*! By fixing my mind on the infinite, by rapidly repeating to myself some selections from the book called *Believe-It-Or-Not*, I might credit the first instance. But two of them together—no, no! It wasn't accident. Therefore it was design, and Boscombe's design."

Hadley took the glass of beer that was handed to him.

"That seems clear enough," he acknowledged. "But the purpose of the design?"

"Wait. The questions to be determined were in their order, 'What is the man trying to do?' And then, 'How?' And then, 'Why?'"

"First of all, this bogus murder-plot of his, which was so easily discovered, and which would have been discovered almost as easily even if Hastings hadn't been there to witness it. I had a good idea of what had happened; most people, with time to think, would have. To top it all, Stanley was ready to blow the gaff at any minute, and inevitably would have done so, which Boscombe knew. But it was a curious thing how little trouble—how very little perfunctory trouble—Boscombe took to conceal a business which might have got him into so much trouble; you might say even that he encouraged discovery, without being so obvious about it as to arouse suspicion. Consider what he did:

"Suppose him to have been telling the truth. Imagine, for the sake of argument, that the bogus plot was *all* he intended. Very well. Something goes wrong; the 'victim' of the joke is inexplicably struck down on his threshold, and he suddenly discovers that he and Stanley are in a nasty position. . . . Well, the natural thing would have been to conceal his bogus plot, and conceal what evidences of it he could.

"But what does he do? He stands there flourishing that gun, which he could easily have concealed; he lets us see it, he draws our attention to it, and then hastens to tell an obviously lame story to account for it. He does more. Although he is no fool, he takes care to let a not over-bright constable—who is in the room telephoning, as he knows—see him make a parade of hiding a pair of shoes and gloves which the policeman would not otherwise have noticed.

"I don't need to recall to you everything Boscombe said and did; but it follows the same line. Why does he want this discovered, then? The wild thought entered my mind—because he really did stab Ames with the clock-hand for a very good reason; and his pretence that he meant to shoot Ames with the revolver for no reason at all, this thin flimsy plot of his, will have the effect of diverting suspicion from himself! In other words, he was blackening his own character in order to whitewash it. There, my children, is the paradox. If he admitted he was waiting for the man with a pistol, we should never be likely to suspect him of having slipped out and killed the same man prematurely with a knife. We don't—to put it another way—suspect a person, even a potential murderer, of upsetting his own plot.

"That in itself was devilishly brilliant, but he made it better yet. Before considering how he made the business foolproof, remember that he couldn't carry the pose of admittedly-attempted murder too far, or it might land him in the dock. Hence the dummy silencer, which he also flourished in our faces. You notice he let out a hint here and there; until finally, perspiring profusely, he broke down and defiantly admitted he never really meant to shoot the man. We were intended to think: 'Filthy little swine! Willing to play bogey and scare Stanley, but without half the guts to carry off a *real* murder; wash him out as a serious suspect.' Again he blackened his character in order to whitewash it, and giggled in his fish-blooded little sleeve all the time.

292

That was what he intended us to think. And I blush to admit, gentlemen, that until late last night I did think so.

"But go back to his real actions in the murder.

"In the question of 'How?' we have first to ask, was Stanley an accomplice in the genuine murder? Obviously not; otherwise there would have been no reason for the hocus-pocus. Stanley was to be a *witness* for him. He was to be the very best and most convincing sort of witness—the one who thinks Boscombe meant to kill the man, but knows positively that he didn't.

"Supposing this to have been so, how could it have been managed? If Boscombe stabbed Ames, surely an innocent witness in the same room couldn't have failed to see it. Then up popped several interesting facts, which had no good reason to account for them. (1) That the room was dark, (2) that Stanley was placed behind a heavy screen arranged by Boscombe, and (3) that on the floor by the legs of Boscombe's huge blue chair there were some curious chalkmarks."

Hadley uttered an exclaimation and leafed back through his notebook.

"Chalk-marks! Damn those chalk-marks; I'd forgotten all about them! Yes—here they are. I remember now. I forgot them. . . ."

"Because you forgot Boscombe," said Melson, wryly.

"I'm afraid I did."

Dr. Fell cleared his throat after a deep pull at the beer.

"Consider first in Boscombe's bogus plan," he went on, "the point about *the necessity for a dark room*, as Boscombe explained it to Stanley in Hastings' evidence. It is weak. So weak that anybody but a man with shattered nerves, like Stanley, wouldn't have been taken in. Boscombe says they must have the room dark when

293

the victim walks upstairs and comes in, 'So that anybody who might be abroad in the hall won't see the light when the victim walks in at the door.' Now, anybody abroad in the hall will see the victim, and the fat's in the fire so far as proving the victim tried to burgle the house, so it's hard to see why Boscombe should be afraid of a little thing like a dim light; but that's not the big weakness. If the plan were what it purported to be, it's a curious way to lure the fly into the spider's parlour. You ask him to come after a suit of clothes, to walk upstairs in the dark, open your door, and—what? See a dark room in a dark house, and casually sit down to wait for somebody to bring you a suit of clothes.

"The reason for putting Stanley behind the screen is even weaker. Behind a screen, *in the dark*! There has never been stated any good reason in the world why Stanley shouldn't be seen in the glare of a Kleig-light, for that matter, since why should the presence of a friend of Boscombe's be so alarming to anybody who had come for cast-off clothes? But not only to keep him in the dark, but keep him behind a screen as well, presupposes a victim whose visual powers combine a cat's eye with an X-ray.

"No matter. You know why it was really done. (1) Darkness, so that Boscombe could move unseen in his *black* pyjamas, and unheard in his felt slippers—"

"Stop a bit!" interposed Hadley. "Hastings was looking down in the moonlight..."

"I'm coming to that presently, as you will see. (2) Stanley behind the screen, so that through the indicated narrow crack Stanley could see only what Boscombe wanted him to see in a certain ruled patch of moonlight, something that would make him swear Boscombe was there all the time. Finally (3) the chalkmarks were vital. They were to show *exactly* where the legs of the chair were to be placed, without any possible mistake, so that the line of vision from any point behind the screen should fall only where Boscombe wanted it to fall.

"But obviously the room could not be altogether dark, or Stanley would see nothing. Hence the skylight had to be opened a little way—just a little way, and as carefully arranged beforehand as a spotlight in a theatre. Hasn't it occurred to you that the meticulous Boscombe would have been a fool not to have covered the whole skylight (on the bare chance that Hastings might be on the roof, although he didn't think it in the least likely) unless Boscombe vitally needed that little light?

"And the ironical thing, in this whole case of ironies, is that the man for whom the whole demonstration was intended—Stanley, the witness—we never questioned at all. It was Hastings who proved . . ."

"That's what we've been asking you," interposed Hadley. "Why didn't Hastings see him slip away? Hastings wasn't lying, was he?"

"Oh no. He was telling the truth. But I've been outlining to you only the things that made me doubt Boscombe's story and believe him guilty. Before we go over the actual killing, let's take the scheme from its inception and see what happened.

"We must understand first of all the real character of Boscombe. I hate that man, Hadley, with a personal hatred. He's the only criminal ever to cross my path in whom I couldn't find a grain—of I won't say good, which means nothing except in a spiritual sense and is begging this particular question—but of likability, of honest human earth and sympathy. Everything in his life was whittled down to a point of icy conceit. There was no pride in it; it was mere conceit. It had undoubtedly come into his decaying brain at one time or other that he would like to do just what he pretended to do in the bogus plot—murder somebody for the pleasure of observing that person's 'reactions' when about to die, and fatten on his own vanity like a vampire-bat fattening on its own blood. But his very conceit made him too lazy to show he was even interested in that—until Eleanor Carver ripped that conceit open, and for the first time in his life he found himself laughed at. So Eleanor Carver had to die.

"In the future, when people write accounts of famous criminals, I can see their handling of him. 'Whey-faced Boscombe, with his sly and grisly smile.' 'Whey-faced Boscombe, clawing back in hysteria before a gun-muzzle when his own scheme was turned against him.' As a psychological monster they will compare him to Neil Cream, with his bald head and his squint-eyed grin, prowling after harlots with the strychnine tablets in his pocket. But Boscombe didn't even have the human weakness to care about harlots, or the forthrightness to use poison. I gave you the hint in the matter of his interest in the Spanish Inquisition. I told you that those old Inquisitors, whatever their wrongs, were at least honest men and sincere men who believed they were saving the soul. Boscombe would simply never have been able to understand that. He could have studied all his life without its ever occurring to him that wrong could be done with honest purpose, or that the human soul even existed as anything but a phantom excuse for hypocritical sadism. Above all, he was fascinated by what he called 'subtlety,' but which we choose merely to call conceit.

"That is the point of character we must grasp if we are to understand this crime at all. When he decided to commit a crime, he had not even the forthrightness to use poison. Eleanor was to die. Very well. But he would never kill a person as you or I might kill, with a sudden shot or blow. Round this murder there must rise a whole fantastic, intricate pattern; the more intricate and unnecessary the strands, then the greater pleasure to his vanity at being able to weave them all. He must spin out his work from small beginnings, and make it grow day by day until it showed at last the figure on the gallows.

"Eleanor—remember?—was the only one who had a flash of insight at his real character. When he decided, patronizingly, that he should make her his mistress for want of something better to do, even experiment with matrimony as an intellectual toy, her laughter suddenly showed him to himself. She *laughed*, gentlemen. And she saw him, briefly, with the mask off. She knew henceforward why he hated her. When she saw a man she thought was Hastings dead at the head of the stairs, remember, she shrieked out instantly that Boscombe had killed him. She knew . . . And this afternoon, when you were asking about people who hated her, Eleanor would have told you so. But you forestalled her. You quoted so much of Lucia Handreth's evidence, you so weighted everything with it, that she naturally jumped to only one conclusion."

Hadley nodded, and the doctor went on:

"Come back to Boscombe. We've already gone over the design to fix the Gamridge murder on Eleanor. That was the inspiration of circumstance, when he was wondering how to proceed. Remember, Carver told us that Boscombe was at Gamridge's early that afternoon, when Carver went to inspect the watches. Carver mentioned that Eleanor would later be there. We know now—from Boscombe's statement—that he remained behind when the others left, if only on the chance of seeing Eleanor. He had no plan yet; he was only dogging her. He may or may not have witnessed the actual murder, but at any rate he knew Eleanor was there, without companion and therefore without alibi; and when he read all the details in the papers next day the plan began to take shape.

"How to turn this knowledge to account? He couldn't go to the police and openly denounce her; that would give him away, and would not be the subtle Boscombe at all; above everything, there was not enough actual evidence to convict her of that crime. On the other hand, he couldn't write an anonymous note to the inspector in charge. It would probably be tossed into the waste-basket like a hundred others. Even if it were investigated, that very investigation might give the show away before he was ready. It wouldn't force *the sort of investigation he wanted*.

"And then——his friend Stanley! Of course. Inspector George Ames was listed in the papers as investigating. Stanley, fond of descanting on his woes and especially on the people who had got him sacked, would naturally have told Boscombe about Ames in the Hope-Hastings case. Ames's tenacity, his not-too-great intelligence, his intense secretiveness. Eureka! If an anonymous person told Ames to come in disguise to a certain place, Ames would not have done it; but what if *Stanley* did?"

"But you say," interposed Hadley, "that Stanley didn't know anything about it! That's Stanley's signature on that letter. He must have known——"

Dr. Fell shook his head.

"You don't need a man to write a typewritten letter for you, I think? All you need is his signature at the bottom of a sheet of paper. And all you need to get his signature is to have him write you a note about anything. At any chemist's you can buy for a couple of bob a bottle of ink-eradicator which will so remove the genuine note that only microphotography (not in use at Scotland Yard) will show it up. So you dispatch a series of notes over Stanley's signature on your own typewriter.

"Now watch little Boscombe work! To watch him work, you will have to consider the fishiest part of Ames's whole report: the third of the three 'coincidences' which are too staggering for belief as such. We've explained the first two. The third says that, while Ames was being informed of the guilt of somebody in this house by a person who refused to help him come into the house after evidence, *still another person* suddenly and conveniently invited him to the house in the middle of the night for a suit of clothes. This is, in a sense, only a corollary of the first coincidence—it brings us round in a circle again, do you see? Because we have already doubted this point when Boscombe stated it, and yet here's Ames stating it! The only conceivable explanations were (a) that the report was a forgery, or (b) that Ames was for some reason not telling the truth.

"I asked you, and you showed it couldn't have been a forgery because Ames took it to the Yard himself. I then asked you, 'Was he above juggling facts a bit, if he thought he did it in a good cause?' And you agreed that he wasn't."

"But," demanded Melson, "why should he have juggled the facts in writing to his own superiors?"

"I'll show you by telling you what happened. Boscombe realizes that he has now a perfect plant for both fake murder and real murder. Fake murder, because months ago—for the pure pleasure of torturing Stanley—he has already mentioned to Stanley the hazy plan of a killing for amusement, which he probably never meant to carry on with. (You notice Hastings never

299

heard mention of it but once.) And real murder, because the stage is set for killing Ames in such a way that Eleanor shall be hanged.

"There is Ames, in his disguise, already watching everybody at the public-house because he has had no definite accusation from 'Stanley' and he is waiting for Stanley to appear in person. And instead there comes to him—Boscombe. He says to Ames, 'I know who you are; I am a friend of Stanley's, and he sent me here.' Ames naturally says: 'What have *you* got to do with it? Why doesn't Stanley come himself?' Boscombe replies, 'You fool, several of them have guessed you're a police officer. If anybody sees Stanley with you, or gets a hint of it, the fat will be in the fire. I'm the person Stanley referred to, who saw those stolen articles in the woman's possession.' He then pitches the yarn exactly as we have it in Ames's report—with one exception. 'I'll get you into the house right enough,' he says, 'but, in the event we don't get the proof and I get into trouble for telling you this, you have got to cover me up. You have got to tell even your superiors, in case I should be laying the foundations for a libel charge, that the man who told you this was *not* the man—I, Calvin Boscombe—who helped you get into the house. If we do find the proof, I shall certainly admit being both. Otherwise, I must have my alibi in black and white . . . or I refuse to help you at all. This is your big case; it means the promotion and pay and everything else if you pull it off. What I ask you is merely nominal, but I insist on it.'

"Well, what could Ames do? He had nothing whatever to lose, by agreeing, and he stood to forfeit everything if he refused. A thin excuse, it was; but he believed it—and he died.

"So they arranged that on Thursday night—Thursday

night, as in any plan Boscombe devised, because the house would be locked up early in Mrs. Gorson's absence and there would be no servants to notice stray visitors from the area—Ames should creep up in the dark to Boscombe's room, *and meet Stanley.* The last touch of reality should be added when Ames, if he were hanging about the house, should at an earlier time see Stanley go in; and he'd got it impressed on that none-too-clever brain of his that he must at no time speak to Stanley. Well, Ames was never to reach Boscombe's room alive.

"In the meantime, Boscombe had been preparing his evidence against Eleanor. A purchased bracelet and ear-rings, even the skull-watch, wouldn't be enough. He must use a pair of gloves apparently belonging to her—but what else that would point straight to Eleanor? Then he had his best inspiration of all in Paull's difficulty—the clock-hands."

"Stop a bit," put in Melson. "That's a snag, isn't it? How did Boscombe learn about it? When Paull talked to Eleanor, either down on the front steps or in the cab, Boscombe couldn't possibly have overheard it! How did he learn?"

"Through Paull's own character. I had a little word with young Christopher tonight. Paull acted exactly as we could have pictured he would. You noticed, probably, that the one person in the house for whom Boscombe had a half-contemptuous tolerance was Paull? Paull amused him, and he could preen his vanity by contrast. Paull, moreover, rather liked Boscombe. He wanted to borrow money—the obvious person to borrow it from was Boscombe, who was rich—but he didn't dare face him. . . ."

"Got it!" said Hadley, softly. "As a last resort, when he was leaving the house that morning, he suddenly thought it might be *easier if he wrote* to Boscombe what he didn't have the nerve to ask—"

"Yes. And Boscombe met him, wormed out the difficulty, and quickly got him out of the way with a cash surety of silence. That was the man to whom Paull wrote the note. If he didn't have to broach the subject to Boscombe face to face, open the ball, he was willing to meet him after Boscombe knew the difficulty. Not an uncommon occurrence, I believe.

"So we come to the last act. Boscombe and Stanley are in the former's room on Thursday night, waiting for the victim. All about Boscombe are the trappings of the fake murder, the trappings he doesn't need. In his bedroom are the trappings he does need.

"On Wednesday night he had stolen the clock-hands, wearing gloves of Eleanor's sort. Man, hadn't you realized all along—hadn't you seen standing out in glory—the glaringly evident fact that Boscombe is the only man in that house with hands small enough to have put on those gloves? A dozen times you've seen his small, delicate hands, which didn't have to go *clear* into the gloves, but only far enough to avoid getting the paint on himself when he removed the clock-hands. One glove, along with the minute-hand and the rest of the evidence, was secreted behind the panel on Thursday, while Eleanor was away at work. He knew he was safe; he knew that in Eleanor's instinctive, deep-rooted dread of the wall-panel she hadn't used it in years. And on Thursday night the trappings he did need, the hour-hand and the right-hand glove, were ready in his bedroom."

"Are you trying to tell me," demanded Hadley, "that the glove was used, after all?"

"I am."

"But, blast it! you yourself proved that neither of those gloves—"

"Haven't you got it a trifle mixed?" enquired Dr. Fell, wrinkling his brow. "I seem to remember that *you* proved it; indeed, as I kept on repeating time after time, it was you who demonstrated it. I don't recall ever saying off my own bat that the right-hand glove wasn't used. All I said was that the left-hand glove, in your ingenious and admirable false solution, was not the one we were looking for. . . . Naturally, my boy, I didn't dare intimate that right was right, so to speak. In your state of mind, it would have been too dangerous. So long as you could prove Eleanor guilty, you would have been quite willing to make her ambidextrous."

"Then you used false evidence," Hadley said, slowly, and squinted down his pencil, "to prove—"

"The truth. Right you are," the doctor agreed, cheerfully. "But then we've both been doing it straight along. . . . Let me show you by a little experiment. You try it, Melson; I don't want this beggar to cheat. Take this paper-cutter; it's quite sharp. Now go over to that sofa and drive it down hard through one of the cushions; they're stuffed with feathers. Never mind, I'll be responsible to the hotel. As soon as you've struck, jerk away, not because you don't want, hum, feathers on your glove, but because you don't want them on your clothes. Like Boscombe. *Now!*"

Melson, hoped nobody would ever take a photograph of him doing this, struck savagely and jerked away.

"Right," said Dr. Fell, affably. "What did you do instantly, as soon as the knife descended?"

"I opened my hand. There's a feather—"

"And that, Hadley, is why there was blood on the palm of the glove and nowhere else; not a great deal, because, except in the case of a severed artery, men don't bleed profusely at the very second of a blow. Your theory would only have been correct if the murderer

303

had withdrawn the weapon from the wound with fist still tightly clenched about it; but not otherwise.

"Let us, then, clear up the last difficulty—why Boscombe wasn't seen leaving his chair by the man at the skylight, and why Hastings was willing to swear he saw him there all the time. It explains itself, if you study the evidence.

"First think of what Boscombe intended Stanley to see so that Stanley could swear to his presence. Mark first the very exceptional height, breadth, and depth of that blue chair. Now, where was the chair? Remember what Hastings said he could see, from his position on the roof: 'I could see just the right-hand side of the chair-back as it faced the door.' In other words, the patch of moonlight was so arranged as to fall just partly down one side of the back and arm, while most of it towards the left (imagining yourself looking down at it) was in shadow. What did Hastings make a point of saying, over and over, when he had looked down for the first time—months ago? That somebody was sitting in the chair; that it was Stanley, but he couldn't be sure of this because he could only see a part of the man's head over the back of the chair; above all, that the only thing he could see of Stanley was the man's hand opening and shutting on the chair-arm. You remember how he emphasized that?

"Now, on Thursday night imagine Stanley peering through the crack in the screen. Most of the chair was in dense shadow; and *all* of the front of it was, because the moonlight would blacken it with the chair's own shadow—all except the outside of the wing and arm. Very well. Stanley was to see Boscombe sit down in that chair when the lights went out. Then what was he to see? What was the one thing that so hypnotized Hastings that night, the thing he dwelt on . . . ?"

"The moonlight shining on the pistol," replied Hadley, "presumably the hand holding it . . . yes, the hand . . . and, by God! now that I come to think of it, how absolutely *still and steady* it was!"

"Exactly. A section of that was what Stanley was supposed to see. Hastings got a better view, but he couldn't see anything more by the very nature of the arrangements. And, by the force of his own testimony, he cannot swear he saw Boscombe in that chair—even though he thinks he did. Remember this: Stanley, six feet two or three, sat in that chair the first night Hastings overheard them talking, and he saw only a part of the top of Stanley's head! Of Stanley, proportionately broad, he could see past the wing only one hand on the arm of the chair. If it was too big for the gigantic Stanley, it must have swallowed the diminutive Boscombe. Then by the nature of Hastings' own testimony he could at most have seen the gun and perhaps part of the 'hand.'

"Boscombe slipped to the left out of the chair, in that dense darkness and in his black pyjamas. How he managed the gun business we do not know at this moment, because he will have disposed of that evidence—but I can guess. Do you remember, Melson, when we first went into his room last night? I, in all innocence, made a move over as though I were going to sit down in the only chair I have ever seen that is almost big enough to allow me relaxation. Boscombe, for no apparent reason, shot over and sat down ahead of me. There was something pushed down in the side of it below the cushion, that is why—something like a bootjack to hold the gun rigid, and draped over the butt of the pistol one of those glaring white cotton gloves of the bogus murder. He needed only a moment to adjust it, while he leaned out of the chair sideways and made a covering

305

shadow with his own body, and a moment to take it away again. Hastings, by the way, did hear the *rustle* as he either left or came back to the chair, and did hear his hard breathing; you remember? But it is not to be wondered that Hastings admired the immovable and extraordinary steadiness of his hand.

"Boscombe didn't really need all that nonsense. Stanley would probably have been willing to swear to his presence through the sheer suggestion of saying that he sat down and remained hidden. It was silly, childish, and horrible—like Boscombe. It was inevitable—for Boscombe.

"So our whey-faced killer slid round to the left, went to the back of the room, followed the rear wall right to his bedroom. He had plenty of time. He had told Ames to ring the bell; to wait, and, if he got no answer in a couple of minutes, to come on upstairs. Boscombe was ready. The moonlight streaming into his bedroom windows gave him light enough to find the prepared clock-hand and the real glove. He was out through the panel, he had struck and vanished and returned; and his alibi was complete. He took no chance of interruption. He chose twelve o'clock—because Eleanor, even in the unlikely event of her going up to the roof, never went up before twelve-fifteen. In both assumptions he was wrong that night; she went up, and she went up before twelve-fifteen. But if luck was against Boscombe in that respect, it favoured him in that she went up first about a quarter to twelve; and then again, after a thorough hunt for the missing key, a few minutes after the murder; just in time to incur suspicion as he intended.

"Finally, having blocked the passage from the landing end by stealing the key, he had already made sure it was blocked from the roof-end. The broken bolt was put in order and bolted. If Eleanor could not wander up, Hastings could not wander down to see why she didn't. He left nothing to chance; he foresaw even eventualities he didn't believe would arise; he held his thousand threads, glorying in his ability never to mishandle one. He was playing a dozen chess games at once, and delighting in it. He was nimble, brilliant, over-ingenious, and unsuccessful, and it does not pain me deeply to think that he will hang."

Hadley drew a deep breath and shut his notebook. The fire was growing lower; again rain had begun to fall; and Melson was already wondering how this brief interlude would have affected his work on Burnet.

"Yes, I fancy that's all," said the chief inspector, taking up his glass again. "Except—what you did this afternoon and this evening. . . ."

"I tried to obtain tangible evidence. Good God! I had nothing whatever against the man! There's a secret panel in his bedroom by which he could get out into the hall; well, what of it? He could have laughed at me. Two witnesses would have sworn, however unwillingly, that he was in the chair all the time. His alibi was unbreakable, yet I had to break it.

"In deference to you, I attempted milder methods first. There was a slight chance that somebody at Gamridge's jewellery counter would remember a man buying duplicates of the stolen articles. I sent two of your men on that lead—but it was a weak one. Even if he is ever identified as a man who bought a bracelet and ear-rings, he will strengthen his *apparent* defence of Eleanor (Lord, he was clever in that!) by simply saying they were for her. We think he's gallantly trying to defend her still, when they're not the articles at all, and there you are. . . . My last mild lead was the 'Stanley' letter. If it had been a letter to Boscombe rubbed out with liquid eraser, I hoped that a microphotographic treatment would bring out the effaced writing and show: 'Dear Boscombe: Here are the books you want,' or whatever the real letter might have been. We might have had him then! I drove to an old French friend of mine who lives at Hampstead, used to be associated with Bencolin at the Prefecture in Paris, and still dabbles in criminology. He tested it. We raised vague words on the letter—enough to prove Stanley's innocence in writing the bogus letter if the worst came to the worst—but nothing pointing to Boscombe.

"Then I was forced to play my last, dangerous, possibly deadly card. I was forced to go to Stanley, the only person Boscombe feared. I had to tell him everything, to concoct this plan with him, and go to the wild extreme of asking a madman to pretend he was mad! I knew he would do it. I knew if he did do it, and we succeeded, you and your department would be out of the whole mess. The great danger was that the man, while agreeing, really would go off his rocker completely and try to get at Boscombe with real bullets. . . . Well, my hair is greyer tonight. I supplied him with the blanks for the gun he produced; I kept it with me, offering excuses, while I drove him to Carver's house— he really arrived with me, you know. Then I took the two policemen into my confidence, rang up the curtain on my show, and nearly turned *your* hair grey. It was a long shot, it was possibly foolish, it was the worst nerve-strain I ever went through when I cracked my whip in the face of a real madman pretending madness. . . .

"But—" He drew a long breath.

The *Daily Trumpeter* said: "Again has been signally demonstrated the efficiency of the law's guardians, even those who have no longer a connection with the institution they reverence in retirement. Only in Britain, we may proudly boast, could such a thing—"

Dr. Fell said: "Well, dammit! it was the only possible way to save all their faces. Have another glass of beer."